THE CLIENT

Also by John Grisham

A TIME TO KILL
THE FIRM
THE PELICAN BRIEF

JOHN GRISHAM

THE CLIENT

DOUBLEDAY
New York London Toronto Sydney Auckland

PUBLISHED BY DOUBLEDAY
a division of Bantam Doubleday Dell Publishing Group, Inc.
666 Fifth Avenue, New York, New York 10103

DOUBLEDAY and the portrayal of an anchor with a dolphin
are trademarks of Doubleday, a division of
Bantam Doubleday Dell Publishing Group, Inc.

All of the characters in this book are fictitious, and any resemblance to actual persons, living or dead, is purely coincidental.

Library of Congress Cataloging-in-Publication Data

Grisham, John.
The client / John Grisham. — 1st ed.
p. cm.
I. Title.
PS3557.R5355C57 1993
813'.54—dc20 92-39079
CIP

ISBN 0-385-42471-X
ISBN 0-385-46865-2 (large print)
ISBN 0-385-47015-0 (limited edition)

Printed in the United States of America
March 1993

7 9 10 8 6

For Ty and Shea

THE CLIENT

ONE

MARK WAS ELEVEN and had been smoking off and on for two years, never trying to quit but being careful not to get hooked. He preferred Kools, his ex-father's brand, but his mother smoked Virginia Slims at the rate of two packs a day, and he could in an average week pilfer ten or twelve from her. She was a busy woman with many problems, perhaps a little naive when it came to her boys, and she never dreamed her eldest would be smoking at the age of eleven.

Occasionally Kevin, the delinquent two streets over, would sell Mark a pack of stolen Marlboros for a dollar. But for the most part he had to rely on his mother's skinny cigarettes.

He had four of them in his pocket this afternoon as he led his brother Ricky, age eight, down the path into the woods behind their trailer park. Ricky was nervous about this, his first smoke. He had caught Mark hiding the cigarettes in a shoe box under his bed yesterday, and threatened to tell all if his big brother didn't show him how to do it. They sneaked along the wooded trail, headed for one of Mark's secret spots where he'd spent many solitary hours trying to inhale and blow smoke rings.

Most of the other kids in the neighborhood were into beer and pot, two vices Mark was determined to avoid. Their ex-father was an alcoholic who'd beaten both boys and their mother, and the beatings always followed his nasty bouts with beer. Mark had seen and felt the effects of alcohol. He was also afraid of drugs.

"Are you lost?" Ricky asked, just like a little brother, as they left the trail and waded through chest-high weeds.

"Just shut up," Mark said without slowing. The only time their father had spent at home was to drink and sleep and abuse them.

He was gone now, thank heavens. For five years Mark had been in charge of Ricky. He felt like an eleven-year-old father. He'd taught him how to throw a football and ride a bike. He'd explained what he knew about sex. He'd warned him about drugs, and protected him from bullies. And he felt terrible about this introduction to vice. But it was just a cigarette. It could be much worse.

The weeds stopped and they were under a large tree with a rope hanging from a thick branch. A row of bushes yielded to a small clearing, and beyond it an overgrown dirt road disappeared over a hill. A highway could be heard in the distance.

Mark stopped and pointed to a log near the rope. "Sit there," he instructed, and Ricky obediently backed onto the log and glanced around anxiously as if the police might be watching. Mark eyed him like a drill sergeant while picking a cigarette from his shirt pocket. He held it with his right thumb and index finger, and tried to be casual about it.

"You know the rules," he said, looking down at Ricky. There were only two rules, and they had discussed them a dozen times during the day, and Ricky was frustrated at being treated like a child. He rolled his eyes away and said, "Yeah, if I tell anyone, you'll beat me up."

"That's right."

Ricky folded his arms. "And I can smoke only one a day."

"That's right. If I catch you smoking more than that, then you're in trouble. And if I find out you're drinking beer or messing with drugs, then—"

"I know, I know. You'll beat me up again."

"Right."

"How many do you smoke a day?"

"Only one," Mark lied. Some days, only one. Some days, three or four, depending on supply. He stuck the filter between his lips like a gangster.

"Will one a day kill me?" Ricky asked.

Mark removed the cigarette from his lips. "Not anytime soon. One a day is pretty safe. More than that, and you could be in trouble."

"How many does Mom smoke a day?"

"Two packs."

"How many is that?"

"Forty."

"Wow. Then she's in big trouble."

"Mom's got all kinds of troubles. I don't think she's worried about cigarettes."

"How many does Dad smoke a day?"

"Four or five packs. A hundred a day."

Ricky grinned slightly. "Then he's gonna die soon, right?"

"I hope so. Between staying drunk and chain-smoking, he'll be dead in a few years."

"What's chain-smoking?"

"It's when you light the new one with the old one. I wish he'd smoke ten packs a day."

"Me too." Ricky glanced toward the small clearing and the dirt road. It was shady and cool under the tree, but beyond the limbs the sun was bright. Mark pinched the filter with his thumb and index finger and sort of waved it before his mouth. "Are you scared?" he sneered as only big brothers can.

"No."

"I think you are. Look, hold it like this, okay?" He waved it closer, then with great drama withdrew it and stuck it between his lips. Ricky watched intently.

Mark lit the cigarette, puffed a tiny cloud of smoke, then held it and admired it. "Don't try to swallow the smoke. You're not ready for that yet. Just suck a little then blow the smoke out. Are you ready?"

"Will it make me sick?"

"It will if you swallow the smoke." He took two quick drags and puffed for effect. "See. It's really easy. I'll teach you how to inhale later."

"Okay." Ricky nervously reached out with his thumb and index finger, and Mark placed the cigarette carefully between them. "Go ahead."

Ricky eased the wet filter to his lips. His hand shook and he took a short drag and blew smoke. Another short drag. The smoke never got past his front teeth. Another drag. Mark watched carefully, hoping he would choke and cough and turn blue, then get sick and never smoke again.

"It's easy," Ricky said proudly as he held the cigarette and admired it. His hand was shaking.

"It's no big deal."

"Tastes kind of funny."

"Yeah, yeah." Mark sat next to him on the log and picked another one from his pocket. Ricky puffed rapidly. Mark lit his, and they sat in silence under the tree enjoying a quiet smoke.

"This is fun," Ricky said, nibbling at the filter.

"Great. Then why are your hands shaking?"

"They're not."

"Sure."

Ricky ignored this. He leaned forward with his elbows on his knees, took a longer drag, then spat in the dirt like he'd seen Kevin and the big boys do behind the trailer park. This was easy.

Mark opened his mouth into a perfect circle and attempted a smoke ring. He thought this would really impress his little brother, but the ring failed to form and the gray smoke dissipated.

"I think you're too young to smoke," he said.

Ricky was busy puffing and spitting, and thoroughly enjoying this giant step toward manhood. "How old were you when you started?" he asked.

"Nine. But I was more mature than you."

"You always say that."

"That's because it's always true."

They sat next to each other on the log under the tree, smoking quietly and staring at the grassy clearing beyond the shade. Mark *was* in fact more mature than Ricky at the age of eight. He was more mature than any kid his age. He'd always been mature. He had hit his father with a baseball bat when he was seven. The aftermath had not been pretty, but the drunken idiot had stopped beating their mother. There had been many fights and many beatings, and Dianne Sway had sought refuge and advice from her eldest son. They had consoled each other and conspired to survive. They had cried together after the beatings. They had plotted ways to protect Ricky. When he was nine, Mark convinced her to file for divorce. He had called the cops when his father showed up drunk after being served with divorce papers. He had testified in court about the abuse and neglect and beatings. He was very mature.

Ricky heard the car first. There was a low, rushing sound coming from the dirt road. Then Mark heard it, and they stopped smoking. "Just sit still," Mark said softly. They did not move.

A long, black, shiny Lincoln appeared over the slight hill and eased toward them. The weeds in the road were as high as the front bumper. Mark dropped his cigarette to the ground and covered it with his shoe. Ricky did the same.

The car slowed almost to a stop as it neared the clearing, then circled around, touching the tree limbs as it moved slowly. It stopped and faced the road. The boys were directly behind it, and hidden from view. Mark slid off the log, and crawled through the weeds to a row of brush at the edge of the clearing. Ricky followed. The rear of the Lincoln was thirty feet away. They watched it carefully. It had Louisiana license plates.

"What's he doing?" Ricky whispered.

Mark peeked through the weeds. "Shhhhh!" He had heard stories around the trailer park of teenagers using these woods to meet girls and smoke pot, but this car did not belong to a teenager. The engine quit, and the car just sat there in the weeds for a minute. Then the door opened, and the driver stepped into the weeds and looked around. He was a chubby man in a black suit. His head was fat and round and without hair except for neat rows above the ears and a black-and-gray beard. He stumbled to the rear of the car, fumbled with the keys, and finally opened the trunk. He removed a water hose, stuck one end into the exhaust pipe, and ran the other end through a crack in the left rear window. He closed the trunk, looked around again as if he were expecting to be watched, then disappeared into the car.

The engine started.

"Wow," Mark said softly, staring blankly at the car.

"What's he doing?" Ricky asked.

"He's trying to kill himself."

Ricky raised his head a few inches for a better view. "I don't understand, Mark."

"Keep down. You see the hose, right? The fumes from the tail pipe go into the car, and it kills him."

"You mean suicide?"

"Right. I saw a guy do it like this in a movie once."

They leaned closer to the weeds and stared at the hose running from the pipe to the window. The engine idled smoothly.

"Why does he want to kill himself?" Ricky asked.

"How am I supposed to know? But we gotta do something."

"Yeah, let's get the hell outta here."

"No. Just be still a minute."

"I'm leaving, Mark. You can watch him die if you want to, but I'm gone."

Mark grabbed his brother's shoulder and forced him lower. Ricky's breathing was heavy and they were both sweating. The sun hid behind a cloud.

"How long does it take?" Ricky asked, his voice quivering.

"Not very long." Mark released his brother and eased onto all fours. "You stay here, okay. If you move, I'll kick your tail."

"What're you doing, Mark?"

"Just stay here. I mean it." Mark lowered his thin body almost to the ground and crawled on elbows and knees through the weeds toward the car. The grass was dry and at least two feet tall. He knew the man couldn't hear him, but he worried about the movement of the weeds. He stayed directly behind the car and slid snakelike on his belly until he was in the shadow of the trunk. He reached and carefully eased the hose from the tail pipe, and dropped it to the ground. He retraced his trail with a bit more speed, and seconds later was crouched next to Ricky, watching and waiting in the heavier grass and brush under the outermost limbs of the tree. He knew that if they were spotted, they could dart past the tree and down their trail and be gone before the chubby man could catch them.

They waited. Five minutes passed, though it seemed like an hour.

"You think he's dead?" Ricky whispered, his voice dry and weak.

"I don't know."

Suddenly, the door opened, and the man stepped out. He was crying and mumbling, and he staggered to the rear of the car where he saw the hose in the grass, and cursed it as he shoved it back into the tail pipe. He held a bottle of whiskey and looked around wildly at the trees, then stumbled back into the car. He mumbled to himself as he slammed the door.

The boys watched in horror.

"He's crazy as hell," Mark said faintly.

"Let's get out of here," Ricky said.

"We can't! If he kills himself, and we saw it or knew about it, then we could get in all kinds of trouble."

Ricky raised his head as if to retreat. "Then we won't tell anybody. Come on, Mark!"

Mark grabbed his shoulder again and forced him to the ground. "Just stay down! We're not leaving until I say we're leaving!"

Ricky closed his eyes tightly and started crying. Mark shook his head in disgust but didn't take his eyes off the car. Little brothers were more trouble than they were worth. "Stop it," he growled through clenched teeth.

"I'm scared."

"Fine. Just don't move, okay. Do you hear me? Don't move. And stop the crying." Mark was back on his elbows, deep in the weeds and preparing to ease through the tall grass once more.

"Just let him die, Mark," Ricky whispered between sobs.

Mark glared at him over his shoulder and eased toward the car, which was still running. He crawled along his same trail of lightly trampled grass so slowly and carefully that even Ricky, with dry eyes now, could barely see him. Ricky watched the driver's door, waiting for it to fly open and the crazy man to lunge out and kill Mark. He perched on his toes in a sprinter's stance for a quick getaway through the woods. He saw Mark emerge under the rear bumper, place a hand for balance on the taillight, and slowly ease the hose from the tail pipe. The grass crackled softly and the weeds shook a little and Mark was next to him again, panting and sweating and, oddly, smiling to himself.

They sat on their legs like two insects under the brush, and watched the car.

"What if he comes out again?" Ricky asked. "What if he sees us?"

"He can't see us. But if he starts this way, just follow me. We'll be gone before he can take a step."

"Why don't we go now?"

Mark stared at him fiercely. "I'm trying to save his life, okay? Maybe, just maybe, he'll see that this is not working, and maybe he'll decide he should wait or something. Why is that so hard to understand?"

"Because he's crazy. If he'll kill himself, then he'll kill us. Why is that so hard to understand?"

Mark shook his head in frustration, and suddenly the door opened again. The man rolled out of the car growling and talking to himself, and stomped through the grass to the rear. He grabbed the end of the hose, stared at it as if it just wouldn't behave, and looked slowly around the small clearing. He was breathing heavily and perspiring. He looked at the trees, and the boys eased to the ground. He looked down, and froze as if he suddenly understood. The grass was slightly trampled around the rear of the car and he knelt as if to inspect it, but then crammed the hose back into the tail pipe instead and hurried back to his door. If someone was watching from the trees, he seemed not to care. He just wanted to hurry up and die.

The two heads rose together above the brush, but just a few inches. They peeked through the weeds for a long minute. Ricky was ready to run, but Mark was thinking.

"Mark, please, let's go," Ricky pleaded. "He almost saw us. What if he's got a gun or something?"

"If he had a gun he'd use it on himself."

Ricky bit his lip and his eyes watered again. He had never won an argument with his brother, and he would not win this one.

Another minute passed, and Mark began to fidget. "I'll try one more time, okay. And if he doesn't give up, then we'll get outta here. I promise, okay?"

Ricky nodded reluctantly. His brother stretched on his stomach and inched his way through the weeds into the tall grass. Ricky wiped the tears from his cheek with his dirty fingers.

The lawyer's nostrils flared as he inhaled mightily. He exhaled slowly and stared through the windshield while trying to determine if any of the precious, deadly gas had entered his blood and begun its work. A loaded pistol was on the seat next to him. A half-empty fifth of Jack Daniels was in his hand. He took a sip, screwed the cap on it, and placed it on the seat. He inhaled slowly and closed his eyes to savor the gas. Would he simply drift away? Would it hurt or burn or make him sick before it finished him off? The note was on the dash above the steering wheel, next to a bottle of pills.

He cried and talked to himself as he waited for the gas to hurry, dammit!, before he'd give up and use the gun. He was a coward, but a very determined one, and he much preferred this sniffing and floating away to sticking a gun in his mouth.

He sipped the whiskey, and hissed as it burned on its descent. Yes, it was finally working. Soon, it would all be over, and he smiled at himself in the mirror because it was working and he was dying and he was not a coward after all. It took guts to do this.

He cried and muttered as he removed the cap of the whiskey bottle for one last swallow. He gulped, and it ran from his lips and trickled into his beard.

He would not be missed. And although this thought should have been painful, the lawyer was calmed by the knowledge that no one would grieve. His mother was the only person in the world who loved him, and she'd been dead four years so this would not hurt her. There was a child from the first disastrous marriage, a daughter he'd not seen in eleven years, but he'd been told she had joined a cult and was as crazy as her mother.

It would be a small funeral. A few lawyer buddies and perhaps a judge or two would be there all dressed up in dark suits and whispering importantly as the piped-in organ music drifted around the near-empty chapel. No tears. The lawyers would sit and glance at their watches while the minister, a stranger, sped through the standard comments used for dear departed ones who never went to church.

It would be a ten-minute job with no frills. The note on the dash required the body to be cremated.

"Wow," he said softly as he took another sip. He turned the bottle up, and while gulping glanced in the rearview mirror and saw the weeds move behind the car.

Ricky saw the door open before Mark heard it. It flew open, as if kicked, and suddenly the large, heavy man with the red face was running through the weeds, holding onto the car and growling. Ricky stood, in shock and fear, and wet his pants.

Mark had just touched the bumper when he heard the door. He

froze for a second, gave a quick thought to crawling under the car, and the hesitation nailed him. His foot slipped as he tried to stand and run, and the man grabbed him. "You! You little bastard!" he screamed as he grabbed Mark's hair and flung him onto the trunk of the car. "You little bastard!" Mark kicked and squirmed, and a fat hand slapped him in the face. He kicked once more, not as violently, and he got slapped again.

Mark stared at the wild, glowing face just inches away. The eyes were red and wet. Fluids dripped from the nose and chin. "You little bastard," he growled through clenched, dirty teeth.

When he had him pinned and still and subdued, the lawyer stuck the hose back into the exhaust pipe, then yanked Mark off the trunk by his collar and dragged him through the weeds to the driver's door, which was open. He threw the kid through the door and shoved him across the black leather seat.

Mark was grabbing at the door handle and searching for the door lock switch when the man fell behind the steering wheel. He slammed the door behind him, pointed at the door handle, and screamed, "Don't touch that!" Then he backhanded Mark in the left eye with a vicious slap.

Mark shrieked in pain, grabbed his eyes and bent over, stunned, crying now. His nose hurt like hell and his mouth hurt worse. He was dizzy. He tasted blood. He could hear the man crying and growling. He could smell the whiskey and see the knees of his dirty blue jeans with his right eye. The left was beginning to swell. Things were blurred.

The fat lawyer gulped his whiskey and stared at Mark, who was all bent over and shaking at every joint. "Stop crying," he snarled.

Mark licked his lips and swallowed blood. He rubbed the knot above his eye and tried to breathe deeply, still staring at his jeans. Again, the man said, "Stop crying," so he tried to stop.

The engine was running. It was a big, heavy, quiet car, but Mark could hear the engine humming very softly somewhere far away. He turned slowly and glanced at the hose winding through the rear window behind the driver like an angry snake sneaking toward them for the kill. The fat man laughed.

"I think we should die together," he announced, all of a sudden very composed.

Mark's left eye was swelling fast. He turned his shoulders and looked squarely at the man, who was even larger now. His face was chubby, the beard was bushy, the eyes were still red and glowed at him like a demon in the dark. Mark was crying. "Please let me out of here," he said, lip quivering, voice cracking.

The driver stuck the whiskey bottle in his mouth and turned it up. He grimaced and smacked his lips. "Sorry, kid. You had to be a cute ass, had to stick your dirty little nose into my business, didn't you? So I think we should die together. Okay? Just you and me, pal. Off to La La Land. Off to see the wizard. Sweet dreams, kid."

Mark sniffed the air, then noticed the pistol lying between them. He glanced away, then stared at it when the man took another drink from the bottle.

"You want the gun?" the man asked.

"No sir."

"So why are you looking at it?"

"I wasn't."

"Don't lie to me, kid, because if you do, I'll kill you. I'm crazy as hell, okay, and I'll kill you." Though tears flowed freely from his eyes, his voice was very calm. He breathed deeply as he spoke. "And besides, kid, if we're gonna be pals, you've got to be honest with me. Honesty's very important, you know? Now, do you want the gun?"

"No sir."

"Would you like to pick up the gun and shoot me with it?"

"No sir."

"I'm not afraid of dying, kid, you understand?"

"Yes sir, but I don't want to die. I take care of my mother and my little brother."

"Aw, ain't that sweet. A real man of the house."

He screwed the cap onto the whiskey bottle, then suddenly grabbed the pistol, stuck it deep into his mouth, curled his lips around it, and looked at Mark, who watched every move, hoping he would pull the trigger and hoping he wouldn't. Slowly, he withdrew the barrel from his mouth, kissed the end of it, then pointed it at Mark.

"I've never shot this thing, you know," he said, almost in a whisper. "Just bought it an hour ago at a pawnshop in Memphis. Do you think it'll work?"

"Please let me out of here."

"You have a choice, kid," he said, inhaling the invisible fumes. "I'll blow your brains out, and it's over now, or the gas'll get you. Your choice."

Mark did not look at the pistol. He sniffed the air and thought for an instant that maybe he smelled something. The gun was close to his head. "Why are you doing this?" he asked.

"None of your damned business, okay, kid. I'm nuts, okay. Over the edge. I planned a nice little private suicide, you know, just me and my hose and maybe a few pills and some whiskey. Nobody looking for me. But, no, you have to get cute. You little bastard!" He lowered the pistol and carefully placed it on the seat. Mark rubbed the knot on his forehead and bit his lip. His hands were shaking and he pressed them between his legs.

"We'll be dead in five minutes," he announced officially as he raised the bottle to his lips. "Just you and me, pal, off to see the wizard."

Ricky finally moved. His teeth chattered and his jeans were wet, but he was thinking now, moving from his crouch onto his hands and knees and sinking into the grass. He crawled toward the car, crying and gritting his teeth as he slid on his stomach. The door was about to fly open. The crazy man, who was large but quick, would leap from nowhere and grab him by the neck, just like Mark, and they'd all die in the long, black car. Slowly, inch by inch, he pushed his way through the weeds.

Mark slowly lifted the pistol with both hands. It was as heavy as a brick. It shook as he raised it and pointed it at the fat man, who leaned toward it until the barrel was an inch from his nose.

"Now, pull the trigger, kid," he said with a smile, his wet face glowing and dancing with delightful anticipation. "Pull the trigger, and I'll be dead and you go free." Mark curled a finger around the trigger. The man nodded, then leaned even closer and bit the tip of the barrel with flashing teeth. "Pull the trigger!" he shouted.

Mark closed his eyes and pressed the handle of the gun with the palms of his hands. He held his breath, and was about to squeeze the trigger when the man jerked it from him. He waved it wildly in front of Mark's face, and pulled the trigger. Mark screamed as the window behind his head cracked into a thousand pieces but did not shatter. "It works! It works!" he yelled as Mark ducked and covered his ears.

Ricky buried his face in the grass when he heard the shot. He was ten feet from the car when something popped and Mark yelled. The fat man was yelling, and Ricky peed on himself again. He closed his eyes and clutched the weeds. His stomach cramped and his heart pounded, and for a minute after the gunshot he did not move. He cried for his brother, who was dead now, shot by a crazy man.

"Stop crying, dammit! I'm sick of your crying!"

Mark clutched his knees and tried to stop crying. His head pounded and his mouth was dry. He stuck his hands between his knees and bent over. He had to stop crying and think of something. On a television show once some nut was about to jump off a building, and this cool cop just kept talking to him and talking to him, and finally the nut started talking back and of course did not jump. Mark quickly smelled for gas, and asked, "Why are you doing this?"

"Because I want to die," the man said calmly.

"Why?" he asked again, glancing at the neat, little round hole in his window.

"Why do kids ask so many questions?"

"Because we're kids. Why do you want to die?" He could barely hear his own words.

"Look, kid, we'll be dead in five minutes, okay? Just you and me, pal, off to see the wizard." He took a long drink from the bottle, now almost empty. "I feel the gas, kid. Do you feel it? Finally."

In the side mirror, through the cracks in the window, Mark saw the weeds move and caught a glimpse of Ricky as he slithered through the weeds and ducked into the bushes near the tree. He closed his eyes and said a prayer.

"I gotta tell you, kid, it's nice having you here. No one wants to die alone. What's your name?"

"Mark."

"Mark who?"

"Mark Sway." Keep talking, and maybe the nut won't jump. "What's your name?"

"Jerome. But you can call me Romey. That's what my friends call me, and since you and I are pretty tight now you can call me Romey. No more questions, okay, kid?"

"Why do you want to die, Romey?"

"I said no more questions. Do you feel the gas, Mark?"

"I don't know."

"You will soon enough. Better say your prayers." Romey sank low into the seat with his beefy head straight back and eyes closed, completely at ease. "We've got about five minutes, Mark, any last words?" The whiskey bottle was in his right hand, the gun in his left.

"Yeah, why are you doing this?" Mark asked, glancing at the mirror for another sign of his brother. He took short, quick breaths through the nose, and neither smelled nor felt anything. Surely Ricky had removed the hose.

"Because I'm crazy, just another crazy lawyer, right. I've been driven crazy, Mark, and how old are you?"

"Eleven."

"Ever tasted whiskey?"

"No," Mark answered truthfully.

Suddenly, the whiskey bottle was in his face, and he took it.

"Take a shot," Romey said without opening his eyes.

Mark tried to read the label, but his left eye was virtually closed and his ears were ringing from the gunshot, and he couldn't concentrate. He sat the bottle on the seat where Romey took it without a word.

"We're dying, Mark," he said almost to himself. "I guess that's tough at age eleven, but so be it. Nothing I can do about it. Any last words, big boy?"

Mark told himself that Ricky had done the trick, that the hose was now harmless, that his new friend Romey here was drunk and crazy, and that if he survived he would have to do so by thinking and talking. The air was clean. He breathed deeply and told himself that he could make it. "What made you crazy?"

Romey thought for a second and decided this was humorous. He snorted and actually chuckled a little. "Oh, this is great. Perfect. For weeks now, I've known something no one else in the entire world knows, except my client, who's a real piece of scum, by the way. You see, Mark, lawyers hear all sorts of private stuff that we can never repeat. Strictly confidential, you understand. No way we can ever tell what happened to the money or who's sleeping with who or where the body's buried, you follow?" He inhaled mightily, and exhaled with enormous pleasure. He sank lower in the seat, eyes still closed. "Sorry I had to slap you." He curled his finger around the trigger.

Mark closed his eyes and felt nothing.

"How old are you, Mark?"

"Eleven."

"You told me that. Eleven. And I'm forty-four. We're both too young to die, aren't we, Mark?"

"Yes sir."

"But it's happening, pal. Do you feel it?"

"Yes sir."

"My client killed a man and hid the body, and now my client wants to kill me. That's the whole story. They've made me crazy. Ha! Ha! This is great, Mark. This is wonderful. I, the trusted lawyer, can now tell you, literally seconds before we float away, where the body is. The body, Mark, the most notorious undiscovered corpse of our time. Unbelievable. I can finally tell!" His eyes were open and glowing down at Mark. "This is funny as hell, Mark!"

Mark missed the humor. He glanced at the mirror, then at the door lock switch a foot away. The handle was even closer.

Romey relaxed again and closed his eyes as if trying desperately to take a nap. "I'm sorry about this, kid, really sorry, but, like I said, it's nice to have you here." He slowly placed the bottle on the dash next to the note and moved the pistol from his left hand to his right, caressing it softly and stroking the trigger with his index finger. Mark tried not to look. "I'm really sorry about this, kid. How old are you?"

"Eleven. You've asked me three times."

"Shut up! I feel the gas now, don't you? Quit sniffing, dammit!

It's odorless, you little dumbass. You can't smell it. I'd be dead now and you'd be off playing GI Joe if you hadn't been so cute. You're pretty stupid, you know."

Not as stupid as you, thought Mark. "Who did your client kill?"

Romey grinned but did not open his eyes. "A United States Senator. I'm telling. I'm telling. I'm spilling my guts. Do you read newspapers?"

"No."

"I'm not surprised. Senator Boyette from New Orleans. That's where I'm from."

"Why did you come to Memphis?"

"Dammit, kid! Full of questions, aren't you?"

"Yeah. Why'd your client kill Senator Boyette?"

"Why, why, why, who, who, who. You're a real pain in the ass, Mark."

"I know. Why don't you just let me go?" Mark glanced at the mirror, then at the hose running into the backseat.

"I might just shoot you in the head if you don't shut up." His bearded chin dropped and almost touched his chest. "My client has killed a lot of people. That's how he makes money, by killing people. He's a member of the Mafia in New Orleans, and now he's trying to kill me. Too bad, ain't it, kid. We beat him to it. Joke's on him."

Romey took a long drink from the bottle and stared at Mark.

"Just think about it, kid, right now, Barry, or Barry The Blade as he's known, these Mafia guys all have cute nicknames, you know, is waiting for me in a dirty restaurant in New Orleans. He's probably got a couple of his pals nearby, and after a quiet dinner he'll want me to get in the car and take a little drive, talk about his case and all, and then he'll pull out a knife, that's why they call him The Blade, and I'm history. They'll dispose of my chubby little body somewhere, just like they did Senator Boyette, and, bam!, just like that, New Orleans has another unsolved murder. But we showed them, didn't we, kid? We showed them."

His speech was slower and his tongue thicker. He moved the pistol up and down on his thigh when he talked. The finger stayed on the trigger.

Keep him talking. "Why does this Barry guy want to kill you?"

"Another question. I'm floating. Are you floating?"

"Yeah. It feels good."

"Buncha reasons. Close your eyes, kid. Say your prayers." Mark watched the pistol and glanced at the door lock. He slowly touched each fingertip to each thumb, like counting in kindergarten, and the coordination was perfect.

"So where's the body?"

Romey snorted and his head nodded. The voice was almost a whisper. "The body of Boyd Boyette. What a question. First U. S. Senator murdered in office, did you know that? Murdered by my dear client Barry The Blade Muldanno, who shot him in the head four times, then hid the body. No body, no case. Do you understand, kid?"

"Not really."

"Why aren't you crying, kid? You were crying a few minutes ago. Aren't you scared?"

"Yes, I'm scared. And I'd like to leave. I'm sorry you want to die and all, but I have to take care of my mother."

"Touching, real touching. Now, shut up. You see, kid, the Feds have to have a body to prove there was a murder. Barry is their suspect, their only suspect, because he really did it, you see, in fact they know he did it. But they need the body."

"Where is it?"

A dark cloud moved in front of the sun and the clearing was suddenly darker. Romey moved the gun gently along his leg as if to warn Mark against any sudden moves. "The Blade is not the smartest thug I've ever met, you know. Thinks he's a genius, but he's really quite stupid."

You're the stupid one, Mark thought again. Sitting in a car with a hose running from the exhaust. He waited as still as could be.

"The body's under my boat."

"Your boat?"

"Yes, my boat. He was in a hurry. I was out of town, so my beloved client took the body to my house and buried it in fresh concrete under my garage. It's still there, can you believe it? The FBI has dug up half of New Orleans trying to find it, but they've never thought about my house. Maybe Barry ain't so stupid after all."

"When did he tell you this?"

"I'm sick of your questions, kid."

"I'd really like to leave now."

"Shut up. The gas is working. We're gone, kid. Gone." He dropped the pistol on the seat.

The engine hummed quietly. Mark glanced at the bullet hole in the window, at the millions of tiny crooked cracks running from it, then at the red face and heavy eyelids. A quick snort, almost a snore, and the head nodded downward.

He was passing out! Mark stared at him and watched his thick chest move. He'd seen his ex-father do this a hundred times.

Mark breathed deeply. The door lock would make noise. The gun was too close to Romey's hand. Mark's stomach cramped and his feet were numb.

The red face emitted a loud, sluggish noise, and Mark knew there would be no more chances. Slowly, ever so slowly, he inched his shaking finger to the door lock switch.

Ricky's eyes were almost as dry as his mouth, but his jeans were soaked. He was under the tree, in the darkness, away from the bushes and the tall grass and the car. Five minutes had passed since he had removed the hose. Five minutes since the gunshot. But he knew his brother was alive because he had darted behind trees for fifty feet until he caught a glimpse of the blond head sitting low and moving about in the huge car. So he stopped crying, and started praying.

He made his way back to the log, and as he crouched low and stared at the car and ached for his brother, the passenger door suddenly flew open, and there was Mark.

Romey's chin dropped onto his chest, and just as he began his next snore Mark slapped the pistol onto the floor with his left hand while unlocking the door with his right. He yanked the handle and rammed his shoulder into the door, and the last thing he heard as he rolled out was another deep snore from the lawyer.

He landed on his knees and grabbed at the weeds as he scratched and clawed his way from the car. He raced low through the grass and within seconds made it to the tree where Ricky watched in muted horror. He stopped at the stump and turned, expecting to see the lawyer lumbering after him with the gun. But the car appeared harmless. The passenger door was open. The engine was running. The exhaust pipe was free of devices. He breathed for the first time in a minute, then slowly looked at Ricky.

"I pulled the hose out," Ricky said in a shrill voice between rapid breaths. Mark nodded but said nothing. He was suddenly much calmer. The car was fifty feet away, and if Romey emerged, they could disappear through the woods in an instant. And hidden by the tree and the cover of the brush, they would never be seen by Romey if he decided to jump out and start blasting away with the gun.

"I'm scared, Mark. Let's go," Ricky said, his voice still shrill, his hands shaking.

"Just a minute." Mark studied the car intently.

"Come on, Mark. Let's go."

"I said just a minute."

Ricky watched the car. "Is he dead?"

"I don't think so."

So the man was alive, and had the gun, and it was becoming obvious that his big brother was no longer scared and was thinking of something. Ricky took a step backward. "I'm leaving," he mumbled. "I want to go home."

Mark did not move. He exhaled calmly and studied the car. "Just a second," he said without looking at Ricky. The voice had authority again.

Ricky grew still and leaned forward, placing both hands on both wet knees. He watched his brother, and shook his head slowly as Mark carefully picked a cigarette from his shirt pocket while staring at the car. He lit it, took a long draw, and blew smoke upward to the branches. It was at this point that Ricky first noticed the swelling.

"What happened to your eye?"

Mark suddenly remembered. He rubbed it gently, then rubbed the knot on his forehead. "He slapped me a couple of times."

"It looks bad."

"It's okay. You know what I'm gonna do?" he said without expecting an answer. "I'm gonna sneak back up there and stick the hose into the exhaust pipe. I'm gonna plug it in for him, the bastard."

"You're crazier than he is. You're kidding, right, Mark?"

Mark puffed deliberately. Suddenly, the driver's door swung open, and Romey stumbled out with the pistol. He mumbled loudly as he faltered to the rear of the car, and once again found the garden hose lying harmlessly in the grass. He screamed obscenities at the sky.

Mark crouched low and held Ricky with him. Romey spun around and surveyed the trees around the clearing. He cursed more, and started crying loudly. Sweat dripped from his hair, and his black jacket was soaked and glued to him. He stomped around the rear of the car, sobbing and talking, screaming at the trees.

He stopped suddenly, wrestled his ponderous bulk onto the top of the trunk, then squirmed and slid backward like a drugged elephant until he hit the rear window. His stumpy legs stretched before him. One shoe was missing. He took the gun, neither slowly nor quickly, almost routinely, and stuck it deep in his mouth. His wild red eyes flashed around, and for a second paused at the trunk of the tree above the boys.

He opened his lips and bit the barrel with his big, dirty teeth. He closed his eyes, and pulled the trigger with his right thumb.

TWO

THE SHOES WERE SHARK, and the vanilla silks ran all the way to the kneecaps where they finally stopped and caressed the rather hairy calves of Barry Muldanno, or Barry The Blade, or simply The Blade, as he liked to be called. The dark green suit had a shine to it and appeared at first glance to be lizard or iguana or some other slimy reptile, but upon closer look it was not animal at all but polyester. Double-breasted with buttons all over the front. It hung handsomely on his well-built frame. And it rippled nicely as he strutted to the pay phone in the rear of the restaurant. The suit was not gaudy, just flashy. He could pass for a well-dressed drug importer or perhaps a hot Vegas bookie, and that was fine because he was The Blade and he expected people to notice, and when they looked at him they were supposed to see success. They were supposed to gawk in fear and get out of his way.

The hair was black and full, colored to hide a bit of gray, slicked down, laden with gel, pulled back fiercely and gathered into a perfect little ponytail that arched downward and touched precisely at the top of the dark green polyester jacket. Hours were spent on the hair. The obligatory diamond earring sparkled from the proper left lobe. A tasteful gold bracelet clung to the left wrist just below the diamond Rolex, and on his right wrist another tasteful gold chain rattled softly as he strutted.

The swagger stopped in front of the pay phone, which was near the rest rooms in a narrow hallway in the back of the restaurant. He stood in front of the phone, and cut his eyes in all directions. To the average person, the sight of Barry The Blade's eyes cutting and darting and searching for violence would loosen the bowels. The eyes were very dark brown, and so close together that if one could stand to look directly into them for more than two seconds, one would swear Barry was cross-eyed. But he wasn't. A neat row of black hair ran from temple to temple without the slightest break for the furrow above the rather long and pointed nose. Solid brow. Puffy brown skin half-circled the eyes from below and said without a doubt that this man enjoyed booze and the fast life. The shady eyes confessed many hangovers, among other things. The Blade loved his eyes. They were legendary.

He punched the number of his lawyer's office, and said rapidly without waiting for a reply, "Yeah, this is Barry! Where's Jerome? He's late. Supposed to meet me here forty minutes ago. Where is he? Have you seen him?"

The Blade's voice was not pleasant either. It had the menacing resonance of a successful New Orleans street thug who had broken many arms and would gladly break one more if you lingered too long in his path or weren't quick enough with your answers. The voice was rude, arrogant, and intimidating, and the poor secretary on the other end had heard it many times and she'd seen the eyes and the slick suits and the ponytail. She swallowed hard, caught her breath, thanked heavens he was on the phone and not in the office standing before her desk cracking his knuckles, and informed Mr. Muldanno that Mr. Clifford had left the office around 9 A.M. and had not been heard from since.

The Blade slammed the phone down and stormed through the hallway, then caught himself and began the strut as he neared the tables and the faces. The restaurant was beginning to fill. It was almost five.

He just wanted a few drinks and then a nice dinner with his lawyer so they could talk about his mess. Just drinks and dinner, that's all. The Feds were watching, and listening. Jerome was paranoid and just last week told Barry he thought they had wired his law office. So they would meet here and have a nice meal without worrying about eavesdroppers and bugging devices.

They needed to talk. Jerome Clifford had been defending prominent New Orleans thugs for fifteen years—gangsters, pushers, politicians—and his record was impressive. He was cunning and corrupt, completely willing to buy people who could be bought. He drank with the judges and slept with their girlfriends. He bribed the cops and threatened the jurors. He schmoozed with the politicians and contributed when asked. Jerome knew what made the system tick, and when a sleazy defendant with money needed help in New Orleans he invariably found his way to the law offices of W. Jerome Clifford, Attorney and Counselor-at-Law. And in that office he found a friend who thrived on the dirt and was loyal to the end.

Barry's case, however, was something different. It was huge, and growing by the moment. The trial was a month away and loomed like an execution. It would be his second murder trial. His first had come at the tender age of eighteen when a local prosecutor attempted to prove, with only one most unreliable witness, that Barry had cut the fingers off a rival thug and slit his throat. Barry's uncle, a well-respected and seasoned mobster, dropped some money here and there, and young Barry's jury could not agree on a verdict and thus simply hung itself.

Barry later served two years in a pleasant federal joint on racketeering charges. His uncle could've saved him again, but he was twenty-five at the time and ready for a brief imprisonment. It looked good on his résumé. The family was proud of him. Jerome Clifford had handled the plea bargain, and they'd been friends ever since.

A fresh club soda with lime awaited Barry as he swaggered to the bar and assumed his position. The alcohol could wait a few hours. He needed steady hands.

He squeezed the lime and watched himself in the mirror. He caught a few stares; after all, at this moment he was perhaps the most famous murder defendant in the country. Four weeks from trial, and people were looking. His face was all over the papers.

This trial was much different. The victim was a Senator, the first ever to be murdered, they alleged, while in office. *United States of America versus Barry Muldanno.* Of course, there was no body, and this presented tremendous problems for the United States of America. No corpse, no pathology reports, no ballistics, no bloody photographs to wave around the courtroom and display for the jury.

But Jerome Clifford was cracking up. He was acting strange—disappearing like this, staying away from the office, not returning calls, always late for court, always mumbling under his breath and drinking too much. He'd always been mean and tenacious, but now he was detached and people were talking. Frankly, Barry wanted a new lawyer.

Just four short weeks, and Barry needed time. A delay, a continuance, something. Why does justice move so quickly when you don't want it to? His life had been lived on the fringes of the law, and he'd seen cases drag on for years. His uncle had once been indicted, but after three years of exhaustive warfare the government finally quit. Barry had been indicted six months ago, and bam!, here's the trial. It wasn't fair. Romey wasn't working. He had to be replaced.

Of course, the Feds had a hole or two in their case. No one saw the killing. There would be a decent circumstantial case against him, with motive, perhaps. But no one actually saw him do it. There was an informant who was unstable and unreliable and expected to be chewed up on cross-examination, if he indeed made it to trial. The Feds were hiding him. And, Barry had his one marvelous advantage—the body, the diminutive, wiry corpse of Boyd Boyette rotting slowly away in concrete. Without it, Reverend Roy could not get a conviction. This made Barry smile, and he winked at two peroxide blondes at a table near the door. Women had been plentiful since the indictment. He was famous.

Reverend Roy's case was weak all right, but it hadn't slowed his nightly sermons in front of the cameras, or his pompous predictions of swift justice, or his blustering interviews with any journalist bored enough to quiz him. He was an oily-voiced, leather-lunged, pious U.S. Attorney with obnoxious political aspirations and a thunderous opinion about everything. He had his very own press agent, a most overworked soul charged with the task of keeping the Reverend in the spotlight so that one day very soon the public would insist he serve them in the United States Senate. From there, only the Reverend knew where God might lead him.

The Blade crunched his ice at the repulsive thought of Roy Foltrigg waving his indictment before the cameras and bellowing all sorts of forecasts of good triumphing over evil. But six months had passed since the indictment, and neither Reverend Roy nor his confederates, the FBI, had found the body of Boyd Boyette. They followed Barry night and day—in fact, they were probably waiting outside right now, as if he were stupid enough to have dinner, then go look at the body just for the hell of it. They had bribed every wino and street bum who claimed to be an informant. They had drained ponds and lakes; they had dragged rivers. They had obtained search warrants for dozens of buildings and sites in the city. They had spent a small fortune on backhoes and bulldozers.

But Barry had it. The body of Boyd Boyette. He would like to move it, but he couldn't. The Reverend and his host of angels were watching.

Clifford was an hour late now. Barry paid for two rounds of club soda, winked at the peroxides in their leather skirts, and left the place cursing lawyers in general and his in particular.

He needed a new lawyer, one who would return his phone calls and meet him for drinks and find some jurors who could be bought. A real lawyer!

He needed a new lawyer, and he needed a continuance or a postponement or a delay, hell, anything to slow this thing down so he could think.

He lit a cigarette and walked casually along Magazine between Canal and Poydras. The air was thick. Clifford's office was four blocks away. His lawyer wanted a quick trial! What an idiot! No one wanted a quick trial in this system, but here was W. Jerome Clifford pushing for one. Clifford had explained not three weeks ago that they should push hard for a trial because there was no corpse, thus no case, et cetera, et cetera. And if they waited, the body might be found, and since Barry was such a lovely suspect and it was a sensational killing with a ton of pressure behind its prosecution, and since Barry had actually performed the killing, was in fact guilty as hell, then they should go to trial immediately. This had shocked Barry. They had argued viciously in Romey's office, and things had not been the same since.

At one point in the discussion, three weeks ago, things got quiet and Barry boasted to his lawyer that the body would never be found. He'd disposed of lots of them, and he knew how to hide them. Boyette had been hidden rather quickly, and though Barry wanted to move the little fella, he was nonetheless secure and resting peacefully without the threat of disturbance from Roy and the Fibbies.

Barry chuckled to himself as he strolled along Poydras.

"So where's the body?" Clifford had asked.

"You don't want to know," Barry had replied.

"Sure I want to know. The whole world wants to know. Come on, tell me if you've got the guts."

"You don't want to know."

"Come on. Tell me."

"You're not gonna like it."

"Tell me."

Barry flicked his cigarette on the sidewalk, and almost laughed out loud. He shouldn't have told Jerome Clifford. It was a childish thing to do, but harmless. The man could be trusted with secrets, attorney-client privilege and all, and he had been wounded when Barry hadn't come clean initially with all the gory details. Jerome Clifford was as crooked and sleazy as his clients, and if they got blood on them he wanted to see it.

"You remember what day Boyette disappeared?" Barry had asked.

"Sure. January 16."

"Remember where you were January 16?"

At this point, Romey had walked to the wall behind his desk and studied his badly scrawled monthly planners. "Colorado, skiing."

"And I borrowed your house?"

"Yeah, you were meeting some doctor's wife."

"That's right. Except she couldn't make it, so I took the Senator to your house."

Romey froze at this point, and glared at his client, mouth open, eyes lowered.

Barry had continued. "He arrived in the trunk, and I left him at your place."

"Where?" Romey had asked in disbelief.

"In the garage."

"You're lying."

"Under the boat that hasn't been moved in ten years."

"You're lying."

The front door of Clifford's office was locked. Barry rattled it and cursed through the window. He lit another cigarette and searched the usual parking places for the black Lincoln. He'd find the fat bastard if it took all night.

Barry had a friend in Miami who was once indicted for an assortment of drug charges. His lawyer was quite good, and had managed to stall and delay for two and a half years until finally the judge lost patience and ordered a trial. The day before jury selection, his friend killed his very fine lawyer, and the judge was forced to grant another continuance. The trial never happened.

If Romey died suddenly, it would be months, maybe years, before the trial.

THREE

RICKY BACKED AWAY from the tree until he was in the weeds, then found the narrow trail and started to run. "Ricky," Mark called, "Hey, Ricky, wait," but it didn't work. He stared once more at the man on the car with the gun still in his mouth. The eyes were half-open and the feet twitched at the heels.

Mark had seen enough. "Ricky," he called again as he jogged toward the trail. His brother was ahead, running slowly in an odd way with both arms stiff and straight down by his legs. He leaned forward at the waist. Weeds hit him in the face. He tripped but didn't fall. Mark grabbed him by the shoulders and spun him around. "Ricky, listen! It's okay." Ricky was zombielike, with pale skin and glazed eyes. He breathed hard and rapidly, and emitted a dull, aching moan. He couldn't talk. He jerked away and resumed his trot, still moaning as the weeds slapped him in the face. Mark followed close behind as they crossed a dry creek bed and headed for home.

The trees thinned just before the crumbling board fence that encircled most of the trailer park. Two small children were throwing rocks at a row of cans lined neatly along the hood of a wrecked car. Ricky ran faster and crawled through a broken section of the fence. He jumped a ditch, darted between two trailers, and ran into the street. Mark was two steps behind. The steady groan grew louder as Ricky breathed even harder.

The Sway mobile home was twelve feet wide and sixty feet long, and parked on a narrow strip on East Street with forty others. Tucker Wheel Estates also included North, South, and West streets, and all four curved and crossed each other several times from all directions. It was a decent trailer park with reasonably clean streets, a few trees, plenty of bicycles, and few abandoned cars. Speed bumps slowed traffic. Loud music or noise brought the police as soon as it was reported to Mr. Tucker. His family owned all the land and most of the trailers, including Number 17 on East Street, which Dianne Sway rented for two hundred and eighty dollars a month.

Ricky ran through the unlocked door and fell onto the couch in the den. He seemed to be crying, but there were no tears. He curled his knees to his stomach as if he were cold, then, very slowly, placed his right thumb in his mouth. Mark watched this intently. "Ricky, talk to me," he said, gently shaking his shoulder. "You gotta talk to me, man, okay, Ricky. It's okay."

He sucked harder on the thumb. He closed his eyes and his body shook.

Mark looked around the den and kitchen, and realized things were exactly as they had left them an hour ago. An hour ago! It seemed like days. The sunlight was fading and the rooms were a bit darker. Their books and backpacks from school were piled, as always, on the kitchen table. The daily note from Mom was on the counter next to the phone. He walked to the sink and ran water in a clean coffee cup. He had a terrible thirst. He sipped the cool water and stared through the window at the trailer next door. Then he heard smacking noises, and looked at his brother. The thumb. He'd seen a show on television where some kids in California sucked their thumbs after an earthquake. All kinds of doctors were involved. A year after it hit the poor kids were still sucking away.

The cup touched a tender spot on his lip, and he remembered the blood. He ran to the bathroom and studied his face in the mirror. Just below the hairline there was a small, barely noticeable knot. His left eye was puffy and looked awful. He ran water in the sink and washed a spot of blood from his lower lip. It was not swollen, but suddenly began throbbing. He'd looked worse after fights at school. He was tough.

He took an ice cube from the refrigerator and held it firmly under his eye. He walked to the sofa and studied his brother, paying particular attention to the thumb. Ricky was asleep. It was almost five-thirty, time for their mother to arrive home after nine long hours at the lamp factory. His ears still rang from the gunshots and the blows he took from his late friend Mr. Romey, but he was beginning to think. He sat next to Ricky's feet and slowly rubbed around his eye with the ice.

If he didn't call 911, it could be days before anyone found the body. The fatal shot had been severely muffled, and Mark was certain no one heard it but them. He'd been to the clearing many times, but suddenly realized he had never seen another person there. It was secluded. Why had Romey chosen the place? He was from New Orleans, right?

Mark watched all kinds of rescue shows on television, and knew for certain that every 911 call was recorded. He did not want to be recorded. He would never tell anyone, not even his mother, what he had just lived through, and he really needed, at this crucial moment, to discuss the matter with his little brother so they could get their lies straight. "Ricky," he said, shaking his brother's leg. Ricky groaned but did not open his eyes. He pulled himself tighter into a knot. "Ricky, wake up!"

There was no response to this, except a sudden shudder as if he were freezing. Mark found a quilt in a closet and covered his brother, then wrapped a handful of ice cubes in a dish towel and placed the pack gingerly over his own left eye. He didn't feel like answering questions about his face.

He stared at the phone and thought of cowboy and Indian movies with bodies lying around and buzzards circling above and everyone concerned about burying the dead before the damned vultures got them. It would be dark in an hour or so. Do buzzards strike at night? Never saw that in a movie.

The thought of the fat lawyer lying out there with the gun in his mouth, one shoe off, probably still bleeding, was horrible enough, but throw in the buzzards ripping and tearing, and Mark picked up the phone. He punched 911 and cleared his throat.

"Yeah, there's a dead man, in the woods, and, well, someone needs to come get him." He spoke in the deepest voice possible, and knew from the first syllable that it was a pitiful attempt at disguise. He breathed hard and the knot on his forehead pounded.

"Who's calling please?" It was a female voice, almost like a robot's.

"Uh, I really don't want to say, okay."

"We need your name, son." Great, she knew he was a kid. He hoped he could at least sound like a young teenager.

"Do you want to know about the body or not?" Mark asked.

"Where is the body?"

This is just great, he thought, already telling someone about it. And not someone to be trusted, but someone who wore a uniform and worked with the police, and he could just hear this taped conversation as it would be repeatedly played before the jury, just like on television. They would do all those voice tests and everyone would know it was Mark Sway on the phone telling about the body when no one else in the world knew about it. He tried to make his voice even deeper.

"It's near Tucker Wheel Estates, and—"

"That's on Whipple Road."

"Yes, that's right. It's in the woods between Tucker Wheel Estates and Highway 17."

"The body is in the woods?"

"Sort of. The body is actually lying on a car in the woods."

"And the body's dead?"

"The guy's been shot, okay. With a gun, in the mouth, and I'm sure the man's dead."

"Have you seen the body?" The woman's voice was losing its professional restraint. It had an edge to it now.

What kind of stupid question is that, Mark thought. Have I seen it? She was stalling, trying to keep him on the line so she could trace it.

"Son, have you seen the body?" she asked again.

"Of course I've seen it."

"I need your name, son."

"Look, there's a small dirt road off Highway 17 that leads to a small clearing in the woods. The car is big and black, and the dead man is lying on it. If you can't find it, well, tough luck. Bye."

He hung up and stared at the phone. The trailer was perfectly still. He walked to the door and peered through the dirty curtains, half-expecting squad cars to come flying in from all directions—loudspeakers, SWAT teams, bulletproof vests.

Get a grip. He shook Ricky again, and, touching his arm, noticed how clammy it was. But Ricky was still sleeping and sucking his thumb. Mark gently grabbed him around the waist and dragged him across the floor, down the narrow hallway to their bedroom where he shoveled him into bed. Ricky mumbled and wiggled a bit along the way, but quickly curled into a ball. Mark covered him with a blanket and closed the door.

Mark wrote a note to his mother, told her Ricky felt bad and was sleeping so please be quiet, and he'd be home in an hour or so. The boys were not required to be home when she arrived, but if they weren't, there'd better be a note.

The distant beat of a helicopter went unnoticed by Mark.

He lit a cigarette along the trail. Two years ago, a new bike had disappeared from a house in the suburbs, not far from the trailer park. It was rumored to have been seen behind one of the mobile homes, and the same rumor held that it was being stripped and repainted by a couple of trailer park kids. The suburb kids enjoyed classifying their lesser neighbors as trailer park kids, the implications being obvious. They attended the same school, and there were daily fights between the two societies. All crime and mischief in the suburbs were automatically blamed on the trailer people.

Kevin, the delinquent on North Street, had the new bike and had shown it to a few of his buddies before it was repainted. Mark had seen it. The rumors flew and the cops poked around, and one night there was a knock at the door. Mark's name had been mentioned in the investigation, and the policeman had a few questions. He sat at the kitchen table and glared down at Mark for an hour. It was very unlike television where the defendant keeps his cool and sneers at the cop.

Mark admitted nothing, didn't sleep for three nights, and vowed to live a clean life and stay away from trouble.

But this was trouble. Real trouble, much worse than a stolen bike. A dead man who told secrets before he died. Was he telling the truth? He was drunk and crazy as hell, talking about the wizard and all. But why would he lie?

Mark knew Romey had a gun, had even held and touched the trigger. And the gun killed the man. It had to be a crime to watch someone commit suicide and not stop it.

He would never tell a soul! Romey had stopped talking. Ricky would have to be dealt with. Mark had kept silent about the bike, and he could do it again. No one would ever know he had been in the car.

There was a siren in the distance, then the steady thump of a helicopter. Mark eased under a tree as the chopper swept close by. He crept through the trees and brush, staying low and in no hurry, until he heard voices.

Lights flashed everywhere. Blue for the cops and red for the ambulance. The white Memphis Police cars were parked around the black Lincoln. The orange-and-white ambulance was arriving on the scene as Mark peeked through the woods. No one seemed anxious or worried.

Romey had not been moved. One cop took pictures while the others laughed. Radios squawked, just like on television. Blood ran from under the body and down across the red-and-white taillights. The pistol was still in his right hand, on top of his bulging stomach. His head slumped to the right, his eyes closed now. The paramedics walked up and looked him over, then made bad jokes and the cops laughed. All four doors were open and the car was being carefully inspected. There was no effort to remove the body. The helicopter made a final pass then flew away.

Mark was deep in the brush, maybe thirty feet from the tree and the log where they had lit the first smokes. He had a perfect view of the clearing, and of the fat lawyer lying up there on the car like a dead cow in the middle of the road. Another cop car arrived, then another ambulance. People in uniform were bumping into each other. Small white bags with unseen things in them were removed with great caution from the car. Two policemen with rubber gloves rolled up the hose. The photographer squatted in each door and flashed away. Occasionally, someone would stop and stare at Romey, but most of them drank coffee from Styrofoam cups and chatted away. A cop laid Romey's shoe on the trunk next to the body, then placed it in a white bag and wrote something on it. Another cop knelt by the license plates and waited with his radio for a report to come back.

Finally, a stretcher emerged from the first ambulance and was carried to the rear bumper and laid in the weeds. Two paramedics grabbed Romey's feet and gently pulled him until two other paramedics could grab his arms. The cops watched and joked about how fat Mr. Clifford was because they knew his name now. They asked if more paramedics were needed to carry his big ass, if the stretcher was reinforced or something, if he would fit in the ambulance. Lots of laughter as they strained to lower him.

A cop put the pistol in a bag. The stretcher was heaved into the ambulance, but the doors were not closed. A wrecker with yellow lights arrived and backed itself to the front bumper of the Lincoln.

Mark thought of Ricky and the thumb-sucking. What if he needed help? Mom would be home soon. What if she tried to wake him and got scared? He would leave in just a minute, and smoke the last cigarette on the way home.

He heard something behind him, but thought nothing of it. Just the snap of a twig, then, suddenly, a strong hand grabbed his neck and a voice said, "What's up, kid?"

Mark jerked around and looked into the face of a cop. He froze and couldn't breathe.

"What're you doing, kid?" the cop asked as he lifted Mark up by the neck. The grip didn't hurt, but the cop meant to be obeyed. "Stand up, kid, okay. Don't be afraid."

Mark stood and the cop released him. The cops in the clearing had heard and were staring.

"What're you doing here?"

"Just watching," Mark said.

The cop pointed with his flashlight to the clearing. The sun was down and it would be dark in twenty minutes. "Let's walk over there," he said.

"I need to go home," Mark said.

The cop placed his arm around Mark's shoulders and led him through the weeds. "What's your name?"

"Mark."

"Last name?"

"Sway. What's yours?"

"Hardy. Mark Sway, huh?" the cop repeated thoughtfully. "You live in Tucker Wheel Estates, don't you?"

He couldn't deny this, but he hesitated for some reason. "Yes sir."

They joined the circle of policemen who were now quiet and waiting to see the kid.

"Hey, fellas, this is Mark Sway, the kid who made the call," Hardy announced. "You did make the call, didn't you, Mark?"

He wanted to lie, but at the moment he doubted a lie would work. "Uh, yes sir."

"How'd you find the body?"

"My brother and I were playing."

"Playing where?"

"Around here. We live over there," he said, pointing beyond the trees.

"Were you guys smoking dope?"

"No sir."

"Are you sure?"

"Yes sir."

"Stay away from drugs, kid." There were at least six policemen in the circle, and the questions were coming from all directions.

"How'd you find the car?"

"Well, we just sort of walked up on it."

"What time was it?"

"I don't remember, really. We were just walking through the woods. We do it all the time."

"What's your brother's name?"

"Ricky."

"Same last name?"

"Yes sir."

"Where were you and Ricky when you first saw the car?"

Mark pointed to the tree behind him. "Under that tree."

A paramedic approached the group and announced they were leaving and taking the body to the morgue. The wrecker was tugging at the Lincoln.

"Where is Ricky now?"

"At home."

"What happened to your face?" Hardy asked.

Mark instinctively reached for his eye. "Oh, nothing. Just got in a fight at school."

"Why were you hiding in the bushes over there?"

"I don't know."

"Come on, Mark, you were hiding for a reason."

"I don't know. It's sort of scary, you know. Seeing a dead man and all."

"You've never seen a dead man before?"

"On television."

One cop actually smiled at this.

"Did you see this man before he killed himself?"

"No sir."

"So you just found him like this?"

"Yes sir. We walked up under that tree and saw the car, then, we, uh, we saw the man."

"Where were you when you heard the gunshot?"

He started to point to the tree again, but caught himself. "I'm not sure I understand."

"We know you heard the gunshot. Where were you when you heard it?"

"I didn't hear the gunshot."

"You sure?"

"I'm sure. We walked up and found him right here, and we took off home and I called 911."

"Why didn't you give your name to 911?"

"I don't know."

"Come on, Mark, there must be a reason."

"I don't know. Scared, I guess."

The cops exchanged looks as if this were a game. Mark tried to breathe normally and act pitiful. He was just a kid.

"I really need to go home. My mom's probably looking for me."

"Okay. One last question," Hardy said. "Was the engine running when you first saw the car?"

Mark thought hard, but couldn't remember if Romey had turned it off before he shot himself. He answered very slowly. "I'm not sure, but I think it was running."

Hardy pointed to a police car. "Get in. I'll drive you home."

"That's okay. I'll just walk."

"No, it's too dark. I'll give you a ride. Come on." He took his arm, and walked him to the car.

FOUR

DIANNE SWAY had called the children's clinic and was sitting on the edge of Ricky's bed, biting her nails and waiting for a doctor to call. The nurse said it would be less than ten minutes. The nurse also said there was a very contagious virus in the schools and they had treated dozens of children that week. He had the symptoms, so don't worry. Dianne checked his forehead for a fever. She shook him gently again, but there was no response. He was still curled tightly, breathing normally and sucking his thumb. She heard a car door slam and went back to the living room.

Mark burst through the door. "Hi, Mom."

"Where have you been?" she snapped. "What's wrong with Ricky?"

Sergeant Hardy appeared in the door, and she froze.

"Good evening, ma'am," he said.

She glared at Mark. "What have you done?"

"Nothing."

Hardy stepped inside. "Nothing serious, ma'am."

"Then why are you here?"

"I can explain, Mom. It's sort of a long story."

Hardy closed the door behind him, and they stood in the small room looking awkwardly at one another.

"I'm listening."

"Well, me and Ricky were back in the woods playing this afternoon, and we saw this big black car parked in a clearing with the motor running, and when we got closer there was this man lying across the trunk with a gun in his mouth. He was dead."

"Dead!"

"Suicide, ma'am," Hardy offered.

"And we ran home as fast as we could and I called 911."

Dianne covered her mouth with her fingers.

"The man's name is Jerome Clifford, male white," Hardy reported officially. "He's from New Orleans, and we have no idea why he came here. Been dead for about two hours now, we think, not very long. He left a suicide note."

"What did Ricky do?" Dianne asked.

"Well, we ran home, and he fell on the couch and started sucking his thumb and wouldn't talk. I took him to his bed and covered him."

"How old is he?" Hardy asked with a frown.

"Eight."

"May I see him?"

"Why?" Dianne asked.

"I'm concerned. He witnessed something awful, and he might be in shock."

"Shock?"

"Yes ma'am."

Dianne walked quickly through the kitchen and down the hall with Hardy behind her and Mark following, shaking his head and clenching his teeth.

Hardy pulled the covers off Ricky's shoulders and touched his arm. The thumb was in the mouth. He shook him, called his name, and the eyes opened for a second. Ricky mumbled something.

"His skin is cold and damp. Has he been ill?" Hardy asked.

"No."

The phone rang, and Dianne raced for it. From the bedroom, Hardy and Mark listened as she told the doctor about the symptoms and the dead body the boys had found.

"Did he say anything when you guys saw the body?" Hardy asked quietly.

"I don't think so. It happened pretty fast. We, uh, we just took off running once we saw it. He just moaned and grunted all the way, ran sort of funny with his arms straight down. I never saw him run like that, and then as soon as we got home he curled up and hasn't spoken since."

"We need to get him to a hospital," Hardy said.

Mark's knees went weak and he leaned on the wall. Dianne hung up and Hardy met her in the kitchen. "The doctor wants him at the hospital," she said in panic.

"I'll call an ambulance," Hardy said, heading for his car. "Pack a few of his clothes." He disappeared and left the door open.

Dianne glared at Mark, who was weak and needed to sit. He fell into a chair at the kitchen table.

"Are you telling the truth?" she asked.

"Yes ma'am. We saw the dead body, and Ricky freaked out I guess, and we just ran home." It would take hours to tell the truth at this point. Once they were alone, he might reconsider and tell the rest of the story, but the cop was here now and it would get too complicated. He was not afraid of his mother, and generally came clean when she pressed. She was only thirty, younger than any of his friends' moms, and they had been through a lot together. Their brutal ordeals fighting off his father had forged a bond much deeper than any ordinary mother-son relationship. It hurt to hide this from her. She was scared and desperate, but the things Romey told him had nothing to do with Ricky's condition. A sharp pain hit him in the stomach and the room spun slowly.

"What happened to your eye?"

"I got in a fight in school. It wasn't my fault."

"It never is. Are you okay?"

"I think so."

Hardy lumbered through the door. "The ambulance'll be here in five minutes. Which hospital?"

"The doctor said to go to St. Peter's."

"Who's your doctor?"

"Shelby Pediatric Group. They said they would call in a children's psychiatrist to meet us at the hospital." She nervously lit a cigarette. "Do you think he's okay?"

"He needs to be looked at, maybe hospitalized, ma'am. I've seen this before with kids who witness shootings and stabbings. It's very traumatic, and it could take time for him to get over it. Had a kid last year who watched his mother get shot by a crack dealer, in one of the projects, and the poor little fella is still in the hospital."

"How old was he?"

"Eight, now he's nine. Won't talk. Won't eat. Sucks his thumb and plays with dolls. Really sad."

Dianne had heard enough. "I'll pack some clothes."

"You'd better pack clothes for yourself too, ma'am. You might have to stay with him."

"What about Mark?" she asked.

"What time does your husband get home?"

"I don't have one."

"Then pack clothes for Mark too. They might want to keep you overnight."

Dianne stood in the kitchen with her cigarette inches from her lips, and tried to think. She was scared and uncertain. "I don't have health insurance," she mumbled to the window.

"St. Peter's will take indigent cases. You need to get packed."

A crowd gathered around the ambulance as soon as it stopped at Number 17 East Street. They waited and watched, whispering and pointing as the paramedics went inside.

Hardy laid Ricky on the stretcher, and they strapped him down under a blanket. Ricky tried to curl, but the heavy Velcro bands kept him straight. He moaned twice, but never opened his eyes. Dianne gently freed his right arm and made the thumb available. Her eyes were watery, but she refused to cry.

The crowd backed away from the rear of the ambulance as the paramedics approached with the stretcher. They loaded Ricky, and Dianne stepped in behind. A few neighbors called out their concerns, but the driver slammed the door before she could answer. Mark sat in the front seat of the police car with Hardy, who hit a switch and suddenly blue lights were fluttering and bouncing off the nearby trailers. The crowd inched away, and Hardy gunned the engine. The ambulance followed.

Mark was too worried and scared to be interested in the radios and mikes and guns and gadgets. He sat still and kept his mouth shut.

"Are you telling the truth, son?" Hardy, suddenly the cop again, asked from nowhere.

"Yes sir. About what?"

"About what you saw?"

"Yes sir. You don't believe me?"

"I didn't say that. It's just a little strange, that's all."

Mark waited a few seconds, and when it was obvious Hardy was waiting for him, he asked, "What's strange?"

"Several things. First, you made the call, but wouldn't give your name. Why not? If you and Ricky just stumbled upon the dead man, why not give your name? Second, why did you sneak back to the scene and hide in the woods. People who hide are afraid. Why didn't you simply return to the scene and tell us what you saw? Third, if you and Ricky saw the same thing, why has he freaked out and you're in pretty good shape, know what I mean?"

Mark thought for a while, and realized he could think of nothing to say. So he said nothing. They were on the interstate headed for downtown. It was neat to watch the other cars get out of the way. The red ambulance lights were close behind.

"You didn't answer my question," Hardy finally said.

"Which question?"

"Why didn't you give your name when you made the call?"

"I was scared, okay. That's the first dead body I ever saw, and it scared me. I'm still scared."

"Then why did you sneak back to the scene? Why were you trying to hide from us?"

"I was scared, you know, but I just wanted to see what was going on. That's not a crime, is it?"

"Maybe not."

They left the expressway, and were now darting through traffic. The tall buildings of downtown Memphis were in sight.

"I just hope you're telling the truth," Hardy said.

"Don't you believe me?"

"I've got my doubts."

Mark swallowed hard and looked in the side mirror. "Why do you have doubts?"

"I'll tell you what I think, kid. You want to hear it?"

"Sure," Mark said slowly.

"Well, I think you kids were in the woods smoking. I found some fresh cigarette butts under that tree with the rope. I figure you were under there having a little smoke and you saw the whole thing."

Mark's heart stopped and his blood ran cold, but he knew the importance of trying to appear calm. Just shrug it off. Hardy wasn't there. He didn't see anything. He caught his hands shaking, so he sat on them. Hardy watched him.

"Do you arrest kids for smoking cigarettes?" Mark asked, his voice a shade weaker.

"No. But kids who lie to cops get in all sorts of trouble."

"I'm not lying, okay. I've smoked cigarettes there before, but not today. We were just walking through the woods, thinking about maybe having a smoke, and we walked up on the car and Romey."

Hardy hesitated slightly, then asked, "Who's Romey?"

Mark braced himself and breathed deeply. In a flash, he knew it was over. He'd blown it. Said too much. Lied too much. He'd lasted less than an hour with his story. Keep thinking, he told himself.

"That's the guy's name, isn't it?"

"Romey?"

"Yeah. Isn't that what you called him?"

"No. I told your mother his name was Jerome Clifford, from New Orleans."

"I thought you said it was Romey Clifford, from New Orleans."

"Who ever heard of the name Romey?"

"Beats me."

The car turned right, and Mark looked straight ahead. "Is this St. Peter's?"

"That's what the sign says."

Hardy parked to the side, and they watched the ambulance back up to the emergency dock.

FIVE

THE HONORABLE J. Roy Foltrigg, United States Attorney for the Southern District of Louisiana at New Orleans, and a Republican, sipped properly from a can of tomato juice and stretched his legs in the rear of his customized Chevrolet van as it raced smoothly along the expressway. Memphis was five hours to the north, straight up Interstate 55, and he could've caught a plane, but there were two reasons why he hadn't. First, the paperwork. He could claim it was official business related to the Boyd Boyette case, and he could stretch things here and there and make it work. But it would take months to get reimbursed and there would be eighteen different forms. Second, and much more important, he didn't like to fly. He could've waited three hours in New Orleans for a flight that would last for an hour and place him in Memphis around 11 P.M., but they would make it by midnight in the van. He didn't confess this fear of flying, and he knew he would one day be forced to see a shrink to overcome it. For the meantime, he had purchased this fancy van with his own money and loaded it down with appliances and gadgets, two phones, a television, even a fax machine. He buzzed around the Southern District of Louisiana in it, always with Wally Boxx behind the wheel. It was much nicer and more comfortable than any limousine.

He slowly kicked off his loafers and watched the night fly by as Special Agent Trumann listened to the telephone stuck in his ear. On the other end of the heavily padded back bench sat Assistant U.S. Attorney Thomas Fink, a loyal Foltrigg subordinate who'd worked on the Boyette case eighty hours a week and would handle most of the trial, especially the nonglamorous grunt work, saving of course the easy and high-profile parts for his boss. Fink was reading a document, as always, and trying to listen to the mumblings of Agent Trumann, who was seated across from him in a heavy swivel seat. Trumann had Memphis FBI on the phone.

Next to Trumann, in an identical swivel recliner, was Special Agent Skipper Scherff, a rookie who'd worked little on the case but happened to be available for this joyride to Memphis. He scribbled on a legal pad, and would do so for the next five hours because in this tight circle of power he had absolutely nothing to say and no one wanted to hear him. He would obediently stare at his legal pad and record orders from his supervisor, Larry Trumann, and, of course, from the general himself, Reverend Roy. Scherff stared intently at his scribbling, avoiding with great diligence even the slightest eye contact with Foltrigg, and tried in vain to discern what Memphis was telling Trumann. The news of Clifford's death had electrified their office only an hour earlier, and Scherff was still uncertain why and how he was sitting in Roy's van speeding along the expressway. Trumann had told him to run home, pack a change of clothes, and go immediately to Foltrigg's office. And this is what he'd done. And here he was, scribbling and listening.

The chauffeur, Wally Boxx, actually had a license to practice law, though he didn't know how to use it. Officially, he was an Assistant United States Attorney, same as Fink, but in reality he was a fetch-and-catch boy for Foltrigg. He drove his van, carried his briefcase, wrote his speeches, and handled the media, which took fifty percent of his time because his boss was gravely concerned with his public image. Boxx was not stupid. He was deft at political maneuvering, quick to the defense of his boss, and thoroughly loyal to the man and his mission. Foltrigg had a great future, and Boxx knew he would be there one day whispering importantly with the great man as only the two of them strolled around Capitol Hill.

Boxx knew the importance of Boyette. It would be the biggest trial of Foltrigg's illustrious career, the trial he'd been dreaming of, the trial to thrust him into the national spotlight. He knew Foltrigg was losing sleep over Barry The Blade Muldanno.

Larry Trumann finished the conversation and replaced the phone. He was a veteran agent, early forties, with ten years to go before retirement. Foltrigg waited for him to speak.

"They're trying to convince Memphis PD to release the car so we can go over it. It'll probably take an hour or so. They're having a hard time explaining Clifford and Boyette and all this to Memphis, but they're making progress. Head of our Memphis office is a guy named Jason McThune, very tough and persuasive, and he's meeting with the Memphis chief right now. McThune's called Washington and Washington's called Memphis, and we should have the car within a couple of hours. Single gunshot wound to the head, obviously self-inflicted. Apparently he tried to do it first with a garden hose in the tail pipe, but for some reason it didn't work. He was taking Dalmane and codeine, and washing it all down with Jack Daniels. No record on the gun, but it's too early. Memphis is checking it. A cheap .38. Thought he could swallow a bullet."

"No doubt it's suicide?" Foltrigg asked.

"No doubt."

"Where did he do it?"

"Somewhere in north Memphis. Drove into the woods in his big black Lincoln, and took care of himself."

"I don't suppose anyone saw it?"

"Evidently not. A couple of kids found the body in a remote area."

"How long had he been dead?"

"Not long. They'll do an autopsy in a few hours, and determine the time of death."

"Why Memphis?"

"Not sure. If there's a reason, we don't know it yet."

Foltrigg pondered these things and sipped his tomato juice. Fink took notes. Scherff scribbled furiously. Wally Boxx hung on every word.

"What about the note?" Foltrigg asked, looking out the window.

"Well, it could be interesting. Our guys in Memphis have a copy of it, not a very good copy, and they'll try and fax it to us in a few minutes. Apparently the note was handwritten in black ink, and the writing is fairly legible. It's a few paragraphs of instructions to his secretary about the funeral—he wants to be cremated—and what to do with his office furniture. The note tells the secretary where to find his will. Nothing about Boyette, of course. Nothing about Muldanno. Then, he apparently tried to add something to the note with a blue Bic pen, but it ran out of ink after he started his message. It's badly scrawled, and hard to read."

"What is it?"

"We don't know. The Memphis Police still have possession of the note, the gun, the pills, all the physical evidence removed from the car. McThune is trying to get it now. They found a Bic pen, no ink, in the car, and it appears to be the same pen he tried to use to add something to the note."

"They'll have it when we arrive, won't they?" Foltrigg asked in a tone that left no doubt he expected to have it all as soon as he got to Memphis.

"They're working on it," Trumann answered. Foltrigg was not his boss, technically, but this case was a prosecution now, not an investigation, and the Reverend was in control.

"So Jerome Clifford drives to Memphis and blows his brains out," Foltrigg said to the window. "Four weeks before trial. Man oh man. What else can go crazy with this case?"

No answer was expected. They rode in silence waiting for Roy to speak again.

"Where's Muldanno?" he finally asked.

"New Orleans. We're watching him."

"He'll have a new lawyer by midnight, and by noon tomorrow he'll file a dozen motions for continuances claiming the tragic death of Jerome Clifford seriously undermines his constitutional right to a fair trial with assistance of counsel. We'll oppose it of course, and the judge will order a hearing for next week, and we'll have the hearing, and we'll lose, and it'll be six months before this case goes to trial. Six months! Can you believe it?"

Trumann shook his head in disgust. "At least it'll give us more time to find the body."

It certainly would, and of course Roy had thought of this. He needed more time, really, he just couldn't admit it because he was the prosecutor, the people's lawyer, the government fighting crime and corruption. He was right, justice was on his side, and he had to be ready to attack evil at any moment, any time, any place. He had pushed hard for a speedy trial, because he was right, and he would get a conviction. The United States of America would win! And

Roy Foltrigg would deliver the victory. He could see the headlines. He could smell the ink.

He also needed to find the damned body of Boyd Boyette, or else there might be no conviction, no front page pictures, no interviews on CNN, no speedy ascent to Capitol Hill. He had convinced those around him that a guilty verdict was possible with no corpse, and this was true. But he didn't want to chance it. He wanted the body.

Fink looked at Agent Trumann. "We think Clifford knew where the body is. Did you know that?"

It was obvious Trumann did not know this. "What makes you think so?"

Fink placed his reading material on the seat. "Romey and I go way back. We were in law school together twenty years ago at Tulane. He was a little crazy back then, but very smart. About a week ago, he called me at home and said he wanted to talk about the Muldanno case. He was drunk, thick-tongued, out of his head, and kept saying he couldn't go through with the trial, which was surprising given how much he loves these big cases. We talked for an hour. He rambled and stuttered—"

"He even cried," Foltrigg interrupted.

"Yeah, cried like a child. I was surprised by all this at first, but then nothing Jerome Clifford did really surprised me anymore, you know. Not even suicide. He finally hung up. He called me at the office at nine the next morning scared to death he'd let something slip the night before. He was in a panic, kept hinting he might know where the body is and fishing to see whether he'd dropped off any clues during his drunken chitchat. Well, I played along, and thanked him for the information he gave me the night before, which was nothing. I thanked him twice, then three times, and I could feel Romey sweating on the other end of the phone. He called twice more that day, at the office, then called me at home that night, drunk again. It was almost comical, but I thought I could string him along and maybe he'd let something slip. I told him I had to tell Roy, and that Roy had told the FBI, and that the FBI was now trailing him around the clock."

"This really freaked him out," Foltrigg added helpfully.

"Yeah, he cussed me out pretty good, but called the next day at the office. We had lunch, and the guy was a nervous wreck. He was too scared to come right out and ask if we knew about the body, and I played it cool. I told him we were certain we'd have the body in plenty of time for the trial, and I thanked him again. He was cracking up before my eyes. He hadn't slept or bathed. His eyes were puffy and red. He got drunk over lunch, and started accusing me of trickery and all sorts of sleazy, unethical behavior. It was an ugly scene. I paid the check and left, and he called me at home that night, remarkably sober. He apologized. I said no problem. I explained to him that Roy was seriously considering an indictment against him for obstruction of justice, and this set him off. He said we couldn't prove it. I said maybe not, but he'd be indicted, arrested, and put on trial, and there would be no way he could represent Barry Muldanno. He screamed and cussed for fifteen minutes, then hung up. I never heard from him again."

"He knows, or he knew, where Muldanno put the body," Foltrigg added with certainty.

"Why weren't we informed?" Trumann asked.

"We were about to tell you. In fact, Thomas and I discussed it this afternoon, just a short time before we got the call." Foltrigg said this with an air of indifference, as if Trumann should not question him about such things. Trumann glanced at Scherff, who was glued to his legal pad, drawing pictures of handguns.

Foltrigg finished his tomato juice and tossed the can in the garbage. He crossed his feet. "You guys need to track Clifford's movements from New Orleans to Memphis. Which route did he take? Are there friends along the way? Where did he stop? Who did he see in Memphis? Surely he must've talked to someone from the time he left New Orleans until he shot himself. Don't you think so?"

Trumann nodded. "It's a long drive. I'm sure he had to stop along the way."

"He knew where the body is, and he obviously planned to commit suicide. There's an outside chance he told someone, don't you think?"

"Maybe."

"Think about it, Larry. Let's say you're the lawyer, heaven forbid. And you represent a killer who's murdered a United States Senator. Let's say that the killer tells you, his lawyer, where he hid the body. So, two, and only two, people in the entire world know this secret. And you, the lawyer, go off the deep end and decide to kill yourself. And you plan it. You know you're gonna die, right? You get pills and whiskey and a gun and a water hose, and you drive five hours from home, and you kill yourself. Now, would you share your little secret with anyone?"

"Perhaps. I don't know."

"There's a chance, right?"

"Slight chance."

"Good. If we have a slight chance, then we must investigate it thoroughly. I'd start with his office personnel. Find out when he left New Orleans. Check his credit cards. Where did he buy gas? Where did he eat? Where did he get the gun and the pills and the booze? Does he have family between here and there? Old lawyer friends along the way? There are a thousand things to check."

Trumann handed the phone to Scherff. "Call our office. Get Hightower on the phone."

Foltrigg was pleased to see the FBI jump when he barked. He grinned smugly at Fink. Between them on the floor was a storage box crammed with files and exhibits and documents all related to *U.S.A. vs. Barry Muldanno.* Four more boxes were at the office. Fink had their contents memorized, but Roy did not. He pulled out a file and flipped through it. It was a thick motion filed by Jerome Clifford two months earlier that still had not been ruled upon. He laid it down, and stared through the window at the dark Mississippi landscape passing in the night. The Bogue Chitto exit was just ahead. Where do they get these names?

This would be a quick trip. He needed to confirm that Clifford was in fact dead, and had in fact died by his own hand. He had to know if any clues were dropped along the way, confessions to friends or loose talk to strangers, perhaps notes with last words that might be of help. Longshots at best. But there had been many dead ends in the search for Boyd Boyette and his killer, and this would not be the last.

SIX

A DOCTOR in a yellow jogging suit ran through the swinging doors at the end of the emergency hallway and said something to the receptionist sitting behind the dirty sliding windows. She pointed, and he approached Dianne and Mark and Hardy as they stood by a Coke machine in one corner of the Admissions lobby of St. Peter's Charity Hospital. He introduced himself to Dianne as Dr. Simon Greenway and ignored the cop and Mark. He was a psychiatrist, he said, and had been called moments earlier by Dr. Sage, the family's pediatrician. She needed to come with him. Hardy said he would stay with Mark.

They hurried away, down the narrow hallway, dodging nurses and orderlies, darting around gurneys and parked beds, and disappeared through the swinging doors. The Admissions lobby was crowded with dozens of sick and struggling patients-to-be. There were no empty chairs. Family members filled out forms. No one was in a hurry. A hidden intercom rattled nonstop somewhere above, paging a hundred doctors a minute.

It was a few minutes after seven. "Are you hungry, Mark?" Hardy asked.

He wasn't, but he wanted to leave this place. "Maybe a little."

"Let's go to the cafeteria. I'll buy you a cheeseburger."

They walked through a busy hallway, down a flight of stairs to the basement where a mass of anxious people roamed the corridor. Another hall led to a large open area, and suddenly they were in a cafeteria, louder and more crowded than the lunchroom at school. Hardy pointed to the only empty table in view, and Mark waited there.

Of particular concern to Mark at this moment was, of course, his little brother. He was worried about Ricky's physical condition, although Hardy had explained that he was in no danger of dying. He said that some doctors would talk to him and try to bring him around. But it could take time. He said that it was terribly important for the doctors to know exactly what happened, the truth and nothing but the truth, and that if the doctors were not told the truth then it could be severely damaging to Ricky and his mental condition. Hardy said Ricky might be locked up in some institution for months, maybe years, if the doctors weren't told the truth about what the boys witnessed.

Hardy was okay, not too bright, and he was making the mistake of talking to Mark as if he were five years old instead of eleven. He described the padded walls, and rolled his eyes around with great exaggeration. He told of patients being chained to beds as if spinning some horror story around the campfire. Mark was tired of it.

Mark could think of little except Ricky and whether he would remove his thumb and start talking. He desperately wanted this to happen, but he wanted to have first crack at Ricky when the shock ended. They had things to discuss.

What if the doctors or, heaven forbid, the cops got to him first, and Ricky told the whole story and they all knew Mark was lying? What would they do to him if they caught him lying? Maybe they wouldn't believe Ricky. Since he'd blanked out and left the world for a while, maybe they would tend to believe Mark instead. This conflict in stories was too awful to think about.

It's amazing how lies grow. You start with a small one that seems easy to cover, then you get boxed in and tell another one. Then another. People believe you at first, and they act upon your lies, and you catch yourself wishing you'd simply told the truth. He could have told the truth to the cops and to his mother. He could have explained in great detail everything that Ricky saw. And the secret would still be safe because Ricky didn't know.

Things were happening so fast he couldn't plan. He wanted to get his mother in a room with the door locked and unload all this, just stop it now before it got worse. If he didn't do something, he might go to jail and Ricky might go to the nuthouse for kids.

Hardy appeared with a tray covered with french fries and cheeseburgers, two for him and one for Mark. He arranged the food neatly and returned the tray.

Mark nibbled on a french fry. Hardy launched into a burger.

"So what happened to your face?" Hardy asked, chomping away.

Mark rubbed the knot and remembered he had been wounded in the fray. "Oh nothing. Just got in a fight in school."

"Who's the other kid?"

Dammit! Cops are relentless. Tell one lie to cover another. He was sick of lying. "You don't know him," he answered, then bit into his cheeseburger.

"I might want to talk to him."

"Why?"

"Did you get in trouble for this fight? I mean, did your teacher take you to the principal's office, or anything like that?"

"No. It happened when school was out."

"I thought you said you got in a fight at school."

"Well, it sort of started at school, okay. Me and this guy got into it at lunch, and agreed to meet when school was out."

Hardy drew mightily on the tiny straw in his milk shake. He swallowed hard, cleared his mouth, and said, "What's the other kid's name?"

"Why do you want to know?"

This angered Hardy and he stopped chewing. Mark refused to look into his eyes, and he bent low over his food and stared at the ketchup.

"I'm a cop, kid. It's my job to ask questions."

"Do I have to answer them?"

"Of course you do. Unless, of course, you're hiding something and afraid to answer. At that point, I'll have to get with your mother and perhaps take the both of you down to the station for more questioning."

"Questioning about what? What exactly do you want to know?"

"Who is the kid you had a fight with today?"

Mark nibbled forever on the end of a long fry. Hardy picked up the second cheeseburger. A spot of mayonnaise hung from the corner of his mouth.

"I don't want to get him in trouble," Mark said.

"He won't get in trouble."

"Then why do you want to know his name?"

"I just want to know. It's my job, okay?"

"You think I'm lying, don't you?" Mark asked, looking pitifully into the bulging face.

The chomping stopped. "I don't know, kid. Your story is full of holes."

Mark looked even more pitiful. "I can't remember everything. It happened so fast. You expect me to give every little detail, and I can't remember it that way."

Hardy stuck a wad of fries in his mouth. "Eat your food. We'd better get back."

"Thanks for the dinner."

Ricky was in a private room on the ninth floor. A large sign by the elevator labeled it as the PSYCHIATRIC WING, and it was much quieter. The lights were dimmer, the voices softer, the traffic much slower. The nurses' station was near the elevator, and those stepping off were scrutinized. A security guard whispered with the nurses and watched the hallways. Down from the elevators, away from the rooms, was a small, dark sitting area with a television, soft drink machines, magazines, and Gideon Bibles.

Mark and Hardy were alone in the waiting area. Mark sipped a Sprite, his third, and watched a rerun of "Hill Street Blues" on cable while Hardy dozed fitfully on the terribly undersized couch. It was almost nine, and half an hour had passed since Dianne had walked him down the hall to Ricky's room for a quick peek. He looked small under the sheets. The IV, Dianne had explained, was to feed him because he wouldn't eat. She assured him Ricky would be all right, but Mark studied her eyes and knew she was worried. Dr. Greenway would return in a bit, and wanted to talk to Mark.

"Has he said anything?" Mark had asked as he studied the IV.

"No. Not a word."

She took his hand and they walked through the dim hallway to the sitting area. At least five times, Mark had almost blurted something out. They had passed an empty room not far from Ricky's and he thought of dragging her inside for a confession. But he didn't. Later, he kept telling himself, I'll tell her later.

Hardy had stopped asking questions. His shift ended at ten, and it was obvious he was tired of Mark and Ricky and the hospital. He wanted to return to the streets.

A pretty nurse in a short skirt walked past the elevators and motioned for Mark to follow her. He eased from his chair, holding his Sprite. She took his hand, and there was something exciting about this. Her fingernails were long and red. Her skin was smooth and tanned. She had blond hair and a perfect smile, and she was young. Her name was Karen, and she squeezed his hand a bit tighter than necessary. His heart skipped a beat.

"Dr. Greenway wants to talk to you," she said, leaning down as she walked. Her perfume lingered, and it was the most wonderful fragrance Mark could remember.

She walked him to Ricky's room, Number 943, and released his hand. The door was closed, so she knocked slightly and opened it. Mark entered slowly, and Karen patted him on the shoulder. He watched her leave through the half-open door.

Dr. Greenway now wore a shirt and tie with a white lab jacket over it. An ID tag hung from the left front pocket. He was a skinny man with round glasses and a black beard, and seemed too young to be doing this.

"Come in, Mark," he said after Mark was already in the room and standing at the foot of Ricky's bed. "Sit here." He pointed to a plastic chair next to a foldaway bed under the window. His voice was low, almost a whisper. Dianne sat with her feet curled under her on the bed. Her shoes were on the floor. She wore blue jeans and a sweater, and stared at Ricky under the sheets with a tube in his arm. A lamp on a table near the bathroom door provided the only light. The blinds were shut tight.

Mark eased into the plastic chair, and Dr. Greenway sat on the edge of the foldaway, not two feet away. He squinted and frowned, and projected such somberness that Mark thought for a second they were all about to die.

"I need to talk to you about what happened," he said. He was not whispering now. It was obvious Ricky was in another world and they were unafraid of waking him. Dianne was behind Greenway, still staring blankly at the bed. Mark wanted her alone so he could talk and work out of this mess, but she was back there in the darkness, behind the doctor, ignoring him.

"Has he said anything?" Mark asked first. The past three hours with Hardy had been nothing but quick questions, and the habit was hard to break.

"No."

"How sick is he?"

"Very sick," Greenway answered, his tiny, dark eyes glowing at Mark. "What did he see this afternoon?"

"Is this in secret?"

"Yes. Anything you tell me is strictly confidential."

"What if the cops want to know what I tell you?"

"I can't tell them. I promise. This is all very secret and confidential. Just you and me and your mother. We're all trying to help Ricky, and I've got to know what happened."

Maybe a good dose of the truth would help everyone, especially Ricky. Mark looked at the small, blond head with hair sticking in all directions on the pillow. Why oh why didn't they just run when the black car pulled up and parked? He was suddenly hit with guilt, and it terrified him. All of this was his fault. He should have known better than to mess with a crazy man.

His lip quivered and his eyes watered. He was cold. It was time to tell all. He was running out of lies and Ricky needed help. Greenway watched every move.

And then Hardy walked slowly by the door. He paused for a second in the hall and locked eyes with Mark, then disappeared. Mark knew he wasn't far away. Greenway had not seen him.

Mark started with the cigarettes. His mother looked at him hard, but if she was angry she didn't convey it. She shook her head once or twice, but never said a word. He spoke in a low voice, his eyes alternating quickly between Greenway and the door, and described the tree with the rope and the woods and the clearing. Then the car. He left out a good chunk of the story, but did admit to Greenway, in a soft voice and in extreme confidence, that he once crawled to the car and removed the hose. And when he did so, Ricky cried and peed in his pants. Ricky begged him not to do it. He could tell Greenway liked this part. Dianne listened without expression.

Hardy walked by again, but Mark pretended not to see him. He paused in his story for a few seconds, then told how the man stormed out of the car, saw the garden hose lying harmlessly in the weeds, and crawled on the trunk and shot himself.

"How far away was Ricky?" Greenway asked.

Mark looked around the room. "You see that door across the hall?" he asked, pointing. "From here to there."

Greenway looked and rubbed his beard. "About forty feet. That's not very far."

"It was very close."

"What exactly did Ricky do when the shot was fired?"

Dianne was listening now. It apparently had just occurred to her that this was a different version from the earlier one. She wrinkled her forehead and looked hard at her eldest.

"I'm sorry, Mom. I was too scared to think. Don't be angry with me."

"You actually saw the man shoot himself?" she asked in disbelief.

"Yes."

She looked at Ricky. "No wonder."

"What did Ricky do when the shot was fired?"

"I wasn't looking at Ricky. I was watching the man with the gun."

"Poor baby," Dianne mumbled in the background. Greenway held up a hand to cut her off.

"Was Ricky close to you?"

Mark glanced at the door, and explained faintly how Ricky had frozen, then started away in an awkward jog, arms straight down, a dull moaning sound coming from his mouth. He told it all with dead accuracy from the point of the shooting to the point of the ambulance, and he left out nothing. He closed his eyes and relived each step, each movement. It felt wonderful to be so truthful.

"Why didn't you tell me you watched the man kill himself?" Dianne asked.

This irritated Greenway. "Please, Ms. Sway, you can discuss it with him later," he said without taking his eyes off Mark.

"What was the last word Ricky said?" Greenway asked.

He thought and watched the door. The hall was empty. "I really can't remember."

□ □ □ □

Sergeant Hardy huddled with his lieutenant and Special Agent Jason McThune of the FBI. They chatted in the sitting area next to the soft drink machines. Another FBI agent loitered suspiciously near the elevator. The hospital security guard glared at him.

The lieutenant explained hurriedly to Hardy that it was now an FBI matter, that the dead man's car and all other physical evidence had been turned over by Memphis PD, that print experts had finished dusting the car and found lots of fingerprints too small for an adult, and they needed to know if Mark had dropped any clues or changed his story.

"No, but I'm not convinced he's telling the truth," Hardy said.

"Has he touched anything we can take?" McThune asked quickly, unconcerned about Hardy's theories or convictions.

"What do you mean?"

"We have a strong suspicion the kid was in the car at some point before Clifford died. We need to lift the kid's prints from something and see if they match."

"What makes you think he was in the car?" Hardy asked with great anticipation.

"I'll explain later," his lieutenant said.

Hardy looked around the sitting area, and suddenly pointed to a trash basket by the chair Mark had sat in. "There. The Sprite can. He drank a Sprite while sitting right there." McThune looked up and down the hall, and carefully wrapped a handkerchief around the Sprite can. He placed it in the pocket of his coat.

"It's definitely his," Hardy said. "This is the only trash basket, and that's the only Sprite can."

"I'll run this to our fingerprint men," McThune said. "Is the kid, Mark, staying here tonight?"

"I think so," Hardy said. "They've moved a portable bed into his brother's room. Looks like they'll all sleep in there. Why is the FBI concerned with Clifford?"

"I'll explain later," said his lieutenant. "Stay here for another hour."

"I'm supposed to be off in ten minutes."

"You need the overtime."

□ □ □ □

Dr. Greenway sat in the plastic chair near the bed and studied his notes. "I'm gonna leave in a minute, but I'll be back early in the morning. He's stable, and I expect little change through the night. The nurses will check in every so often. Call them if he wakes up." He flipped a page of notes and read the chicken scratch, then looked at Dianne. "It's a severe case of acute post-traumatic stress disorder."

"What does that mean?" Mark asked. Dianne rubbed her temples and kept her eyes closed.

"Sometimes a person sees a terrible event and cannot cope with it. Ricky was badly scared when you removed the garden hose from the tail pipe, and when he saw the man shoot himself he was suddenly exposed to a terrifying experience that he couldn't handle. It triggered a response in him. He sort of snapped. It shocked his mind and body. He was able to run home, which is quite remarkable because normally a person traumatized like Ricky would immediately become numb and paralyzed." He paused and placed his notes on the bed. "There's not a lot we can do right now. I expect him to come around tomorrow, or the next day at the latest, and we'll start talking about things. It may take some time. He'll have nightmares of the shooting, and flashbacks. He'll deny it happened, then he'll blame himself for it. He'll feel isolated, betrayed, bewildered, maybe even depressed. You just never know."

"How will you treat him?" Dianne asked.

"We have to make him feel safe. You must stay here at all times. Now, you said the father is of no use."

"Keep him away from Ricky," Mark said sternly. Dianne nodded.

"Fine. And there are no grandparents or relatives nearby."

"No."

"Very well. It's imperative that both of you stay in this room as much as possible for the next several days. Ricky must feel safe and secure. He'll need emotional and physical support from you. He and I will talk several times a day. It will be important for Mark and Ricky to talk about the shooting. They need to share and compare their reactions."

"When do you think we might go home?" Dianne asked.

"I don't know, but as soon as possible. He needs the safety and familiarity of his bedroom and surroundings. Maybe a week. Maybe two. Depends on how quickly he responds."

Dianne pulled her feet under her. "I, uh, I have a job. I don't know what to do."

"I'll have my office contact your employer first thing in the morning."

"My employer runs a sweatshop. It is not a nice, clean corporation with benefits and sympathy. They will not send flowers. I'm afraid they won't understand."

"I'll do the best I can."

"What about school?" Mark asked.

"Your mother has given me the name of the principal. I'll call first thing in the morning and talk to your teachers."

Dianne was rubbing her temples again. A nurse, not the pretty one, knocked while entering. She handed Dianne two pills and a cup of water.

"It's Dalmane," Greenway said. "It should help you rest. If not, call the nurses' station and they'll bring something stronger."

The nurse left and Greenway stood and felt Ricky's forehead. "See you guys in the morning. Get some sleep." He smiled for the first time, then closed the door behind him.

They were alone, the tiny Sway family, or what was left of it. Mark moved closer to his mother, and leaned on her shoulder. They looked at the small head on the large pillow less than five feet away.

She patted his arm. "It'll be all right, Mark. We've been through worse." She held him tight and he closed his eyes.

"I'm sorry, Mom." His eyes watered, and he was ready for a cry. "I'm so sorry about all this." She squeezed him, and held him tight for a long minute. He sobbed quietly with his face buried in her shirt.

She gently lay down with Mark still in her arms, and they curled together on the cheap foam mattress. Ricky's bed was two feet higher. The window was above them. The lights were low. Mark stopped the crying. It was something he was lousy at anyway.

The Dalmane was working, and she was exhausted. Nine hours of packing plastic lamps into cardboard boxes, five hours of a full-blown crisis, and now the Dalmane. She was ready for a deep sleep.

"Will you get fired, Mom?" Mark asked. He worried about the family finances as much as she did.

"I don't think so. We'll worry about it tomorrow."

"We need to talk, Mom."

"I know we do. But let's do it in the morning."

"Why can't we talk now?"

She relaxed her grip and breathed deeply, eyes already closed. "I'm very tired and sleepy, Mark. I promise we'll have a long talk first thing in the morning. You have some questions to answer, don't you? Now go brush your teeth and let's try and sleep."

Mark was suddenly tired too. The hard line of a metal brace protruded through the cheap mattress, and he crept closer to the wall and pulled the lone sheet over him. His mother rubbed his arm. He stared at the wall, six inches away, and decided he could not sleep like this for a week.

Her breathing was much heavier and she was completely still. He thought of Romey. Where was he now? Where was the chubby little body with the bald head? He remembered the sweat and how it poured from his shiny scalp and ran down in all directions, some dripping from his eyebrows and some soaking his collar. Even his ears were wet. Who would get his car? Who would clean it up and wash the blood off? Who would get the gun? Mark realized for the first time that his ears were no longer ringing from the gunfire in the car. Was Hardy still out there in the sitting room trying to sleep? Would the cops return tomorrow with more questions? What if they asked about the garden hose? What if they asked a thousand questions?

He was wide awake now, staring at the wall. Lights from the outside trickled through the blinds. The Dalmane worked well because his mother was breathing very slow and heavy. Ricky had not moved. He stared at the dim light above the table, and thought of Hardy and the police. Were they watching him? Was he under surveillance, like on television? Surely not.

He watched them sleep for twenty minutes, and got bored with it. It was time to explore. When he was a first-grader, his father came home drunk late one night, and started raising hell with Dianne. They fought and the trailer shook, and Mark eased open the shoddy window in his room and slid to the ground. He went for a long walk around the neighborhood, then through the woods. It was a hot, sticky night with plenty of stars, and he rested on a hill overlooking the trailer park. He prayed for the safety of his mother. He asked God for a family in which everyone could sleep without fear of abuse. Why couldn't they just be normal? He rambled for two hours. All was quiet when he returned home, and thus began a habit of nighttime excursions that had brought him much pleasure and peace.

Mark was a thinker, a worrier, and when sleep came and went or wouldn't come at all, he went for long secret walks. He learned much. He wore dark clothing and moved like a thief through the shadows of Tucker Wheel Estates. He witnessed petty crimes of theft and vandalism, but he never told. He saw lovers sneak from windows. He loved to sit on the hill above the park on clear nights and enjoy a quiet smoke. The fear of getting caught by his mother had vanished years ago. She worked hard and slept sound.

He was not afraid of strange places. He pulled the sheet over his mother's shoulder, did the same for Ricky, and quietly closed the door behind him. The hall was dark and empty. Karen the gorgeous was busy at the nurses' desk. She smiled beautifully at him and stopped her writing. He wanted to go for some orange juice in the cafeteria, he said, and he knew how to get there. He'd be back in a minute. Karen grinned at him as he walked away, and Mark was in love.

Hardy was gone. The sitting room was empty but the television was on. "Hogan's Heroes." He took the empty elevator to the basement.

The cafeteria was deserted. A man with casts on both legs sat stiffly in a wheelchair at one table. The casts were shiny and clean. An arm was in a sling. A band of thick gauze covered the top of his head and it looked as though the hair had been shaven. He was terribly uncomfortable.

Mark paid for a pint of juice, and sat at a table near the man. He grimaced in pain, and shoved his soup away in frustration. He sipped juice through a straw, and noticed Mark.

"What's up?" Mark asked with a smile. He could talk to anyone and felt sorry for the guy.

The man glared at him, then looked away. He grimaced again and tried to adjust his legs. Mark tried not to stare.

A man with a white shirt and tie appeared from nowhere with a tray of food and coffee, and sat at a table on the other side of the injured guy. He didn't appear to notice Mark. "Bad injury," he said with a large smile. "What happened?"

"Car wreck," came the somewhat anguished reply. "Got hit by an Exxon truck. Nut ran a stop sign."

The smile grew even larger and the food and coffee were ignored. "When did it happen?"

"Three days ago."

"Did you say Exxon truck?" The man was standing and moving quickly to the guy's table, pulling something out of his pocket. He took a chair and was suddenly sitting within inches of the casts.

"Yeah," the guy said warily.

The man handed him a white card. "My name's Gill Teal. I'm a lawyer, and I specialize in auto accidents, especially cases involving large trucks." Gill Teal said this very rapidly, as if he'd hooked a large fish and had to work quickly or it might get away. "That's my specialty. Big-truck cases. Eighteen wheelers. Dump trucks. Tankers. You name it, and I go after them." He thrust his hand across the table. "Name's Gill Teal."

Luckily for the guy, his good arm was his right one, and he lamely slung it over the table to shake hands with this hustler. "Joe Farris."

Gill pumped it furiously, and eagerly moved in for the kill. "What you got—two broke legs, concussion, coupla puncture wounds?"

"And broken collarbone."

"Great. Then we're looking at permanent disability. What type work you do?" Gill asked, rubbing his chin in careful analysis. The card was lying on the table, untouched by Joe. They were unaware of Mark.

"Crane operator."

"Union?"

"Yeah."

"Wow. And the Exxon truck ran a stop sign. No doubt about who's at fault here?"

Joe frowned and shifted again, and even Mark could tell he was rapidly tiring of Gill and this intrusion. He shook his head no.

Gill made frantic notes on a napkin, then smiled at Joe and announced, "I can get you at least six hundred thousand. I take only a third, and you walk away with four hundred thousand. Minimum. Four hundred grand, tax free, of course. We'll file suit tomorrow."

Joe took this as if he'd heard it before. Gill hung in mid-air with his mouth open, proud of himself, full of confidence.

"I've talked to some other lawyers," Joe said.

"I can get you more than anybody. I do this for a living, nothing but truck cases. I've sued Exxon before, know all their lawyers and corporate people locally, and they're terrified of me because I go for the jugular. It's warfare, Joe, and I'm the best in town. I know how to play their dirty games. Just settled a truck case for almost half a million. They threw money at my client once he hired me. Not bragging, Joe, but I'm the best in town when it comes to these cases."

"A lawyer called me this morning and said he could get me a million."

"He's lying. What was his name? McFay? Ragland? Snodgrass? I know these guys. I kick their asses all the time, Joe, and anyway I said six hundred thousand is a minimum. Could be much more. Hell, Joe, if they push us to trial, who knows how much a jury might give us. I'm in trial every day, Joe, kicking ass all over Memphis. Six hundred is a minimum. Have you hired anybody yet? Signed a contract?"

Joe shook his head no. "Not yet."

"Wonderful. Look, Joe, you've got a wife and kids, right?"

"Ex-wife, three kids."

"So you've got child support, man, now listen to me. How much child support?"

"Five hundred a month."

"That's low. And you've got bills. Here's what I'll do. I'll advance you a thousand bucks a month to be applied against your settlement. If we settle in three months, I withhold three thousand. If it takes two years, and it won't, but if it does I'll withhold twenty-four thousand. Or whatever. You follow me, Joe? Cash now on the spot."

Joe shifted again and stared at the table. "This other lawyer came by my room yesterday and said he'd advance two thousand now and float me two thousand a month."

"Who was it? Scottie Moss? Rob LaMoke? I know these guys, Joe, and they're trash. Can't find their way to the courthouse. You can't trust them. They're incompetent. I'll match it—two thousand now, and two thousand a month."

"This other guy with some big firm offered ten thousand up front and a line of credit for whatever I needed."

Gill was crushed, and it was at least ten seconds before he could speak. "Listen to me, Joe. It's not a matter of advance cash, okay. It's a matter of how much money I can get for you from Exxon. And nobody, I repeat, nobody will get more than me. Nobody. Look. I'll advance five thousand now, and allow you to draw what you need to pay bills. Fair enough?"

"I'll think about it."

"Time is critical, Joe. We must move fast. Evidence disappears. Memories fade. Big corporations move slow."

"I said I'll think about it."

"Can I call you tomorrow?"

"No."

"Why not?"

"Hell, I can't sleep now for all the damned lawyers calling. I can't eat a meal without you guys bargin' in. There are more lawyers around this damned place than doctors."

Gill was unmoved. "There are a lot of sharks out here, Joe. A lot of really lousy lawyers who'll screw up your case. Sad but true. The profession is overcrowded, so lawyers are everywhere trying to find business. But don't make a mistake, Joe. Check me out. Look in the yellow pages. There's a full-page, three-color ad for me, Joe. Look up Gill Teal, and you'll see who's for real."

"I'll think about it."

Gill came forth with another card and handed it to Joe. He said good-bye and left, never touching the food or coffee on his tray.

Joe was suffering. He grabbed the wheel with his right arm, and slowly rolled himself away. Mark wanted to help, but thought better of asking. Both of Gill's cards were on the table. He finished his juice, glanced around, and picked up one of the cards.

Mark told Karen, his sweetheart, that he couldn't sleep and would be watching television if anyone needed him. He sat on the couch in the waiting area and flipped through the phone book while watching "Cheers" reruns. He sipped another Sprite. Hardy, bless his heart, had given him eight quarters after dinner.

Karen brought him a blanket and tucked it around his legs. She patted his arm with her long, thin hands, and glided away. He watched every step.

Mr. Gill Teal did indeed have a full-page ad in the Attorneys section of the Memphis yellow pages, along with a dozen other lawyers. There was a nice picture of him standing casually outside a courthouse with his jacket off and sleeves rolled up. "I FIGHT FOR YOUR RIGHTS!" it said under the photo. In bold red letters across the top, the question HAVE YOU BEEN INJURED? cried out. Thick green print answered just below, IF SO, CALL GILL TEAL—HE'S FOR REAL. Farther down, in blue print Gill listed all the types of cases he handled, and there were hundreds. Lawnmowers, electrical shock, deformed babies, car wrecks, exploding water heaters. Eighteen years' experience in all courts. A small map in the corner of the ad directed the world to his office, which was just across the street from the courthouse.

Mark heard a familiar voice, and suddenly there he was, Gill Teal himself, on television standing beside a hospital emergency entrance talking about injured loved ones and crooked insurance companies. Red lights flashed in the background. Paramedics ran behind him. But Gill had the situation under control, and he would take your case for nothing down. No fee unless he recovered.

Small world! In the past two hours, Mark had seen him in person, picked up one of his business cards, was literally looking at his face in the yellow pages, and now, here he was speaking to him from the television.

He closed the phone book and laid it on the cluttered coffee table. He pulled the blanket over him and decided to go to sleep.

Tomorrow he might call Gill Teal.

SEVEN

FOLTRIGG LIKED TO BE ESCORTED. He especially enjoyed those priceless moments when the cameras were rolling and waiting for him, and at just the right moment he would stroll majestically through the hall or down the courthouse steps with Wally Boxx in front like a pit bull and Thomas Fink or another assistant by his side brushing off idiotic questions. He spent many quiet moments watching videos of himself darting in and out of courthouses with a small entourage. His timing was usually perfect. He had the walk perfected. He held his hands up patiently as if he would love to answer questions but, being a man of great importance, he just didn't have the time. Soon thereafter, Wally would call the reporters in for an orchestrated press conference in which Roy himself would break from his brutal work schedule and spend a few moments in the lights. A small library in the U.S. Attorney's suite had been converted to a press room, complete with floodlights and a sound system. Roy kept makeup in a locked cabinet.

As he entered the Federal Building on Main Street in Memphis, a few minutes after midnight, he had an escort of sorts with Wally and Fink and agents Trumann and Scherff, but there were no anxious reporters. In fact, not a soul waited for him until he entered the offices of the FBI where Jason McThune sipped stale coffee with two other weary agents. So much for grand entrances.

Introductions were handled quickly as they walked to McThune's cramped office. Foltrigg took the only available seat. McThune was a twenty-year man who'd been shipped to Memphis four years earlier against his wishes and was counting the months until he could leave for the Pacific Northwest. He was tired and irritated because it was late. He'd heard of Foltrigg, but never met him. The rumors described him as a pompous ass.

An agent who was unidentified and unintroduced closed the door, and McThune fell into his seat behind the desk. He covered the basics: the finding of the car, the contents of it, the gun, the wound, the time of death, and on and on. "Kid's name is Mark Sway. He told Memphis PD he and his younger brother happened upon the body and ran to call the authorities. They live about a half a mile away in a trailer park. The younger kid is in the hospital now suffering from what appears to be traumatic shock. Mark Sway and his mother, Dianne, divorced, are also at the hospital. The father lives here in the city, and has a record of petty stuff. DUI's, fights, and the like. Sophisticated criminal. Low-class white people. Anyway, the kid's lying."

"I couldn't read the note," Foltrigg interrupted, dying to say something. "The fax was bad." He said this as if McThune and the Memphis FBI were inept because he, Roy Foltrigg, had received a bad fax in his van.

McThune glanced at Larry Trumann and Skipper Scherff standing against the wall, and continued. "I'll get to that in a minute. We know the kid's lying because he says they arrived on the scene after Clifford shot himself. Looks doubtful. First, the kid's fingerprints are all over the car, inside and out. On the dash, on the door, on the whiskey bottle, on the gun, everywhere. We lifted a print from him about two hours ago, and we've had our people all over the car. They'll finish up tomorrow, but it's obvious the kid was inside. Doing what, well, we're not yet certain. We've also found prints all around the rear taillights just above the exhaust pipe. And there were also three fresh cigarette butts under a tree near the car. Virginia Slims, the same brand used by Dianne Sway. We figure the kids were being kids, took the cigarettes from their mother, and went for a smoke. They were minding their own business when Clifford appears from nowhere. They hide and watch him—it's a dense area and hiding is no problem. Maybe they sneak around and pull out the hose, we're not sure and the kids aren't telling. The little boy can't talk right now, and Mark evidently is lying. Anyway, it's obvious the hose didn't work. We're trying to match prints on it, but it's tedious work. May be impossible. I'll have photos in the morning to show the location of the hose when Memphis PD arrived."

McThune lifted a yellow notepad from the wreckage on his desk. He spoke to it, not to Foltrigg. "Clifford fired at least one shot from inside the car. The bullet exited through the center, almost exactly, of the front passenger window, which cracked but did not shatter. No idea why he did this, and no idea when it was done. The autopsy was finished an hour ago, and Clifford was full of Dalmane, codeine, and Percodan. Plus his blood alcohol content was point two-two, so he was drunk as a skunk, as these people say down here. My point being, not only was he off his rocker enough to kill himself, but he was also drunk and stoned, so there's no way to figure out a lot of this. We're not tracking a rational mind."

"I understand that." Roy nodded impatiently. Wally Boxx hovered behind him like a well-trained terrier.

McThune ignored him. "The gun's a cheap .38 he purchased illegally at a pawnshop here in Memphis. We've questioned the owner, but he won't talk without his lawyer present, so we'll do that in the morning, or this morning I should say. A Texaco receipt shows a purchase of gasoline in Vaiden, Mississippi, about an hour and a half from here. The clerk is a kid who says she thinks he stopped around 1 P.M. No other evidence of any stops. His secretary says he left the office around 9 A.M., said he had an errand to run and she didn't hear a word until we called. Frankly, she was not very upset at the news. It looks as though he left New Orleans shortly after nine, drove to Memphis in five or six hours, stopped once for gas, stopped to buy the gun, and drove off and shot himself. Maybe he stopped for lunch, maybe to buy whiskey, maybe a lot of things. We're digging."

"Why Memphis?" Wally Boxx asked. Foltrigg nodded, obviously approving the question.

"Because he was born here," McThune said solemnly while staring at Foltrigg, as if everyone prefers to die in the place of their birth. It was a humorous response delivered by a serious face, and Foltrigg missed it all. McThune had heard he was not too bright.

"Evidently, the family moved away when he was a child," he explained after a pause. "He went to college at Rice and law school at Tulane."

"We were in law school together," Fink said proudly.

"That's great. The note was handwritten and dated today, or yesterday I should say. Handwritten with a black felt tip pen of some sort—the pen wasn't found on him or in the car." McThune picked up a sheet of paper and leaned across the desk. "Here. This is the original. Be careful with it."

Wally Boxx leaped at it and handed it to Foltrigg, who studied it. McThune rubbed his eyes and continued. "Just funeral arrangements and directions to his secretary. Look at the bottom. It looks as though he tried to add something with a blue ballpoint pen, but the pen was out of ink."

Foltrigg's nose got closer to the note. "It says 'Mark, Mark where are,' and I can't make out the rest of it."

"Right. The handwriting is awful and the pen ran out of ink, but our expert says the same thing. 'Mark, Mark where are.' He also thinks that Clifford was drunk or stoned or something when he tried to write this. We found the pen in the car. Cheap Bic. No doubt it's the pen. He has no children, nephews, brothers, uncles, or cousins by the name of Mark. We're checking his close friends—his secretary said he had none—but as of now we haven't found a Mark."

"So what does it mean?"

"There's one other thing. A few hours ago, Mark Sway rode to the hospital with a Memphis cop by the name of Hardy. Along the way, he let it slip that Romey said or did something. Romey. Short for Jerome, according to Mr. Clifford's secretary. In fact, she said more people called him Romey than Jerome. How would the kid know the nickname unless Mr. Clifford himself told him?"

Foltrigg listened with his mouth open. "What do you think?" he asked.

"Well, my theory is that the kid was in the car before Clifford shot himself, and that he was there for some time because of all the prints, and that he and Clifford talked about something. Then, at some point, the kid leaves the car, Clifford tries to add something to his note, and shoots himself. The kid is scared. His little brother goes into shock, and here we are."

"Why would the kid lie?"

"One, he's scared. Two, he's a kid. Three, maybe Clifford told him something he doesn't need to know."

McThune's delivery was perfect, and the dramatic punch line left a heavy silence in the room. Foltrigg was frozen. Boxx and Fink stared blankly at the desk with open mouths.

Because his boss was temporarily at a loss, Wally Boxx moved in defensively and asked a stupid question. "Why do you think this?"

McThune's patience with U.S. Attorneys and their little flunkies had been exhausted about twenty years ago. He'd seen them come and go. He'd learned to play their games and manipulate their egos. He knew the best way to handle their banalities was simply to respond. "Because of the note, the prints, and the lies. The poor kid doesn't know what to do."

Foltrigg placed the note on the desk, and cleared his throat. "Have you talked to the kid?"

"No. I went to the hospital two hours ago, but did not see him. Sergeant Hardy of Memphis PD talked to him."

"Do you plan to?"

"Yes, in a few hours. Trumann and I will go to the hospital around nine or so and talk to the kid and maybe his mother. I'd also like to talk to the little brother, but it'll depend on his doctor."

"I'd like to be there," Foltrigg said. Everyone knew it was coming.

McThune shook his head. "Not a good idea. We'll handle it." He was abrupt and left no doubt that he was in charge. This was Memphis, not New Orleans.

"What about the kid's doctor? Have you talked to him?"

"No, not yet. We'll try this morning. I doubt if he'll say much."

"Do you think these kids would tell the doctor?" Fink asked innocently.

McThune rolled his eyes at Trumann as if to say, "What kind of dumbasses have you brought me?" "I can't answer that, sir. I don't know what the kids know. I don't know the doctor's name. I don't know if he's talked to the kids. I don't know if the kids will tell him anything."

Foltrigg frowned at Fink, who shrank with embarrassment. McThune glanced at his watch and stood. "Gentlemen, it's late. Our people will finish with the car by noon, and I suggest we meet then."

"We must know everything Mark Sway knows," Roy said without moving. "He was in that car, and Clifford talked to him."

"I know that."

"Yes, Mr. McThune, but there are some things you don't know. Clifford knew the location of the body, and he was talking about it."

"There are a lot of things I don't know, Mr. Foltrigg, because this is a New Orleans case, and I work Memphis, you understand. I don't want to know any more about poor Mr. Boyette and poor Mr. Clifford. I'm up to my ass in dead bodies here. It's almost 1 A.M., and I'm sitting here in my office working on a case that's not mine, talking to you fellas and answering your questions. And I'll work on the case until noon tomorrow, then my pal Larry Trumann here can have it. I'll be finished."

"Unless, of course, you get a call from Washington."

"Yes, unless of course I get a call from Washington, then I'll do whatever Mr. Voyles tells me."

"I talk to Mr. Voyles every week."

"Congratulations."

"The Boyette case is the FBI's top priority at this moment, according to him."

"So I've heard."

"And I'm sure Mr. Voyles will appreciate your efforts."

"I doubt it."

Roy stood slowly and stared at McThune. "It is imperative that we know everything Mark Sway knows. Do you understand?"

McThune returned the stare and said nothing.

EIGHT

KAREN CHECKED ON MARK throughout the night, and brought him orange juice around eight. He was alone in the small waiting room. She woke him gently.

In spite of his many problems at the moment, he was falling hopelessly in love with this beautiful nurse. He sipped the juice and looked into her sparkling brown eyes. She patted the blanket covering his legs.

"How old are you?" he asked.

She smiled even wider. "Twenty-four. Thirteen years older than you. Why do you ask?"

"Just a habit. Are you married?"

"No." She gently removed the blanket and began folding it. "How was the sofa?"

Mark stood, stretched, and watched her. "Better than that bed Mom had to sleep on. Did you work all night?"

"From eight to eight. We're doing twelve-hour shifts, four days a week. Come with me. Dr. Greenway is in the room and wants to see you." She took his hand, which helped immensely, and they walked to Ricky's room. Karen left and closed the door behind her.

Dianne looked tired. She stood at the foot of Ricky's bed with an unlit cigarette in her trembling hand. Mark stood next to her, and she put her arm on his shoulder. They watched as Greenway rubbed Ricky's forehead and spoke to him. His eyes were closed and he was not responding.

"He doesn't hear you, Doctor," Dianne said finally. It was difficult to listen to Greenway chat away in baby talk. He ignored her. She wiped a tear from her cheek. Mark smelled fresh soap and noticed her hair was wet. She had changed clothes. But there was no makeup and her face was different.

Greenway stood straight. "A most severe case," he said properly, almost to himself while staring at the closed eyes.

"What's next?" she asked.

"We wait. His vital signs are stable, so there's no physical danger. He'll come around, and when he does, it's imperative that you be in this room." Greenway was looking at them now, rubbing his beard, deep in thought. "He must see his mother when he opens his eyes, do you understand this?"

"I'm not leaving."

"You, Mark, can come and go a bit, but it's best if you stay here as much as possible too."

Mark nodded his head. The thought of spending another minute in the room was painful.

"The first moments can be crucial. He'll be frightened when he looks around. He needs to see and feel his mother. Hold him and reassure him. Call the nurse immediately. I'll leave instructions. He'll be very hungry, so we'll try and get some food in him. The nurse'll remove the IV, so he can walk around the room. But the important thing is to hold him."

"When do you—"

"I don't know. Probably today or tomorrow. There's no way to predict."

"Have you seen cases like this before?"

Greenway looked at Ricky, and decided to go for the truth. He shook his head. "Not quite this bad. He's almost comatose, which is a bit unusual. Normally, after a period of good rest, they'll be awake and eating." He almost managed a smile. "But, I'm not concerned. Ricky will be all right. It'll just take some time."

Ricky seemed to hear this. He grunted and stretched, but did not open his eyes. They watched intently, hoping for a mumble or word. Though Mark preferred that he remain silent about the shooting until they discussed it alone, he desperately wanted his little brother to wake up and start talking about other matters. He was tired of looking at him curled up on the pillow, sucking that damned thumb.

Greenway reached into his bag and produced a newspaper. It was the *Memphis Press,* the morning paper. He laid it on the bed, and handed Dianne a card. "My office is in the building next door. Here's the phone number, just in case. Remember, the moment he wakes up, call the nurses' station, and they'll call me immediately. Okay?"

Dianne took the card and nodded. Greenway unfolded the newspaper on Ricky's bed in front of them. "Have you seen this?"

"No," she answered.

At the bottom of the front page was a headline about Romey. NEW ORLEANS LAWYER COMMITS SUICIDE IN NORTH MEMPHIS. Under the headline to the right was a big photo of W. Jerome Clifford, and to the left was the smaller headline—FLAMBOYANT CRIMINAL LAWYER WITH SUSPECTED MOB TIES. The word "Mob" jumped at Mark. He stared at Romey's face, and suddenly needed to vomit.

Greenway leaned forward and lowered his voice. "It seems as though Mr. Clifford was a rather well-known lawyer in New Orleans. He was involved in the Senator Boyette case. Apparently, he was the attorney for the man charged with the murder. Have you kept up with it?"

Dianne actually put the unlit cigarette in her mouth. She shook her head no.

"Well, it's a big case. The first U.S. Senator to be murdered in office. You can read this after I leave. There are police and FBI downstairs. They were waiting when I arrived an hour ago." Mark grabbed the railing on the foot of the bed. "They want to talk to Mark, and of course they want you present."

"Why?" she asked.

Greenway looked at his watch. "The Boyette case is complicated. I think you'll understand more after you read the story here. I told them you and Mark could not speak with them until I say so. Is this all right?"

"Yes," Mark blurted. "I don't want to talk to them." Dianne and Greenway looked at him. "I may end up like Ricky if these cops keep bugging me." For some reason, Mark knew the police would return with a lot of questions. They were not finished with him. But the photo on the front page of the paper and the mention of the FBI suddenly sent chills over him, and he needed to sit down.

"Keep them away for now," Dianne said to Greenway.

"They asked if they could see you at nine, and I said no. But they won't go away." He looked at his watch again. "I'll be here at noon. Perhaps we should talk to them then."

"Whatever you think," she said.

"Very well. I'll put them off until twelve. My office has called your employer and the school. Try not to worry about that. Just stay by this bed until I return." He almost smiled as he closed the door behind him.

Dianne ran to the bathroom and lit her cigarette. Mark punched the remote control by Ricky's bed until the television was on and he found the local news. Nothing but weather and sports.

Dianne finished the story about Mr. Clifford and placed the paper on the floor under the foldaway bed. Mark watched anxiously.

"His client killed a United States Senator," she said in awe.

No kidding. There were about to be some tough questions, and Mark was suddenly hungry. It was past nine. Ricky hadn't moved. The nurses had forgotten about them. Greenway seemed like ancient history. The FBI was waiting somewhere in the darkness. The room was growing smaller by the minute, and the cheap cot on which he was sitting was ruining his back.

"I wonder why he did that," he said because he could think of nothing else to say.

"It says Jerome Clifford had ties with the New Orleans mob, and that his client is widely thought to be a member."

He'd seen *The Godfather* on cable. In fact, he'd even seen the first sequel to *The Godfather,* and he knew all about the mob. Scenes from the movies flashed before his eyes, and the pains in his stomach grew sharper. His heart pounded. "I'm hungry, Mom. Are you hungry?"

"Why didn't you tell me the truth, Mark?"

"Because the cop was in the trailer, and it wasn't a good time to talk. I'm sorry, Mom. I promise I'm sorry. I planned to tell you as soon as we were alone, I promise."

She rubbed her temples and looked so sad. "You never lie to me, Mark."

Never say never. "Can we talk about this later, Mom? I'm really hungry. Give me a couple of bucks and I'll run down to the cafeteria and get some doughnuts. I'd love a doughnut. I'll get you some coffee." He was on his feet waiting for the money.

Fortunately, she was not in the mood for a serious talk about truthfulness and such. The Dalmane lingered and her thoughts were slow. Her head pounded. She opened her purse and gave him a five-dollar bill. "Where's the cafeteria?"

"Basement. Madison Wing. I've been there twice."

"Why am I not surprised? I suppose you've been all over this place."

He took the money and crammed it in the pocket of his jeans. "Yes ma'am. We're on the quietest floor. The babies are in the basement and it's a circus down there."

"Be careful."

He closed the door behind him. She waited, then took the bottle of Valium from her purse. Greenway had sent it.

Mark ate four doughnuts during "Donahue" and watched his mother try to nap on the bed. He kissed her on the forehead, and told her he needed to roam around a bit. She told him not to leave the hospital.

He used the stairs again because he figured Hardy and the FBI and the rest of the gang might be hanging around somewhere downstairs waiting for him to happen by.

Like most big-city charity hospitals, St. Peter's had been built over time whenever funds could be squeezed, with little thought of architectural symmetry. It was a sprawling and bewildering configuration of additions and wings, with a maze of hallways and corridors and mezzanines trying desperately to connect everything. Elevators and escalators had been added wherever they would fit. At some point in history, someone had realized the difficulty of moving from one point to another without getting hopelessly lost, and a dazzling array of color-coded signs had been implemented for the orderly flow of traffic. Then more wings were added. The signs became obsolete, but the hospital failed to remove them. Now they only added to the confusion.

Mark darted through now familiar territory and exited the hospital through a small lobby on Monroe Avenue. He'd studied a map of downtown in the front of the phone book, and he knew Gill

Teal's office was within easy walking distance. It was on the third floor of a building four blocks away. He moved quickly. It was Tuesday, a school day, and he wanted to avoid truant officers. He was the only kid on the street, and he knew he was out of place.

A new strategy was developing. What was wrong, he asked himself as he stared at the sidewalk and avoided eye contact with the pedestrians passing by, with making an anonymous phone call to the cops or FBI and telling them exactly where the body was? The secret would no longer belong only to him. If Romey wasn't lying, then the body would be found and the killer would go to jail.

There were risks. His phone call to 911 yesterday had been a disaster. Anybody on the other end of the phone would know he was just a kid. The FBI would record him and analyze his voice. The Mafia wasn't stupid.

Maybe it wasn't such a good idea.

He turned on Third Street, and darted into the Sterick Building. It was old and very tall. The lobby was tile and marble. He entered the elevator with a crowd of others, and punched the button for the third floor. Four other buttons were pushed by people wearing nice clothes and carrying briefcases. They chatted quietly, in the normal hushed tones of elevator talk.

His stop was first. He stepped into a small lobby with hallways running left, right, and straight ahead. He went left, and roamed about innocently, trying to appear calm, as if lawyer shopping were a chore he'd done many times. There were plenty of lawyers in the building. Their names were etched on distinguished bronze plates screwed into the doors, and some doors were covered with rather long and intimidating names with lots of initials followed by periods. J. Winston Buckner. F. MacDonald Durston. I. Hempstead Crawford. The more names Mark read, the more he longed for plain old Gill Teal.

He found Mr. Teal's door at the end of the hall, and there was no bronze plate. The words GILL TEAL—THE PEOPLE'S LAWYER were painted in bold black letters from the top of the door to the bottom. Three people waited in the hall beside it.

Mark swallowed, and entered the office. It was packed. The small waiting room was filled with sad people suffering from all sorts of injuries and wounds. Crutches were everywhere. Two people sat in wheelchairs. There were no empty seats, and one poor man in a neck brace sat on the cluttered coffee table, his head wobbling around like a newborn's. A lady with a dirty cast on her foot cried softly. A small girl with a horribly burned face clung to her mother. War could not have been more pitiful. It was worse than the emergency room at St. Peter's.

Mr. Teal certainly had been busy rounding up clients. Mark decided to leave, when someone called out rudely, "What do you want?"

It was a large lady behind the receptionist's window. "You, kid, you want something?" Her voice boomed around the room, but no one noticed. The suffering continued unabated. He stepped to the window and looked at the scowling, ugly face.

"I'd like to see Mr. Teal," he said softly, looking around.

"Oh you would. Do you have an appointment?" She picked a clipboard and studied it.

"No ma'am."

"What's your name?"

"Uh, Mark Sway. It's a very private matter."

"I'm sure it is." She glared at him from head to toe. "What type of injury is it?"

He thought about the Exxon truck and how it had excited Mr. Teal, but he knew he couldn't pull it off. "I, uh, I don't have an injury."

"Well, you're in the wrong place. Why do you need a lawyer?"

"It's a long story."

"Look, kid, you see these people? They've all got appointments to see Mr. Teal. He's a very busy man, and he only takes cases involving death or injuries."

"Okay." Mark was already retreating and thinking about the mine field of canes and crutches behind him.

"Now please go bother someone else."

"Sure. And if I get hit by a truck or something, I'll come back to see you." He walked through the carnage, and made a quick exit.

He took the stairs down and explored the second floor. More lawyers. On one door he counted twenty-two bronze names. Lawyers on top of lawyers. Surely one of these guys could help him. He passed a few of them in the hall. They were too busy to notice.

A security guard suddenly appeared and walked slowly toward him. Mark glanced at the next door. The words REGGIE LOVE—LAWYER were painted on it in small letters, and he casually turned the knob and stepped inside. The small reception area was quiet and empty. Not a single client was waiting. Two chairs and a sofa sat around a glass table. The magazines were arranged neatly. Soft music came from above. A pretty rug covered the hardwood floor. A young man with a tie but no coat stood from his desk behind some potted trees, and walked a few steps forward. "May I help you?" he asked, quite pleasantly.

"Yes. I need to see a lawyer."

"You're a bit young to need a lawyer, aren't you?"

"Yes, but I'm having some problems. Are you Reggie Love?"

"No. Reggie's in the back. I'm her secretary. What's your name?"

He was her secretary. Reggie was a she. The secretary was a he. "Uh, Mark Sway. You're a secretary?"

"And a paralegal, among other things. Why aren't you in school?" A nameplate on the desk identified him as Clint Van Hooser.

"So you're not a lawyer?"

"No. Reggie's the lawyer."

"Then I need to speak with Reggie."

"She's busy right now. You can have a seat." He waved at the sofa.

"How long will it be?" Mark asked.

"I don't know." The young man was amused by this kid needing a lawyer. "I'll tell her you're here. Maybe she can see you for a minute."

"It's very important."

The kid was nervous and sincere. His eyes glanced at the door as if someone had followed him here. "Are you in trouble, Mark?" Clint asked.

"Yes."

"What type of trouble? You need to tell me a little about it, or Reggie won't talk to you."

"I'm supposed to talk to the FBI at noon, and I think I need a lawyer."

This was good enough. "Have a seat. It'll be a minute."

Mark eased into a chair, and as soon as Clint disappeared he opened a yellow phone book and flipped through the pages until he found the attorneys. There was Gill Teal again in his full-page spread. Pages and pages of huge ads, all crying out for injured people. Photos of busy and important men and women holding thick law books or sitting behind wide desks or listening intently to the telephones stuck in their ears. Then half-page ones, then quarter. Reggie Love was not there. What kind of lawyer was she?

Reggie Love was one of thousands in the Memphis yellow pages. She couldn't be much of a lawyer if the yellow pages thought so little of her, and the thought of racing from the office crossed his mind. But then there was Gill Teal, the one for real, the people's lawyer, the star of the yellow pages who also had enough fame to get himself on television, and just look at his office down the hall. No, he quickly decided, he'd take his chances with Reggie Love. Maybe she needed clients. Maybe she had more time to help him. The idea of a woman lawyer suddenly appealed to him because he'd seen one on "L.A. Law" once and she had ripped up some cops pretty good. He closed the book and returned it carefully to the magazine rack beside the chair. The office was cool and pretty. There were no voices.

Clint closed the door behind him and eased across the Persian rug to her desk. Reggie Love was on the phone, listening more than talking. Clint placed three phone messages before her, and gave the standard hand signal to indicate someone was waiting in the reception area. He sat on the corner of the desk, straightening a paper clip and watching her.

There was no leather in the office. The walls were papered with light floral shades of rose and pink. A spotless desk of glass and chrome covered one corner of the rug. The chairs were sleek and upholstered with a burgundy fabric. This, without a doubt, was the office of a woman. A very neat woman.

Reggie Love was fifty-two years old, and had been practicing law for less than five years. She was of medium build with very short, very gray hair that fell in bangs almost to the top of her perfectly round, black-framed glasses. The eyes were green, and they glowed at Clint as if something funny had been said. Then she rolled them and shook her head. "Good-bye, Sam," she finally said, and hung up.

"Got a new client for you," Clint said with a smile.

"I don't need new clients, Clint. I need clients who can pay. What's his name?"

"Mark Sway. He's just a kid, ten maybe twelve years old. And he says he's supposed to meet with the FBI at noon. Says he needs a lawyer."

"He's alone?"

"Yeah."

"How'd he find us?"

"I have no idea. I'm just the secretary, remember. You'll have to ask some questions yourself."

Reggie stood and walked around the desk. "Show him in. And rescue me in fifteen minutes, okay. I've got a busy morning."

"Follow me, Mark," Clint said, and Mark followed him through a narrow door and down a hallway. Her office door was covered with stained glass, and a small brass plate again said REGGIE LOVE—LAWYER. Clint opened the door, and motioned for Mark to enter.

The first thing he noticed about her was her hair. It was gray and shorter than his; very short above the ears and in the back, a bit thicker on top with bangs halfway down. He'd never seen a woman with gray hair worn so short. She wasn't old and she wasn't young.

She smiled appropriately as they met at the door. "Mark, I'm Reggie Love." She offered her hand, he took it reluctantly, and she squeezed hard and shook firm. Shaking hands with women was not something he did often. She was neither tall nor short, thin nor heavy. Her dress was straight and black and she wore black and gold bracelets on both wrists. They rattled.

"Nice to meet you," he said weakly as they shook. She was already leading him to a corner of the office where two soft chairs faced a table with picture books on it.

"Have a seat," she said. "I only have a minute."

Mark sat on the edge of his seat, and was suddenly terrified. He'd lied to his mother. He'd lied to the police. He'd lied to Dr. Greenway. He was about to lie to the FBI. Romey had been dead less than a day, and he was lying right and left to everyone who asked. Tomorrow he would certainly lie to the next person. Maybe it was time to come clean for a change. Sometimes it was frightening to tell the truth, but he usually felt better afterward. But the thought of unloading all this baggage on a stranger made his blood run cold.

"Would you like something to drink?"

"No ma'am."

She crossed her legs. "Mark Sway, right? Please do not call me ma'am, all right? My name is not Ms. Love or any of that, my name is Reggie. I'm old enough to be your grandmother, but you call me Reggie, okay?"

"Okay."

"How old are you, Mark? Tell me a little about yourself."

"I'm eleven. I'm in the fifth grade at Willow Road."

"Why aren't you in school this morning?"

"It's a long story."

"I see. And you're here because of this long story?"

"Yes."

"Do you want to tell me this long story?"

"I think so."

"Clint said you're supposed to meet with the FBI at noon. Is this true?"

"Yes. They want to ask me some questions at the hospital."

She picked up a legal pad from the table and wrote something on it. "The hospital?"

"It's part of the long story. Can I ask you something, Reggie?" It was strange calling this lady by a baseball name. He'd watched a cheap TV movie about the life of Reggie Jackson, and remembered the crowd chanting Reggie! Reggie! in perfect unison. Then there was the Reggie candy bar.

"Sure." She grinned a lot, and it was obvious she enjoyed this scene with the kid who needed a lawyer. Mark knew the smiles would disappear if he made it through the story. She had pretty eyes, and they sparkled at him.

"If I tell you something, will you ever repeat it?" he asked.

"Of course not. It's privileged, confidential."

"What does that mean?"

"It means simply that I can never repeat anything you tell me, unless you tell me I can repeat it."

"Never?"

"Never. It's like talking to your doctor or minister. The conversations are secret and held in trust. Do you understand?"

"I think so. Under no circumstances—"

"Never. Under no circumstances can I tell anyone what you tell me."

"What if I told you something that no one else knows?"

"I can't repeat it."

"Something the police really want to know?"

"I can't repeat it." She at first was amused by these questions, but his determination made her wonder.

"Something that could get you in a lot of trouble."

"I can't repeat it."

Mark looked at her without blinking for a long minute, and convinced himself she could be trusted. Her face was warm and her eyes were comforting. She was relaxed and easy to talk to.

"Any more questions?" she asked.

"Yeah. Where'd you get the name Reggie?"

"I changed my name several years ago. It was Regina, and I was married to a doctor, and then all sorts of bad things happened so I changed my name to Reggie."

"You're divorced?"

"Yes."

"My parents are divorced."

"I'm sorry."

"Don't be sorry. My brother and I were really happy when they got a divorce. My father drank a lot and beat us. Beat Mom too. Me and Ricky always hated him."

"Ricky's your brother?"

"Yes. He's the one in the hospital."

"What's the matter with him?"

"It's part of the long story."

"When would you like to tell me this story?"

Mark hesitated a few seconds and thought about a few things. He wasn't quite ready to tell all. "How much do you charge?"

"I don't know. What kind of case is it?"

"What kind of cases do you take?"

"Mostly cases involving abused or neglected children. Some abandoned children. Lots of adoptions. A few medical malpractice cases involving infants. But mainly abuse cases. I get some pretty bad cases."

"Good, because this is a really bad one. One person is dead. One is in the hospital. The police and FBI want to talk to me."

"Look, Mark, I assume you don't have a lot of money to hire me, do you?"

"No."

"Technically, you're supposed to pay me something as a retainer, and once this is done I'm your lawyer and we'll go from there. Do you have a dollar?"

"Yes."

"Then why don't you give it to me as a retainer."

Mark pulled a one-dollar bill from his pocket and handed it to her. "This is all I've got."

Reggie didn't want the kid's dollar, but she took it because ethics were ethics and because it would probably be his last payment. And he was proud of himself for hiring a lawyer. She would somehow return it to him.

She laid the bill on the table, and said, "Okay, now I'm the lawyer and you're the client. Let's hear the story."

He reached into his pocket again and pulled out the folded clipping from the newspaper Greenway had given them. He handed it to her. "Have you seen this?" he asked. "It's in this morning's paper." His hand was trembling and the paper shook.

"Are you scared, Mark?"

"Sort of."

"Try to relax, okay."

"Okay. I'll try. Have you seen this?"

"No, I haven't seen the paper yet." She took the clipping and read it. Mark watched her eyes closely.

"Okay," she said when she finished.

"It mentions the body was found by two boys. Well, that's me and Ricky."

"Well, I'm sure that must've been awful, but it's no crime to find a dead body."

"Good. Because there's much more to the story."

Her smile had disappeared. The pen was ready. "I want to hear it now."

Mark breathed deeply and rapidly. The four doughnuts churned away in his stomach. He was scared, but he also knew he would feel much better when it was over. He settled deep in the chair, took a long breath, and looked at the floor.

He started with his career as a smoker, and Ricky catching him, and going to the woods. Then the car, the water hose, the fat man who turned out to be Jerome Clifford. He spoke slowly because he wanted to remember it all, and because he wanted his new lawyer to write it all down.

Clint attempted to interrupt after fifteen minutes, but Reggie frowned at him. He quickly closed the door and disappeared.

The first account took twenty minutes with few interruptions from Reggie. There were gaps and holes, none the fault of Mark, just soft spots that she picked through during the second pass, which took another twenty minutes. They broke for coffee and ice water, all fetched by Clint, and Reggie moved the conversation to her desk where she spread out her notes and prepared for the third run-through of this remarkable story. She filled one legal pad, and started another. The smiles were long gone. The friendly, patronizing chitchat from the grandmother to her grandchild had been replaced with pointed questions picking for details.

The only details Mark withheld were the ones describing the exact location of the body of Senator Boyd Boyette, or rather Romey's story about the body. As the secret and confidential conversation unfolded, it became obvious to Reggie that Mark knew where the body was allegedly buried, and she skillfully and fearfully danced around this information. Maybe she would ask, maybe she wouldn't. But it would be the last thing discussed.

An hour after they started, she took a break and read the newspaper story twice. Then again. It seemed to fit. He knew too many details to be lying. This was not a story a hyperactive mind could fabricate. And the poor kid was scared to death.

Clint interrupted again at eleven-thirty to inform Reggie her next appointment had been waiting for an hour. "Cancel it," Reg-

said without looking from her notes, and Clint was gone. Mark walked around her office as she read. He stood in her window and watched the traffic on Third Street below. Then he returned to his seat and waited.

His lawyer was deeply troubled, and he almost felt sorry for her. All those names and faces in the yellow pages, and he had to drop this bomb on Reggie Love.

"What are you afraid of, Mark?" she asked, rubbing her eyes.

"Lots of things. I've lied to the police about this, and I think they know I'm lying. And that scares me. My little brother's in a coma because of me. It's all my fault. I lied to his doctor. And all that scares me. I don't know what to do, and I guess that's why I'm here. What should I do?"

"Have you told me everything?"

"No, but almost."

"Have you lied to me?"

"No."

"Do you know where the body is buried?"

"I think so. I know what Jerome Clifford told me."

For a split second, Reggie was terrified he would blurt it out. But he didn't, and they stared at each other for a long time.

"Do you want to tell me where it is?" she finally asked.

"Do you want me to?"

"I'm not sure. What keeps you from telling me?"

"I'm scared. I don't want anybody to know that I know, because Romey told me his client had killed many people and was planning on killing Romey too. If he's killed lots of people, and if he thinks I know this secret, he'll come after me. And if I tell this stuff to the cops then he'll come after me for sure. He's in the Mafia, and that really scares me. Wouldn't it scare you?"

"I think so."

"And the cops have threatened me if I don't tell the truth, and they think I'm lying anyway, and I just don't know what to do. Do you think I should tell the police and the FBI?"

Reggie stood and walked slowly to the window. She had no wonderful advice at this point. If she suggested that her newest client spill his guts to the FBI, and he followed her advice, his life could indeed be in danger. There was no law requiring him to tell.

Obstruction of justice, maybe, but he was just a kid. They didn't know for certain what he knew, and if they couldn't prove it, he was safe.

"Let's do this, Mark. Don't tell me where the body is, okay? For now anyway. Maybe later, but not now. And let's meet with the FBI and listen to them. You won't have to say a word. I'll do the talking, and we'll both do the listening. And when it's over, you and I will decide what to do next."

"Sounds good to me."

"Does your mother know you're here?"

"No. I need to call her."

Reggie found the number in the phone book and dialed the hospital. Mark explained to Dianne that he had gone for a walk and would be there in a minute. He was a smooth liar, Reggie noticed. He listened for a while and looked disturbed. "How is he?" he asked. "I'll be there in a minute."

He hung up and looked at Reggie. "Mom's upset. Ricky's coming out of the coma and she can't find Dr. Greenway."

"I'll walk with you to the hospital."

"That would be nice."

"Where does the FBI want to meet?"

"I think at the hospital."

She checked her watch and threw two fresh legal pads into her briefcase. She was suddenly nervous. Mark waited by the door.

NINE

THE SECOND LAWYER hired by Barry The Blade Muldanno to defend him on these obnoxious murder charges was another angry hatchet man by the name of Willis Upchurch, a rising star among the gang of boisterous mouthpieces trotting across the country performing for crooks and cameras. Upchurch had offices in Chicago and Washington, and any other city where he could hook a famous case and rent space. As soon as he talked with Muldanno after breakfast, he was on a plane to New Orleans to, first, organize a press conference, and, second, meet with his famous new client and plot a noisy defense. He had become somewhat rich and noted in Chicago for his passionate defense of mob assassins and drug traffickers, and in the past decade or so had been called in by mob brass around the country for all sorts of representation. His record was average, but it was not his won/lost ratio that attracted clients. It was his angry face and bushy hair and thunderous voice. Upchurch was a lawyer who wanted to be seen and heard in magazine articles, news stories, advice columns, quickie books, and gossip shows. He had opinions. He was unafraid of predictions. He was radical and would say anything, and this made him a favorite of the loony daytime TV talk shows.

He took only sensational cases with lots of headlines and cameras. Nothing was too repulsive for him. He preferred rich clients who could pay, but if a serial killer needed help, Upchurch would be there with a contract giving himself exclusive book and movie rights.

Though he enjoyed his notoriety immensely, and received some praise from the far left for his vigorous defense of indigent murderers, Upchurch was little more than a Mafia lawyer. He was owned by the mob, yanked around by their strings, and paid whenever they decided. He was allowed to roam a bit and spout at the mouth, but if they called, he came running.

And when Johnny Sulari, Barry's uncle, called at four in the morning, Willis Upchurch came running. The uncle explained the scarce facts about the untimely death of Jerome Clifford. Upchurch drooled into the receiver as Sulari asked him to fly immediately to New Orleans. He skipped to the bathroom at the thought of defending Barry The Blade Muldanno in front of all those cameras. He whistled in the shower when he thought of all the ink the case had already generated, and how he would now be the star. He grinned at himself in the mirror as he tied his ninety-dollar tie and thought of spending the next six months in New Orleans with the press at his beck and call.

This was why he went to law school!

The scene was frightening at first. The IV had been removed because Dianne was in the bed clutching Ricky and rubbing his head. She hugged him fiercely and wrapped her legs around his. He was moaning and grunting, twisting and jerking. His eyes were open, then shut. Dianne pressed her head to his and spoke softly through her tears. "It's okay, baby. It's okay. Mommy's here. Mommy's here."

Greenway stood close by, arms folded, rubbing his beard. He appeared puzzled, as if he hadn't seen this before. A nurse held the other side of the bed.

Mark entered the room slowly and no one noticed. Reggie had stopped at the nurses' station. It was almost noon, time for the FBI and all, but Mark knew immediately that no one in the room was remotely concerned with the cops and their questions.

"It's okay, baby. It's okay. Mommy's here."

Mark inched to the foot of the bed for a closer look. Dianne managed a quick, uncomfortable smile, then closed her eyes and kept whispering to Ricky.

After a few long minutes of this, Ricky opened his eyes, seemed to notice and recognize his mother, and grew still. She kissed him a dozen times on the forehead. The nurse smiled and patted his shoulder and cooed something at him.

Greenway looked at Mark and nodded at the door. Mark followed him outside, into the quiet hallway. They walked slowly toward the end of it, away from the nurses' station.

"He woke up about two hours ago," the doctor explained. "It looks like he's coming out of it slowly."

"Has he said anything yet?"

"Like what?"

"Well, you know, like about what happened yesterday."

"No. He's mumbled a lot, which is a good sign, but he hasn't made any words yet."

This was comforting, in a sense. Mark would have to stick close to the room just in case. "So he's gonna be okay?"

"I didn't say that." The lunch cart stopped in the middle of the hall and they walked around it. "I think he'll be okay, but it could take time." There was a long pause in which Mark worried if Greenway expected him to say something.

"How strong is your mother?"

"Pretty strong, I guess. We've been through a lot."

"Where's the family? She'll need plenty of help."

"There's no family. She has a sister in Texas, but they don't get along. And her sister has problems too."

"Your grandparents?"

"No. My ex-father was an orphan. I figure his parents probably dumped him somewhere when they got to know him. My mother's father is dead, and her mother lives in Texas too. She's sick all the time."

"I'm sorry."

They stopped at the end of the hall and looked through a dirty window at downtown Memphis. The Sterick Building stood tall.

"The FBI is bugging me," Greenway said.

Join the club, Mark thought. "Where are they?"

"Room 28. It's a small conference room on the second floor that's seldom used. They said they'd be expecting me, you, and your mother at exactly noon, and they sounded very serious." Greenway glanced at his watch, and started to walk back to the room. "They are quite anxious."

"I'm ready for them," Mark said in a weak effort at boldness.

Greenway frowned at him. "How's that?"

"I've hired us a lawyer," he said proudly.

"When?"

"This morning. She's here now, down the hall."

Greenway looked ahead but the nurses' station was around a bend in the corridor. "The lawyer's here?" he asked in disbelief.

"Yep."

"How'd you find a lawyer?"

"It's a long story. But I paid her myself."

Greenway pondered this as he shuffled along. "Well, your mother cannot leave Ricky right now, under any circumstances. And I certainly need to stay close."

"No problem. Me and the lawyer will handle it."

They stopped at Ricky's door, and Greenway hesitated before pushing it open. "I can put them off until tomorrow. In fact, I can order them out of the hospital." He was attempting to sound tough, but Mark knew better.

"No, thanks. They won't go away. You take care of Ricky and Mom, and me and the lawyer'll take care of the FBI."

Reggie had found an empty room on the eighth floor, and they hurried down the stairs to use it. They were ten minutes late. She closed the door quickly, and said, "Pull up your shirt."

He froze, and stared at her.

"Pull up your shirt!" she insisted, and he began pulling at his bulky Memphis State Tigers sweatshirt. She opened her briefcase and removed a small, black recorder and a strip of plastic and Velcro. She checked the micro-cassette tape, then punched the buttons. Mark watched every move. She'd used this device many times before, he could tell. She pressed it to his stomach, and said, "Hold it right here." Then she threaded the plastic strap through a clip on the recorder, wrapped it around his mid-section and back, and fastened it snugly with the Velcro ends. "Breathe deeply," she said, and he did.

He tucked the sweatshirt into his jeans. Reggie took a step back and stared at his stomach. "Perfect," she said.

"What if they frisk me?"

"They won't. Let's go."

She grabbed her briefcase, and they were out the door.

"How do you know they won't frisk me?" he asked again, very anxious. He walked fast to keep up with her. A nurse looked at them suspiciously.

"Because they're here to talk, not to arrest. Just trust me."

"I trust you, but I'm really scared."

"You'll do fine, Mark. Just remember what I told you."

"Are you sure they can't see this thing?"

"I'm positive." She pushed hard through a door and they were back in the stairwell, descending quickly on green concrete steps. Mark was one step behind. "What if the beeper goes off or something and they freak out and pull guns? What then?"

"No beeper." She took his hand, squeezed it hard, and zigzagged downward to the second floor. "And they don't shoot kids."

"They did in a movie once."

The second floor of St. Peter's had been built many years before the ninth. It was gray and dirty, and the narrow corridors were swarming with the usual anxious traffic of nurses, doctors, technicians, and orderlies pushing stretchers, and patients rolling along in wheelchairs, and dazed families walking to nowhere in particular and trying to stay awake. Corridors met from all directions in chaotic little junctions, then branched out again in a hopeless labyrinth. Reggie asked three nurses about the location of Room 28, and the third pointed and talked but never stopped walking. They found a neglected hallway with ancient carpet and bad lighting, and six doors down to the right was their room. The door was cheap wood with no window.

"I'm scared, Reggie," Mark said, staring at the door.

She held his hand firmly. If she was nervous, it was not apparent. Her face was calm. Her voice was warm and reassuring. "Just do as I told you, Mark. I know what I'm doing."

They retreated a step or two, and Reggie opened an identical door to Room 24. It was an abandoned coffee room now used for haphazard storage. "I'll wait in here. Now, go knock on the door."

"I'm scared, Reggie."

She carefully felt the recorder, and worked her fingers around it until she pushed the button. "Now go," she instructed and pointed down the hall.

Mark took a deep breath and knocked on the door. He could hear chairs move inside. "Come in," someone said, and the voice was not friendly. He opened the door slowly, stepped inside, and closed it behind him. The room was narrow and long, just like the table in the center of it. No windows. No smiles from the two men who stood on each side of the table near the end. They could pass for twins—white button-down shirts, red-and-blue ties, dark pants, short hair.

"You must be Mark," one said as the other stared at the door.

Mark nodded, but could not speak.

"Where's your mother?"

"Uh, who are you?" Mark managed to get it out.

The one on the right said, "I'm Jason McThune, FBI, Memphis." He stuck out his hand and Mark shook it limply. "Nice to meet you, Mark."

"Yeah, my pleasure."

"And I'm Larry Trumann," said the other. "FBI, New Orleans." Mark allowed Trumann the same feeble handshake. The agents exchanged nervous looks, and for an awkward second neither knew what to say.

Trumann finally pointed to the chair at the end of the table. "Have a seat, Mark." McThune nodded his agreement and almost smiled. Mark carefully sat down, terrified the Velcro would break away and the damned thing would somehow fall off. They'd handcuff his little butt so fast and throw him in the car and he'd never see his mother again. What would Reggie do then? They moved toward him in their rolling chairs. They slid their notepads on the table to within inches of him.

They were breathing on him, and Mark figured it was part of the game. Then he almost smiled. If they wanted to sit this close, fine. But the black recorder would get it all. No fading voices.

"We, uh, we really expected your mother and Dr. Greenway to be here," Trumann said, glancing at McThune.

"They're with my brother."

"How is he?" McThune asked gravely.

"Not too good. Mom can't leave his room right now."

"We thought she'd be here," Trumann said again and looked at McThune as if uncertain how to proceed.

"Well, we can wait a day or two until she's available," Mark offered.

"No, Mark, we really need to talk now."

"Maybe I can go get her."

Trumann took his pen from his shirt pocket, and smiled at Mark. "No, let's talk a few minutes, Mark. Just the three of us. Are you nervous?"

"A little. What do you want?" He was still stiff with fear but breathing better. The recorder hadn't beeped or shocked him.

"Well, we want to ask you some questions about yesterday."

"Do I need a lawyer?"

They looked at each other with perfectly symmetrical open mouths, and at least five seconds passed before McThune cocked his head at Mark and said, "Of course not."

"Why not?"

"Well, we just, you know, want to ask you a few questions. That's all. If you decide you want your mother, then we'll go get her. Or something. But you don't need a lawyer. Just a few questions, that's all."

"I've already talked to the cops once. In fact, I talked to the cops for a long time last night."

"We're not cops. We're FBI agents."

"That's what scares me. I think maybe I need a lawyer to, you know, protect my rights and all."

"You've been watching too much TV, kid."

"The name's Mark, okay? Can you at least call me Mark?"

"Sure. Sorry. But you don't need a lawyer."

"Yeah," Trumann chimed in. "Lawyers just get in the way. You have to pay them money, and they object to everything."

"Don't you think we should wait until my mother can be here?"

They exchanged matching little smiles, and McThune said, "Not really, Mark. I mean, we can wait if you want to, but you're a smart kid and we're really in a hurry here, and we just have a few quick questions for you."

"Okay. I guess. If I have to."

Trumann looked at his notepad, and went first. "Good. You told the Memphis Police that Jerome Clifford was already dead when you and Ricky found the car yesterday. Now, Mark, is this really the truth?" He sort of sneered toward the end of the question as if he knew damned well it wasn't the truth.

Mark fidgeted and looked straight ahead. "Do I have to answer the question?"

"Sure you do."

"Why?"

"Because we need to know the truth, Mark. We're the FBI, and we're investigating this thing, and we must know the truth."

"What happens if I don't answer?"

"Oh, lots of things. We might be forced to take you down to our office, in the backseat of the car of course, no handcuffs, and ask some really tough questions. May have to bring along your mother too."

"What will happen to my mother? Can she get in trouble?"

"Maybe."

"What kind of trouble?"

They paused for a second and exchanged nervous looks. They had started on shaky ground, and things were getting shakier by the minute. Children are not to be interviewed without first talking to the parents.

But what the hell. His mother didn't show. He had no father. He was a poor kid, and here he was all alone. It was perfect, really. They couldn't ask for a better situation. Just a couple of quick questions.

McThune cleared his throat and went into a deep frown. "Mark, have you ever heard of obstruction of justice?"

"I don't think so."

"Well, it's a crime, okay. A federal offense. A person who knows something about a crime, and withholds this information from the FBI or the police, might be found guilty of obstruction of justice."

"What happens then?"

"Well, if found guilty, such a person might be punished. You know, sent to jail or something like that."

"So, if I don't answer your questions, me and Mom might go to jail?"

McThune retreated a bit and looked at Trumann. The ice was getting thinner. "Why don't you want to answer the question, Mark?" Trumann asked. "Are you hiding something?"

"I'm just scared. And it doesn't seem fair since I'm just eleven years old and you're the FBI, and my mom's not here. I don't know what to do, really."

"Can't you just answer the questions, Mark, without your mother? You saw something yesterday, and your mother was not around. She can't help you answer the questions. We just want to know what you saw."

"If you were in my place, would you want a lawyer?"

"Hell no," McThune said. "I would never want a lawyer. Pardon my language, son, but they're just a pain in the ass. A real pain. If you have nothing to hide, you don't need a lawyer. Just answer our questions truthfully, and everything will be fine." He was becoming angry, and this did not surprise Mark. One of them had to be angry. It was the good guy–bad guy routine Mark had seen a thousand times on television. McThune would get ugly, and Trumann would smile a lot and sometimes even frown at his partner for Mark's benefit, and this would somehow endear Trumann to Mark. McThune would then get disgusted and leave the room, and Mark would then be expected to spill his guts all over the table.

Trumann leaned to him with a drippy smile. "Mark, was Jerome Clifford already dead when you and Ricky found him?"

"I take the Fifth Amendment."

The drippy smile vanished. McThune's face reddened, and he shook his head in absolute frustration. There was a long pause as the agents stared at each other. Mark watched an ant crawl across the table and disappear under a notepad.

Trumann, the good guy, finally spoke. "Mark, I'm afraid you've been watching too much television."

"You mean, I can't take the Fifth Amendment?"

"Lemme guess," McThune snarled. "You watch 'L.A. Law,' right?"

"Every week."

"Figures. Are you gonna answer any questions, Mark? Because if you're not, then we have to do other things."

"Like what?"

"Go to court. Talk to the judge. Convince him to require you to talk to us. It's pretty nasty, really."

"I need to go to the rest room," Mark said as he slid his chair away from the table and stood.

"Uh, sure, Mark," Trumann said, suddenly afraid they'd made him sick. "I think it's just down the hall." Mark was at the door.

"Take five minutes, Mark, we'll wait. No hurry."

He left the room and closed the door behind him.

For seventeen minutes, the agents made small talk and played with their pens. They weren't worried. They were experienced agents with many tricks. They'd been here before. He would talk.

A knock, and McThune said, "Come in." The door opened, and an attractive lady of fifty or so walked in and closed the door as if this were her office. They scrambled to their feet just as she said, "Keep your seats."

"We're in a meeting," Trumann said officially.

"You're in the wrong room," McThune said rudely.

She placed her briefcase on the table and handed each agent a white card. "I don't think so," she said. "My name is Reggie Love. I'm an attorney, and I represent Mark Sway."

They took it well. McThune inspected the card while Trumann just stood there, arms dangling by his legs, trying to say something.

"When did he hire you?" McThune said, looking wildly at Trumann.

"That's really none of your business, is it now? I'm not hired. I'm retained. Sit down."

She eased gracefully into her seat and rolled it to the table. They backed awkwardly into theirs, and kept their distance.

"Where's, uh, where's Mark?" Trumann asked.

"He's off somewhere taking the Fifth. Can I see your ID, please?"

They instantly reached for their jackets, fished around desperately, and simultaneously produced their badges. She held both, studied them carefully, then wrote something on a legal pad.

When she finished, she slid them across the table and asked, "Did you in fact attempt to interrogate this child outside the presence of his mother?"

"No," said Trumann.

"Of course not," said McThune, shocked at this suggestion.

"He tells me you did."

"He's confused," said McThune. "We initially approached Dr. Greenway, and he agreed to this meeting, which was supposed to include Mark, Dianne Sway, and the doctor."

"But the kid showed up alone," Trumann added quickly, very anxious to explain things. "And we asked where his mother was, and he said she couldn't make it right now, and we sort of thought she was on her way or something, so we were just chitchatting with the kid."

"Yeah, while we waited for Ms. Sway and the doctor," McThune chimed in helpfully. "Where were you during this?"

"Don't ask questions that are irrelevant. Did you advise Mark to talk to a lawyer?"

The agents locked eyes and searched each other for help. "It wasn't mentioned," Trumann said, shrugging innocently.

It was easier to lie because the kid wasn't there. And he was just a scared little kid who'd gotten things confused, and they were, after all, FBI agents, so she'd eventually believe them.

McThune cleared his throat and said, "Uh, yeah, once, Larry, remember Mark said something, or maybe I said something about 'L.A. Law,' and then Mark said he might need a lawyer, but he was sort of kidding and we, or at least I, took it as a joke. Remember, Larry?"

Larry now remembered. "Oh, sure, yeah, something about 'L.A. Law.' Just a joke though."

"Are you sure?" Reggie asked.

"Of course I'm sure," Trumann protested. McThune frowned and nodded along with his partner.

"He didn't ask you guys if he needed a lawyer?"

They shook their heads and tried hopelessly to remember. "I don't remember it that way. He's just a kid, and very scared, and I think he's confused," McThune said.

"Did you advise him of his Miranda rights?"

Trumann smiled at this and was suddenly more confident. "Of course not. He's not a suspect. He's just a kid. We need to ask him a few questions."

"And you did not attempt to interrogate him without his mother's presence or consent?"

"No."

"Of course not."

"And you did not tell him to avoid lawyers after he asked your advice?"

"No ma'am."

"No way. The kid's lying if he told you otherwise."

Reggie slowly opened her briefcase and lifted out the black recorder and the micro-cassette tape. She sat them in front of her, and placed the briefcase on the floor. Special Agents McThune and Trumann stared at the devices and seemed to shrink a bit in their seats.

Reggie rewarded each with a bitchy smile, and said, "I think we know who's lying."

McThune slid two fingers down the bridge of his nose. Trumann rubbed his eyes. She let them suffer for a moment. The room was silent.

"It's all right here on tape, fellas. You boys attempted to interrogate a child outside the presence of his mother and without her consent. He specifically asked you if you shouldn't wait until she was available and you said no. You attempted to coerce the child with the threat of criminal prosecution not only for the child but also for his mother. He told you he was scared, and twice he specifically asked you if he needed a lawyer. You advised him not to get a lawyer, giving as one of your reasons the opinion that lawyers are a pain in the ass. Gentlemen, the pain is here."

They sunk lower. McThune pressed four fingers against his forehead and gently rubbed. Trumann stared in disbelief at the tape, but was careful not to look at this woman. He thought of grabbing it, and ripping it to shreds, and stomping on it because it could be his career, but for some reason he believed with all his troubled heart that this woman had made a copy of it.

Getting slapped with a lie was bad enough, but their problems ran much deeper. There could be serious disciplinary proceedings. Reprimands. Transfers. Crap in the record. And at this moment, Trumann also believed that this woman knew all there was to know about the disciplining of wayward FBI agents.

"You wired the kid," Trumann said meekly to no one in particular.

"Why not? No crime. You're the FBI, remember. You boys run more wire than AT&T."

What a smartass! But then, she was a lawyer, wasn't she? McThune leaned forward, cracked his knuckles, and decided to offer some resistance. "Look, Ms. Love, we—"

"It's Reggie."

"Okay, okay. Reggie, uh, look, we're sorry. We, uh, got a little carried away, and, well, we apologize."

"A little carried away? I could have your jobs for this."

They were not about to argue with her. She was probably right, and even if there was room for debate they simply were not up to it.

"Are you taping this?" Trumann asked.

"No."

"Okay, we were out of line. We're sorry." He could not look at her.

Reggie slowly placed the tape in her coat pocket. "Look at me, fellas." They slowly lifted their eyes to hers, but it was painful. "You've already proven to me that you'll lie, and that you'll lie quickly. Why should I trust you?"

Trumann suddenly slapped the table, hissed, and made a noisy show of standing and pacing to the end of the table. He threw up his hands. "This is incredible. We came here with just a few questions for the kid, just doing our jobs, and now we're fighting with you. The kid didn't tell us he had a lawyer. If he'd told us, then we would have backed off. Why'd you do this? Why'd you deliberately pick this fight? It's senseless."

"What do you want from the kid?"

"The truth. He's lying about what he saw yesterday. We know he's lying. We know he talked to Jerome Clifford before Clifford killed himself. We know the kid was in the car. Maybe I don't blame him for lying. He's just a kid. He's scared. But dammit, we need to know what he saw and heard."

"What do you suspect he saw and heard?"

The nightmare of explaining this to Foltrigg suddenly hit Trumann, and he leaned against the wall. This is exactly why he hated lawyers—Foltrigg, Reggie, the next one he met. They made life so complicated.

"Has he told you everything?" McThune asked.

"Our conversations are extremely private."

"I know that. But do you realize who Clifford was, and Muldanno and Boyd Boyette? Do you know the story?"

"I read the paper this morning. I've kept up with the case in New Orleans. You boys need the body, don't you?"

"You could say that," Trumann said from the end of the table. "But at this moment we really need to talk to your client."

"I'll think about it."

"When might you reach a decision?"

"I don't know. Are you boys busy this afternoon?"

"Why?"

"I need to talk to my client some more. Let's say we'll meet in my office at 3 P.M." She took her briefcase and placed the recorder in it. It was obvious this meeting was over. "I'll keep the tape to myself. It'll just be our little secret, okay?"

McThune nodded his agreement, but knew there was more.

"If I need something from you boys, like the truth or a straight answer, I expect to get it. If I catch you lying again, I'll use the tape."

"That's blackmail," said Trumann.

"That's exactly what it is. Indict me." She stood and grabbed the doorknob. "See you boys at three."

McThune followed her. "Uh, listen, Reggie, there's this guy who'll probably want to be at the meeting. His name is Roy Foltrigg, and he's—"

"Mr. Foltrigg is in town?"

"Yes. He arrived last night, and he'll insist on attending this meeting at your office."

"Well, well. I'm honored. Please invite him."

TEN

THE FRONT PAGE STORY in the *Memphis Press* about Clifford's death was written top to bottom by Slick Moeller, a veteran police reporter who had been covering crime and cops in Memphis for thirty years. His real name was Alfred, but no one knew it. His mother called him Slick, but not even she could remember the nickname's origins. Three wives and a hundred girlfriends had called him Slick. He did not dress exceptionally well, did not finish high school, did not have money, was blessed with average looks and build, drove a Mustang, could not keep a woman, and so no one knew why he was called Slick.

Crime was his life. He knew the drug dealers and pimps. He drank beer at the topless bars and gossiped with the bouncers. He kept charts on the who's who of motorcycle gangs that supplied the city with drugs and strippers. He could move deftly through the toughest projects of Memphis without a scratch. He knew the rank and file of the street gangs. He had busted no less than a dozen stolen car rings by tipping the police. He knew the ex-cons, especially the ones who returned to crime. He could spot a fencing operation simply by watching the pawnshops. His cluttered downtown apartment was most unremarkable except for an entire wall of emergency scanners and police radios. His Mustang had more junk than a police cruiser, except for a radar gun, and he didn't want one.

Slick Moeller lived and moved in the dark shadows of Memphis. He was often on the crime scene before the cops. He moved freely about the morgues and hospitals and black funeral parlors. He had nurtured thousands of contacts and sources, and they talked to Slick because he could be trusted. If it was off the record, then it was off the record. Background was background. An informant would never be compromised. Tips were guarded zealously. Slick was a man of his word, and even the street gang leaders knew it.

He was also on a first-name basis with virtually every cop in the city, many of whom referred to him with great admiration as the Mole. Mole Moeller did this. Mole Moeller said that. Since Slick had become his real name, the added nickname did not bother him. Nothing bothered Slick much. He drank coffee with cops in a hundred all-night diners around town. He watched them play softball, knew when their wives filed for divorce, knew when they got themselves reprimanded. He was at Central Headquarters at least twenty hours a day, it seemed, and it was not uncommon for cops to stop him and ask what was going on. Who got shot? Where was the holdup? Was the driver drunk? How many were killed? Slick told them as much as he could. He helped them whenever possible. His name was often mentioned in classes at the Memphis Police Academy.

And so it was no surprise to anyone that Slick spent the entire morning fishing around Central. He'd made his calls to New Orleans and knew the basics. He knew Roy Foltrigg and New Orleans FBI were in town, and that everything had been turned over to them. This intrigued him. It was not just a simple suicide; there were too many blank faces and "no comments." There was a note of some sort, and all questions about it were met with sudden denials. He could read the faces of some of these cops, been doing it for years. He knew about the boys and that the younger one was in bad shape. There were some fingerprints, some cigarette butts.

He left the elevator on the ninth floor and walked away from the nurses' station. He knew the number of Ricky's room, but this was the psychiatric ward and he was not about to go barging in with his questions. He didn't want to scare anyone, especially an eight-year-old kid who was in shock. He stuck two quarters in the soft drink machine and sipped on a diet Coke as if he'd been there all night walking the floors. An orderly in a light blue jacket pushed a cart of cleaning supplies to the elevator. He was a male, about twenty-five, long hair, and certainly bored with his menial job.

Slick stepped to the elevators, and when the door opened he

followed the orderly onto it. The name Fred was sewn into the jacket above the pocket. They were alone.

"You work the ninth floor?" Slick asked, bored but with a smile.

"Yeah." Fred did not look at him.

"I'm Slick Moeller with the *Memphis Press,* working on a story about Ricky Sway in Room 943. You know, the shooting and all." He'd learned early in his career that it was best to tell them up front who and what.

Fred was suddenly interested. He stood erect and looked at Slick as if to say "Yeah, I know plenty, but you're not getting it from me." The cart between them was filled with Ajax, Comet, and twenty bottles of generic hospital supplies. A bucket of dirty rags and sponges covered the bottom tray. Fred was a toilet scrubber, but in a flash, he became a man with the inside scoop. "Yeah," he said calmly.

"Have you seen the kid?" Slick asked nonchalantly while watching the numbers light up above the door.

"Yeah, just left there."

"I hear it's severe traumatic shock."

"Don't know," Fred said smugly as if his secrets were crucial. But he wanted to talk, and this never ceased to amaze Slick. Take an average person, tell him you're a reporter, and nine times out of ten he'll feel obligated to talk. Hell, he'll want to talk. He'll tell you his deepest secrets.

"Poor kid," Slick mumbled to the floor as if Ricky were terminal. He said nothing else for a few seconds, and this was too much for Fred. What kind of a reporter was he? Where were the questions? He, Fred, knew the kid, had just left his room, had talked to his mother. He, Fred, was a player in this game.

"Yeah, he's in bad shape," Fred said, also to the floor.

"Still in a coma?"

"In and out. May take a long time."

"Yeah. That's what I heard."

The elevator stopped on the fifth floor, but Fred's cart blocked the door and no one entered. The door closed.

"There's not much you can do for a kid like that," Slick explained. "I see it all the time. Kid sees something horrible in a split second, goes into shock, and it takes months to drag him out. All kinds of shrinks and stuff. Really sad. This Sway kid ain't that bad, is he?"

"I doubt it. Dr. Greenway thinks he'll snap out in a day or two. It'll take some therapy, but he'll be fine. I see it all the time. Thinking about med school myself."

"Have the cops been snooping around?"

Fred cut his eyes around as if the elevator were bugged. "Yeah, FBI was here all day. The family has already hired a lawyer."

"You don't say."

"Yeah, cops are real interested in this case, and they're talking to the kid's brother. Somehow a lawyer's got in the middle of it."

The elevator stopped on the second floor, and Fred grabbed the handles on his cart.

"Who's the lawyer?" Slick asked.

The door opened and Fred pushed forward. "Reggie somebody. I haven't seen him yet."

"Thanks," Slick said as Fred disappeared and the elevator filled. He rode it to the ninth floor to search for another fish.

By noon, the Reverend Roy Foltrigg and his sidekicks, Wally Boxx and Thomas Fink, had become a collective nuisance around the offices of the United States Attorney for the Western District of Tennessee. George Ord had held the office for seven years, and he did not care for Roy Foltrigg. He had not invited him to Memphis. Ord had met Foltrigg before at numerous conferences and seminars where the various U.S. Attorneys gather and plot ways to protect the government. Foltrigg usually spoke at these forums, always anxious to share his opinions and strategies and great victories with anyone who would listen.

After McThune and Trumann returned from the hospital and broke the frustrating news about Mark and his new lawyer, Foltrigg, along with Boxx and Fink, had once again situated himself in Ord's office to analyze the latest. Ord sat in his heavy leather chair behind his massive desk, and listened as Foltrigg interrogated the agents and occasionally barked orders to Boxx.

"What do you know about this lawyer?" he asked Ord.

"Never heard of her."

"Surely someone in your office has dealt with her?" Foltrigg asked. The question was nothing short of a challenge for Ord to find someone with the scoop on Reggie Love. He left his office and consulted with an assistant. The search began.

Trumann and McThune sat very quietly in one corner of Ord's office. They had decided to tell no one of the tape, at least for the moment. Maybe later. Maybe, they hoped, never.

A secretary brought sandwiches, and lunch was eaten amid aimless speculation and chatter. Foltrigg was anxious to return to New Orleans, but more anxious to hear from Mark Sway. The fact that the kid had somehow obtained the services of an attorney was most troublesome. He was afraid to talk. Foltrigg was convinced Clifford had told him something, and as the day wore on he became more convinced the kid knew about the body. He was never one to hesitate before drawing conclusions. By the time the sandwiches were finished, he had persuaded himself and everyone in the room that Mark Sway knew precisely where Boyette was buried.

David Sharpinski, one of Ord's many assistants, presented himself at the office and explained he'd gone to law school at Memphis State with Reggie Love. He sat next to Foltrigg, in Wally's seat, and answered questions. He was busy and would rather have been working on a case.

"We finished law school together four years ago," Sharpinski said.

"So she's only practiced for four years," Foltrigg surmised quickly. "What kind of work does she do? Criminal law? How much criminal law? Does she know the ropes?"

McThune glanced at Trumann. They'd been nailed by a four-year lawyer.

"A little criminal stuff," Sharpinski replied. "We're pretty good friends. I see her around from time to time. Most of her work is with abused children. She's, well, she's had a pretty rough time of it."

"What do you mean by that?"

"It's a long story, Mr. Foltrigg. She's a very complex person. This is her second life."

"You know her well, don't you?"

"I do. We were in law school together for three years, off and on."

"What do you mean, off and on?"

"Well, she had to drop out, let's say, emotional problems. In her first life, she was the wife of a prominent doctor, an ob-gyn. They were rich and successful, all over the society pages, charities, country clubs, you name it. Big house in Germantown. His and her Jaguars. She was on the board of every garden club and social organization in Memphis. She had worked as a schoolteacher to put him through med school, and after fifteen years of marriage he decided to trade her in for a new model. He started chasing women, and became involved with a younger nurse, who eventually became wife number two. Reggie's name back then was Regina Cardoni. She took it hard, filed for divorce, and things got nasty. Dr. Cardoni played hardball, and she slowly cracked up. He tormented her. The divorce dragged along. She felt publicly humiliated. Her friends were all doctors' wives, country club types, and they ran for cover. She even attempted suicide. It's all in the divorce papers in the clerk's office. He had a truckload of lawyers, and they pulled strings and had her committed to an institution. Then he cleaned her out."

"Children?"

"Two, a boy and a girl. They were young teenagers, and of course he got custody. He gave them their freedom and enough money to finance it, and they turned their backs on their mother. He and his lawyers kept her in and out of mental institutions for two years, and by then it was all over. He got the house, kids, the trophy wife, everything."

Describing this tragic history of a friend troubled Sharpinski, and he was obviously uncomfortable telling it all to Mr. Foltrigg. But most of it was public record.

"So how'd she become a lawyer?"

"It wasn't easy. The court order prohibited visitation with the children. She lived with her mother, who, I think, probably saved her life. I'm not sure, but I've heard that her mother mortgaged her home to finance some pretty heavy therapy. It took years, but she slowly pieced her life back together. She pulled out of it. The kids grew up and left Memphis. The boy went to prison for selling drugs. The daughter lives in California."

"What kind of law student was she?"

"At times, very astute. She was determined to prove to herself she could succeed as a lawyer. But she continued to battle depression. She struggled with booze and pills, and finally dropped out halfway through. Then she came back, clean and dry, and finished with a vengeance."

As usual, Fink and Boxx scribbled furiously on legal pads, trying importantly to take down every word as if Foltrigg would later quiz them on their notes. Ord listened but was more concerned with the pile of past due work on his desk. With each minute, he resented Foltrigg and this intrusion more and more. He was just as busy and important as Foltrigg.

"What kind of lawyer is she?" Roy asked.

Mean as hell, thought McThune. Shrewd as the devil, thought Trumann. Quite talented with electronics.

"She works hard, doesn't make much money, but then I don't think money is important to Reggie."

"Where in the world did she get a name like Reggie?" Foltrigg asked, thoroughly baffled by it. Perhaps it comes from Regina, Ord thought to himself.

Sharpinski started to speak, then thought for a second. "It would take hours to tell what I know about her, and I really don't want to. It's not important, is it?"

"Maybe," Boxx snapped.

Sharpinski glared at him, then looked at Foltrigg. "When she started law school, she tried to erase most of her past, especially the painful years. She took back her maiden name of Love. I guess she got Reggie from Regina, but I've never asked. But she did it legally, court orders and all, and there's no trace of the old Regina Cardoni, at least not on paper. She didn't talk about her past in law school, but she was the topic of a lot of conversation. Not that she gives a damn."

"Is she still sober?"

Foltrigg wanted the dirt, and this irritated Sharpinski. To McThune and Trumann she appeared remarkably sober.

"You'll have to ask her, Mr. Foltrigg."

"How often do you see her?"

"Once a month, maybe twice. We talk on the phone occasionally."

"How old is she?" Foltrigg asked the question with a great deal of suspicion, as if perhaps Sharpinski and Reggie had a little thing going on the side.

"You'll have to ask her that too. Early fifties, I'd guess."

"Why don't you call her now, ask her what's going on, just friendly small talk, you know. See if she mentions Mark Sway."

Sharpinski gave Foltrigg a look that would sour butter. Then he looked at Ord, his boss, as if to say "Can you believe this nut?" Ord rolled his eyes and began refilling a stapler.

"Because she's not stupid, Mr. Foltrigg. In fact, she's quite smart, and if I call she'll immediately know the reason why."

"Perhaps you're right."

"I am."

"I would like for you to go with us at three to her office, if you can work it in."

Sharpinski looked at Ord for guidance. Ord was deeply involved with the stapler. "I can't do it. I'm very busy. Anything else?"

"No. You can go now," Ord suddenly said. "Thanks, David." Sharpinski left the office.

"I really need him to go with me," Foltrigg said to Ord.

"He said he was busy, Roy. My boys work," he said, looking at Boxx and Fink. A secretary knocked and entered. She brought a two-page fax to Foltrigg, who read it with Boxx. "It's from my office," he explained to Ord as if he and he alone had such technology at his fingertips. They read on, and Foltrigg finally finished. "Ever hear of Willis Upchurch?"

"Yes. He's a big shot defense lawyer from Chicago, lot of mob work. What's he done?"

"It says he just finished a press conference before a lot of cameras in New Orleans, and that he's been hired by Muldanno, that the case will be postponed, his client will be found not guilty, etc., etc."

"That sounds like Willis Upchurch. I can't believe you haven't heard of him."

"He's never been to New Orleans," Foltrigg said with authority, as if he remembered every lawyer who dared to step on his turf.

"Your case just became a nightmare."

"Wonderful. Just wonderful."

ELEVEN

THE ROOM WAS DARK because the shades were pulled. Dianne was curled along the end of Ricky's bed, napping. After a morning of mumbling and thrashing and getting everyone's hopes aroused, he had drifted away again after lunch and had returned to the now familiar position of knees pulled to his chest, IV in the arm, thumb in the mouth. Greenway assured her repeatedly that he was not in pain. But after squeezing and kissing him for four hours, she was convinced her son was hurting. She was exhausted.

Mark sat on the foldaway bed with his back against the wall under the window, and stared at his brother and his mother in the bed. He, too, was exhausted, but sleep was not possible. Events were whirling around his overworked brain, and he tried to keep thinking. What was the next move? Could Reggie be trusted? He'd seen all those lawyer shows and movies on TV, and it seemed as if half the lawyers could be trusted and the other half were snakes. When should he tell Dianne and Dr. Greenway? If he told them everything, would it help Ricky? He thought about this for a long time. He sat on the bed listening to the quiet voices in the hallway as the nurses went about their work, and debated with himself about how much to tell.

The digital clock next to the bed gave the time as two thirty-two. It was impossible to believe that all this crap had happened in less than twenty-four hours. He scratched his knees and made the decision to tell Greenway everything that Ricky could have seen and heard. He stared at the blond hair sticking out from under the sheet, and he felt better. He would come clean, stop the lying, and do all he could to help Ricky. The things Romey told him in the car were not heard by anyone else, and, for the moment, and subject to advice from his lawyer, he would hold them private for a while.

But not for long. These burdens were getting heavy. This was not a game of hide-and-seek played by trailer park kids in the woods and ravines around Tucker Wheel Estates. This was not a sly little escape from his bedroom for a moonlit walk through the neighborhood. Romey stuck a real gun in his mouth. These were real FBI agents with real badges, just like the true crime stories on television. He had hired a real lawyer who'd stuck a real tape recorder to his stomach so she could outfox the FBI. The man who killed the Senator was a professional killer who'd murdered many others, according to Romey, and was a member of the Mafia, and those people would think nothing of rubbing out an eleven-year-old kid.

This was just too much for him to handle alone. He should be at school right now, fifth period, doing math which he hated but suddenly missed. He'd have a long talk with Reggie. She'd arrange a meeting with the FBI, and he'd tell them every stinking detail Romey had unloaded on him. Then they would protect him. Maybe they would send in bodyguards until the killer went to jail, or maybe they would arrest him immediately and all would be safe. Maybe.

Then he remembered a movie about a guy who squealed on the Mafia and thought the FBI would protect him, but suddenly he was on the run with bullets flying over his head and bombs going off. The FBI wouldn't return his phone calls because the guy didn't say something right in the courtroom. At least twenty times during the movie someone said, "The mob never forgets." In the final scene, this guy's car was blown to bits just as he turned the key, and he landed a half a mile away with no legs. As he took his final breath, a dark figure stood over him and said, "The mob never forgets." It wasn't much of a movie, but its message was suddenly clear to Mark.

He needed a Sprite. His mother's purse was on the floor under the bed, and he slowly unzipped it. There were three bottles of pills. There were two packs of cigarettes and for a split second he was tempted. He found the quarters and left the room.

A nurse whispered to an old man in the waiting area. Mark

opened his Sprite and walked to the elevators. Greenway had asked him to stay in the room as much as possible, but he was tired of the room and tired of Greenway, and there seemed little chance of Ricky waking anytime soon. He entered the elevator and pushed the button to the basement. He would check out the cafeteria, and see what the lawyers were doing.

A man entered just before the doors closed, and seemed to look at him a bit too long. "Are you Mark Sway?" he asked.

This was getting old. Starting with Romey, he'd met enough strangers in the past twenty-four hours to last for months.

He was certain he'd never seen this guy before. "Who are you?" he asked cautiously.

"Slick Moeller, with the *Memphis Press,* you know, the newspaper. You're Mark Sway, aren't you?"

"How'd you know?"

"I'm a reporter. I'm supposed to know these things. How's your brother?"

"He's doing great. Why do you want to know?"

"Working on a story about the suicide and all, and your name keeps coming up. Cops say you know more than you're telling."

"When's it gonna be in the paper?"

"I don't know. Tomorrow maybe."

Mark felt weak again, and stopped looking at him. "I'm not answering any questions."

"That's fine." The elevator door suddenly opened and a swarm of people entered. Mark could no longer see the reporter. Seconds later it stopped on the fifth floor, and Mark darted out between two doctors. He hit the stairs and walked quickly to the sixth floor.

He'd lost the reporter. He sat on the steps in the empty stairwell, and began to cry.

Foltrigg, McThune, and Trumann arrived in the small but tasteful reception area of Reggie Love, Attorney-at-Law, at exactly 3 P.M., the appointed hour. They were met by Clint, who asked them to be seated, then offered coffee or tea, all of which they stiffly declined. Foltrigg informed Clint right properly that he was the United States Attorney for the Southern District of Louisiana, New Orleans, and that he was now present in this office and did not expect to wait. It was a mistake.

He waited for forty-five minutes. While the agents flipped through magazines on the sofa, Foltrigg paced the floor, glanced at his watch, fumed, scowled at Clint, even barked at him twice and each time was informed Reggie was on the phone with an important matter. As if Foltrigg was there for an unimportant matter. He wanted to leave so badly. But he couldn't. For one of the rare times in his life he had to absorb a subtle ass-kicking without a fight.

Finally, Clint asked them to follow him to a small conference room lined with shelves of heavy law books. Clint instructed them to be seated, and explained that Reggie would be right with them.

"She's forty-five minutes late," Foltrigg protested.

"That's quite early for Reggie, sir," Clint said with a smile as he closed the door. Foltrigg sat at one end of the table with an agent close to each side. They waited.

"Look, Roy," Trumann said with hesitation, "you need to be careful with this gal. She might be taping this."

"What makes you think so?"

"Well, uh, you just never—"

"These Memphis lawyers do a lot of taping," McThune added helpfully. "I don't know about New Orleans, but it's pretty bad up here."

"She has to tell us up front if she's taping, doesn't she?" Foltrigg asked, obviously without a clue.

"Don't bet on it," said Trumann. "Just be careful, okay."

The door opened and Reggie entered, forty-eight minutes late. "Keep your seats," she said as Clint closed the door behind her. She offered a hand to Foltrigg, who was half-standing. "Reggie Love, you must be Roy Foltrigg."

"I am. Nice to meet you."

"Please be seated." She smiled at McThune and Trumann, and for a brief second all three of them thought about the tape. "Sorry I'm late," she said as she sat alone at her end of the conference table. They were eight feet away, huddled together like wet ducks.

"No problem," Foltrigg said loudly as if it was very much a problem.

She pulled a large tape recorder from a hidden drawer in the table and sat it in front of her. "Mind if I tape this little conference?" she asked as she plugged in the microphone. The little conference would be taped whether they liked it or not. "I'll be happy to provide you with a copy of the tape."

"Fine with me," Foltrigg said, pretending he had a choice.

McThune and Trumann stared at the tape recorder. How nice of her to ask! She smiled at the two of them as they smiled at her, then all three smiled at the recorder. She was as subtle as a rock through a window. The damnable micro-cassette could not be far away.

She pushed a button. "Now, what's up?"

"Where's your client?" Foltrigg asked. He leaned forward and it was clear he would do all the talking.

"At the hospital. The doctor wants him to stay in the room near his brother."

"When can we talk to him?"

"You're assuming that you will in fact talk to him." She looked at Foltrigg with very confident eyes. Her hair was gray and cut like a boy's. The face was quite colorful. The eyebrows were dark. The lips were soft red and meticulously painted. The skin was smooth and free of heavy makeup. It was a pretty face, with bangs, and eyes that glowed with a calm steadiness. Foltrigg looked at her, and thought of all the misery and suffering she'd seen. She covered it well.

McThune opened a file and flipped through it. In the past two hours they had assembled a two-inch-thick dossier on Reggie Love, aka Regina L. Cardoni. They had copied the divorce papers and commitment proceedings from the clerk's office in the county courthouse. The mortgage papers and land records on her mother's home were in the folder. Two Memphis agents were attempting to obtain her law school transcripts.

Foltrigg loved the trash. Whatever the case and whoever the opponent, Foltrigg always wanted the dirt. McThune read the sordid legal history of the divorce with its allegations of adultery and alcohol and dope and unfitness and, ultimately, the attempted suicide. He read it carefully, though, without being seen. He did not, under any circumstances, want to make this woman angry.

"We need to talk to your client, Ms. Love."

"It's Reggie. Okay, Roy?"

"Whatever. We think he knows something, plain and simple."

"Such as?"

"Well, we're convinced little Mark was in the car with Jerome Clifford prior to his death. We think he spent more than a few seconds with him. Clifford was obviously planning to kill himself, and we have reason to believe he wanted to tell someone where his client, Mr. Muldanno, had disposed of the body of Senator Boyette."

"What makes you think he wanted to tell?"

"It's a long story, but he had contacted an assistant in my office on two occasions and hinted that he might be willing to cut some deal and get out. He was scared. And he was drinking a lot. Very erratic behavior. He was sliding off the deep end, and wanted to talk."

"Why do you think he talked to my client?"

"There's just a chance, okay. And we must look under every stone. Surely you understand."

"I sense a bit of desperation."

"A lot of desperation, Reggie. I'm leveling with you. We know who killed the Senator, but, frankly, I'm not ready for trial without a corpse." He paused and smiled warmly at her. Despite his many obnoxious flaws, Roy had spent hours before juries and he knew how and when to act sincere.

And she'd spent many hours in therapy, and she could spot a fake. "I'm not telling you that you cannot talk to Mark Sway. You cannot talk to him today, but maybe tomorrow. Maybe the next day. Things are moving fast. Mr. Clifford's body is still warm. Let's slow down a bit, and take it one step at a time. Okay?"

"Okay."

"Now, convince me Mark Sway was in the car with Jerome Clifford prior to the shooting."

No problem. Foltrigg looked at a notepad, and reeled off the many places where fingerprints were matched. Rear taillights, trunk, front passenger door handle and lock switch, dash, gun, bottle of Jack Daniels. There was a tentative match on the hose, but it was not definite. They were working on it. Foltrigg was the prosecutor now, building a case with indisputable evidence . . .

Reggie took pages of notes. She knew Mark had been in the car, but she had no idea he'd left such a wide trail.

"The whiskey bottle?" she asked.

Foltrigg flipped a page for the details. "Yes, three definite prints. No question about it."

Mark had told her about the gun, but not about the bottle. "Seems a bit strange, doesn't it?"

"It's all strange at this point. The police officers who talked to him do not recall smelling alcohol, so I don't think he drank any of it. I'm sure he could explain it, you know, if only we could talk to him."

"I'll ask him."

"So he didn't tell you about the bottle?"

"No."

"Did he explain the gun?"

"I cannot divulge what my client has explained to me."

Foltrigg waited desperately for a hint, and this really angered him. Trumann likewise waited breathlessly. McThune stopped reading the report of a court-appointed psychiatrist.

"So he hasn't told you everything?" Foltrigg asked.

"He's told me a lot. It's possible he missed some of the details."

"These details could be crucial."

"I'll determine what's crucial and what's not. What else do you have?"

"Hand her the note," Foltrigg instructed Trumann, who produced it from a file and handed it to her. She read it slowly, then read it again. Mark had not mentioned the note.

"Obviously two different pens," Foltrigg explained. "We found the blue one in the car, a cheap Bic, out of ink. Just speculating, it looks as though Clifford tried to add something after Mark left the car. The word 'where' seems to indicate the boy was gone. It's obvious they talked, exchanged names, and that the kid was in the car long enough to touch everything."

"No prints on this?" she asked, waving the note.

"None. We've checked it thoroughly. The kid did not touch it."

She calmly placed it next to her legal pad and folded her hands together. "Well, Roy, I think the big question is, How did you guys match his fingerprints? How did you obtain one of his to match with the ones in the car?" She asked this with the same confident sneer Trumann and McThune had seen when she produced the tape less than four hours ago.

"Very simple. We lifted one off a soft drink can at the hospital last night."

"Did you ask either Mark Sway or his mother before doing so?"

"No."

"So you invaded the privacy of an eleven-year-old child."

"No. We are trying to obtain evidence."

"Evidence? Evidence for what? Not for a crime, I dare say. The crime has been committed and the body has been disposed of. You just can't find it. What other crime do we have here? Suicide? Watching a suicide?"

"Did he watch the suicide?"

"I can't tell you what he did or saw because he has confided in me as his lawyer. Our talks are privileged, you know that, Roy. What else have you taken from this child?"

"Nothing."

She snorted as if she didn't believe this. "What else do you have?"

"This is not enough?"

"I want it all."

Foltrigg flipped pages back and forth and did a slow burn. "You've seen the puffy left eye and the knot on his forehead. The police said there was a trace of blood on his lip when they found him at the scene. Clifford's autopsy revealed a spot of blood on the back of his right hand, and it's not his type."

"Let me guess. It's Mark's."

"Probably so. Same blood type."

"How do you know his blood type?"

Foltrigg dropped the legal pad and rubbed his face. The most effective defense lawyers are those who keep the fighting away from the issues. They bitch and throw rocks over the tiny subplots of a case and hope the prosecution and the jury are diverted away from the obvious guilt of their clients. If there's something to hide, then scream at the other guy for violating technicalities. Right now they should be nailing down the facts of what, if anything, Clifford said to Mark. It should be so simple. But now the kid had a lawyer, and here they were trying to explain how they obtained certain crucial information. There was nothing wrong with lifting prints from a can without asking. Good police work. But from the mouth of a defense lawyer, it's suddenly a vicious invasion of privacy. Next she would threaten a lawsuit. And now, the blood.

She was good. He found it difficult to believe she'd been practicing only four years.

"From his brother's hospital admission records."

"And how did you obtain the hospital records?"

"We have ways."

Trumann braced for a reprimand. McThune hid behind the file. They had been burned by this temper. She'd made them stutter and stammer and sweat blood, and now it was time for old Roy to take a few punches. It was almost funny.

But she kept her cool. She slowly extended a skinny finger with white nail polish and pointed it at Roy. "If you get near my client again and attempt to obtain anything from him without my permission, I'll sue you and the FBI. I'll file an ethics complaint with the state bar in Louisiana and Tennessee, and I'll haul your ass into Juvenile Court here and ask the judge to lock you up." The words were spoken in an even voice, no emotion, but so matter-of-factly that everyone in the room, including Roy Foltrigg, knew that she would do exactly as she promised.

He smiled and nodded. "Fine. Sorry if we've gotten a bit out of line. But we're anxious, and we must talk to your client."

"Have you told me everything you know about Mark?"

Foltrigg and Trumann checked their notes. "Yes, I think so."

"What's that?" she insisted, pointing to the file McThune was lost in. He was reading about her suicide attempt, by pills, and it was alleged in the pleadings, sworn under oath, that she'd been in a coma for four days before pulling out. Evidently, her ex-husband, Dr. Cardoni, a real piece of scum according to the pleadings, was a nasty sort with all the money and lawyers, and as soon as Regina/Reggie here took the pills he ran to court with a pile of motions to get the kids. Looking at the dates stamped on the papers, it was obvious the good doctor was filing requests and asking for hearings while she was lost in a coma and fighting for her life.

McThune didn't panic. He looked at her innocently and said,

"Just some of our internal stuff." It was not a lie, because he was afraid to lie to her. She had the tape, and had sworn them to truthfulness.

"About my client?"

"Oh no."

She studied her legal pad. "Let's meet again tomorrow," she said. It was not a suggestion, but a directive.

"We're really in a hurry, Reggie," Foltrigg pleaded.

"Well I'm not. And I guess I'm calling the shots, aren't I?"

"I guess you are."

"I need time to digest this and talk with my client."

This was not what they wanted, but it was painfully clear this was all they would get. Foltrigg dramatically screwed the top onto his pen and slid his notes into his briefcase. Trumann and McThune followed his lead and for a minute the table shook as they shuffled paper and files and restuffed everything.

"What time tomorrow?" Foltrigg asked, slamming his briefcase and pushing away from the table.

"Ten. In this office."

"Will Mark Sway be here?"

"I don't know."

They stood and filed out of the room.

TWELVE

WALLY BOXX called the office in New Orleans at least four times every hour. Foltrigg had forty-seven Assistant U.S. Attorneys fighting all sorts of crime and protecting the interests of the government, and Wally was in charge of relaying orders from the boss in Memphis. In addition to Thomas Fink, three other attorneys were working on the Muldanno case, and Wally felt the need to call them every fifteen minutes with instructions, and the latest on Clifford. By noon, the entire office knew of Mark Sway and his little brother. The place buzzed with gossip and speculation. How much did the kid know? Would he lead them to the body? Initially, these questions were pondered in hushed whispers by the three Muldanno prosecutors, but by mid-afternoon the secretaries in the coffee room were exchanging wild theories about the suicide note and what was told to the kid before Clifford ate his bullet. All other work virtually stopped as Foltrigg's office waited for Wally's next call.

Foltrigg had been burned by leaks before. He'd fired people he suspected of talking too much. He'd required polygraphs for all lawyers, paralegals, investigators, and secretaries who worked for him. He kept sensitive information under lock and key for fear of leakage by his own people. He lectured and threatened.

But Roy Foltrigg was not the sort of person to inspire intense loyalty. He was not appreciated by many of the assistants. He played the political game. He used cases for his own raw ambition. He hogged the spotlight and took credit for all the good work, and blamed his subordinates for all the bad. He sought marginal indictments against elected officials for a few cheap headlines. He investigated his enemies and dragged their names through the press. He was a political whore whose only talent with the law was in the courtroom where he preached to juries and quoted scripture. He was a Reagan appointee with one year left, and most of the assistant attorneys were counting the days. They encouraged him to run for office. Any office.

The reporters in New Orleans began calling at 8 A.M. They wanted an official comment about Clifford from Foltrigg's office. They did not get one. Then Willis Upchurch performed at two o'clock, with Muldanno glowering at his side, and more reporters came snooping around the office. There were hundreds of phone calls to Memphis and back.

People talked.

They stood before the dirty window at the end of the hall on the ninth floor, and watched the rush-hour traffic of downtown. Dianne nervously lit a Virginia Slim, and blew a heavy cloud of smoke. "Who is this lawyer?"

"Her name is Reggie Love."

"How'd you find her?"

He pointed to the Sterick Building four blocks away. "I went to her office in that building right there, and I talked to her."

"Why, Mark?"

"These cops scare me, Mom. The police and FBI are crawling all over this place. And reporters. I had one catch me in the elevator this afternoon. I think we need some legal advice."

"Lawyers don't work for free, Mark. You know we can't afford a lawyer."

"I've already paid her," he said like a tycoon.

"What? How can you pay a lawyer?"

"She wanted a small retainer, and she got one. I gave her a dollar from that five that went for doughnuts this morning."

"She's working for a dollar? She must be a great lawyer."

"She's pretty good. I've been impressed so far."

Dianne shook her head in amazement. During her nasty divorce, Mark, then age nine, had constantly criticized her lawyer. He watched hours of reruns of "Perry Mason" and never missed "L.A. Law." It had been years since she'd won an argument with him.

"What has she done so far?" Dianne asked, as if she were emerging from a dark cave and seeing sunlight for the first time in a month.

"At noon, she met with some FBI agents, and ripped them up pretty good. And later, she met with them again in her office. I haven't talked with her since then."

"What time is she coming here?"

"Around six. She wants to meet you and talk to Dr. Greenway. You'll really like her, Mom."

Dianne filled her lungs with smoke, and exhaled. "But why do we need her, Mark? I don't understand why she's entered the picture. You've done nothing wrong. You and Ricky saw the car, you tried to help the man, but he shot himself anyway. And you guys saw it. Why do you need a lawyer?"

"Well, I did lie to the cops at first, and that scares me. And I was afraid we might get in trouble because we didn't stop the man from shooting himself. It's all pretty scary, Mom."

She watched him intently as he explained this, and he avoided her eyes. There was a long pause. "Have you told me everything?" She asked this very slowly, as if she knew.

At first he'd lied to her at the trailer while they waited on the ambulance, with Hardy lingering nearby, all ears. Then last night, in Ricky's room, under cross-examination by Greenway, he had told the first version of the truth. He remembered how sad she had been when she heard this revised story, and later how she'd said, "You never lie to me, Mark."

They'd been through so much together, and here he was dancing around the truth, dodging questions, telling Reggie more than he'd told his mother. It made him sick.

"Mom, it all happened so fast yesterday. It was all a blur in my mind last night, but I've been thinking about it today. Thinking hard. I've gone through each step, minute by minute, and I'm remembering things now."

"Such as?"

"Well, you know how this has affected Ricky. I think it shocked me sort of like that. Not as bad, but I'm remembering things now that I should have remembered last night when I talked to Dr. Greenway. Does this make sense?"

Actually, it did make sense. Dianne was suddenly concerned.

Two boys see the same event. One goes into shock. It's reasonable to believe the other would be affected. She hadn't thought of this. She leaned down next to him. "Mark, are you all right?"

He knew he had her. "I think so," he said with a frown, as if a migraine were upon him.

"What have you remembered?" she asked cautiously.

He took a deep breath. "Well, I remember—"

Greenway cleared his throat and appeared from nowhere. Mark whirled around. "I need to be going," Greenway said, almost as an apology. "I'll check back in a couple of hours."

Dianne nodded but said nothing.

Mark decided to get it over with. "Look, Doctor, I was just telling Mom that I'm remembering things now for the first time."

"About the suicide?"

"Yes sir. All day long I've been seeing flashes and recalling details. I think some of it might be important."

Greenway looked at Dianne. "Let's go back to the room and talk," he said.

They walked to the room, closed the door behind them, and listened as Mark tried to fill in the gaps. It was a relief to unload this baggage, though he did most of the talking in the direction of the floor. It was an act, this painful pulling of scenes from a shocked and badly scarred mind and he carried it off with finesse. He paused quite often, long pauses in which he searched for words to describe what was already firmly etched in his memory. He glanced at Greenway occasionally, and the doctor's expression never changed. He glanced at his mother from time to time, and she didn't appear to be disappointed. She maintained a look of motherly concern.

But when he got to the part about Clifford grabbing him, he could see them fidget. He kept his troubled eyes on the floor. Dianne sighed when he talked about the gun. Greenway shook his head when he told of the gunshot through the window. At times, he thought they were about to yell at him for lying last night, but he plowed ahead, obviously disturbed and deep in thought.

He carefully replayed every single event that Ricky could have seen and heard. The only details he kept to himself were Clifford's confessions. He vividly recalled the crazy stuff: La La Land and floating off to see the wizard.

When he finished, Dianne was sitting on the foldaway bed rubbing her head, talking about Valium. Greenway sat in a chair, hanging on every word. "Is this all of it, Mark?"

"I don't know. It's all I can remember right now," he mumbled, as if he had a toothache.

"You were actually in the car?" Dianne said without opening her eyes.

He pointed to his slightly swollen left eye. "You see this. This is where he slapped me when I tried to get out of the car. I was dizzy for a long time. Maybe I was unconscious, I don't know."

"You told me you were in a fight at school."

"I don't remember telling you that, Mom, and if I did, well, maybe I was in shock or something." Dammit. Trapped by another lie.

Greenway stroked his beard. "Ricky saw you get grabbed, thrown in the car, the gunshot. Wow."

"Yeah. It's coming back to me, real clear. I'm sorry I didn't remember it sooner, but my mind just went blank. Sort of like Ricky here."

Another long pause.

"Frankly, Mark, I find it hard to believe you couldn't remember some of this last night," Greenway said.

"Gimme a break, would you? Look at Ricky here. He saw what happened to me, and it drove him to the ozone. Did we talk last night?"

"Come on, Mark," Dianne said.

"Of course we talked," Greenway said with at least four new wrinkles across his forehead.

"Yeah, I guess we did. Don't remember much of it though."

Greenway frowned at Dianne and their eyes locked. Mark walked into the bathroom and drank water out of a paper cup.

"It's okay," Dianne said. "Have you told the police this?"

"No. I just remembered it. Remember?"

Dianne nodded slowly and managed a very slight grin at Mark. Her eyes were narrow, and his suddenly found the floor. She believed all of his story about the suicide, but this sudden surge of clear memory did not fool her. She would deal with him later.

Greenway had his doubts too, but he was more concerned with

treating his patient than reprimanding Mark. He gently stroked his beard and studied the wall. There was a long pause.

"I'm hungry," Mark finally said.

Reggie arrived an hour late with apologies. Greenway had left for the day. Mark stumbled through the introductions. She smiled warmly at Dianne as they shook hands, then sat beside her on the bed. She asked her a dozen questions about Ricky. She was an immediate friend of the family, anxious and properly concerned about everything. What about her job? School? Money? Clothes?

Dianne was tired and vulnerable, and it was nice to talk to a woman. She opened up, and they went on for a while about Greenway saying this and that, about everything unrelated to Mark and his story and the FBI, the only reason for Reggie's being there.

Reggie had a sack of deli sandwiches and chips, and Mark spread them on a crowded table by Ricky's bed. He left the room to get drinks. They hardly noticed.

He bought two Dr Peppers in the waiting area and returned to the room without being stopped by cops, reporters, or Mafia gunmen. The women were deep into a conversation about McThune and Trumann trying to interrogate Mark. Reggie was telling the story in such a manner that Dianne had no choice but to mistrust the FBI. They were both shocked. Dianne was alive and animated for the first time in many hours.

Jack Nance and Associates was a quiet firm that advertised itself as security specialists, but was in fact nothing more than a couple of private investigators. Its ad in the yellow pages was one of the smallest in town. It did not want the run-of-the-mill divorce cases in which one spouse was sleeping around and the other wanted photos. It did not own a polygraph. It did not snatch children. It did not track down thieving employees.

Jack Nance himself was an ex-con with an impressive record who'd managed to avoid trouble for ten years. His associate was Cal Sisson, also a convicted felon who'd run a terrific scam with a bogus roofing company. Together they scratched out a nice living doing dirty work for rich people. They had once broken both hands of the teenaged boyfriend of a rich client's daughter after the kid slapped her. They had once deprogrammed a couple of Moonies, the children of another rich client. They were not afraid of violence. More than once, they had beaten a business rival who'd taken money from a client. They had once burned the downtown love nest of a client's wife and her lover.

There was a market for their brand of investigative work, and they were known in small circles as two very nasty and efficient men who would take your cash, do your dirty work, and leave no trail. They achieved amazing results. Every client came by referral.

Jack Nance was in his cluttered office after dark when someone knocked on the door. The secretary had left for the day. Cal Sisson was stalking a crack dealer who'd hooked the son of a client. Nance was around forty, not a big man, but compact and extremely agile. He walked through the secretary's office and opened the front door. The face was a strange one.

"Looking for Jack Nance," the man said.

"That's me."

The man stretched out his hand, and they shook. "My name's Paul Gronke. Can I come in?"

Nance opened the door wider and motioned for Gronke to enter. They stood in front of the secretary's desk. Gronke looked around the cramped and messy room.

"It's late," Nance said. "What do you want?"

"I need some fast work."

"Who referred you?"

"I've heard of you. Word gets around."

"Give me a name."

"Okay. J. L. Grainger. I think you helped him on a business deal. He also mentioned a Mr. Schwartz who was also quite pleased with your work."

Nance thought about this for a second as he studied Gronke. He was a burly man with a thick chest, late thirties, badly dressed but didn't know it. Because of his clipped drawl, Nance immediately knew he was from New Orleans. "I get a two-thousand-dollar retainer up front, nonrefundable, all in cash, before I lift a finger." Gronke pulled a roll of bills from his left front pocket and peeled off twenty big ones. Nance relaxed. It was his fastest retainer in ten years. "Sit down," he said, taking the money and waving at a sofa. "I'm listening."

Gronke took a folded newspaper clipping from his jacket and handed it to Nance. "Did you see this in today's paper?"

Nance looked at it. "Yeah. I read it. How are you involved?"

"I'm from New Orleans. In fact, Mr. Muldanno is an old pal, and he's very disturbed to see his name suddenly show up here in the Memphis paper. It says he has Mafia ties and all. Can't believe a word in the newspapers. The press is going to ruin this country."

"Was Clifford his lawyer?"

"Yeah. But now he has a new one. That's not important, though. Lemme tell you what's worrying him. He has a good source telling him these two boys know something."

"Where are the boys?"

"One's in the hospital, a coma or something. He freaked out when Clifford shot himself. His brother was actually in the car with Clifford prior to the shooting, and we're afraid this kid might know something. He's already hired a lawyer, and is refusing to talk to the FBI. Looks real suspicious."

"Where do I fit in?"

"We need someone with Memphis connections. We need to see the kid. We need to know where he is at all times."

"What's his name?"

"Mark Sway. He's at the hospital, we think, with his mother. Last night they stayed in the room with the younger brother, a kid named Ricky Sway. Ninth floor at St. Peter's. Room 943. We want you to find the kid, determine his location as of now, and then watch him."

"Easy enough."

"Maybe not. There are cops and probably FBI agents watching too. The kid's attracting a crowd."

"I get a hundred bucks an hour, cash."

"I know that."

She called herself Amber, which along with Alexis happened to be the two most popular acquired names among strippers and whores in the French Quarter. She answered the phone, then carried it a few feet to the tiny bathroom where Barry Muldanno was brushing his teeth. "It's Gronke," she said, handing it to him. He took it, turned off the water, and admired her naked body as she crawled under the sheets. He stepped into the doorway. "Yeah," he said into the phone.

A minute later, he placed the phone on the table next to the bed, and quickly dried himself off. He dressed in a hurry. Amber was somewhere under the covers.

"What time are you going to work?" he asked, tying his tie.

"Ten. What time is it?" Her head appeared between the pillows.

"Almost nine. I gotta run an errand. I'll be back."

"Why? You got what you wanted."

"I might want some more. I pay the rent here, sweetheart."

"Some rent. Why don't you move me outta this dump? Get me a nice place?"

He tugged his sleeves from under his jacket, and admired himself in the mirror. Perfect, just perfect. He smiled at Amber. "I like it here."

"It's a dump. If you treated me right, you'd get me a nice place."

"Yeah, yeah. See you later, sweetheart." He slammed the door. Strippers. Get them a job, then an apartment, buy some clothes, feed them nice dinners, and then they get culture and start making demands. They were an expensive habit, but one he could not break.

He bounced down the steps in his alligator loafers, and opened the door onto Dumaine. He looked right and left, certain that someone was watching, and took off around the corner onto Bourbon. He moved in shadows, crossing and recrossing the street, then turned corners and retraced some of his steps. He zigzagged for eight blocks, then disappeared into Randy's Oysters on Decatur. If they stuck to him, they were supermen.

Randy's was a sanctuary. It was an old-fashioned New Orleans eatery, long and narrow, dark and crowded, off-limits for tourists, owned and operated by the family. He ran up the cramped staircase to the second floor where reserved seating was required and only a select few could get reservations. He nodded to a waiter, grinned at a beefy thug, and entered a private room with four tables. Three were empty, and at the fourth a solitary figure sat in virtual darkness reading by the light of a real candle. Barry approached, stopped, and waited to be invited. The man saw him and waved at a chair. Barry obediently took a seat.

Johnny Sulari was the brother of Barry's mother, and the undisputed head of the family. He owned Randy's, along with a hundred other assorted ventures. As usual, he was working tonight, reading financial statements by candlelight and waiting for dinner. This was Tuesday, just another night at the office. On Friday, Johnny would be here with an Amber or an Alexis or a Sabrina, and on Saturday he would be here with his wife.

He did not appreciate the interruption. "What is it?" he asked.

Barry leaned forward, well aware that he was not wanted here at this moment. "Just talked to Gronke in Memphis. Kid's hired a lawyer, and is refusing to talk to the FBI."

"I can't believe you're so stupid, Barry, you know that?"

"We've had this conversation, okay?"

"I know. And we'll have it again. You're a dumbass, and I just want you to know that I think you're a real dumbass."

"Okay. I'm a dumbass. But we need to make a move."

"What?"

"We need to send Bono and someone else, maybe Pirini, maybe the Bull, I don't care, but we need a couple of men in Memphis. And we need them now."

"You want to hit the kid?"

"Maybe. We'll see. We need to find out what he knows, okay? If he knows too much, then maybe we'll take him out."

"I'm embarrassed we're related by blood, Barry. You're a complete fool, you know that?"

"Okay. But we need to move fast."

Johnny picked up a stack of papers, and began reading. "Send Bono and Pirini, but no more stupid moves. Okay? You're a idiot, Barry, an imbecile, and I don't want anything done up there until I say so. Understand?"

"Yes sir."

"Leave now." Johnny waved his hand, and Barry jumped to his feet.

THIRTEEN

BY TUESDAY EVENING, George Ord and his staff had managed to confine the activities of Foltrigg, Boxx, and Fink to the expansive library in the center of the offices. Here they'd set up camp. They had two phones. Ord loaned them a secretary and an intern. All other assistant attorneys were ordered to stay out of the library. Foltrigg kept the doors closed and spread his papers and mess over the sixteen-foot conference table in the middle of the room. Trumann was allowed to come and go. The secretary fetched coffee and sandwiches whenever the Reverend ordered.

Foltrigg had been a mediocre student of the law, and had managed to avoid the drudgery of legal research for the past fifteen years. He had learned to hate libraries in law school. Research was to be done by egghead scholars; that was his theory. Law could be practiced only by real lawyers who could stand before juries and preach.

But out of sheer boredom, here he was in George Ord's library with Boxx and Fink, nothing to do but wait at the beck and call of one Reggie Love, and so he, the great Roy Foltrigg, lawyer extraordinaire, had his nose stuck in a thick law book with a dozen more stacked around him on the table. Fink, the egghead scholar, was on the floor between two shelves of books with his shoes off and research materials littered about. Boxx, also a lightweight legal intellect, went through the motions at the other end of Foltrigg's table. Boxx had not opened a law book in years, but for the moment there was simply nothing else to do. He wore his only clean pair of boxer shorts and hoped like hell they left Memphis tomorrow.

At issue, at the heart of their research, was the question of how Mark Sway could be made to divulge information if he didn't want to. If someone possesses information crucial to a criminal prosecution, and that person chooses not to talk, then how can the information be obtained? For issue number two, Foltrigg wanted to know if Reggie Love could be made to divulge whatever Mark Sway had told her. The attorney-client privilege is almost sacred, but Roy wanted it researched anyway.

The debate over whether or not Mark Sway knew anything had ended hours ago with Foltrigg clearly victorious. The kid had been in the car. Clifford was crazy and wanted to talk. The kid had lied to the cops. And now the kid had a lawyer because the kid knew something and was afraid to talk. Why didn't Mark Sway simply come clean and tell all? Why? Because he was afraid of the killer of Boyd Boyette. Plain and simple.

Fink still had doubts, but was tired of arguing. His boss was not bright and was very stubborn, and when he closed his mind it remained closed forever. And there was a lot of merit to Foltrigg's arguments. The kid was making strange moves, especially for a kid.

Boxx, of course, stood firm behind his boss and believed everything he said. If Roy said the kid knew where the body was, then it was the gospel. Pursuant to one of his many phone calls, a half dozen Assistant U.S. Attorneys were doing identical research in New Orleans.

Larry Trumann knocked and entered the library around ten Tuesday night. He'd been in McThune's office for most of the evening. Following Foltrigg's orders, they had begun the process of obtaining approval to offer Mark Sway safety under the Federal Witness Protection Program. They had made a dozen phone calls to Washington, twice speaking with the Director of the FBI, F. Denton Voyles. If Mark Sway didn't give Foltrigg the answers he wanted in the morning, they would be ready with a most attractive offer.

Foltrigg said it would be an easy deal. The kid had nothing to lose. They would offer his mother a good job in a new city, one of her choosing. She would earn more than the six lousy bucks an hour she got at the lamp factory. The family would live in a house with a foundation, not a cheap trailer. There would be a cash incentive, maybe a new car.

Mark sat in the darkness on the thin mattress, and stared at his mother lying above him next to Ricky. He was sick of this room and this hospital. The foldaway bed was ruining his back. Tragically, Karen the beautiful was not at the nurses' station. The hallways were empty. No one waited for the elevators.

A solitary man occupied the waiting area. He flipped through a magazine and ignored the "M*A*S*H" reruns on the television. He was on the sofa, which happened to be the spot Mark had planned to sleep. Mark stuck two quarters in the machine, and pulled out a Sprite. He sat in a chair and stared at the TV. The man was about forty, and looked tired and worried. Ten minutes passed, and "M*A*S*H" went away. Suddenly, there was Gill Teal, the people's lawyer, standing calmly at the scene of a car wreck talking about defending rights and fighting insurance companies. Gill Teal, he's for real.

Jack Nance closed the magazine and picked up another. He glanced at Mark for the first time, and smiled. "Hi there," he said warmly, then looked at a *Redbook.*

Mark nodded. The last thing he needed in his life was another stranger. He sipped his drink, and prayed for silence.

"What're you doing here?" the man asked.

"Watching television," Mark answered, barely audible.

The man stopped smiling and began reading an article. The midnight news came on, and there was a huge story about a typhoon in Pakistan. There were live pictures of dead people and dead animals piled along the shore like driftwood. It was the kind of footage one had to watch.

"That's awful, isn't it," Jack Nance said to the TV as a helicopter hovered over a pile of human debris.

"It's gross," Mark said, careful not to get friendly. Who knows—this guy could be just another hungry lawyer waiting to pounce on wounded prey.

"Really gross," the man said, shaking his head at the suffering. "I guess we have much to be thankful for. But it's hard to be thankful in a hospital, know what I mean?" He was suddenly sad again. He looked painfully at Mark.

"What's the matter?" Mark couldn't help but ask.

"It's my son. He's in real bad shape." The man threw the magazine on the table and rubbed his eyes.

"What happened?" Mark asked. He felt sorry for this guy.

"Car wreck. Drunk driver. My boy was thrown out of the car."

"Where is he?"

"ICU, first floor. I had to leave and get away. It's a zoo down there, people screaming and crying all the time."

"I'm very sorry."

"He's only eight years old." He appeared to be crying, but Mark couldn't tell.

"My little brother's eight. He's in a room around the corner."

"What's wrong with him?" the man asked without looking.

"He's in shock."

"What happened?"

"It's a long story. And getting longer. He'll make it, though. I sure hope your kid pulls through."

Jack Nance looked at his watch and suddenly stood. "Me too. I need to go check on him. Good luck to you, uh, what's your name?"

"Mark Sway."

"Good luck, Mark. I gotta run." He walked to the elevators and disappeared.

Mark took his place on the couch, and within minutes was asleep.

FOURTEEN

THE PHOTOS on the front page of Wednesday's edition of the *Memphis Press* had been lifted from the yearbook at Willow Road Elementary School. They were a year old—Mark was in the fourth grade and Ricky the first. They were next to each other on the bottom third of the page, and under the cute, smiling faces were the names. Mark Sway. Ricky Sway. To the left was a story about Jerome Clifford's suicide and the bizarre aftermath in which the boys were involved. It was written by Slick Moeller, and he had pieced together a suspicious little story. The FBI was involved; Ricky was in shock; Mark had called 911 but hadn't given his name; the police had tried to interrogate Mark but he hadn't talked yet; the family had hired a lawyer, one Reggie Love (female); Mark's fingerprints were all over the inside of the car, including the gun. The story made Mark look like a cold-blooded killer.

Karen brought it to him around six as he sat in an empty semiprivate room directly across the hall from Ricky's. Mark was watching cartoons and trying to nap. Greenway wanted everyone out of the room except Ricky and Dianne. An hour earlier, Ricky had opened his eyes and asked to use the bathroom. He was back in the bed now, mumbling about nightmares and eating ice cream.

"You've hit the big time," Karen said as she handed him the front section and put his orange juice on the table.

"What is it?" he asked, suddenly staring at his face in black and white. "Damn!"

"Just a little story. I'd like your autograph when you have time."

Very funny. She left the room and he read it slowly. Reggie had told him about the fingerprints and the note. He'd dreamed about the gun, but through a legitimate lapse in memory had forgotten about touching the whiskey bottle.

There was something unfair here. He was just a kid who'd been minding his own business, and now suddenly his picture was on the front page and fingers were pointed at him. How can a newspaper dig up old yearbook photos and run them whenever it chooses? Wasn't he entitled to a little privacy?

He threw the paper to the floor and walked to the window. It was dawn, drizzling outside, and downtown Memphis was slowly coming to life. Standing in the window of the empty room, looking at the blocks of tall buildings, he felt completely alone. Within an hour, a half million people would be awake, reading about Mark and Ricky Sway while sipping their coffee and eating their toast. The dark buildings would soon be filled with busy people gathering around desks and coffeepots, and they would gossip and speculate wildly about him and what happened with the dead lawyer. Surely the kid was in the car. There are fingerprints everywhere! How did the kid get in the car? How did he get out? They would read Slick Moeller's story as if every word were true, as if Slick had the inside dope.

It was not fair for a kid to read about himself on the front page and not have parents to hide behind. Any kid in this mess needed the protection of a father and the sole affection of a mother. He needed a shield against cops and FBI agents and reporters, and god forbid, the mob. Here he was, eleven years old, alone, lying, then telling the truth, then lying some more, never certain what to do next. The truth can get you killed—he'd seen that in a movie one time, and always remembered it when he felt the urge to lie to someone in authority. How could he get out of this mess?

He retrieved the paper from the floor and entered the hall. Greenway had stuck a note on Ricky's door forbidding anyone from entering, including nurses. Dianne was having back pains from sitting in his bed and rocking, and Greenway had ordered another round of pills for her discomfort.

Mark stopped at the nurses' station, and handed the paper to Karen. "Nice story, huh," she said with a smile. The romance was gone. She was still beautiful but now playing hard to get, and he just didn't have the energy.

"I'm going to get a doughnut," he said. "You want one?"

"No thanks."

He walked to the elevators, and pushed the Call button. The middle door opened and he stepped in.

At that precise second, Jack Nance turned in the darkness of the waiting room and whispered into his radio.

The elevator was empty. It was just a few minutes past six, a good half an hour before the rush hit. The elevator stopped at floor number eight. The door opened, and one man stepped in. He wore a white lab jacket, jeans, sneakers, and a baseball cap. Mark did not look at his face. He was tired of meeting new people.

The door closed, and suddenly the man grabbed Mark and pinned him in a corner. He clenched his fingers around Mark's throat. The man fell to one knee and pulled something from a pocket. His face was inches from Mark's, and it was a horrible face. He was breathing heavy. "Listen to me, Mark Sway," he growled. Something clicked in his right hand, and suddenly a shiny switchblade entered the picture. A very long switchblade. "I don't know what Jerome Clifford told you," he said urgently. The elevator was moving. "But if you repeat a single word of it to anyone, including your lawyer, I'll kill you. And I'll kill your mother and your little brother. Okay? He's in Room 943. I've seen the trailer where you live. Okay? I've seen your school at Willow Road." His breath was warm and had the smell of creamed coffee, and he aimed it directly at Mark's eyes. "Do you understand me?" he sneered with a nasty smile.

The elevator stopped, and the man was on his feet by the door with the switchblade hidden by his leg. Although Mark was paralyzed, he was able to hope and pray that someone would get on the damned elevator with him. It was obvious he was not getting off at this point. They waited ten seconds at the sixth floor, and nobody entered. The doors closed, and they were moving again.

The man lunged at him again, this time with the switchblade an inch or two from Mark's nose. He pinned him in the corner with a heavy forearm, and suddenly jabbed the shiny blade at Mark's waist. Quickly and efficiently, he cut a belt loop. Then a second one. He'd already delivered his message, without interruption, and now it was time for a little reinforcement.

"I'll slice your guts out, do you understand me?" he demanded, and then released Mark.

Mark nodded. A lump the size of a golf ball clogged his dry throat, and suddenly his eyes were wet. He nodded yes, yes, yes.

"I'll kill you. Do you believe me?"

Mark stared at the knife, and nodded some more. "And if you tell anyone about me, I'll get you. Understand?" Mark kept nodding, only faster now.

The man slid the knife into a pocket and pulled a folded eight by ten color photograph from under the lab jacket. He stuck it in Mark's face. "You seen this before?" he asked, smiling now.

It was a department store portrait taken when Mark was in the second grade, and for years now it had hung in the den above the television. Mark stared at it.

"Recognize it?" the man barked at him.

Mark nodded. There was only one such photograph in the world.

The elevator stopped on the fifth floor, and the man moved quickly, again by the door. At the last second, two nurses stepped in, and Mark finally breathed. He stayed in the corner, holding the railings, praying for a miracle. The switchblade had come closer with each assault, and he simply could not take another one. On the third floor, three more people entered and stood between Mark and the man with the knife. In an instant, Mark's assailant was gone; through the door as it was closing.

"Are you okay?" A nurse was staring at him, frowning and very concerned. The elevator kicked and started down. She touched his forehead and felt a layer of sweat between her fingers. His eyes were wet. "You look pale," she said.

"I'm okay," he mumbled weakly, holding the railings for support.

Another nurse looked down at him in the corner. They studied his face with much concern. "Are you sure?"

He nodded, and the elevator door suddenly opened on the second floor. He darted through bodies and was in a narrow corridor dodging gurneys and wheelchairs. His well-worn Nike hightops squeaked on the clean linoleum as he ran to a door with an EXIT sign over it. He pushed through the door, and was in the stairwell. He grabbed the rails and started up, two steps at a time, churning and churning. The pain hit his thighs at the sixth floor, but he ran harder. He passed a doctor on the eighth floor, but never slowed. He ran, climbing the mountain at a record pace until the stairwell stopped on the fifteenth floor. He collapsed on a landing under a fire hose, and sat in the semidarkness until the sun filtered through a tiny painted window above him.

Pursuant to his agreement with Reggie, Clint opened the office at exactly eight, and after turning on the lights, made the coffee. It was Wednesday, southern pecan day. He looked through the countless one-pound bags of coffee beans in the refrigerator until he found southern pecan, and measured four perfect scoops into the grinder. She would know in an instant if he'd missed the measurement by half a teaspoon. She would take the first sip like a wine connoisseur, smack her lips like a rabbit, then pass judgment on the coffee. He added the precise quantity of water, flipped the switch, and waited for the first black drops to hit the canister. The aroma was delicious.

Clint enjoyed the coffee almost as much as his boss, and the meticulous routine of making it was only half-serious. They began each morning with a quiet cup as they planned the day and talked about the mail. They had met in a detox center eleven years ago when she was forty-one and he was seventeen. They had started law school at the same time, but he flunked out after a nasty round with coke. He'd been perfectly clean for five years, she for six. They had leaned on each other many times.

He sorted the mail and placed it carefully on her clean desk. He poured his first cup of coffee in the kitchen, and read with great interest the front page story about her newest client. As usual, Slick had his facts. And, as usual, the facts were stretched with a good dose of innuendo thrown in. The boys favored each other, but Ricky's hair was a shade lighter. He smiled with several teeth missing.

Clint placed the front page in the center of Reggie's desk.

□ □ □ □

Unless she was expected in court, Reggie seldom made it to the office before 9 A.M. She was a slow starter who usually hit her stride around four in the afternoon and preferred to work late.

Her mission as a lawyer was to protect abused and neglected children, and she did this with great skill and passion. The juvenile courts routinely called her for indigent work representing kids who needed lawyers but didn't know it. She was a zealous advocate for small clients who could not say thanks. She had sued fathers for molesting daughters. She had sued uncles for raping their nieces. She had sued mothers for abusing their babies. She had investigated parents for exposing their children to drugs. She served as legal guardian for more than twenty children. And she worked the Juvenile Court as appointed counsel for kids in trouble with the law. She performed pro bono work for children in need of commitment to mental facilities. The money was adequate, but not important. She had money once, lots of it, and it had brought nothing but misery.

She sipped the southern pecan, pronounced it good, and planned the day with Clint. It was a ritual adhered to whenever possible.

As she picked up the newspaper, the buzzer rang as the door opened. Clint jumped to answer it. He found Mark Sway standing in the reception room, wet from the drizzle and out of breath.

"Good morning, Mark. You're all wet."

"I need to see Reggie." His bangs stuck to his forehead and water dripped from his nose. He was in a daze.

"Sure." Clint backed away from him, and returned with a hand towel from the rest room. He wiped Mark's face, and said, "Follow me."

Reggie was waiting in the center of her office. Clint closed the door and left them alone.

"What's the matter?" she asked.

"I think we need to talk." She pointed, and he sat in a wingback chair and she sat on the sofa.

"What's going on, Mark?" His eyes were red and tired. He stared at the flowers on the coffee table.

"Ricky snapped out of it early this morning."

"That's great. What time?"

"A couple of hours ago."

"You look tired. Would you like some hot cocoa?"

"No. Did you see the paper this morning?"

"Yeah, I saw it. Does it scare you?"

"Of course it scares me." Clint knocked on the door, then opened it and brought the hot cocoa anyway. Mark thanked him and held it with both hands. He was cold and the warm cup helped. Clint closed the door and was gone.

"When do we meet with the FBI?" he asked.

"In an hour. Why?"

He sipped the cocoa and it burned his tongue. "I'm not sure I want to talk to them."

"Okay. You don't have to, you know. I've explained all this."

"I know. Can I ask you something?"

"Of course, Mark. You look scared."

"It's been a rough morning." He took another tiny sip, then another. "What would happen to me if I never told anyone what I know?"

"You've told me."

"Yeah, but you can't tell. And I haven't told you everything, right?"

"That's right."

"I've told you that I know where the body is, but I haven't told—"

"I know, Mark. I don't know where it is. There's a big difference, and I certainly understand it."

"Do you want to know?"

"Do you want to tell me?"

"Not really. Not now."

She was relieved but didn't show it. "Okay, then I don't want to know."

"So what happens to me if I never tell?"

She'd thought about this for hours, and still had no answer. But she'd met Foltrigg, had watched him under pressure, and was convinced he would try all legal means to extract the information from her client. As much as she wanted to, she could not advise him to lie.

A lie would work just fine. One simple lie, and Mark Sway could live the rest of his life without regard to what happened in New Orleans. And why should he worry about Muldanno and Foltrigg and the late Boyd Boyette? He was just a kid, guilty of neither crime nor major sin.

"I think that an effort will be made to force you to talk."

"How does it work?"

"I'm not sure. It's very rare, but I believe steps can be taken in court to force you to testify about what you know. Clint and I have been researching it."

"I know what Clifford told me, but I don't know if it's the truth."

"But you think it's the truth, don't you, Mark?"

"I think so, I guess. I don't know what to do." He was mumbling softly, at times barely audible, unwilling to look at her. "Can they make me talk?" he asked.

She answered carefully. "It could happen. I mean, a lot of things could happen. But, yes, a judge in a courtroom one day soon could order you to talk."

"And if I refused?"

"Good question, Mark. It's a gray area. If an adult refuses a court order, he's in contempt of court and runs the risk of being locked up. I don't know what they'd do with a child. I've never heard of it before."

"What about a polygraph?"

"What do you mean?"

"Well, let's say they drag me into court, and the judge tells me to spill my guts, and I tell the story but leave out the most important part. And they think I'm lying. What then? Can they strap me in the chair and start asking questions? I saw it in a movie one time."

"You saw a child take a polygraph?"

"No. It was some cop who got caught lying. But, I mean, can they do it to me?"

"I doubt it. I've never heard of it, and I'd be fighting like crazy to stop it."

"But it could happen."

"I'm not sure. I doubt it." These were hard questions coming at her like gunfire, and she had to be careful. Clients often heard what they wanted to hear, and missed the rest. "But I must warn you, Mark, if you lie in court you could be in big trouble."

He thought about this for a second, and said, "If I tell the truth I'm in bigger trouble."

"Why?"

She waited a long time for a response. Every twenty seconds or so, he would take a sip of the cocoa, but he was not at all interested in answering this question. The silence did not bother him. He stared at the table, but his mind whirled away somewhere else.

"Mark, last night you indicated you were ready to talk to the FBI and tell them your story. Now, it's obvious you've changed your mind. Why? What's happened?"

Without a word, he gently placed the cup on the table and covered his eyes with his fists. His chin dropped to his chest, and he started crying.

The door opened into the reception area and a Federal Express lady ran in with a box three inches thick. All smiles and perfect efficiency, she handed it to Clint and showed him where to sign. She thanked him, wished him a nice day, and vanished.

The package was expected. It was from Print Research, an amazing little outfit in D.C. that did nothing but scan two hundred daily newspapers nationwide and catalogue the stories. The news was clipped, copied, computerized, and readily available within twenty-four hours for those willing to pay. Reggie didn't want to pay, but she needed quick background on Boyette et al. Clint had placed the order yesterday, as soon as Mark left and Reggie had herself a new client. The search was limited to the New Orleans and Washington papers.

He removed the contents, a neat stack of eight and a half by eleven Xerox copies of newspaper stories, headlines, and photos, all arranged in perfect chronological order, all copied with the columns straight and the photos clean.

Boyette was an old Democrat from New Orleans, and he'd served several terms as an undistinguished rank and file member of the U.S. House, when one day Senator Dauvin, an antebellum relic from the Civil War, suddenly died in office at the age of ninety-one.

Boyette pulled strings and twisted arms, and in keeping with the great tradition of Louisiana politics rounded up some cash and found a home for it. He was appointed by the Governor to fill the unexpired portion of Dauvin's term. The theory was simple: If a man had enough sense to accumulate a bunch of cash, then he would certainly make a worthy U.S. Senator.

Boyette became a member of the world's most exclusive club, and with time proved himself quite capable. Over the years he narrowly missed a few indictments, and evidently learned his lessons. He survived two close reelections, and finally reached a point attained by most southern senators where he was simply left alone. When this happened, Boyette slowly mellowed, and changed from a hell-raising segregationist to a rather liberal and open-minded statesman. He lost favor with three straight governors in Louisiana, and in doing so became an outcast with the petroleum and chemical companies that had ruined the ecology of the state.

So Boyd Boyette became a radical environmentalist, something unheard of among southern politicians. He railed against the oil and gas industry, and it vowed to defeat him. He held hearings in small bayou towns devastated by the oil boom and bust, and made enemies in the tall buildings in New Orleans. Senator Boyette embraced the crumbling ecology of his beloved state, and studied it with a passion.

Six years ago, someone in New Orleans had floated out a proposal to build a toxic waste dump in Lafourche Parish, about eighty miles southwest of New Orleans. It was quickly killed for the first time by local authorities. As is true with most ideas created by rich, corporate minds, it didn't go away, but rather came back a year later with a different name, a different set of consultants, new promises of local jobs, and a new mouthpiece doing the presenting. It was voted down by the locals for the second time, but the vote was much closer. A year passed, some money changed hands, cosmetic changes were made to the plans, and it was suddenly back on the agenda. The folks who lived around the site were hysterical. Rumors were rampant, especially a persistent one that the New Orleans mob was behind the dump and would not stop until it was a reality. Of course, millions were at stake.

The New Orleans papers did a credible job of linking the mob to the toxic waste site. A dozen corporations were involved, and names and addresses led to several known and undisputed crime figures.

The stage was set, the deal was done, the dump was to be approved, then Senator Boyd Boyette came crashing in with an army of federal regulators. He threatened investigations by a dozen agencies. He held weekly press conferences. He made speeches all over southern Louisiana. The advocates of the waste site ran for cover. The corporations issued terse statements of no comment. Boyette had them on the ropes, and he was enjoying himself immensely.

On the night of his disappearance, the Senator had attended an angry meeting of local citizens at a packed high school gymnasium in Houma. He left late, and alone, as was his custom, for the hour drive to his home near New Orleans. Years earlier, Boyette had grown weary of the constant small talk and incessant ass kissing of aides, and he preferred to drive by himself whenever possible. He was studying Russian, his fourth language, and he cherished the solitude of his Cadillac and the language tapes.

By noon the next day, it was determined the Senator was missing. The splashy headlines from New Orleans told the story. Bold headlines in the *Washington Post* suspected foul play. Days went by and the news was scarce. No body was found. A hundred old photos of the Senator were dug up and used by the newspapers. The story was becoming old when, suddenly, the name of Barry Muldanno was linked to the disappearance and this set off a frenzy of Mafia dirt and trash. A rather frightening mug shot of a young Muldanno ran on page one in New Orleans. The paper rehashed its earlier stories about the waste site and the mob. The Blade was a known hit man with a criminal record. And on and on.

Roy Foltrigg made a grand entrance into the story when he stepped in front of the cameras to announce the indictment of Barry Muldanno for the murder of Senator Boyd Boyette. He, too, got the front page in both New Orleans and Washington, and Clint remembered a similar photo in the Memphis paper. Big news, but no body. This, however, did not throttle Mr. Foltrigg. He ranted against organized crime. He predicted certain victory. He preached his carefully prepared remarks with the flair of a veteran stage actor, shouting at all the right moments, pointing his finger, waving the indictment. He had no comment about the absence of a corpse, but hinted that he knew something he couldn't tell and said he had no doubt the remains of the late Senator would be found.

There were pictures and stories when Barry Muldanno was arrested, or rather, turned himself in to the FBI. He spent three days in jail before bail was arranged, and there were photos of him leaving just as he had arrived. He wore a dark suit and smiled at the cameras. He was innocent, he proclaimed. It was a vendetta.

There were photos of bulldozers, taken from a distance, as the FBI trenched its way through the soggy soil of New Orleans searching for the body. More of Foltrigg performing for the press. More investigative reports of New Orleans's rich history of organized crime. The story seemed to lose steam as the search continued.

The Governor, a Democrat, appointed a crony to serve the remaining year and a half of Boyette's term. The New Orleans paper ran an analysis of the many politicians waiting anxiously to run for the Senate. Foltrigg was one of two Republicans rumored to be interested.

He sat next to her on the sofa, and wiped his eyes. He hated himself for crying, but it could not be helped. Her arm was around his shoulder, and she patted him gently.

"You don't have to say a word," she repeated quietly.

"I really don't want to. Maybe later, if I have to, but not now. Okay?"

"Okay, Mark."

There was a knock at the door. "Come in," Reggie said just loud enough to be heard. Clint appeared holding a stack of papers and looking at his watch.

"Sorry to interrupt. But it's almost ten, and Mr. Foltrigg will be here in a minute." He placed the papers on the coffee table in front of her. "You wanted to see these before the meeting."

"Tell Mr. Foltrigg we have nothing to discuss," Reggie said.

Clint frowned at her and looked at Mark. He sat close to her as if he needed protecting. "You're not going to see him?"

"No. Tell him the meeting's been canceled because we have nothing to say," she said, and nodded at Mark.

Clint glanced at his watch again and backed awkwardly to the door. "Sure," he said with a smile as if he suddenly enjoyed the idea of telling Foltrigg to take a hike. He closed the door behind him.

"Are you okay?" she asked.

"Not really."

She leaned forward and began flipping through the copies of the clippings. Mark sat in a daze, tired and drained, still frightened after talking things over with his lawyer. She scanned the pages, reading the headlines and captions and pulling the photographs closer to her. About a third of the way through, she suddenly stopped and leaned back on the sofa. She handed Mark a close-up of Barry Muldanno as he smiled at the camera. It was from the New Orleans paper. "Is this the man?"

Mark looked without touching it. "No. Who is it?"

"It's Barry Muldanno."

"That's not the man who grabbed me. I guess he's got a lot of friends."

She placed the copy in the stack on the coffee table, and patted him on the leg.

"What're you gonna do?" he asked.

"Make a few calls. I'll talk to the administrator of the hospital and arrange security around Ricky's room."

"You can't tell him about this guy, Reggie. They'll kill us. We can't tell anybody."

"I won't. I'll explain to the hospital that there have been some threats. It's routine in criminal cases. They'll place a few guards on the ninth floor around the room."

"I don't want to tell Mom either. She's stressed out with Ricky, and she's taking pills to sleep and pills to do this and that, and I just don't think she can handle this right now."

"You're right." He was a tough little kid, raised on the streets and wise beyond his years. She admired his courage.

"Do you think Mom and Ricky are safe?"

"Of course. These men are professionals, Mark. They won't do anything stupid. They'll lay low and listen. They may be bluffing." She did not sound sincere.

"No, they're not bluffing. I saw the knife, Reggie. They're here in Memphis for one reason, and that's to scare the hell out of me. And it's working. I ain't talking."

FIFTEEN

FOLTRIGG YELLED ONLY ONCE, then stormed from the office making threats and slamming the door. McThune and Trumann were frustrated, but also embarrassed at his antics. As they left, McThune rolled his eyes at Clint as if he wanted to apologize for this pompous loudmouth. Clint relished the moment, and when the dust settled he walked to Reggie's office.

Mark had pulled a chair to the window, and sat watching it rain on the street and sidewalk below. Reggie was on the phone with the hospital administrator discussing security on the ninth floor. She covered the phone, and Clint whispered that they were gone. He left to get more cocoa for Mark, who never moved.

Within minutes, Clint took a call from George Ord, and he buzzed Reggie on the intercom. She'd never met the U.S. Attorney from Memphis, but was not surprised that he was now on the phone. She allowed him to hold for one full minute, then picked up the phone. "Hello."

"Ms. Love, this is—"

"It's Reggie, okay. Just Reggie. And you're George, right?" She called everyone by their first name, even stuffy judges in their proper little courtrooms.

"Right, Reggie. This is George Ord. Roy Foltrigg is in my office, and—"

"What a coincidence. He just left mine."

"Yeah, and that's why I'm calling. He didn't get a chance to talk to you and your client."

"Give him my apologies. My client has nothing to say to him." She was talking and looking at the back of Mark's head. If he were listening, she couldn't tell. He was frozen in the chair at the window.

"Reggie, I think it would be wise if you at least meet with Mr. Foltrigg again."

"I have no desire to meet with Roy, nor does my client." She could picture Ord speaking gravely into the phone with Foltrigg pacing around the office waving his arms.

"Well, this will not be the end of it, you know?"

"Is that a threat, George?"

"It's more of a promise."

"Fine. You tell Roy and his boys that if anyone attempts to contact my client or his family I'll have their asses. Okay, George?"

"I'll relay the message."

It was really sort of funny—it was not, after all, his case—but Ord could not laugh. He returned the receiver to its place, smiled to himself, and said, "She says she ain't talking, the kid ain't talking, and if you or anyone else contacts the kid or his family she'll, uh, have your asses, as she put it."

Foltrigg bit his lip and nodded at every word as if this was fine because he could play hardball with the best of them. He had regained his composure and was already implementing Plan B. He paced around the office as if in deep thought. McThune and Trumann stood by the door like sentries. Bored sentries.

"I want the kid followed, okay," Foltrigg finally snapped at McThune. "We're leaving for New Orleans, and I want you guys to tail him twenty-four hours a day. I want to know what he does, and, more importantly, he needs to be protected from Muldanno and his henchmen."

McThune did not take orders from any U.S. Attorney, and at this moment he was sick of Roy Foltrigg. And the idea of using three or four overworked agents to follow an eleven-year-old kid was quite stupid. But, it was not worth the fight. Foltrigg had a hot line to Director Voyles in Washington, and Director Voyles wanted the body and he wanted a conviction almost as bad as Foltrigg.

"Okay," he said. "We'll get it done."

"Paul Gronke's already here somewhere," Foltrigg said as though he'd just heard fresh gossip. They knew the flight number and his time of arrival eleven hours ago. They had, however, managed to lose his trail once he left the Memphis airport. They had discussed it with Ord and Foltrigg and a dozen other FBI agents for two hours this morning. At this very moment, no less than eight agents were trying to find Gronke in Memphis.

"We'll find him," McThune said. "And we'll watch the kid. Why don't you get your ass back to New Orleans."

"I'll get the van ready," Trumann said officially as if the van was in fact *Air Force One*.

Foltrigg stopped pacing in front of Ord's desk. "We're leaving, George. Sorry for the intrusion. I'll probably be back in a couple of days."

What wonderful news, Ord thought. He stood, and they shook hands. "Anytime," he said. "If we can help, just call."

"I'll meet with Judge Lamond first thing in the morning. I'll let you know."

Ord offered his hand again for one final shake. Foltrigg took it and headed for the door. "Watch out for these thugs," he advised McThune. "I don't think he's dumb enough to touch the kid, but who knows." McThune opened the door and waved him through. Ord followed.

"Muldanno's heard something," Foltrigg continued, "and they're just snooping around here." He was in the outer office where Wally Boxx and Thomas Fink waited. "But keep an eye on them, okay, George? These guys are really dangerous. And follow the kid, too, and watch his lawyer. And thanks a million. I'll call you tomorrow. Where's the van, Wally?"

After an hour of watching the sidewalks, sipping hot cocoa, and listening to his lawyer practice law, Mark was ready for a move. Reggie had called Dianne and explained that Mark was in her office killing time and helping with the paperwork. Ricky was much better, sleeping again. He'd consumed half a gallon of ice cream while Greenway asked him a hundred questions.

At eleven, Mark parked himself at Clint's desk and inspected the dictating equipment. Reggie had a client, a woman who desperately wanted a divorce, and they needed to plot strategy for an hour.

Clint typed away on long paper and grabbed the phone every five minutes.

"How'd you become a secretary?" Mark asked, very bored with this candid view of the practice of law.

Clint turned and smiled at him. "It was an accident."

"Did you want to be a secretary when you were a kid?"

"No. I wanted to build swimming pools."

"What happened?"

"I don't know. I got messed up on drugs, almost flunked out of high school, then went to college, then went to law school."

"You have to go to law school to be a secretary in a law office?"

"No. I flunked out of law school, and Reggie gave me a job. It's fun, most of the time."

"Where'd you meet Reggie?"

"It's a long story. We were friends in law school. We've been friends for a long time. She'll probably tell you about it when you meet Momma Love."

"Momma who?"

"Momma Love. She hasn't told you about Momma Love?"

"No."

"Momma Love is Reggie's mother. They live together, and she loves to cook for the kids Reggie represents. She fixes inside-out ravioli and spinach lasagna and all sorts of delicious Italian food. Everyone loves it."

After two days of doughnuts and green Jell-O, the mention of thick, cheesy dishes cooked at someone's home was terribly inviting. "When do you think I might meet Momma Love?"

"I don't know. Reggie takes most of her clients home, especially the younger ones."

"Does she have any kids?"

"Two, but they're grown and live away."

"Where does Momma Love live?"

"In midtown, not far from here. It's an old house she's owned for years. In fact, it's the house Reggie grew up in."

The phone rang. Clint took the message and returned to his typewriter. Mark watched intently.

"How'd you learn to type so fast?"

The typing stopped, and he slowly turned and looked at Mark.

He smiled, and said, "In high school. I had this teacher who was like a drill sergeant. We hated her, but she made us learn. Can you type?"

"A little. I've had three years of computer at school."

Clint pointed to his Apple next to the typewriter. "We've got all sorts of computers around here."

Mark glanced at it, but was not impressed. Everybody had computers. "So how'd you get to be a secretary?"

"It wasn't planned. When Reggie finished law school, she didn't want to work for anybody, so she opened this office. It was about four years ago. She needed a secretary, and I volunteered. Have you seen a male secretary before?"

"No. Didn't know men could be secretaries. How's the money?"

Clint chuckled at this. "It's okay. If Reggie has a good month, then I have a good month. We're sort of like partners."

"Does she make a lot of money?"

"Not really. She doesn't want a lot of money. A few years ago she was married to a doctor, and they had a big house and lots of money. Everything went to hell, and she blames the money for most of it. She'll probably tell you about it. She's very honest about her life."

"She's a lawyer and she doesn't want money?"

"Unusual, isn't it?"

"I'll say. I mean, I've seen a lot of lawyer shows on television, and all they do is talk about money. Sex and money."

The phone rang. It was a judge, and Clint got real nice and chatted with him for five minutes. He hung up and returned to his typing. As he reached full speed, Mark asked, "Who's that woman in there?"

Clint stopped, stared at the keys, and slowly turned around. His chair squeaked. He forced a quick smile. "In there with Reggie?"

"Yeah."

"Norma Thrash."

"What's her problem?"

"She's got a bunch of them, really. She's in the middle of a nasty divorce. Husband's a real jerk."

Mark was curious about how much Clint knew. "Does he beat her up?"

"I don't think so," he answered slowly.

"Do they have kids and all?"

"Two. I really can't say much about it. It's confidential, you know?"

"Yeah, I know. But you probably know everything, don't you? I mean, after all, you type it up."

"I know most of what goes on. Sure. But Reggie doesn't tell me everything. For example, I have no idea what you've told her. I assume it's pretty serious, but she'll keep it to herself. I've read the newspaper. I've seen the FBI and Mr. Foltrigg, but I don't know the details."

This was exactly what Mark wanted to hear. "Do you know Robert Hackstraw? They call him Hack."

"He's a lawyer, isn't he?"

"Yeah. He represented my mother in her divorce a couple of years ago. A real moron."

"You weren't impressed with her lawyer?"

"I hated Hack. He treated us like dirt. We'd go to his office and wait for two hours. Then he'd talk to us for ten minutes, and tell us he was in a big hurry, had to get to court because he was so important. I tried to convince Mom to get another lawyer, but she was too stressed out."

"Did it go to trial?"

"Yeah. My ex-father thought he should get one kid, didn't really care which one but he preferred Ricky 'cause he knew I hated him, so he hired a lawyer, and for two days my mother and my father trashed each other in court. They tried to prove each other was unfit. Hack was a complete fool in the courtroom, but my ex-father's lawyer was even worse. The judge hated both lawyers, and said he wasn't about to separate me and Ricky. I asked him if I could testify. He thought about it during lunch on the second day, and decided he wanted to hear what I had to say. I had asked Hack the same question, and he said something smart, like I was too young and dumb to testify."

"But you testified."

"Yeah, for three hours."

"How'd it go?"

"I was pretty good, really. I just told about the beatings, the bruises, the stitches. I told him how much I hated my father. The judge almost cried."

"And it worked?"

"Yeah. My father wanted some visitation rights, and I spent a lot of time explaining to the judge that I had no desire to ever see the man again once the trial was over. And, that Ricky was terrified of him. So the judge not only cut off all visitation, but also told my father to stay away from us."

"Have you seen him since?"

"No. But I will one day. When I grow up, we'll catch him somewhere, me and Ricky, and we'll beat the living hell out of him. Bruise for bruise. Stitch for stitch. We talk about it all the time."

Clint was no longer bored with this little conversation. He listened to every word. The kid was so casual about his plans for beating his father. "You might go to jail."

"He didn't go to jail when he beat us. He didn't go to jail when he stripped my mother naked and threw her in the street with blood all over her. That's when I hit him with the baseball bat."

"You what?"

"He was drinking one night at home, and we could tell he was about to get out of hand. We could always tell. Then he left to buy more beer. I ran down the street and borrowed an aluminum tee ball bat from Michael Moss. I hid it under my bed, and I remember praying for a good car wreck so he wouldn't come home. But he did. Mom was in their bedroom, hoping he would just pass out, which he did all the time. Ricky and I stayed in our room, waiting for the explosion."

The phone rang again, and Clint quickly took the message and returned to the story.

"About an hour later there was all this yelling and cussing. The trailer was shaking. We locked the door. Ricky was under the bed, crying. Then Mom started yelling for me. I was seven years old, and Mom wanted me to rescue her. He was just beating the hell out of her, throwing her around, kicking her, ripping her shirt off, calling her a whore and a slut. I didn't even know what those words meant. I walked to the kitchen. I guess I was too scared to move.

He saw me and threw a beer can at me. She tried to run outside, but he caught her and tore her pants off. God, he was hitting her so hard. Then he ripped off her underwear. Her lip was busted and there was blood everywhere. He threw her outside, completely naked, and dragged her into the street where, of course, the neighbors were watching. Then he laughed at her, and left her lying there. It was horrible."

Clint leaned forward and hung on every word. Mark was speaking in a monotone, showing absolutely no emotion.

"When he came back to the trailer, the door was of course open, and I was waiting. I had pulled a kitchen chair beside the door, and I damned near took his head off with the baseball bat. A perfect shot to his nose. I was crying and scared to death, but I'll always remember the sound of the bat crunching his face. He fell on the sofa, and I hit him once in the stomach. I was trying to land a good one in the crotch, because I figured that would hurt the most. Know what I mean? I was swinging like crazy. I hit him once more on the ear, and that was all she wrote."

"What happened?" Clint snapped.

"He got up, slapped me in the face, knocked me down, cussed me, then started kicking me. I remember being so scared I couldn't fight. His face was a bloody mess. He smelled awful. He was growling and slapping and tearing my clothes off. I started kicking like crazy when he pulled at my underwear, but he got them off and threw me outside. Not a bit of clothing. I guess he wanted me in the street with my mother, but about that time she made it to the door and fell on me."

He told it all so calmly, as if he'd done it a hundred times and the script was memorized. No emotion, just the facts in short clipped sentences. He would look at the desk, then stare at the door without missing a word.

"What happened?" Clint asked, almost out of breath.

"One of the neighbors had called the cops. I mean, you can hear everything in the next trailer, so our neighbors had suffered through this with us. And that was not the first fight, not by a long shot. I remember seeing blue lights in the street, and he disappeared somewhere inside the trailer. Me and Mom got up real quick and ran inside and got dressed. Some of the neighbors saw me naked, though. We tried to wash the blood off before the cops came in. My father had settled down quite a bit, and was suddenly real friendly with the cops. Me and Mom waited in the kitchen. His nose was the size of a football, and the cops were more concerned with his face than with me and Mom. He called one of the cops Frankie as if they were buddies. There were two cops, and they got everybody separated. Frankie took him to the bedroom to cool him off. The other cop sat with Mom at the kitchen table. This is what they always did. I went to our room, and got Ricky out from under the bed. Mom told me later that he got real chummy with the cops, said it was just a family fight, nothing serious, and that most of it was my fault because I, for no reason, had attacked him with a baseball bat. The cops referred to it as just another domestic disturbance, same thing they always said. No charges were filed. They took him to the hospital where he spent the night. Had to wear this ugly white mask for a while."

"What'd he do to you?"

"He didn't drink for a long time after that. He apologized to us, promised it would never happen again. Sometimes he was okay when he wasn't drinking. But then he got worse. More beatings and all. Mom finally filed for divorce."

"And he tried to get custody—"

"Yeah. He lied in court, and he was doing a pretty good job of it. He didn't know I was going to testify, so he denied a bunch of it and said Mom was lying about the rest. He was real cocky and cool in court, and our dumbass lawyer couldn't do anything with him. But, when I testified and told about the baseball bat and getting my clothes ripped off, that's when the judge had tears in his eyes. He got real mad at my ex-father, accused him of lying. Said he ought to throw his sorry ass in jail for lying. I told him I thought that's exactly what he should do." He paused for a second.

The sentences were a bit slower, and Mark was losing steam. Clint was still mesmerized.

"Of course, Hack took full credit for another brilliant courtroom victory. Then he threatened to sue Mom if she didn't pay him. She had a bunch of bills, and he was calling twice a week wanting the rest of his fee, so she had to file for bankruptcy. Then she lost her job."

"So you've been through a divorce, and then a bankruptcy?"

"Yeah. The bankruptcy lawyer was a real bozo too."

"But you like Reggie?"

"Yeah. Reggie's cool."

"That's good to hear."

The phone rang, and Clint picked it up. A lawyer from Juvenile Court wanted some information on a client, and the conversation dragged on. Mark left to find the hot cocoa. He passed the conference room with pretty books covering the walls. He found the tiny kitchen next to the rest room.

There was a Sprite in the refrigerator, and he unscrewed the top. Clint was amazed by his story, he could tell. He had left out many of the details, but it was all true. He was proud of it, in a way, proud of defending his mother, and the story always amazed people.

Then the tough little kid with the baseball bat remembered the knife attack in the elevator, and the folded photograph of the poor, fatherless family. He thought of his mother at the hospital, all alone and unprotected. He was suddenly scared again.

He tried to open a package of saltines, but his hands shook and the plastic wouldn't open. The shaking got worse and he couldn't stop it. He slumped to the floor and spilled the Sprite.

SIXTEEN

THE LIGHT RAIN had stopped in time for the rush of secretaries who moved in hurried groups of three and four along the damp sidewalks in pursuit of lunch. The sky was gray and the streets were wet. Clouds of mist boiled and hissed behind each passing car along Third Street. Reggie and her client turned on Madison. Her briefcase was in her left hand, and with her right she held his hand and guided him through the crowd. She had places to go and walked quickly.

From a generic white Ford van parked almost directly in front of the Sterick Building, Jack Nance watched and radioed ahead. When they turned on Madison and were lost from sight, he listened. Within minutes, Cal Sisson, his partner, had them and was watching as they headed for the hospital, as expected. Five minutes later, they were in the hospital.

Nance locked the van and jaywalked across Third. He entered the Sterick Building, rode the elevator to the second floor, and gently turned the knob of the door with REGGIE LOVE—LAWYER on it. It was unlocked, which was a pleasant surprise. Eleven minutes had passed since noon. Virtually every lawyer with a nickel and dime solo practice in this city broke for lunch and locked the office. He opened the door and stepped inside as a hideous buzzer went off above his head and announced his arrival. Dammit! He'd hoped to enter through a locked door, something he was very proficient at, and dig through files without being interrupted. It was easy work. Most of these small outfits thought nothing of security. The big firms were a different story, although in the off-hours Nance could enter any one of a thousand law offices in Memphis and find whatever he wanted. He'd done it at least a dozen times. There were two things ham and egg lawyers did not have at their offices—cash and security devices. They locked their doors, and that was it.

A young man appeared from the back, and said, "Yes. Can I help you?"

"Yeah," Nance said without a smile. All business. Rough day. "I'm with the *Times-Picayune,* you know the paper in New Orleans. Looking for Reggie Love."

Clint stopped ten feet away. "She's not here."

"When might she return?"

"Don't know. You have any identification?"

Nance was headed for the door. "You mean, like little white cards you lawyers throw on the sidewalks. No, pal, I don't carry business cards. I'm a reporter."

"Fine. What's your name?"

"Arnie Carpentier. Tell her I'll catch her later." He opened the door, the buzzer worked again, and he was gone. Not a productive visit, but he'd met Clint and seen the front room and reception area. The next visit would take longer.

The ride to the ninth floor was uneventful. Reggie held his hand, which normally would have irritated him but was rather comforting under the circumstances. He studied his feet as they ascended. He was afraid to look up, afraid of more strangers. He squeezed her hand.

They spilled into the lobby on the ninth floor and had taken no more than ten steps before three people rushed them from the direction of the waiting area. "Ms. Love! Ms. Love," one of them yelled. Reggie at first was startled, but gripped Mark's hand tighter and kept walking. One had a microphone, one a notepad, and one a camera. The one with the notepad said, "Ms. Love, just a few quick questions."

They walked faster toward the nurses' station. "No comment."

"Is it true your client is refusing to cooperate with the FBI and the police?"

"No comment," she said, looking ahead. They followed like bloodhounds. She leaned quickly to Mark, and said, "Don't look at them and don't say a word."

"Is it true the U.S. Attorney from New Orleans was in your office this morning?"

"No comment."

Doctors, nurses, patients, everybody vacated the center of the hallway as Reggie and her famous client raced along followed by the yelping dogs.

"Did your client talk to Jerome Clifford before he died?"

She squeezed his hand harder and walked faster. "No comment."

As they neared the end of the hall, the clown with the camera suddenly dashed in front of them, knelt low as he backpedaled, and managed to get a shot before he landed on his ass. The nurses laughed. A security guard stepped forward at the nurses' station and raised his hands at the yelpers. They had met him before.

As Reggie and Mark rounded a bend in the hall, one called out, "Is it true your client knows where Boyette is buried?"

There was a slight hesitation in her step. The shoulders jumped and the back arched, then she was over it and she and her client were gone.

Two overweight security guards in uniform sat in folding chairs by Ricky's door. They had pistols on their hips, and Mark noticed the pistols before anything else. One had a newspaper, which he promptly lowered as they approached. The other stood to greet them. "Can I help you?" he asked Reggie.

"Yes. I'm the attorney for the family, and this is Mark Sway, the patient's brother." She spoke in a professional whisper as if she had a right to be there and they didn't, so be quick with the questions because she had things to do. "Dr. Greenway is expecting us," she said as she walked to the door and knocked. Mark stood behind her, staring at the pistol, which was remarkably similar to the one poor Romey had used.

The security guard returned to his seat and his partner returned to his paper. Greenway opened the door and stepped outside, followed by Dianne, who had been crying. She hugged Mark and placed her arm on his shoulder.

"He's asleep," Greenway said quietly to Reggie and Mark. "Doing much better, but very tired."

"He was asking about you," Dianne whispered to Mark.

He looked at the moist eyes and asked, "What's the matter, Mom?"

"Nothing. We'll talk about it later."

"What's happened?"

Dianne looked at Greenway, then at Reggie, then at Mark. "It's nothing," she said.

"Your mother was fired this morning, Mark," Greenway said. He looked at Reggie. "These people sent a letter by courier informing her she'd been fired. Can you believe it? Had it delivered to the nurses here on the ninth floor, and one of them delivered it about an hour ago."

"Let me see the letter," Reggie said. Dianne pulled it from a pocket. Reggie unfolded it and read slowly. Dianne hugged Mark, and said, "It'll be all right, Mark. We've managed before. I'll find another job."

Mark bit his lip and wanted to cry.

"Can I keep this?" Reggie said as she stuffed it in her briefcase. Dianne nodded yes.

Greenway studied his watch as if he couldn't determine the correct time. "I'm gonna grab a quick sandwich, and I'll be back here in twenty minutes. I want to spend a couple of hours with Ricky and Mark, alone."

Reggie glanced at her watch. "I'll be back around four. There are reporters here, and I want you to ignore them." She was talking to all three of them.

"Yeah, just say no comment, no comment," Mark added helpfully. "It's really fun."

Dianne missed the fun. "What do they want?"

"Everything. They've seen the newspaper. The rumors are rampant. They smell a story, and they'll do anything to get information. I saw a television van on the street, and I suspect they're somewhere close by. I think it's best if you stay here with Mark."

"Okay," Dianne said.

"Where's a telephone?" Reggie asked.

Greenway pointed in the direction of the nurses' station. "Come on. I'll show you."

"I'll see you guys at four, okay?" she said to Dianne and Mark. "Remember, not a word to anyone. And stay close to this room."

She and Greenway disappeared around the bend. The security guards were half-asleep. Mark and his mother entered the dark room and sat on the bed. A stale doughnut caught his attention, and he devoured it in four bites.

Reggie called her office, and Clint answered. "You remember that lawsuit we filed last year on behalf of Penny Patoula?" she asked softly, looking around for the bloodhounds. "It was sex discrimination, wrongful discharge, harassment, the works. I think we threw in everything. Circuit Court. Yeah, that's it. Pull the file. Change the name from Penny Patoula to Dianne Sway. The defendant will be Ark-Lon Fixtures. I want you to name the president individually. His name is Chester Tanfill. Yeah, make him a defendant too, and sue for wrongful discharge, labor violations, sexual harassment, throw in an equal rights charge, and ask for a million or two in damages. Do it now, and quickly. Prepare a summons, and a check for the filing fee. Run over to the courthouse and file it. I'll be there in about thirty minutes to pick it up, so hurry. I'll personally deliver it to Mr. Tanfill."

She hung up and thanked the nearest nurse. The reporters were loitering near the soft drink machine, but she was through the door to the stairwell before they saw her.

Ark-Lon Fixtures was a series of metal connected buildings on a street of such structures in a minimum wage industrial park near the airport. The front building was a faded orange in color, and expansion had taken place in every direction except toward the street. The newer additions were of the same general architecture but with different shades of orange. Trucks waited near a loading dock in the rear. An enclosed chain-link fence protected rolls of steel and aluminum.

Reggie parked near the front in a space reserved for visitors. She held her briefcase, and opened the door. A chesty woman with black hair and a long cigarette ignored her and listened to the phone stuck in her ear. Reggie stood before her, waiting impatiently. The room was dusty, dirty, and clouded with blue cigarette smoke. Matted pictures of beagles adorned the walls. Half the fluorescent lights were out.

"May I help you?" the receptionist asked as she lowered the phone.

"I need to see Chester Tanfill."

"He's in a meeting."

"I know. He's a very busy man, but I have something for him."

The receptionist placed the phone on the desk. "I see. And what might that be?"

"It's really none of your business. I need to see Chester Tanfill. It's urgent."

This really pissed her off. The nameplate declared her to be Louise Chenault. "I don't care how urgent it is, ma'am. You can't just barge in here and demand to see the president of this company."

"This company is a sweatshop, and I've just sued it for two million bucks. And I've also sued Chester boy for a couple of million, and I'm telling you to find his sorry ass and get him out here immediately."

Louise jumped to her feet, and backed away from the desk. "Are you some kind of lawyer?"

Reggie pulled the lawsuit and the summons from the briefcase. She looked at it, ignored Louise, and said, "I am indeed a lawyer. And I need to serve these papers on Chester. Now find him. If he's not here in five minutes, I'll amend it and ask for five million in damages."

Louise bolted from the room and ran through a set of double doors. Reggie waited a second, then followed. She walked through a room filled with tacky, cramped cubicles. Cigarette smoke seemed to ooze from every opening. The carpet was ancient shag and badly worn. She caught a glimpse of Louise's round rump darting into a door on the right, and she followed.

Chester Tanfill was in the process of standing behind his desk when Reggie barged in. Louise was speechless. "You can leave now," Reggie said rudely. "I'm Reggie Love, Attorney-at-Law," she said, glaring at Chester.

"Chester Tanfill," he said without offering a hand. She wouldn't have taken it. "This is a bit rude, Ms. Love."

"The name is Reggie, okay, Chester? Tell Louise to leave."

He nodded and Louise gladly left, closing the door behind her.

"What do you want?" he snapped. He was wiry and gaunt, around fifty, with a spotted face and puffy eyes partially hidden behind wire-rimmed glasses. A drinking problem, she thought. The clothes were Sears or Penney's. His neck was turning dark red.

She threw the lawsuit and the summons on his desk. "I'm serving you with this lawsuit."

He smirked at it, a man unafraid of lawyers and their games. "For what?"

"I represent Dianne Sway. You fired her this morning, and we're suing you this afternoon. How's that for swift justice?"

Chester's eyes narrowed and he looked at the lawsuit again. "You're kidding."

"You're a fool if you think I'm kidding. It's all right there, Chester. Wrongful discharge, sexual harassment, the works. A couple of million in damages. I file these things all the time. I must say, however, that this is one of the best I've seen. This poor woman has been at the hospital for two days with her son. Her doctor says she cannot leave his bedside. In fact, he's called here and explained her situation, but no, you assholes fire her for missing work. I can't wait to explain this to a jury."

It sometimes took Chester's lawyer two days to return a phone call, and this woman, Dianne Sway, files a full-blown lawsuit within hours of being terminated. He slowly picked up the papers and studied the front page. "I'm named personally?" he asked as if his feelings were hurt.

"You fired her, Chester. Don't worry though, when the jury returns a verdict against you individually, you can simply file for bankruptcy."

Chester pulled his chair under him and carefully sat down. "Please, sit," he said, waving at a chair.

"No thanks. Who's your attorney?"

"Uh, geez, uh, Findley and Baker. But just wait a minute. Let me think about this." He flipped the page and scanned the pleadings. "Sexual harassment?"

"Yeah, that's a fertile field these days. Seems as though one of your supervisors has put the move on my client. Always suggesting things they might do in the rest room during lunch. Always telling dirty jokes. Lots of crude talk. It'll all come out at trial. Who should I call at Findley and Baker?"

"Just wait a minute." He flipped the pages, then laid them on the desk. She stood next to his desk, glaring down. He rubbed his temples. "I don't need this."

"Neither did my client."

"What does she want?"

"A little dignity. You run a sweatshop here. You prey on single working mothers who can barely feed their children on what you pay. They cannot afford to complain."

He was rubbing his eyes now. "Skip the lecture, okay. I just don't need this. There could, well, there might be some trouble at the top."

"I couldn't care less about you and your troubles, Chester. A copy of this lawsuit will be hand delivered to the *Memphis Press* this afternoon, and I'm sure it'll run tomorrow. The Sways are getting more than their share of ink these days."

"What does she want?" he asked again.

"Are you trying to bargain?"

"Maybe. I don't think you can win this case, Ms. Love, but I don't need the headache."

"It'll be more than a headache, I promise. She makes nine hundred dollars a month, and takes home around six-fifty. That's eleven thousand bucks a year, and I promise your legal costs on this lawsuit will run five times that much. I'll obtain access to your personnel records. I'll take the depositions of other female employees. I'll open up your financial books. I'll subpoena all your records. And if I see anything the least bit improper, I'll notify the Equal Employment Opportunity Commission, the National Labor Relations Board, the IRS, OSHA, and anybody else who might be interested. I'll make you lose sleep, Chester. You'll wish a thousand times you hadn't fired my client."

He slapped the table with both palms. "What does she want, dammit!"

Reggie picked up her briefcase, and walked to the door. "She wants her job. A raise would be nice, say from six bucks an hour to nine, if you can spare it. And if you can't, then do it anyway. Transfer her to another section, away from the dirty supervisor."

Chester listened carefully. This was not too bad.

"She'll be in the hospital for a few weeks. She has bills, so I want the payroll checks to keep coming. In fact, Chester, I want the payroll checks delivered to the hospital, just like you clowns delivered her termination letter this morning. Every Friday, I want the check delivered. Okay?"

He slowly nodded yes.

"You have thirty days to answer the lawsuit. If you behave and do as I say, I'll dismiss it on the thirtieth day. You have my word. You don't have to tell your lawyers about it. Is it a deal?"

"Deal."

Reggie opened the door. "Oh, and send some flowers. Room 943. A card would be nice. In fact, send some fresh flowers every week. Okay, Chester?"

He was still nodding.

She slammed the door and left the grungy corporate offices of Ark-Lon Fixtures.

Mark and Ricky sat on the end of the foldaway bed and looked up into the bearded and intense face of Dr. Greenway less than two feet away. Ricky wore a pair of Mark's hand-me-down pajamas with a blanket draped over his shoulders. He was cold, as usual, and scared, and uncertain about this first venture out of his bed, even though it was inches away. And he preferred his mother to be present, but the doctor had gently insisted on talking to the boys by themselves. Greenway had spent almost twelve hours now trying to win Ricky's confidence. He sat close to his big brother, who was bored with this little chat before it started.

The shades were pulled, the lights were dim, the room was dark except for a small lamp on a table by the bathroom. Greenway leaned forward with his elbows on his knees.

"Now, Ricky, I would like to talk about the other day when you and Mark went to the woods for a smoke. Okay?"

This frightened Ricky. How did Greenway know they were smoking? Mark leaned over an inch or two and said, "It's okay, Ricky. I've already told them about it. Mom's not mad at us."

"Do you remember going for a smoke?" Greenway asked.

Slowly, he nodded his head yes. "Yes sir."

"Why don't you tell me what you remember about you and Mark in the woods smoking a cigarette."

He pulled the blanket tighter around him and knotted it with his hands at his stomach. "I'm really cold," he muttered, his teeth chattering.

"Ricky, the temperature is almost seventy-eight degrees in here. And you've got the blanket and wool pajamas. Try and think about being warm, okay?"

He tried but it didn't help. Mark gently placed his arm around Ricky's shoulder, and this seemed to help.

"Do you remember smoking a cigarette?"

"I think so. Uh-huh."

Mark glanced up at Greenway, then at Ricky.

"Okay. Do you remember seeing the big black car when it pulled up in the grass?"

Ricky suddenly stopped shaking and stared at the floor. He mumbled the word "Yes," and that would be his last word for twenty-four hours.

"And what did the big black car do when you first saw it?"

The mention of the cigarette had scared him, but the image of the black car and the fear it brought were simply too much. He bent over at the waist and placed his head on Mark's knee. His eyes were shut tightly, and he began sobbing, but with no tears.

Mark rubbed his hair, and repeated, "It's okay, Ricky. It's okay. We need to talk about it."

Greenway was unmoved. He crossed his bony legs and scratched his beard. He had expected this, and had warned Mark and Dianne that this first little session would not be productive. But it was very important.

"Ricky, listen to me," he said in a childlike voice. "Ricky, it's okay. I just want to talk to you. Okay, Ricky."

But Ricky had had enough therapy for one day. He began to curl under the blanket, and Mark knew the thumb could not be far behind. Greenway nodded at him as if all was well. He stood, carefully lifted Ricky, and placed him in the bed.

SEVENTEEN

WALLY BOXX stopped the van in heavy traffic on Camp Street, and ignored the horns and fingers as his boss and Fink and the FBI agents made a quick exit onto the sidewalk in front of the Federal Building. Foltrigg walked importantly up the steps with his entourage behind. In the lobby, a couple of bored reporters recognized him and began asking questions, but he was all business and had nothing but smiles and no comments.

He entered the offices of the United States Attorney for the Southern District of Louisiana, and the secretaries sprang to life. His assigned space in the building was a vast suite of small offices connected by hallways, and large open areas where the clerical staff performed, and smaller rooms where cubicles allowed some privacy for law clerks and paralegals. In all, forty-seven Assistant U.S. Attorneys labored here under the commands of Reverend Roy. Another thirty-eight underlings plowed through the drudgery and paperwork and boring research and tedious attention to mindless details, all in an effort to protect the legal interests of Roy's client, the United States of America.

The largest office of course belonged to Foltrigg, and it was richly decorated with heavy wood and deep leather. Whereas most lawyers allow themselves only one Ego Wall with pictures and plaques and awards and certificates for Rotary Club memberships, Roy had covered no less than three of his with framed photographs and yellow fill-in-the-blank attendance diplomas from a hundred judicial conferences. He threw his jacket on the burgundy leather sofa, and headed directly for the main library where a meeting awaited him.

He had called six times during the five-hour trip from Memphis. There had been three faxes. Six assistants were waiting around a thirty-foot oak conference table covered with open law books and countless legal pads. All jackets were off and all sleeves rolled up.

He said hello to the group and took a chair at the center of the table. They each had a copy of a summarization of the FBI's findings in Memphis. The note, the fingerprints, the gun, everything. There was nothing new Foltrigg or Fink could tell them except that Gronke was in Memphis, and this was irrelevant to this group.

"What do you have, Bobby?" Foltrigg asked dramatically, as if the future of the American legal system rested upon Bobby and whatever he had uncovered in his research. Bobby was the dean of the assistants, a thirty-two-year veteran who hated courtrooms but loved libraries. In times of crisis when answers were needed for complex questions, they all turned to Bobby.

He rubbed his thick, gray hair and adjusted his black-rimmed glasses. Six months until retirement, when he would be through with the likes of Roy Foltrigg. He'd seen a dozen of them come and go, most never heard from again. "Well, I think we've narrowed it down," he said, and most of them smiled. He began every report with the same line. To Bobby, legal research was a game of clearing away the piles of debris heaped upon even the simplest of issues, and narrowing the focus to that which is quickly grasped by judges and juries. Everything got narrowed down when Bobby handled the research.

"There are two avenues, neither very attractive but one or both might work. First, I suggest the Juvenile Court approach in Memphis. Under the Tennessee Youth Code, a petition can be filed with the Juvenile Court alleging certain misconduct by the child. There are various categories of wrongdoing, and the petition must classify the child as either a delinquent or a child in need of supervision. A hearing is held, the Juvenile Court judge hears the proof and makes a determination as to what happens to the child. The same can be done for abused or neglected children. Same procedure, same court."

"Who can file the petition?" Foltrigg asked.

"Well, the statute is very broad, and I think it's a terrible flaw in the law. But it plainly says that a petition can be filed by, and I quote, 'any interested party.' End of quote."

"Can that be us?"

"Maybe. It depends on what we allege in our petition. And here's the sticky part—we must allege the kid has done, or is doing, something wrong, violating the law in some way. And the only violation even remotely touching this kid's behavior is, of course, obstruction of justice. So we must allege things we're not sure of, such as the kid's knowledge of where the body is. This could be tricky, since we're not certain."

"The kid knows where the body is," Foltrigg said flatly. Fink studied some notes and pretended not to hear, but the other six repeated the words to themselves. Did Foltrigg know things he hadn't yet told them? There was a pause as this apparent statement of fact settled in around the table.

"Have you told us everything?" Bobby asked, glancing at his cohorts.

"Yes," Foltrigg replied. "But I'm telling you the kid knows. It's my gut feeling."

Typical Foltrigg. Creating facts with his guts, and expecting those under him to follow on faith.

Bobby continued. "A Juvenile Court summons is served on the child's mother, and a hearing is held within seven days. The child must have a lawyer, and I understand one has already been obtained. The child has a right to be at the hearing and may testify if he so chooses." Bobby wrote something on his legal pad. "Frankly, this is the quickest way to get the kid to talk."

"What if he refuses to talk on the witness stand?"

"Very good question," Bobby said like a professor pandering a first-year law student. "It is completely discretionary with the judge. If we put on a good case and convince the judge the kid knows something, he has the authority to order the kid to talk. If the kid refuses, he may be in contempt of court."

"Let's say he's in contempt. What happens then?"

"Difficult to say at this point. He's only eleven years old, but the judge could, as a last resort, incarcerate the child in a youth court facility until he purges himself of contempt."

"In other words, until he talks."

It was so easy to spoon-feed Foltrigg. "That is correct. Mind you, this would be the most drastic course the judge could take. We have yet to find any precedent for the incarceration of an eleven-year-old child for contempt of court. We haven't checked all fifty states, but we've covered most of them."

"It won't go that far," Foltrigg predicted calmly. "If we file a petition as an interested party, serve the kid's mother with papers, drag his little butt into court with his lawyer in tow, then I think he'll be so scared he'll tell what he knows. What about you, Thomas?"

"Yeah, I think it'll work. And what if it doesn't? What's the downside?"

"There's little risk," Bobby explained. "All Juvenile Court proceedings are closed. We can even ask that the petition be kept under lock and key. If it's dismissed initially for lack of standing or whatever, no one will know it. If we proceed to the hearing and A, the kid talks but doesn't know anything, or B, the judge refuses to make him talk, then we haven't lost anything. And C, if the kid talks out of fear or under threat of contempt, then we've gotten what we wanted. Assuming the kid knows about Boyette."

"He knows," Foltrigg said.

"The plan would not be so attractive if the proceedings were made public. We would look weak and desperate if we lost. It could, in my opinion, seriously undermine our chances at trial here in New Orleans if we try this and fail, and if it's in some way publicized."

The door opened and Wally Boxx, fresh from having successfully parked the van, entered and seemed irritated that they had proceeded without him. He sat next to Foltrigg.

"But you're certain it can be done in private?" Fink asked.

"That's what the law says. I don't know how they apply it in Memphis, but the confidentiality is explicit in the code sections. There are even penalties for disclosure."

"We'll need local counsel, someone in Ord's office," Foltrigg said to Fink as if the decision had already been made. Then he turned to the group. "I like the sound of this. Right now the kid and his lawyer are probably thinking it's all over. This will be a wake-up call. They'll know we're serious. They'll know they're headed for court. We'll make it plain to his lawyer that we'll not rest until we have the truth from the kid. I like this. Little downside risk. It'll take place three hundred miles from here, away from these morons with cameras we have around here. If we try it and fail, no big deal. No one will know. I like the idea of no cameras and no reporters." He paused as if deep in thought, the field marshal surveying the plains, deciding where to send his tanks.

To everyone except Boxx and Foltrigg, the humor in this was delicious. The idea of the Reverend plotting strategies that did not include cameras was unheard of. He, of course, did not realize it. He bit his lip and nodded his head. Yes, yes, this was the best course. This would work.

Bobby cleared his throat. "There is one other possible approach, and I don't like it but it's worth mentioning. A real longshot. If you assume the kid knows—"

"He knows."

"Thank you. Assuming this, and assuming he has confided in his lawyer, there is the possibility of a federal indictment against her for obstruction of justice. I don't have to tell you the difficulty in piercing the attorney-client privilege; it's virtually impossible. The indictment would, of course, be used to sort of scare her into cutting some deal. I don't know. As I said, a real longshot."

Foltrigg chewed on this for a second, but his mind was still churning over the first plan and it simply couldn't digest the second.

"A conviction might be difficult," Fink said.

"Yep," Bobby agreed. "But a conviction would not be the goal. She would be indicted here, a long way from home, and I think it would be quite intimidating. Lots of bad press. Couldn't keep this one quiet, you know. She'd be forced to hire a lawyer. We could string it out for months, you know, the works. You might even consider obtaining the indictment, keeping it sealed, breaking the news to her, and offering some deal in return for its dismissal. Just a thought."

"I like it," Foltrigg said to no one's surprise. It had the stench of the government's jackboot, and these strategies always appealed to him. "And we can always dismiss the indictment anytime we want."

Ah yes! The Roy Foltrigg Special. Get the indictment, hold the press conference, beat the defendant to the ground with all sorts of threats, cut the deal, then quietly dismiss the indictment a year later. He'd done it a hundred times in seven years. He'd also eaten a few of his Specials when the defendant and/or his lawyer refused to deal and insisted on a trial. When this happened Foltrigg was always too busy with more important prosecutions, and the file was thrown at one of the younger assistants who invariably got his ass kicked. Invariably, Foltrigg placed the blame squarely on the assistant. He'd even fired one for losing the trial brought about by a Roy Foltrigg Special.

"That's Plan B, okay, on hold for right now," he said, very much in control. "Plan A is to file a petition in Juvenile Court first thing tomorrow morning. How long will it take to prepare it?"

"An hour," answered Tank Mozingo, a burly assistant with the ponderous name of Thurston Alomar Mozingo, thus known simply as Tank. "The petition is set out in the code. We simply add the allegations and fill in the blanks."

"Get it done." He turned to Fink. "Thomas, you'll handle this. Get on the phone to Ord and ask him to help us. Fly to Memphis tonight. I want the petition filed first thing in the morning, after you talk to the judge. Tell him how urgent this is." Papers shuffled around the table as the research group began cleaning its mess. Their work was over. Fink took notes as Boxx darted for a legal pad. Foltrigg spewed forth instructions like King Solomon dictating to his scribes. "Ask the judge for an expedited hearing. Explain how much pressure is behind this. Ask for complete confidentiality, including the closing of the petition and all other pleadings. Stress this, you understand. I'll be sitting by the phone in case I'm needed."

Bobby was buttoning his cuffs. "Look, Roy, there's something else we need to mention."

"What is it?"

"We're playing hardball with this kid. Let's not forget the danger he's in. Muldanno is desperate. There are reporters everywhere. A leak here and a leak there, and the mob could silence the kid before he talks. There's a lot at stake."

Roy flashed a confident smile. "I know that, Bobby. In fact,

Muldanno's already sent his boys to Memphis. The FBI up there is tracking them, and they're also watching the boy. Personally, I don't think Muldanno's stupid enough to try something, but we're not taking chances." Roy stood and smiled around the room. "Good work, men. I appreciate it."

They mumbled their thank-yous and left the library.

On the fourth floor of the Radisson Hotel in downtown Memphis, two blocks from the Sterick Building and five blocks from St. Peter's, Paul Gronke played a monotonous game of gin rummy with Mack Bono, a Muldanno grunt from New Orleans. A heavily marked score sheet was on the floor under the table, abandoned. They had been playing for a dollar a game, but now no one cared. Gronke's shoes were on the bed. His shirt was unbuttoned. Heavy cigarette smoke clung to the ceiling. They were drinking bottled water because it was not yet five, but almost, and when the magic hour hit they'd call room service. Gronke checked his watch. He looked through the window at the buildings across Union Avenue. He played a card.

Gronke was a childhood friend of Muldanno's, a most trusted partner in many of his dealings. He owned a few bars and a tourist tee shirt shop in the Quarter. He'd broken his share of legs and had helped The Blade do the same. He did not know where Boyd Boyette was buried, and he wasn't about to ask, but if he pressed hard his friend would probably tell him. They were very close.

Gronke was in Memphis because The Blade had called him. And he was bored as hell sitting in this hotel room playing cards with his shoes off, drinking water and eating sandwiches, smoking Camels and waiting on the next move by an eleven-year-old kid.

Across the double beds, an open door led to the next room. It too had two beds and a cloud of smoke whirling around the ceiling vents. Jack Nance stood in the window watching the rush-hour traffic leave downtown. A radio and a cellular phone stood ready on a nearby table. Any minute Cal Sisson would call from the hospital with the latest about Mark Sway. A thick briefcase was open on one bed, and Nance in his boredom had spent most of the afternoon playing with his bugging devices.

He had a plan to drop a bug in Room 943. He had seen the

lawyer's office, absent of special locks on the door, absent of cameras overhead, absent of any security devices. Typical lawyer. Wiring it would be easy. Cal Sisson had visited the doctor's office and found pretty much the same. A receptionist at a front desk. Sofas and chairs for the patients to wait for their shrink. A couple of drab offices down a hall. No special security. The client, this clown who liked to be called The Blade, had approved the wiring of the telephones in both the doctor's and lawyer's office. He also wanted files copied. Easy work. He also wanted a bug planted in Ricky's room. Easy work too, but the difficult part was receiving the transmission once the bug was in place. Nance was working on this.

As far as Nance was concerned, it was simply a surveillance job, nothing more or less. The client was paying top dollar in cash. If he wanted a child followed, it was easy. If he wanted to eavesdrop, no problem as long as he was paying.

But Nance had read the newspapers. And he had heard the whispers in the room next door. There was more here than simple surveillance. Broken legs and arms were not being discussed over gin rummy. These guys were deadly, and Gronke had already mentioned calling New Orleans for more help.

Cal Sisson was ready to bolt. He was fresh off probation, and another conviction would send him back for decades. A conviction for conspiracy to commit murder would send him away for life. Nance had convinced him to hold tight for one more day.

The cellular phone rang. It was Sisson. The lawyer just arrived at the hospital. Mark Sway's in Room 943 with his mother and lawyer.

Nance placed the phone on the table, and walked into the other room.

"Who was it?" Gronke asked with a Camel in his mouth.

"Cal. Kid's still at the hospital, now with his mother and his lawyer."

"Where's the doctor?"

"He left an hour ago." Nance walked to the dresser and poured a glass of water.

"Any sign of the Feds?" Gronke grunted.

"Yeah. Same two are hanging around the hospital. Doing the same thing we are, I guess. The hospital's keeping two security guards by the door, and another one close by."

"You think the kid told them about meeting me this morning?" Gronke asked for the hundredth time of the day.

"He told someone. Why else would they suddenly surround his room with security guards?"

"Yeah, but the security guards are not Fibbies, are they? If he'd told the Fibbies, then they'd be sitting in the hall, don't you think?"

"Yeah." This conversation had been repeated throughout the day. Who did the kid tell? Why were there suddenly guards by the door? And on and on. Gronke couldn't get enough of it.

Despite his arrogance and street punk posture, he seemed to be a man of patience. Nance figured it went with the territory. Killers had to be cold-blooded and patient.

EIGHTEEN

THEY LEFT THE HOSPITAL in her Mazda RX-7, his first ride in a sports car. The seats were leather but the floor was dirty. The car was not new, but it was cool, with a stick shift that she worked like a veteran race car driver. She said she liked to drive fast, which was fine with Mark. They darted through traffic as they left downtown and headed east. It was almost dark. The radio was on but barely audible, some FM station specializing in easy listening.

Ricky was awake when they left. He was staring at cartoons but saying little. A sad little tray of hospital food sat on the table, untouched by either Ricky or Dianne. Mark had not seen his mother eat three bites in two days. He felt sorry for her sitting there on the bed, staring at Ricky, worrying herself to death. The news from Reggie about the job and the raise had made her smile. Then it made her cry.

Mark was sick of the crying and the cold peas and the dark, cramped room, and he felt guilty for leaving but was delighted to be here in this sports car headed, he hoped, for a plate of hot, heavy food with warm bread. Clint had mentioned inside-out ravioli and spinach lasagna, and for some reason visions of these rich, meaty dishes had stuck in his mind. Maybe there would be a cake and some cookies. But if Momma Love served green Jell-O, he might throw it at her.

He thought of these things as Reggie thought of being trailed. Her eyes went from the traffic to the mirror, and back again. She drove much too fast, zipping between cars and changing lanes, which didn't bother Mark one bit.

"You think Mom and Ricky are safe?" he asked, watching the cars in front.

"Yes. Don't worry about them. The hospital promised to keep guards at the door." She had talked to George Ord, her new pal, and explained her concern about the safety of the Sway family. She did not mention any specific threats, though Ord had asked. The family was getting unwanted attention, she had explained. Lots of rumors and gossip, most of it generated by a frustrated media. Ord had talked to McThune, then called her back and said the FBI would stay close to the room, but out of sight. She thanked him.

Ord and McThune were amused by it. The FBI already had people in the hospital. Now they had been invited.

She suddenly turned to the right at an intersection, and the tires squealed. Mark chuckled, and she laughed as though it was all fun but her stomach was flipping. They were on a smaller street with old homes and large oaks.

"This is my neighborhood," she said. It was certainly nicer than his. They turned again, to another narrower street where the houses were smaller but still two and three stories tall with deep lawns and manicured hedgerows.

"Why do you take your clients home?" he asked.

"I don't know. Most of my clients are children who come from awful homes. I feel sorry for them, I guess. I get attached to them."

"Do you feel sorry for me?"

"A little. But you're lucky, Mark, very lucky. You have a mother who's a good woman and who loves you very much."

"Yeah, I guess so. What time is it?"

"Almost six. Why?"

Mark thought a second and counted the hours. "Forty-nine hours ago Jerome Clifford shot himself. I wish we'd simply run away when we saw his car."

"Why didn't you?"

"I don't know. It was like I just had to do something once I realized what was going on. I couldn't run away. He was about to die, and I just couldn't ignore it. Something kept pulling me to his car. Ricky was crying and begging me to stop, but I just couldn't. This is all my fault."

"Maybe, but you can't change it, Mark. It's done." She glanced at her mirror and saw nothing.

"Do you think we're gonna be okay? I mean, Ricky and me and Mom? When this is all over, will things be like they were?"

She slowed and turned into a narrow driveway lined with thick, untrimmed hedges. "Ricky will be fine. It might take time, but he'll be all right. Kids are tough, Mark. I see it every day."

"What about me?"

"Everything will work out, Mark. Just trust me." The Mazda stopped beside a large two-story house with a porch around the front of it. Shrubs and flowers grew to the windows. Ivy covered one end of the porch.

"Is this your house?" he asked, almost in awe.

"My parents bought it fifty-three years ago, the year before I was born. This is where I grew up. My daddy died when I was fifteen, but Momma Love, bless her heart, is still here."

"You call her Momma Love?"

"Everyone calls her Momma Love. She's almost eighty, and in better shape than me." She pointed to a garage straight ahead, behind the house. "You see those three windows above the garage? That's where I live."

Like the house, the garage needed a good coat of paint on the trim. Both were old and handsome, but there were weeds in the flower beds and grass growing in the cracks of the driveway.

They entered through a side door, and the aroma from the kitchen hit Mark hard. He was suddenly starving. A small woman with gray hair in a tight ponytail and dark eyes met them and hugged Reggie.

"Momma Love, meet Mark Sway," Reggie said, waving at him. He and Momma Love were exactly the same height, and she gently hugged him and pecked him on the cheek. He stood stiff, uncertain how to greet a strange eighty-year-old woman.

"Nice to meet you, Mark," she said in his face. Her voice was strong and sounded much like Reggie's. She took his arm and led him to the kitchen table. "Have a seat right here, and I'll get you something to drink."

Reggie grinned at him as if to say "Just do as she says because you have no choice." She hung her umbrella on a rack behind the door and laid her briefcase on the floor.

The kitchen was small and cluttered with cabinets and shelves along three walls. Steam rose from the gas stove. A wooden table with four chairs sat squarely in the center of the room with pots and pans hanging from a beam above it. The kitchen was warm and created instant hunger.

Mark took the nearest chair and watched Momma Love scoot around, grabbing a glass from the cabinet, opening the refrigerator, filling the glass with ice, pouring tea from a pitcher.

Reggie kicked off her shoes and was stirring something in a pot on the stove. She and Momma Love chatted back and forth, the usual routine of how the day went and who'd called. A cat stopped at Mark's chair and examined him.

"That's Axle," Momma Love said as she served the ice tea with a cloth napkin. "She's seventeen years old, and very gentle."

Mark drank the tea and left Axle alone. He was not fond of cats.

"How's your little brother?" Momma Love asked.

"He's doing much better," he said, and suddenly wondered how much Reggie had told her mother. Then he relaxed. If Clint knew very little, Momma Love probably knew even less. He took another sip. She waited for a longer answer. "He started talking today."

"That's wonderful!" she exclaimed with a huge smile and patted him on the shoulder.

Reggie poured her tea from a different pitcher, and doctored it with sweetener and lemon. She sat across from Mark at the table, and Axle jumped into her lap. She sipped tea, rubbed the cat, and began slowly removing her jewelry. She was tired.

"Are you hungry?" Momma Love asked, suddenly darting around the kitchen, opening the oven, stirring the pot, closing a drawer.

"Yes ma'am."

"It's so nice to hear a young man with manners," she said as she stopped for a second and smiled at him. "Most of Reggie's kids have no manners. I haven't heard a 'yes ma'am' in this house in years." Then she was off again, wiping out a pan and placing it in the sink.

Reggie winked at him. "Mark's been eating hospital food for

three days, Momma Love, so he wants to know what you're cooking."

"It's a surprise," she said, opening the oven and releasing a thick aroma of meat and cheese and tomatoes. "But I think you'll like it, Mark."

He was certain he would like it. Reggie winked at him again as she twisted her head and removed a set of small diamond earrings. The pile of jewelry in front of her now included half a dozen bracelets, two rings, a necklace, a watch, and the earrings. Axle was watching it too. Momma Love was suddenly hacking away with a large knife on a cutting board. She whirled around and laid a basket of bread, hot and buttery, in front of him. "I bake bread every Wednesday," she said, patting his shoulder again, then off to the stove.

Mark grabbed the biggest slice and took a bite. It was soft and warm, unlike any bread he'd eaten. The butter and garlic melted instantly on his tongue.

"Momma Love is full-blooded Italian," Reggie said, stroking Axle. "Both her parents were born in Italy and immigrated to this country in 1902. I'm half Italian."

"Who was Mr. Love?" Mark asked, chomping away, butter on his lips and fingers.

"A Memphis boy. They were married when she was sixteen—"

"Seventeen," Momma Love corrected without turning around.

Momma Love was now setting the table with plates and flatware. Reggie and her jewelry were in the way, so she gathered it all up and kicked and nudged Axle to the floor. "When do we eat, Momma Love?" she asked.

"In a minute."

"I'm going to run and change clothes," she said. Axle sat on Mark's foot and rubbed the back of her head on his shin.

"I'm very sorry about your little brother," Momma Love said, glancing at the door to make sure Reggie was indeed gone.

Mark swallowed a mouthful of bread, and wiped his mouth with the napkin. "He'll be okay. We've got good doctors."

"And you've got the best lawyer in the world," she said sternly with no smile. She waited for verification.

"We sure do," Mark said slowly.

She nodded her approval and started for the sink. "What on earth did you boys see out there?"

Mark sipped his tea and stared at the gray ponytail. This could be a long night with plenty of questions. It would be best to stop it now. "Reggie told me not to talk about it." He bit into another piece of bread.

"Oh, Reggie always says that. But you can talk to me. All her kids do."

In the last forty-nine hours, he'd learned much about interrogation. Keep the other guy on his heels. When the questions get old, dish out a few of your own. "How often does she bring a kid home?"

She slid the pot off the burner, and thought a second. "Maybe twice a month. She wants them to eat good food, so she brings them to Momma Love's. Sometimes they spend the night. One little girl stayed a month. She was so pitiful. Name was Andrea. The court took her away from her parents because they were Satan worshipers, doing animal sacrifices and all that mess. She was so sad. She lived upstairs here in Reggie's old bedroom, and she cried when she had to leave. Broke my heart too. I told Reggie 'No more kids,' after that. But Reggie does what Reggie wants. She really likes you, you know."

"What happened to Andrea?"

"Her parents got her back. I pray for her every day. Do you go to church?"

"Sometimes."

"Are you a good Catholic?"

"No. It's a little, well, I'm not sure what kind of church it is. But it's not Catholic. Baptist, I think. We go every now and then."

Momma Love listened to this with deep concern, terribly puzzled by the fact that he wasn't sure what kind of church he attended.

"Maybe I should take you to my church. St. Luke's. It's a beautiful church. Catholics know how to build beautiful churches, you know."

He nodded but could think of nothing to say. In a flash, she'd forgotten about churches and was back to the stove, opening the oven door and studying the dish with the concentration of Dr.

Greenway. She mumbled to herself and it was obvious she was pleased.

"Go wash your hands, Mark, right down the hall there. Kids nowadays don't wash their hands enough. Go along." Mark crammed the last bite of bread into his mouth and followed Axle to the bathroom.

When he returned, Reggie was seated at the table, flipping through a stack of mail. The bread basket had been replenished. Momma Love opened the oven and pulled out a deep dish covered with aluminum foil. "It's lasagna," Reggie said to him with a trace of anticipation.

Momma Love launched into a brief history of the dish while she cut it into sections and dug out great hunks with a large spoon. Steam boiled from the pan. "The recipe has been in my family for centuries," she said, staring at Mark as if he cared about the lasagna's pedigree. He wanted it on his plate. "Came over from the old country. I could bake it for my daddy when I was ten years old." Reggie rolled her eyes a bit and winked at Mark. "It has four layers, each with a different cheese." She covered their plates with perfect squares of it. The four different cheeses ran together and oozed from the thick pasta.

The phone on the countertop rang, and Reggie answered. "Go on and eat, Mark, if you want," Momma Love said as she majestically set his plate in front of him. She nodded at Reggie's back. "She might talk forever." Reggie was listening and talking softly into the phone. It was obvious they were not supposed to hear.

Mark cut a huge bite with his fork, blew on it just enough to knock off the steam, and carefully raised it to his mouth. He chewed slowly, savoring the rich meat sauce, the cheeses, and who knew what else. Even the spinach was divine.

Momma Love watched and waited. She'd poured herself a second glass of wine, and held it halfway between the table and her lips as she waited for a response to her great-grandmother's secret recipe.

"It's great," he said going for the second bite. "Just great." His only experience with lasagna had been a year or so earlier when his mother had pulled a plastic tray from the microwave and served it for dinner. Swanson's frozen, or something like that. He remembered a rubbery taste, nothing like this.

"You like it," Momma Love said, taking a sip of her wine.

He nodded with a mouthful, and this pleased her. She took a small bite.

Reggie hung up and turned to the table. "Gotta run downtown. The cops just picked up Ross Scott for shoplifting again. He's in jail crying for his mother, but they can't find her."

"How long will you be gone?" Mark asked, his fork still.

"Couple of hours. You finish eating and visit with Momma Love. I'll take you to the hospital later." She patted his shoulder, and then she was out the door.

Momma Love was silent until she heard Reggie's car start, then she said, "What on earth did you boys see out there?"

Mark took a bite, chewed forever as she waited, then took a long drink of tea. "Nothing. How do you make this stuff? It's great."

"Well, it's an old recipe."

She sipped the wine, and rattled on for ten minutes about the sauce. Then the cheeses.

Mark didn't hear a word.

He finished the peach cobbler and ice cream while she cleared the table and loaded the dishwasher. He thanked her again, said it was delicious for the tenth time, and stood with an aching stomach. He'd been sitting for an hour. Dinner at the trailer was usually a ten-minute affair. Most of the time they ate microwave meals on trays in front of the television. Dianne was too tired to cook.

Momma Love admired his empty bowl, and sent him to the den while she finished cleaning. The TV was color, but without remote control. No cable. A large family portrait hung above the sofa. He noticed it, then walked closer. It was an old photograph of the Love family, matted and framed by thick, curly wood. Mr. and Mrs. Love were on a small sofa in some studio with two boys in tight collars standing beside them. Momma Love had dark hair and a beautiful smile. Mr. Love was a foot taller, and sat rigid and unsmiling. The boys were stiff and awkward, obviously not happy to be dressed in starched shirts and ties. Reggie was between her parents, in the center of the portrait. She had a wonderful, smirky smile, and it was obvious she was the center of the family's attention and enjoyed this immensely. She was ten or eleven, about Mark's age, and the face of this pretty little girl caught his attention and took his breath. He stared at her face and she seemed to laugh at him. She was full of mischief.

"Beautiful children, huh?" It was Momma Love, easing beside him and admiring her family.

"When was this?" Mark asked, still staring.

"Forty years ago," she said slowly, almost sadly. "We were all so young and happy then." She stood next to him, their arms touching, shoulder to shoulder.

"Where are the boys?"

"Joey, on the right there, is the oldest. He was a test pilot for the Air Force, and was killed in 1964 in a plane crash. He's a hero."

"I'm very sorry," Mark whispered.

"Bennie, on the left, is a year younger than Joey. He's a marine biologist in Vancouver. He never comes to see his mother. He was here about two years ago for Christmas, then off again. He's never married, but I think he's okay. No grandkids by him either. Reggie's got the only grandkids." She was reaching for a framed five by seven next to a lamp on an end table. She handed it to Mark. Two graduation photos with blue caps and gowns. The girl was pretty. The boy had mangy hair, a teenager's beard, and a look of sheer hatred in his eyes.

"These are Reggie's kids," Momma Love explained without the slightest trace of either love or pride. "The boy was in prison last time we heard anything. Selling dope. He was a good boy when he was little, but then his father got him and just ruined him. This was after the divorce. The girl is out in California trying to be an actress or singer or something, or so she says, but she's had drug problems too and we don't hear much. She was a sweet child too. I haven't seen her in almost ten years. Can you believe it? My only granddaughter. It's so sad."

Momma Love was now sipping her third glass of wine, and the tongue was loose. If she could talk about her family long enough, then maybe she'd get around to his. And once they'd covered the families, perhaps they might discuss exactly what on earth the boys saw out there.

"Why haven't you seen her in ten years?" Mark asked, but only because he needed to say something. It was really a dumb question because he knew the answer might take hours. His stomach ached from the feast and he wanted to simply lie on the couch and be left alone.

"Regina, I mean, Reggie, lost her when she was about thirteen. They were going through this nightmare of a divorce, he was chasing other women and had girlfriends all over town, they even caught him with a cute little nurse at the hospital, but the divorce was a horrible nightmare and Reggie got to where she couldn't handle it. Joe, her ex-husband, was a good boy when they got married, but then made a bunch of money and got the doctor's attitude, you know, and he changed. Money went to his head." She paused and took a sip. "Awful, just awful. I do miss them, though. They're my only grandbabies."

They didn't look like grandbabies, especially the boy. He was nothing but a punk.

"What happened to him?" Mark asked after a few seconds of silence.

"Well." She sighed as if she hated to tell, but would do it anyway. "He was sixteen when his father got him, wild and rotten already, I mean, his father was an ob-gyn and never had time for the kids and a boy needs a father, don't you think; and the boy, Jeff is his name, and he was out of control early. Then his father, who had all the money and all the lawyers, got Regina sent away and took the kids, and when this happened Jeff was pretty much on his own. With his father's money, of course. He finished high school almost at gunpoint, and within six months got caught with a bunch of drugs." She stopped suddenly, and Mark thought she was about to cry. She took a sip. "The last time I hugged him was when he graduated from high school. I saw his picture in the newspaper when he got in trouble, but he never called or anything. It's been ten years, Mark. I know I'll die without ever seeing them again." She quickly rubbed her eyes, and Mark looked for a hole to crawl in.

She took his arm. "Come with me. Let's go sit on the porch."

He followed through a narrow foyer, through the front door, and they sat in the swing on the front porch. It was dark and the air was cool. They rocked gently in silence. Momma Love sipped the wine.

She decided to continue the saga. "You see, Mark, once Joe got the kids, he just ruined them. Gave them plenty of money. Kept his old sleazy girlfriends around the house. Flaunted it in front of the kids. Bought them cars. Amanda got pregnant in high school, and he arranged the abortion."

"Why'd Reggie change her name?" he asked politely. Maybe when she answered, this saga would be finished.

"She spent several years in and out of institutions. This was after the divorce, and bless her heart, she was in bad shape, Mark. I cried myself to sleep every night worrying about my daughter. She lived with me most of the time. It took years, but she finally came through. Lots of therapy. Lots of money. Lots of love. And then she decided one day that the nightmare was over, that she would pick up the pieces and move on, and that she would create a new life. That's why she changed her name. She went to court and had it done legally. She fixed up the apartment over the garage. She gave me all these pictures, because she refuses to look at them. She went to law school. She became a new person with a new identity and a new name."

"Is she bitter?"

"She fights it. She lost her children, and no mother can ever recover from that. But she tries not to think about them. They were brainwashed by their father, so they have no use for her. She hates him, of course, and I think it's probably healthy."

"She's a very good lawyer," he said as if he'd personally hired and fired many.

Momma Love moved closer, too close to suit Mark. She patted his knee and this irritated the hell out of him, but she was a sweet old woman and meant nothing by it. She'd buried a son and lost her only grandson, so he gave her a break. There was no moon. A soft wind gently rustled the leaves of the huge black oaks between the porch and the street. He was not anxious to return to the hospital, and so he decided this was pleasant after all. He smiled at Momma Love, but she was staring blankly into the darkness, lost in some deep thought. A heavy, folded quilt padded the swing.

He assumed she would work her way back to the shooting of

Jerome Clifford, and this he wanted to avoid. "Why does Reggie have so many kids for clients?"

She kept patting his knee. "Because some kids need lawyers, though most of them don't know it. And most lawyers are too busy making money to worry about kids. She wants to help. She'll always blame herself for losing her kids, and she just wants to help others. She's very protective of her little clients."

"I didn't pay her very much money."

"Don't worry, Mark. Every month, Reggie takes at least two cases for free. They're called pro bono, which means the lawyer does the work without a fee. If she didn't want your case, she wouldn't have taken it."

He knew about pro bono. Half the lawyers on television were laboring away on cases they wouldn't get paid for. The other half were sleeping with beautiful women and eating in fancy restaurants.

"Reggie has a soul, Mark, a conscience," she continued, still patting gently. The wineglass was empty, but the words were clear and the mind was sharp. "She'll work for no fee if she believes in the client. And some of her poor clients will break your heart, Mark. I cry all the time over some of these little fellas."

"You're very proud of her, aren't you?"

"I am. Reggie almost died, Mark, a few years ago when the divorce was going on. I almost lost her. Then I almost went broke trying to get her back on her feet. But look at her now."

"Will she ever get married again?"

"Maybe. She's dated a couple of men, but nothing serious. Romance is not at the top of her list. Her work comes first. Like tonight. It's almost eight o'clock, and she's at the city jail talking to a little troublemaker they picked up for shoplifting. Wonder what'll be in the newspaper in the morning."

Sports, obituaries, the usual. Mark shifted uncomfortably and waited. It was obvious he was supposed to speak. "Who knows."

"What was it like having your picture on the front page of the paper?"

"I didn't like it."

"Where'd they get those pictures?"

"They're school pictures."

There was a long pause. The chains above them squeaked as the swing moved slowly back and forth. "What was it like walking up on that dead man who'd just shot himself?"

"Pretty scary, but to be honest, my doctor told me not to discuss it because it stresses me out. Look at my little brother, you know. So, I'd better not say anything."

She patted harder. "Of course. Of course."

Mark pressed with his toes, and the swing moved a bit faster. His stomach was still packed and he was suddenly sleepy. Momma Love was humming now. The breeze picked up, and he shivered.

Reggie found them on the dark porch, in the swing, rocking quietly back and forth. Momma Love sipped black coffee and patted him on the shoulder. Mark was curled in a knot beside her, his head resting in her lap, a quilt over his legs.

"How long has he been asleep?" she whispered.

"An hour or so. He got cold, then he got sleepy. He's a sweet child."

"He sure is. I'll call his mother at the hospital, and see if he can stay here tonight."

"He ate until he was stuffed. I'll fix him a good breakfast in the morning."

NINETEEN

THE IDEA WAS TRUMANN'S, and it was a wonderful idea, one that would work and thus would be snared immediately by Foltrigg and claimed as his own. Life with Reverend Roy was a series of stolen ideas and credits when things worked. And when things went to hell, Trumann and his office took the blame, along with Foltrigg's underlings, and the press, and the jurors, and the corrupt defense bar, everybody but the great man himself.

But Trumann had quietly massaged and manipulated the egos of prima donnas before, and he could certainly handle this idiot.

It was late, and as he picked at the lettuce in his shrimp rémoulade in the dark corner of a crowded oyster bar, the idea hit him. He called Foltrigg's private office number, no answer. He dialed the number in the library, and Wally Boxx answered. It was nine-thirty, and Wally explained he and his boss were still buried deep in the law books, just a couple of workaholics slaving over the details and enjoying it. All in a day's work. Trumann said he'd be there in ten minutes.

He left the noisy café and walked hurriedly through the crowds on Canal Street. September was just another hot, sticky summer month in New Orleans. After two blocks he removed his jacket and walked faster. Two more blocks, and his shirt was wet and clinging to his back and chest.

He darted through the crowds of tourists lumbering along Canal with their cameras and gaudy tee shirts, and wondered for the thousandth time why these people came to this city to spend hard-earned money on cheap entertainment and overpriced food. The average tourist on Canal Street wore black socks and white sneakers, was forty pounds overweight, and Trumann figured these people would return home and brag to their less fortunate friends about the delightful cuisine they had uniquely discovered and gorged themselves on in New Orleans. He bumped into a hefty woman with a small black box stuck in her face. She was actually standing near the curb and filming the front of a cheap souvenir store with suggestive street signs displayed for sale in the window. What sort of person would watch a video of a tacky souvenir shop in the French Quarter? Americans no longer experience vacations. They simply Sony them so they can ignore them for the rest of the year.

Trumann was in for a transfer. He was sick of tourists, traffic, humidity, crime, and he was sick of Roy Foltrigg. He turned by Rubinstein Brothers and headed for Poydras.

Foltrigg was not afraid of hard work. It came natural to him. He'd realized in law school that he was not a genius, and that to succeed he'd need to put in more hours. He studied his ass off, and finished somewhere in the middle of the pack. But he'd been elected president of the student body, and there was a certificate declaring this achievement framed in oak somewhere on one of his walls. His career as a political animal started at the moment when his law school classmates chose him as their president, a position most did not know existed and couldn't have cared less about. Job offers had been scarce for young Roy, and at the last minute he jumped at the chance to be an assistant city prosecutor in New Orleans. Fifteen thousand bucks a year in 1975. In two years he handled more cases than all the other city prosecutors combined. He worked. He put in long hours in a dead end job because he was going places. He was a star but no one noticed.

He began dabbling in local Republican politics, a lonely hobby, and learned to play the game. He met people with money and clout, and landed a job with a law firm. He put in incredible hours and became a partner. He married a woman he didn't love because she had the right credentials and a wife brought respectability. Roy was on the move. There was a game plan.

He was still married to her but they slept in different rooms. The kids were now twelve and ten. A pretty family portrait.

He preferred the office to his home, which suited his wife just fine because she didn't like him but did enjoy his salary.

Roy's conference table was once again covered with law books and legal pads. Wally had shed his tie and jacket. Empty coffee cups littered the room. They were both tired.

The law was quite simple: Every citizen owes to society the duty of giving testimony to aid in the enforcement of the law. And, a witness is not excused from testifying because of his fear of reprisal threatening his and/or his family's lives. It was black letter law, as they say, carved in stone over the years by hundreds of judges and justices. No exceptions. No exemptions. No loopholes for scared little boys. Roy and Wally had read dozens of cases. Many were copied and highlighted and thrown about on the table. The kid would have to talk. If the Juvenile Court approach in Memphis fell through, Foltrigg planned to issue a subpoena for Mark Sway to appear before the grand jury in New Orleans. It would scare the little punk to death, and loosen his tongue.

Trumann walked through the door and said, "You guys are working late."

Wally Boxx pushed away from the table and stretched his arms mightily above his head. "Yeah, a lot of stuff to cover," he said, exhausted, waving his hand proudly at the piles of books and notes.

"Have a seat," Foltrigg said, pointing at a chair. "We're finishing up." He stretched too, then cracked his knuckles. He loved his reputation as a workaholic, a man of importance unafraid of painful hours, a family man whose calling went beyond wife and kids. The job meant everything. His client was the United States of America.

Trumann had heard this eighteen-hour-a-day crap for seven years now. It was Foltrigg's favorite subject—talking about himself and the hours at the office and the body that needed no sleep. Lawyers wear their loss of sleep like a badge of honor. Real macho machines grinding it out around the clock.

"I've got an idea," Trumann said, sitting across the table. "You told me earlier about the hearing in Memphis tomorrow. In Juvenile Court."

"We're filing a petition," Roy corrected. "I don't know when the hearing will take place. But we'll ask for a quick one."

"Yeah, well, what about this? Just before I left the office this afternoon, I talked to K. O. Lewis, Voyles's number-one deputy."

"I know K.O.," Foltrigg interrupted. Trumann knew this was coming. In fact, he paused just a split second so Foltrigg could interrupt and set him straight about how close he was to K.O., not Mr. Lewis, but simply K.O.

"Right. Well, he's in St. Louis attending a conference, and he asked about the Boyette case and Jerome Clifford and the kid. I told him what we knew. He said feel free to call if he could do anything. Said Mr. Voyles wants daily reports."

"I know all this."

"Right. Well, I was just thinking. St. Louis is an hour's flight from Memphis, right. What if Mr. Lewis presented himself to the Juvenile Court judge in Memphis first thing in the morning when the petition is filed, and what if Mr. Lewis has a little chat with the judge and leans on him? We're talking about the number-two man in the FBI. He tells the judge what we think this kid knows."

Foltrigg began nodding his approval, and when Wally saw this he began nodding too, only faster.

Trumann continued. "And there's something else. We know Gronke is in Memphis, and it's safe to assume he's not there to visit Elvis's grave. Right? He's been sent there by Muldanno. So I was thinking, what if we assume the kid is in danger, and Mr. Lewis explains to the Juvenile Court judge that it's in the best interests of the kid for us to take him into custody? You know, for his own protection?"

"I like this," Foltrigg said softly. Wally liked it too.

"The kid'll crack under the pressure. First, he's taken into custody by order of the Juvenile Court, same as any other case, and that'll scare the hell out of him. Might also wake up his lawyer. Hopefully the judge orders the kid to talk. At that point, the kid'll crack, I believe. If not, he's in contempt, maybe. Don't you think?"

"Yeah, he's in contempt, but we can't predict what the judge will do at that point."

"Right. So Mr. Lewis tells the judge about Gronke and his connections with the mob, and that we believe he's in Memphis to harm the kid. Either way, we get the kid in custody, away from his lawyer. The bitch."

Foltrigg was wired now. He scribbled something on a legal pad. Wally stood and began pacing thoughtfully around the library, deep in thought as if things were conspiring to force him to make a significant decision.

Trumann could call her a bitch here in the privacy of an office in New Orleans. But he remembered the tape. And he would be happy to remain in New Orleans, far away from her. Let McThune deal with Reggie in Memphis.

"Can you get K.O. on the phone?" Foltrigg asked.

"I think so." Trumann pulled a scrap of paper from a pocket and began punching numbers on the phone.

Foltrigg met Wally in the corner, away from the agent. "It's a great idea," Wally said. "I'm sure this Juvenile Court judge is just some local yokel who'll listen to K.O. and do whatever he wants, don't you think?"

Trumann had Mr. Lewis on the phone. Foltrigg watched him while listening to Wally. "Maybe, but regardless, we get the kid in court quickly and I think he'll fold. If not, he's in custody, under our control and away from his lawyer. I like it."

They whispered for a while as Trumann talked to K. O. Lewis. Trumann nodded at them, gave the okay sign with a big smile, and hung up. "He'll do it," he said proudly. "He'll catch an early morning flight to Memphis and meet with Fink. Then they'll get with George Ord and descend on the judge." Trumann was walking toward them, very proud of himself. "Think about it. The U.S. Attorney on one side, K. O. Lewis on the other, and Fink in the middle, first thing in the morning when the judge gets to the office. They'll have the kid talking in no time."

Foltrigg flashed a wicked smile. He loved those moments when the power of the federal government shifted into high gear and landed hard on small, unsuspecting people. Just like that, with one phone call, the second in command of the FBI had entered the picture. "It just might work," he said to his boys. "It just might work."

In one corner of the small den above the garage, Reggie flipped through a thick book under a lamp. It was midnight, but she couldn't sleep, so she curled under a quilt and sipped tea while reading a book Clint had found titled *Reluctant Witnesses.* As far as law books go, it was quite thin. But the law was quite clear: Every witness has a duty to come forth and assist those authorities investigating a crime. A witness cannot refuse to testify on the grounds that he or she feels threatened. The vast majority of the cases cited in the book dealt with organized crime. Seems the Mafia has historically frowned on its people schmoozing with the cops, and has often threatened wives and children. The Supreme Court has said more than once that wives and children be damned. A witness must talk.

At some point in the very near future, Mark would be forced to talk. Foltrigg could issue a subpoena and compel his attendance before a grand jury in New Orleans. She, of course, would be able to attend. If Mark refused to testify before the grand jury, a quick hearing would be held before the trial judge who would undoubtedly order him to answer Foltrigg's questions. If he refused, the wrath of the court would be severe. No judge tolerates being disobeyed, but federal judges can be especially nasty when their orders fall on deaf ears.

There are places to put eleven-year-old kids who find themselves in disfavor with the system. At the moment, she had no less than twenty clients scattered about in various training schools in Tennessee. The oldest was sixteen. All were secured behind fences with guards pacing about. They were called reform schools not long ago. Now they're training schools.

When ordered to talk, Mark would undoubtedly look to her. And this was why she couldn't sleep. To advise him to disclose the location of the Senator's body would be to jeopardize his safety. His mother and brother would be at risk. These were not people who could become instantly mobile. Ricky might be hospitalized for weeks. Any type of witness protection program would be postponed until he was healthy again. Dianne would be a sitting duck, if Muldanno were so inclined.

It would be proper and ethical and moral to advise him to cooperate, and that would be the easy way out. But what if he got hurt? He would point a finger at her. What if something happened to Ricky or Dianne? She, the lawyer, would be blamed.

Children make lousy clients. The lawyer becomes much more

than a lawyer. With adults, you simply lay the pros and cons of each option on the table. You advise this way and that. You predict a little, but not much. Then you tell the adult it's time for a decision and you leave the room for a bit. When you return, you are handed a decision and you run with it. Not so with kids. They don't understand lawyerly advice. They want a hug and someone to make decisions. They're scared and looking for friends.

She'd held many small hands in courtrooms. She'd wiped many tears.

She imagined this scene: A huge, empty federal courtroom in New Orleans with the doors locked and two marshals guarding it; Mark on the witness stand; Foltrigg in all his glory strutting around on his home turf, prancing back and forth for the benefit of his little assistants and perhaps an FBI agent or two; the judge in a black robe. He was handling it delicately, and he probably disliked Foltrigg immensely because he was forced to see him all the time. He, the judge, asks Mark if he in fact refused to answer certain questions before the grand jury that very morning in a room just a short distance down the hall. Mark, looking upward at His Honor, answers yes. What was the first question? the judge asks Foltrigg, who's on his feet with a legal pad, strutting and prancing as if the room were filled with cameras. I asked him, Your Honor, if Jerome Clifford, prior to the suicide, said anything about the body of Senator Boyd Boyette. And he refused to answer, Your Honor. Then I asked him if Jerome Clifford in fact told him where the body is buried. And he refused to answer this question as well, Your Honor. And the judge leans down even closer to Mark. There is no smile. Mark stares at his lawyer. Why didn't you answer these questions? the judge asks. Because I don't want to, Mark answers, and it's almost funny. But there are no smiles. Well, the judge says, I am ordering you to answer these questions before the grand jury, do you understand me, Mark? I'm ordering you to return to the grand jury room right now and answer all of Mr. Foltrigg's questions, do you understand this? Mark says nothing and doesn't move a muscle. He stares at his trusted lawyer, thirty feet away. What if I don't answer the questions? he finally asks, and this irritates the judge. You have no choice, young man. You must answer because I'm ordering it. And if I don't? Mark asks, terrified. Well, then, I'll find you in contempt and I'll probably incarcerate you until you do as I say. For a very long time, the judge growls.

Axle rubbed against the chair and startled her. The courtroom scene was gone. She closed the book and walked to the window. The best advice to Mark would be simply to lie. Tell a big one. At the critical moment, just explain how the late Jerome Clifford said nothing about Boyd Boyette. He was crazy and drunk and stoned, and said nothing, really. Who in the world could ever know the difference?

Mark was a cool liar.

He awoke in a strange bed between a soft mattress and a heavy layer of blankets. A dim lamp from the hallway cast a narrow light through the slit in the doorway. His battered Nikes were in a chair by the door, but the rest of his clothing was still on. He slid the blankets to his knees and the bed squeaked. He stared at the ceiling and vaguely remembered being escorted to this room by Reggie and Momma Love. Then he remembered the swing on the porch and being very tired.

Slowly, he swung his feet from the bed and sat on the edge of it. He remembered being led and pushed up the stairs. Things were clearing up. He sat in the chair and laced his sneakers. The floor was wooden and creaked softly as he walked to the door and opened it. The hinges popped. The hallway was still. Three other doors opened into it, and they were all closed. He eased to the stairway, and tiptoed down, in no hurry.

A light from the kitchen caught his attention, and he walked faster. The clock on the wall gave the time as two-twenty. He now remembered that Reggie didn't live here; she was above the garage. Momma Love was probably sound asleep upstairs, so he stopped the creeping along and crossed the foyer, unlocked the front door, and found his spot in the swing. The air was cool and the front lawn was pitch black.

For a moment, he was frustrated with himself for falling asleep and being put to bed in this house. He belonged at the hospital with his mother, sleeping on the same crippling bed, waiting for Ricky to snap out of it so they could leave and go home. He assumed Reggie had called Dianne, so his mother probably wasn't worried. In fact, she was probably pleased that he was here at this moment, eating good food and sleeping well. Mothers are like that.

He'd missed two days of school, according to his calculations. Today would be Thursday. Yesterday, he'd been attacked by the man with the knife in the elevator. The man with the family portrait. And the day before that, Tuesday, he had hired Reggie. That, too, seemed like a month ago. And the day before that, Monday, he had awakened like any normal kid and gone off to school with no idea all this was about to happen. There must be a million kids in Memphis, and he would never understand how and why he was selected to meet Jerome Clifford just seconds before he put the gun in his mouth.

Smoking. That was the answer. Hazardous to your health. You could say that again. He was being punished by God for smoking and harming his body. Damn! What if he'd been caught with a beer.

A silhouette of a man appeared on the sidewalk, and stopped for a second in front of Momma Love's house. The orange glow of a cigarette flared in front of his face, then he walked very slowly out of sight. A little late for an evening stroll, Mark thought.

A minute passed, and he was back. Same man. Same slow walk. Same hesitation between the trees as he looked at the house. Mark held his breath. He was sitting in darkness and he knew he could not be seen. But this man was more than a nosy neighbor.

At exactly 4 A.M., a plain white Ford van with the license plates temporarily removed eased into Tucker Wheel Estates and turned onto East Street. The trailers were dark and quiet. The streets were deserted. The little village was peacefully asleep and would be for two more hours until dawn.

The van stopped in front of Number 17. The lights and engine were turned off. No one noticed it. After a minute, a man in a uniform opened the driver's door and stood in the street. The uniform resembled that of a Memphis cop—navy trousers, navy shirt, wide black belt with black holster, some type of gun on the hip, black boots, but no cap or hat. A decent imitation, especially at four in the morning when no one was watching. He held a rectangular cardboard container about the size of two shoe boxes. He glanced around, then carefully watched and listened to the trailer next door to Number 17. Not a sound. Not even the bark of a dog. He smiled to himself, and walked casually to the door of Number 17.

If he detected movement in a nearby trailer, he would simply knock slightly on the door and go through the routine of being a frustrated messenger looking for Ms. Sway. But it wasn't necessary. Not a peep from the neighbors. So he quickly sat the box against the door, got in the van, and drove away. He had come and gone without a trace, leaving behind his little warning.

Exactly thirty minutes later, the box exploded. It was a quiet explosion, carefully controlled. The ground didn't shake and the porch didn't shatter. The door was blown open, and the flames were directed at the interior of the trailer. Lots of red and yellow flames and black smoke rolling through the rooms. The matchbox construction of the walls and floors was nothing more than kindling for the fire.

By the time Rufus Bibbs next door could punch 911, the Sway trailer was engulfed and beyond help. Rufus hung up the phone, and ran to find his garden hose. His wife and kids were running wild, trying to dress and get out of the trailer. Screams and shouts echoed on the street as the neighbors ran to the fire in an amazing array of pajamas and robes. Dozens of them watched the fire as garden hoses came from all directions and water was applied to the trailers next door. The fire grew and the crowd grew, and windows popped in the Bibbs trailer. The domino effect. More screams as more windows popped. Then sirens and red lights.

The crowd moved back as the firemen laid lines and pumped water. The other trailers were saved, but the Sway home was nothing but rubble. The roof and most of the floor were gone. The rear wall stood with a solitary window still intact.

More people arrived as the firemen sprayed the ruins. Walter Deeble, a loudmouth from South Street, started babbling about how cheap these damned trailers were with aluminum wiring and all. Hell, we all live in firetraps, he said with the pitch of a street preacher, and what we ought to do is sue that sonofabitch Tucker and force him to provide safe housing. He just might see his lawyer about it. Personally, he had eight smoke and heat detectors in his trailer because of the cheap aluminum wiring and all, and he just might talk to his lawyer.

By the Bibbs trailer, a small crowd gathered and thanked God the fire didn't spread.

Those poor Sways. What else could happen to them?

TWENTY

AFTER A BREAKFAST of cinnamon rolls and chocolate milk, they left the house and headed for the hospital. It was seven-thirty, much too early for Reggie but Dianne was waiting. Ricky was doing much better.

"What do you think'll happen today?" Mark asked.

For some reason this struck her as being funny. "You poor child," she said when she finished chuckling. "You've been through a lot this week."

"Yeah. I hate school, but it'd be nice to go back. I had this wild dream last night."

"What happened?"

"Nothing. I dreamed everything was normal again, and I made it through a whole day with nothing happening to me. It was wonderful."

"Well, Mark, I'm afraid I have some bad news."

"I knew it. What is it?"

"Clint called a few minutes ago. You've made the front page again. It's a picture of both of us, evidently taken by one of those clowns at the hospital yesterday when we got off the elevator."

"Great."

"There's a reporter at the *Memphis Press* by the name of Slick Moeller. Everyone calls him the Mole. Mole Moeller. He covers the crime beat, sort of a legend around town. He's hot on this case."

"He wrote the story yesterday."

"That's right. He has a lot of contacts within the police department. It sounds as if the cops believe Mr. Clifford told you everything before he killed himself, and now you're refusing to cooperate."

"Pretty accurate, wouldn't you say?"

She glanced at the rearview mirror. "Yeah. It's spooky."

"How does he know this stuff?"

"The cops talk to him, off the record of course, and he digs and digs until he puts the pieces together. And if the pieces don't fit perfectly, then Slick just sort of fills in the gaps. According to Clint, the story is based on unnamed sources within the Memphis Police Department, and there's a great deal of suspicion about how much you know. The theory is that since you've hired me, you must be hiding something."

"Let's stop and get a newspaper."

"We'll get one at the hospital. We'll be there in a minute."

"Do you think those reporters'll be waiting again?"

"Probably. I told Clint to find a back entrance somewhere, and to meet us in the parking lot."

"I'm really sick of this. Just sick of it. All my buddies are in school today, having a good time, being normal, fighting with girls during recess, playing jokes on the teachers, you know, the usual stuff. And look at me. Running around town with my lawyer, reading about my adventures in the newspapers, looking at my face on the front page, hiding from reporters, dodging killers with switchblades. It's like something out of a movie. A bad movie. I'm just sick of it. I don't know if I can take anymore. It's just too much."

She watched him between glances at the street and traffic. His jaws were tight. He stared straight ahead, but saw nothing.

"I'm sorry, Mark."

"Yeah, me too. So much for pleasant dreams, huh."

"This could be a very long day."

"What else is new? They were watching the house last night, did you know that?"

"I beg your pardon."

"Yeah, somebody was watching the house. I was on the porch at two-thirty this morning, and I saw a guy walking along the sidewalk. He was real casual, you know, just smoking a cigarette and looking at the house."

"Could be a neighbor."

"Right. At two-thirty in the morning."

"Maybe someone was out for a walk."

"Then why did he walk by the house three times in fifteen minutes?"

She glanced at him again and hit her brakes to avoid a car in front of them.

"Do you trust me, Mark?" she asked.

He looked at her as if surprised by the question. "Of course I trust you, Reggie."

She smiled and patted his arm. "Then stick with me."

One advantage of an architectural horror like St. Peter's was the existence of lots of doors and exits few people knew about it. With additions stuck here, and wings added over there as an afterthought, there had been created over the course of time little nooks and alleys seldom used and rarely discovered by lost security guards.

When they arrived, Clint had been hustling around the hospital for thirty minutes with no success. He'd managed to become lost himself three different times. He was sweating and apologizing as they met at the parking lot.

"Just follow me," Mark said, and they darted across the street and entered through the emergency gate. They wove through heavy, rush-hour hall traffic and found an ancient escalator going down.

"I hope you know where you're going," Reggie said, obviously in doubt and half-jogging in an effort to keep up with him. Clint was sweating even harder. "No problem," Mark said, and opened a door leading to the kitchen.

"We're in the kitchen, Mark," Reggie said, looking around.

"Just be cool. Act like you're supposed to be here."

He punched a button by a service elevator and the door opened instantly. He punched another button on the inside panel, and they lurched upward, headed for floor number ten. "There are eighteen floors in the main section, but this elevator stops at number ten. It will not stop at nine. Figure it out." He watched the numbers above the door and explained this like a bored tour guide.

"What happens on ten?" Clint asked between breaths.

"Just wait."

The door opened on ten, and they stepped into a huge closet with rows of shelves filled with towels and bedsheets. Mark was off, darting between the aisles. He opened a heavy metal door and they were suddenly in the hallway with patient rooms right and left. He pointed to his left, kept walking, and stopped before an emergency exit door with red and yellow alarm warnings all over it. He grabbed the bar handle across the front of it, and Reggie and Clint stopped cold.

He pushed the door open, and nothing happened. "Alarms don't work," he said nonchalantly and bounded down the steps to the ninth floor. He opened another door, and suddenly they were in a quiet hallway with thick industrial carpet and no traffic. He pointed again, and they were off, past patient rooms, around a bend, and by the nurses' station where they glanced down another hall and saw the loiterers by the elevators.

"Good morning, Mark," Karen the beautiful called out as they hurried by. But she said this without a smile.

"Hi, Karen," he answered without slowing.

Dianne was sitting in a folding chair in the hall with a Memphis cop kneeling before her. She was crying, and had been for some time. The two security guards were standing together twenty feet away. Mark saw the cop and the tears and ran for his mother. She grabbed him and they hugged.

"What's the matter, Mom?" he asked, and she cried harder.

"Mark, your trailer burned last night," the cop said. "Just a few hours ago."

Mark glared at him in disbelief, then squeezed his mother around the neck. She was wiping tears and trying to compose herself.

"How bad?" Mark asked.

"Real bad," the cop said sadly as he stood and held his cap with both hands. "Everything's gone."

"What started the fire?" Reggie asked.

"Don't know right now. The fire inspector will be on the scene this morning. Could be electrical."

"I need to talk to the fire inspector, okay," Reggie insisted, and the cop looked her over.

"And who are you?" he asked.

"Reggie Love, attorney for the family."

"Ah, yes. I saw the paper this morning."

She handed him a card. "Please ask the fire inspector to call me."

"Sure, lady." The cop carefully placed the hat on his head and looked down again at Dianne. He was sad again. "Ms. Sway, I'm very sorry about this."

"Thank you," she said, wiping her face. He nodded at Reggie and Clint, backed away, and left in a hurry. A nurse appeared and stood by just in case.

Dianne suddenly had an audience. She stood and stopped crying, even managed a smile at Reggie.

"This is Clint Van Hooser. He works for me," Reggie said.

Dianne smiled at Clint. "I'm very sorry," he said.

"Thank you," Dianne said softly. A few seconds of awkward silence followed as she finished wiping her face. Her arm was around Mark, who was still dazed.

"Did he behave?" Dianne asked.

"He was wonderful. He ate enough for a small army."

"That's good. Thanks for having him over."

"How's Ricky?" Reggie asked.

"He had a good night. Dr. Greenway stopped by this morning, and Ricky was awake and talking. Looks much better."

"Does he know about the fire?" Mark asked.

"No. And we're not telling him, okay?"

"Okay, Mom. Could we go inside and talk, just me and you?"

Dianne smiled at Reggie and Clint, and led Mark into the room. The door was closed, and the tiny Sway family was all alone with all its worldly possessions.

The Honorable Harry Roosevelt had presided over the Shelby County Juvenile Court for twenty-two years now, and despite the dismal and depressing nature of the court's business he had conducted its affairs with a great deal of dignity. He was the first black Juvenile Court judge in Tennessee, and when he'd been appointed by the Governor in the early seventies, his future was brilliant and there were glowing predictions of higher courts for him to conquer.

The higher courts were still there, and Harry Roosevelt was still here, in the deteriorating building known simply as Juvenile Court. There were much nicer courthouses in Memphis. On Main Street the Federal Building, always the newest in town, housed the elegant and stately courtrooms. The federal boys always had the best —rich carpet, thick leather chairs, heavy oak tables, plenty of lights, dependable air conditioning, lots of well-paid clerks and assistants. A few blocks away, the Shelby County Courthouse was a beehive of judicial activity as thousands of lawyers roamed its tiled and marbled corridors and worked their way through well-preserved and well-scrubbed courtrooms. It was an older building, but a beautiful one with paintings on the walls and a few statues scattered about. Harry could have had a courtroom over there, but he said no. And not far away was the Shelby County Justice Center with a maze of fancy new modern courtrooms with bright fluorescent lights and sound systems and padded seats. Harry could have had one of those too, but he turned it down.

He remained here, in the Juvenile Court Building, a converted high school blocks away from downtown with little parking and few janitors and more cases per judge than any other docket in the world. His court was the unwanted stepchild of the judicial system. Most lawyers shunned it. Most law students dreamed of plush offices in tall buildings and wealthy clients with thick wallets. Never did they dream of slugging their way through the roach-infested corridors of Juvenile Court.

Harry had turned down four appointments, all to courts where the heating systems worked in the winter. He had been considered for these appointments because he was smart and black, and he turned them down because he was poor and black. They paid him sixty thousand a year, lowest of any court in town, so he could feed his wife and four teenagers and live in a nice home. But he'd known hunger as a child, and those memories were vivid. He would always think of himself as a poor black kid.

And that's exactly the reason the once promising Harry Roosevelt remained a simple Juvenile Court judge. To him, it was the most important job in the world. By statute, he had exclusive jurisdiction over delinquent, unruly, dependent, and neglected children. He determined paternity of children born out of wedlock and enforced his own orders for their support and education, and in a county where half the babies were born to single mothers, this accounted for most of his docket. He terminated parental rights and placed abused children in new homes. Harry carried heavy burdens.

He weighed somewhere between three and four hundred pounds, and wore the same outfit every day—black suit, white cotton shirt, and a bow tie which he tied himself and did so poorly. No one knew if Harry owned one black suit or fifty. He always looked the same. He was an imposing figure on the bench, glaring down over his reading glasses at deadbeat fathers who refused to support their children. Deadbeat fathers, black and white alike, lived in fear of Judge Roosevelt. He would track them down and throw them in jail. He found their employers and tapped their paychecks. If you messed with Harry's subjects, or Harry's Kids, as they were known, you could find yourself handcuffed and standing pitifully before him with a bailiff on each side.

Harry Roosevelt was a legend in Memphis. The county fathers had seen fit to give him two more judges to help with the caseload, but he maintained a brutal work schedule. He usually arrived before seven and made his own coffee. He started court promptly at nine and god help the lawyer who was late for court. He'd thrown several of them in jail over the years.

At eight-thirty, his secretary hauled in a box of mail and informed Harry that there was a group of men waiting outside who desperately needed to speak with him.

"What else is new?" he asked, eating the last bite of an apple Danish.

"You might want to meet with these gentlemen."

"Oh really. Who are they?"

"One is George Ord, our distinguished U.S. Attorney."

"I taught George in law school."

"Right. That's what he said, twice. There's also an Assistant U. S. Attorney from New Orleans, a Mr. Thomas Fink. And a Mr. K. O. Lewis, Deputy Director of the FBI. And a couple of FBI agents."

Harry looked up from a file and thought about this. "A rather distinguished group. What do they want?"

"They wouldn't say."

"Well, show them in."

She left, and seconds later Ord, Fink, Lewis, and McThune filed into the crowded and cluttered office and introduced themselves to His Honor. Harry and the secretary moved files from the chairs and everyone looked for a seat. They exchanged brief pleasantries, and after a few minutes of this Harry looked at his watch and said, "Gentlemen, I am scheduled to hear seventeen cases today. What can I do for you?"

Ord cleared his throat first. "Well, Judge, I'm sure you've seen the papers the last two mornings, especially the front page stories about a boy by the name of Mark Sway."

"Very intriguing."

"Mr. Fink here is prosecuting the man accused of killing Senator Boyette, and the case is scheduled for trial in New Orleans in a few weeks."

"I'm aware of this. I've read the stories."

"We are almost certain that Mark Sway knows more than he is telling. He's lied to the Memphis Police on several occasions. We think he talked at length with Jerome Clifford before the suicide. We know without a doubt he was in the car. We've tried to talk to the kid, but he has been very uncooperative. Now he's hired a lawyer and she's stonewalling."

"Reggie Love is a regular in my court. A very competent attorney. Sometimes a bit overprotective of her clients, but there's nothing wrong with that."

"Yes sir. We're very suspicious of the boy, and we feel quite strongly that he is withholding valuable information."

"Such as?"

"Such as the location of the Senator's body."

"How can you assume this?"

"There's a lot to the story, Your Honor. And it would take a while to explain it."

Harry played with his bow tie and gave Ord one of his patented scowls. He was thinking. "So you want me to bring the kid in and ask him questions."

"Sort of. Mr. Fink has brought with him a petition alleging the child to be a delinquent."

This did not sit well with Harry. His shiny forehead was suddenly wrinkled. "A rather serious allegation. What type of offense has the child committed?"

"Obstruction of justice."

"You got any law?"

Fink had a file open, and he was on his feet handing a thin brief across the desk. Harry took it, and began reading slowly. The room was silent. K. O. Lewis had yet to say anything, and this bothered him because he was, after all, the number-two man at the FBI. And this judge seemed not to care.

Harry flipped a page and glanced at his watch. "I'm listening," he said in Fink's direction.

"It's our position, Your Honor, that through his misrepresentations Mark Sway has obstructed the investigation into this matter."

"Which matter? The murder or the suicide?"

Excellent point, and as soon as he heard the question Fink knew Harry Roosevelt would not be a pushover. They were investigating a murder, not a suicide. There was no law against suicide, nor was there a law against witnessing one. "Well, Your Honor, the suicide has some very direct links to the murder of Boyette, we think, and it's important for the kid to cooperate."

"What if the kid knows nothing?"

"We can't be certain until we ask him. Right now he's impeding the investigation, and, as you well know, every citizen has a duty to assist law enforcement officials."

"I'm well aware of that. It just seems a bit severe to allege the kid is a delinquent without any proof."

"The proof will come, Your Honor, if we can get the kid on the witness stand, under oath, in a closed hearing and ask some questions. That's all we're trying to do."

Harry tossed the brief into a pile of papers and removed his reading glasses. He chewed on a stem.

Ord leaned forward and spoke solemnly. "Look, Judge, if we can take the kid into custody, then have an expedited hearing, we think this matter will be resolved. If he states under oath that he knows nothing about Boyd Boyette, then the petition is dismissed, the kid goes home, and the matter is over. It's routine. No proof, no finding of delinquency, no harm. But if he knows something relevant to the location of the body, then we have a right to know and we think the kid will tell us during the hearing."

"There are two ways to make him talk, Your Honor," Fink added. "We can file this petition in your court and have a hearing, or we can subpoena the kid to face the grand jury in New Orleans. Staying here seems to be the quickest and best route, especially for the kid."

"I do not want this kid subpoenaed before a grand jury," Harry said sternly. "Is that understood?"

They all nodded quickly, and they all knew full well that a federal grand jury could subpoena Mark Sway anytime it chose, regardless of the feelings of a local judge. This was typical of Harry. Immediately throwing his protective blanket around any child within reach of his jurisdiction.

"I'd much rather deal with it in my court," he said, almost to himself.

"We agree, Your Honor," Fink said. They all agreed.

Harry picked up his daily calendar. As usual, it was filled with more misery than he could possibly handle in one day. He studied it. "These allegations of obstruction are rather shaky, in my opinion. But I can't prevent you from filing the petition. I suggest we hear this matter at the earliest possible time. If the kid in fact knows nothing, and I suspect this to be the case, then I want it over and done with. Quickly."

This suited everyone.

"Let's do it during lunch today. Where is the kid now?"

"At the hospital," Ord said. "His brother will be there for an unspecified period of time. The mother is confined to the room. Mark just sort of roams about. Last night he stayed with his lawyer."

"That sounds like Reggie," Harry said with affection. "I see no need to take him into custody."

Custody was very important to Fink and Foltrigg. They wanted the kid picked up, hauled away in a police car, placed in a cell of some sort, and in general frightened to the point of talking.

"Your Honor, if I may," K.O. finally said. "We think custody is urgent."

"Oh you do? I'm listening."

McThune handed Judge Roosevelt a glossy eight by ten. Lewis handled the narration. "The man in the picture is Paul Gronke. He's a thug from New Orleans, and a close associate of Barry Muldanno. He's been in Memphis since Tuesday night. That photo was taken as he entered the airport in New Orleans. An hour later he was in Memphis, and unfortunately we lost him when he left the airport here." McThune produced two smaller photos. "The guy with the dark shades is Mack Bono, a convicted murderer with strong mob ties in New Orleans. The guy in the suit is Gary Pirini, another Mafia thug who works for the Sulari family. Bono and Pirini arrived in Memphis last night. They didn't come here to eat barbecued ribs." He paused for dramatic effect. "The kid's in serious danger, Your Honor. The family home is a house trailer in north Memphis, in a place called Tucker Wheel Estates."

"I'm very familiar with the place," Harry said, rubbing his eyes.

"About four hours ago, the trailer burned to the ground. The fire looks suspicious. We think it's intimidation. The kid has been roaming at will since Monday night. There's no father, and the mother cannot leave the younger son. It's very sad, and it's very dangerous."

"So you've been watching him."

"Yes sir. His lawyer asked the hospital to provide security guards outside the brother's room."

"And she called me," Ord added. "She is very concerned about the kid's safety, and asked me to request FBI protection at the hospital."

"And we complied," added McThune. "We've had at least two agents near the room for the past forty-eight hours. These guys are killers, Your Honor, and they're taking orders from Muldanno. And the kid's just roaming around oblivious to the danger."

Harry listened to them carefully. It was a well-rehearsed full court press. By nature, he was suspicious of police and their kind, but this was not a routine case. "Our laws certainly provide for the child to be taken into custody after the petition is filed," he said to no one in particular. "What happens to the kid if the hearing does not produce what you want, if the kid is in fact not obstructing justice?"

Lewis answered. "We've thought about this, Your Honor, and

we would never do anything to violate the secrecy of your hearings. But, we have ways of getting word to these thugs that the kid knows nothing. Frankly, if he comes clean and knows nothing, the matter is closed and Muldanno's boys will lose interest in him. Why should they threaten him if he knows nothing?"

"That makes sense," Harry said. "But what do you do if the kid tells you what you want to hear. He's a marked little boy at that point, don't you think? If these guys are as dangerous as you say, then our little pal could be in serious trouble."

"We're making preliminary arrangements to place him in the witness protection program. All of them, Mark, his mother, and brother."

"Have you discussed this with his attorney?"

"No sir," Fink answered. "The last time we were in her office she refused to meet with us. She's been difficult too."

"Let me see your petition."

Fink whipped it out and handed it to him. He carefully put on his reading glasses and studied it. When he finished, he handed it back to Fink.

"I don't like this, gentlemen. I just don't like the smell of it. I've seen a million cases, and never one involving a minor and a charge of obstructing justice. I have an uneasy feeling."

"We're desperate, Your Honor," Lewis confessed with a great deal of sincerity. "We have to know what the kid knows, and we fear for his safety. This is all on the table. We're not hiding anything, and we're damned sure not trying to mislead you."

"I certainly hope not." Harry glared at them. He scribbled something on scratch paper. They waited and watched his every move. He glanced at his watch.

"I'll sign the order. I want the kid taken directly to the Juvenile Wing and placed in a cell by himself. He'll be scared to death, and I want him handled with velvet gloves. I'll personally call his lawyer later in the morning."

They stood in unison and thanked him. He pointed to the door, and they left quickly without handshakes or farewells.

TWENTY-ONE

KAREN KNOCKED LIGHTLY and entered the dark room with a basket of fruit. The card brought get-well messages from the congregation of Little Creek Baptist Church. The apples and bananas and grapes were wrapped in green cellophane, and looked pretty sitting next to a rather large and expensive arrangement of colorful flowers sent by the concerned friends at Ark-Lon Fixtures.

The shades were drawn, the television was off, and when Karen closed the door to leave none of the Sways had moved. Ricky had changed positions, and was now lying on his back with his feet on the pillows and his head on the blankets. He was awake, but for the last hour had been staring blankly at the ceiling without saying a word or moving an inch. This was something new. Mark and Dianne sat next to each other on the foldaway bed with their feet tucked under them and whispered about such things as clothing and toys and dishes. There was fire insurance, but Dianne didn't know the extent of the coverage.

They spoke in hushed voices. It would be days or weeks before Ricky knew of the fire.

At some point in the morning, about an hour after Reggie and Clint left, the shock of the news wore off and Mark started thinking. It was easy to think in this dark room because there was nothing else to do. The television could be used only when Ricky wanted it. The shades remained closed if there was a chance he was sleeping. The door was always shut.

Mark had been sitting in a chair under the television, eating a stale chocolate chip cookie, when it occurred to him that maybe the fire was not an accident. Earlier, the man with the knife had somehow entered the trailer and found the portrait. His intent had been to wave the knife and wave the portrait, and forever silence little Mark Sway. And he had been most successful. What if the fire was just another reminder from the man with the switchblade? Trailers were easy to burn. The neighborhood was usually quiet at four in the morning. He knew this from experience.

This thought had stuck like a thick knot in his throat, and his mouth was suddenly dry. Dianne didn't notice. She'd been sipping coffee and patting Ricky.

Mark had wrestled with it for a while, then had taken a short walk to the nurses' station where Karen showed him the morning paper.

The thought was so horrible it seared itself into his mind, and after two hours of thinking about it he was convinced the fire was intentional.

"What will the insurance cover?" he asked.

"I'll have to call the agent. There are two policies, if I remember correctly. One is paid by Mr. Tucker on the trailer, because he owns it, and the other is paid by us for the contents of the trailer. The monthly rent is supposed to include the premium for the insurance on the contents. I think that's how it works."

This worried Mark immensely. There were many awful memories from the divorce, and he remembered his mother's inability to testify about any of the financial affairs of the family. She knew nothing. His ex-father paid the bills and kept the checkbook and filed the tax returns. Twice in the past two years the telephone had been cut off because Dianne had forgotten to pay the bills. Or so she said. He suspected each time that there was no money to pay the bills.

"But what will the insurance pay for?" he asked.

"Furniture, clothes, kitchen utensils, I guess. That's what it usually covers."

There was a knock on the door, but it did not open. They waited, then another knock. Mark opened it slightly, and saw two new faces peering through the crack.

"Yes," he said, expecting trouble because the nurses and security guards allowed no one to get this far. He opened the door a bit wider.

"Looking for Dianne Sway," said the nearest face. There was volume to this, and Dianne started for the door.

"Who are you?" Mark asked, opening the door and walking into the hall. The two security guards were standing together to the right, and three nurses were standing together to the left, and all five appeared frozen as if witnessing a horrible event. Mark locked eyes with Karen, and knew instantly something was terribly wrong.

"Detective Nassar, Memphis PD. This is Detective Klickman."

Nassar wore a coat and tie, and Klickman wore a black jogging suit with sparkling new Nike Air Jordans. They were both young, probably early thirties, and Mark immediately thought of the old "Starsky and Hutch" reruns. Dianne opened the door and stood behind her son.

"Are you Dianne Sway?" Nassar asked.

"I am," she answered quickly.

Nassar pulled papers from his coat pocket and handed them over Mark's head to his mother. "These are from Juvenile Court, Ms. Sway. It's a summons for a hearing at noon today."

Her hands shook wildly and the papers rattled as she tried hopelessly to make sense of this.

"Could I see your badges?" Mark asked, rather coolly under the circumstances. They both grabbed and reached and presented their identification under Mark's nose. He studied them carefully, and sneered at Nassar. "Nice shoes," he said to Klickman.

Nassar tried to smile. "Ms. Sway, the summons requires us to take Mark Sway into custody at this time."

There was a heavy pause of two or three seconds as the word "custody" settled in.

"What!" Dianne yelled at Nassar. She dropped the papers. The "What!" echoed down the hallway. There was more anger in her voice than fear.

"It's right here on the front page," Nassar said, picking up the summons. "Judge's orders."

"You what!" she yelled again, and it shot through the air like the crack of a bullwhip. "You can't take my son!" Dianne's face was red and her body, all hundred and fifteen pounds, was tense and coiled.

Great, thought Mark. Another ride in a patrol car. Then his mother yelled, "You son of a bitch!" and Mark tried to calm her.

"Mom, don't yell. Ricky can hear you."

"Over my dead body!" she yelled at Nassar, just inches away. Klickman backed away one step, as if to say this wild woman belonged to Nassar.

But Nassar was a pro. He'd arrested thousands. "Look, Ms. Sway, I understand how you feel. But I have my orders."

"Whose orders!"

"Mom, please don't yell," Mark pleaded.

"Judge Harry Roosevelt signed the order about an hour ago. We're just doing our job, Ms. Sway. Nothing's gonna happen to Mark. We'll take care of him."

"What's he done? Just tell me what's he done?" Dianne turned to the nurses. "Can somebody help me here?" she pleaded and sounded so pitiful. "Karen, do something, would you? Call Dr. Greenway. Don't just stand there."

But Karen and the nurses just stood there. The cops had already warned them.

Nassar was still trying to smile. "If you'll read these papers, Ms. Sway, you'll see that a petition has been filed in Juvenile Court alleging Mark here to be a delinquent because he won't cooperate with the police and FBI. And Judge Roosevelt wants to have a hearing at noon today. That's all."

"That's all! You asshole! You show up here with your little papers and take away my son and you say 'That's all'!"

"Not so loud, Mom," Mark said. He'd hadn't heard such language from her since the divorce.

Nassar stopped trying to smile and pulled at the corners of his mustache. Klickman for some reason was glaring at Mark as if he were a serial killer they'd been tracking for years. There was a long pause. Dianne kept both hands on Mark's shoulders. "You can't have him!"

Finally, Klickman said his first words. "Look, Ms. Sway, we have no choice. We have to take your son."

"Go to hell," she snapped. "If you take him, you whip me first."

Klickman was a meathead with little finesse, and for a split second his shoulders flinched as if he would accept this challenge. Then he relaxed and smiled.

"It's okay, Mom. I'll go. Call Reggie and tell her to meet me at the jail. She'll probably sue these clowns by lunch and have them fired by tomorrow."

The cops grinned at each other. Cute little kid.

Nassar then made the very sad mistake of reaching for Mark's arm. Dianne lunged and struck like a cobra. Whap! She slapped him on his left cheek and screamed, "Don't touch him! Don't touch him!"

Nassar grabbed his face, and Klickman instantly grabbed her arm. She wanted to strike again, but was suddenly spun around, and somehow in the midst of this her feet and Mark's feet became tangled and they hit the floor. "You son of a bitch!" she kept screaming. "Don't touch him."

Nassar reached down for some reason, and Dianne kicked him on the thigh. But she was barefoot and there was little damage. Klickman was reaching down, and Mark was scrambling to get up, and Dianne was kicking and swinging and yelling, "Don't touch him!" The nurses rushed forward and the security guards joined in as Dianne got to her feet.

Mark was pulled from the fracas by Klickman. Dianne was held by the two security guards. She was twisting and crying. Nassar was rubbing his face. The nurses were soothing and consoling and trying to separate everyone.

The door opened, and Ricky stood in it holding a stuffed rabbit. He stared at Mark, whose wrists were being held by Klickman. He stared at his mother, whose wrists were being held by the security guards. Everyone froze and stared at Ricky. His face was as white as the sheets. His hair stuck out in all directions. His mouth was open, but he said nothing.

Then he started the low, mournful groan that only Mark had heard before. Dianne yanked her wrists free and picked him up. The nurses followed her into the room and they tucked him in the bed. They patted his arms and legs, but the groaning continued. Then the thumb went in his mouth and he closed his eyes. Dianne lay beside him in the bed and began humming "Winnie the Pooh" and patting his arm.

"Let's go, kid," Klickman said.

"You gonna handcuff me?"

"No. This is not an arrest."

"Then what the hell is it?"

"Watch your language, kid."

"Kiss my ass, you big stupid jock." Klickman stopped cold and glared down at Mark.

"Watch your mouth, kid," Nassar warned.

"Look at your face, hotshot. I think it's turning blue. Mom coldcocked you. Ha, Ha. I hope she broke your teeth."

Klickman bent over and put his hands on his knees. He stared Mark directly in the eyes. "Are you going with us, or shall we drag you out of here?"

Mark snorted and glared at him. "You think I'm scared of you, don't you? Let me tell you something, meathead, I've got a lawyer who'll have me out in ten minutes. My lawyer is so good that by this afternoon you'll be looking for another job."

"I'm scared to death. Now let's go."

They started walking, a cop on each side of the defendant.

"Where are we going?"

"Juvenile Detention Center."

"Is it sort of a jail?"

"It could be if you don't watch your smart mouth."

"You knocked my mother down, you know that. She'll have your job for that."

"She can have my job," Klickman said. "It's a rotten job because I have to deal with little punks like you."

"Yeah, but you can't find another one, can you? There's no demand for idiots these days."

They passed a small crowd of orderlies and nurses, and suddenly Mark was a star. The center of attention. He was an innocent man being led away to the slaughter. He swaggered a bit. They turned the corner, and then he remembered the reporters.

And they remembered him. A flash went off as they got to the elevators, and two of the loiterers with pencils and pads were suddenly standing next to Klickman. They waited for the elevator.

"Are you a cop?" one of them asked, staring at the glow-in-the-dark Nikes.

"No comment."

"Hey, Mark, where you going?" another asked from just a few feet behind. There was another flash.

"To jail," he said loudly without turning around.

"Shut up, kid," Nassar scolded. Klickman put a heavy arm on his shoulder. The photographer was beside them, almost to the elevator door. Nassar held up an arm to block his view. "Get away," he growled.

"Are you under arrest, Mark?" one of them yelled.

"No," Klickman snapped just as the door opened. Nassar shoved Mark inside while Klickman blocked the door until it started to close.

They were alone in the elevator. "That was a stupid thing to say, kid. Really stupid." Klickman was shaking his head.

"Then arrest me."

"Really stupid."

"Is it against the law to talk to the press?"

"Just keep your mouth shut, okay?"

"Why don't you just beat the hell out of me, okay, meathead?"

"I'd love to."

"Yeah, but you can't, right? Because I'm just a little kid, and you're a big stupid cop and if you touch me you'll get fired and sued and all that. You knocked my mother down, meathead, and you haven't heard the last of it."

"Your mother slapped me," Nassar said.

"Good for her. You clowns have no idea what she's been through. You show up to get me and act like it's no big deal, like just because you're cops and you've got this piece of paper then my mother is supposed to get happy and send me off with a kiss. A couple of morons. Just big, dumb, meatheaded cops."

The elevator stopped, opened, and two doctors entered. They stopped talking and looked at Mark. The door closed behind them, and they continued down. "Can you believe these clowns are arresting me?" he asked the doctors.

They frowned at Nassar and Klickman.

"Juvenile Court offender," Nassar explained. Why couldn't the little punk just shut up?

Mark nodded at Klickman. "This one here with the cute shoes knocked my mother down about five minutes ago. Can you believe it?"

Both doctors looked at the shoes.

"Just shut up, Mark," Klickman said.

"Is your mother okay?" one of the doctors asked.

"Oh she's great. My little brother's in the psychiatric ward. Our trailer burned to the ground a few hours ago. And then these thugs show up and arrest me right in front of my mother. Bigfoot here knocks her to the floor. She's doing great."

The doctors stared at the cops. Nassar watched his feet and Klickman closed his eyes. The elevator stopped and a small crowd boarded. Klickman stayed close to Mark.

When all was quiet and they were moving again, Mark said loudly, "My lawyer'll sue you jerks, you know that, don't you? You'll be unemployed this time tomorrow." Eight sets of eyes looked down in the corner, then up at the pained face of Detective Klickman. Silence.

"Just shut up, Mark."

"And what if I don't? You gonna rough me up like you did my mother. Throw me down, kick me a few times. You're just another meathead cop, you know that, Klickman? Just another fat cop with a gun. Why don't you lose a few pounds?"

Neat rows of sweat broke out across Klickman's forehead. He caught the eyes darting at him from the crowd. The elevator was barely moving. He could have strangled Mark.

Nassar was pressed into the other rear corner, and his ears were now ringing from the slap to the head. He couldn't see Mark Sway, but he could certainly hear him.

"Is your mother all right?" a nurse asked. She was standing next to Mark, looking down and very concerned.

"Yeah, she's having a great day. She'd be a lot better, of course, if these cops would leave her alone. They're taking me to jail, you know that?"

"What for?"

"I don't know. They won't tell me. I was just minding my own business, trying to console my mother because our trailer burned to the ground this morning and we lost everything we own, when they showed up with no warning, and here I am on the way to jail."

"How old are you?"

"Only eleven. But that's not important to these guys. They'd arrest a four-year-old."

Nassar groaned softly. Klickman kept his eyes closed.

"This is awful," the nurse said.

"You should've seen it when they had me and my mother on the floor. Happened just a few minutes ago on the Psychiatric Wing. It'll be on the news tonight. Watch the papers. These clowns will be fired tomorrow. Then the lawsuit."

They stopped on the ground floor, and the elevator emptied.

He insisted on riding in the rear seat, like a real criminal. The car was an unmarked Chrysler but he spotted it a hundred yards away in the parking lot. Nassar and Klickman were afraid to speak to him. They rode in the front seat in complete silence, hoping he might do the same. They were not so lucky.

"You forgot to read me my rights," he said as Nassar drove as fast as possible.

No response from the front seat.

"Hey, you clowns up there. You forgot to read me my rights."

No response. Nassar drove faster.

"Do you know *how* to read me my rights?"

No response.

"Hey, meathead. Yeah, you with the shoes. Do you know how to read me my rights?"

Klickman's breathing was labored, but he was determined to ignore him. Oddly, Nassar had a crooked smile barely noticeable under the mustache. He stopped at a red light, looked both ways, then gunned the engine.

"Listen to me, meathead, okay. I'll do it to myself, okay. I have the right to remain silent. Did you catch that? And, if I say anything, you clowns can use it against me in court. Get that, meathead? Of course, if I said anything you dumbasses would forget it. Then there's something about the right to a lawyer. Can you help with this one, meathead? Yo! meathead. What's the bit about the lawyer? I've seen it on television a million times."

Meathead Klickman cracked his window so he could breathe. Nassar glanced at the shoes and almost laughed. The criminal sat low in the rear seat with his legs crossed.

"Poor meathead. Can't even read me my rights. This car stinks, meathead. Why don't you clean this car? It smells like cigarette smoke."

"I hear you like cigarette smoke," Klickman said, and felt much better about himself. Nassar giggled to help his friend. They'd taken enough crap off this brat.

Mark saw a crowded parking lot next to a tall building. Patrol cars were parked in rows next to the building. Nassar turned into the lot and parked in the driveway.

They rushed him through the entrance doors and down a long hallway. He had finally stopped talking. He was on their turf. Cops were everywhere. Signs directed traffic to the DUI Holding Tank, the Jail, the Visitors' Room, the Receiving Room. Plenty of signs and rooms. They stopped at a desk with a row of closed-circuit monitors behind it, and Nassar signed some papers. Mark studied the surroundings. Klickman almost felt sorry for him. He looked even smaller.

They were off again. The elevator took them to the fourth floor, and again they stopped at a desk. A sign on the wall pointed to the Juvenile Wing, and Mark figured he was getting close.

A uniformed lady with a clipboard and a plastic tag declaring her to be Doreen stopped them. She looked at some papers, then at the clipboard. "Says here Judge Roosevelt wants Mark Sway in a private room," she said.

"I don't care where you put him," Nassar said. "Just take him."

She was frowning and looking at her clipboard. "Of course, Roosevelt wants all juveniles in private rooms. Thinks this is the Hilton."

"It's not?"

She ignored this, and pointed at a piece of paper for Nassar to sign. He scribbled his name hurriedly, and said, "He's all yours. God help you."

Klickman and Nassar left without a word.

"Empty your pockets, Mark," the lady said as she handed him a large metal container. He pulled out a dollar bill, some change, and a pack of gum. She counted it and wrote something on a card, which she then inserted on the end of the metal box. In a corner above the desk, two cameras captured Mark, and he could see himself on one of the dozen screens on the wall. Another lady in a uniform was stamping papers.

"Is this the jail?" Mark asked, cutting his eyes in all directions.

"We call it a detention center," she said.

"What's the difference?"

This seemed to irritate her. "Listen, Mark, we get all kinds of smart mouths up here, okay. You'll get along much better if you keep your mouth shut." She leaned into his face with these words of warning, and her breath was stale cigarettes and black coffee.

"I'm sorry," he said, and his eyes watered. It suddenly hit him. He was about to be locked in a room far away from his mother, far away from Reggie.

"Follow me," Doreen said, proud of herself for restoring a little authority to the relationship. She whisked away with a ring of keys dangling and rattling from her waist. They opened a heavy, wooden door and started through a hallway with gray metal doors spaced evenly apart on both sides of the corridor. Each little room had a number beside it. Doreen stopped at Number 16, and unlocked it with one of her keys. "In here," she said.

Mark walked in slowly. The room was about twelve feet wide and twenty feet long. The lights were bright and the carpet was clean. Two bunk beds were to his right. Doreen patted the top bunk. "You can have either bed," she said, ever the hostess. "Walls are cinder block and windows are nonbreakable, so don't try anything." There were two windows—one in the door and one above the lavatory, and neither was big enough to stick his head through. "Toilet's over there, stainless steel. Can't use ceramic anymore. Had a kid break one and slice his wrists with a piece of it. But that was in the old building. This place is much nicer, don't you think?"

It's gorgeous, Mark almost said. But he was sinking fast. He sat on the bottom bunk and rested his elbows on his knees. The carpet was pale green, the same type of commercial blend he'd been studying at the hospital.

"You okay, Mark?" Doreen asked without the slightest trace of sympathy. This was her job.

"Can I call my mother?"

"Not yet. You can make a few calls in about an hour."

"Well, can you call her and just tell her I'm okay? She's worried sick."

Doreen smiled and the makeup cracked around her eyes. She patted his head. "Can't do it, Mark. Regulations. But she knows you're fine. My goodness, you'll be in court in a couple of hours."

"How long do kids stay in here?"

"Not long. A few weeks occasionally, but this is sort of a holding area until the kids are processed and either sent back home or to a training school." She was rattling her keys. "Listen, I have to go now. The door locks automatically when it's closed, and if it opens without my little key here, then an alarm goes off and there's big trouble. So don't get any ideas, okay, Mark?"

"Yes ma'am."

"Can I get you anything?"

"A telephone."

"In just a little while, okay."

Doreen closed the door behind her. There was a loud click, then silence.

He stared at the doorknob for a long time. This didn't seem like jail. There were no bars on the windows. The beds and floor were clean. The cinder block walls were painted a pleasant shade of yellow. He'd seen worse, in the movies.

There was so much to worry about. Ricky groaning like that again, the fire, Dianne slowly unraveling, cops and reporters glued to him. He didn't know where to start.

He stretched on the top bunk and studied the ceiling. Where in the world was Reggie?

TWENTY-TWO

THE CHAPEL was cold and damp. It was a round building stuck to the side of a mausoleum like a cancerous growth. It was raining outside, and two television crews from New Orleans huddled beside their vans and hid under umbrellas.

The crowd was respectable, especially for a man with no family. His remains were packaged tastefully in a porcelain urn sitting on a mahogany table. Hidden speakers from above brought forth one dreary dirge after another as the lawyers and judges and a few clients ventured in and sat near the rear. Barry The Blade strutted down the aisle with two thugs in tow. He was properly dressed in a black double-breasted suit with a black shirt and a black tie. Black lizard shoes. His ponytail was immaculate. He arrived late, and enjoyed the stares from the mourners. After all, he'd known Jerome Clifford for a long time.

Four rows back, the Right Reverend Roy Foltrigg sat with Wally Boxx and scowled at the ponytail. The lawyers and judges looked at Muldanno, then at Foltrigg, then back at Muldanno. Strange, seeing them in the same room.

The music stopped, and a minister of some generic faith appeared in the small pulpit behind the urn. He started with a lengthy obituary of Walter Jerome Clifford, and threw in everything but the names of his childhood pets. This was not unexpected because when the obituary was over there would be little to say.

It was a brief service, just as Romey had asked for in his note. The lawyers and judges glanced at their watches. Another mournful lamentation started from above, and the minister excused everyone.

Romey's last hurrah was over in fifteen minutes. There were no tears. Even his secretary kept her composure. His daughter was not present. Very sad. He lived forty-four years and no one cried at his funeral.

Foltrigg kept his seat and scowled at Muldanno as he strutted down the aisle and out the door. Foltrigg waited until the chapel was empty, then made an exit with Wally behind him. The cameras were there, and that's exactly what he wanted. Earlier, Wally had leaked a juicy tidbit about the great Roy Foltrigg attending the service, and also that there was a chance Barry The Blade Muldanno would be present. Neither Wally nor Roy had any idea whether Muldanno would attend, but it was only a leak so who cared if it was accurate. It was working.

A reporter asked for a couple of minutes, and Foltrigg did what he always did. He glanced at his watch, looked terribly frustrated by this intrusion, and sent Wally after the van. Then he said what he always said, "Okay, but make it quick. I'm due in court in fifteen minutes." He hadn't been to court in three weeks. He usually went about once a month, but to hear him talk he lived in courtrooms, battling the bad guys, protecting the interests of the American taxpayers. A hard-charging crimebuster.

He squeezed under an umbrella and looked at the mini-cam. The reporter waved a microphone in his face. "Jerome Clifford was a rival. Why did you attend his memorial service?"

He was suddenly sad. "Jerome was a fine lawyer, and a friend of mine. We faced each other many times, but always respected each other." What a guy. Gracious even in death. He hated Jerome Clifford and Jerome Clifford hated him, but the camera saw only the heartbreak of a grieving pal.

"Mr. Muldanno has hired a new lawyer and filed a motion for a continuance. What is your response to this?"

"As you know, Judge Lamond has scheduled a hearing on the continuance request for tomorrow morning at 10 A.M. The decision will be his. The United States will be ready for trial whenever he sets it."

"Do you expect to find the body of Senator Boyette before trial?"

"Yes. I think we're getting close."

"Is it true you were in Memphis just hours after Mr. Clifford shot himself?"

"Yes." He sort of shrugged as if it was no big deal.

"There are news reports in Memphis that the kid who was with Mr. Clifford when he shot himself may know something about the Boyette case. Any truth to this?"

He smiled sheepishly, another trademark. When the answer was yes, but he couldn't say it, but he wanted to send the message anyway, he just grinned at the reporters and said, "I can't comment on that."

"I can't comment on that," he said, glancing around as if time was up and his busy trial calendar was calling.

"Does the boy know where the body is?"

"No comment," he said with irritation. The rain grew harder, and splashed on his socks and shoes. "I have to be going."

After an hour in jail, Mark was ready to escape. He inspected both windows. The one above the lavatory had some wire in it, but that did not matter. What was troubling, though, was the fact that any object exiting through this window, including a boy, would fall directly down at least fifty feet, and the fall would be stopped by a concrete sidewalk lined with chain-link fencing and barbed wire. Also, both windows were thick and too small for escape, he determined.

He would be forced to make his break when they transported him, maybe take a hostage or two. He'd seen some great movies about jailbreaks. His favorite was *Escape from Alcatraz* with Clint Eastwood. He'd figure it out.

Doreen knocked on the door, jangled her keys, and stepped inside. She held a directory and a black phone, which she plugged into the wall. "It's yours for ten minutes. No long distance." Then she was gone, the door clicking loudly behind her, the cheap perfume floating heavy in the air and burning his eyes.

He found the number for St. Peter's, asked for Room 943, and was informed that no calls were being put through to that room. Ricky's asleep, he thought. Must be bad. He found Reggie's number, and listened to Clint's voice on the recorder. He called Greenway's office, and was informed the doctor was at the hospital. Mark explained exactly who he was, and the secretary said she believed the doctor was seeing Ricky. He called Reggie again. Same recording. He left an urgent message—"Get me out of jail, Reggie!" He called her home number, and listened to another recording.

He stared at the phone. With about seven minutes left, he had to do something. He flipped through the directory, and found the listings for the Memphis Police Department. He picked the North Precinct and dialed the number.

"Detective Klickman," he said.

"Just a minute," said the voice on the other end. He held for a few seconds, then a voice said, "Who're you holding for?"

He cleared his throat and tried to sound gruff. "Detective Klickman."

"He's on duty."

"When will he be in?"

"Around lunch."

"Thanks." Mark hung up quickly, and wondered if the lines were bugged. Probably not. After all, these phones were used by criminals and people like himself to call their lawyers and talk business. There had to be privacy.

He memorized the precinct phone number and address, then flipped to the yellow pages under Restaurants. He punched a number, and a friendly voice said, "Domino's Pizza. May I take your order."

He cleared his throat and tried to sound hoarse. "Yes, I'd like to order four of your large supremes."

"Is that all?"

"Yes. Need them delivered at noon."

"Your name?"

"I'm ordering them for Detective Klickman, North Precinct."

"Delivered where?"

"North Precinct—3633 Allen Road. Just ask for Klickman."

"We've been there before, believe me. Phone number?"

"It's 555-8989."

There was a short pause as the adding machine rang it up. "That'll be forty-eight dollars and ten cents."

"Fine. Don't need it until noon."

Mark hung up, his heart pounding. But he'd done it once, and he could do it again. He found the Pizza Hut numbers, there were seventeen in Memphis, and started placing orders. Three said they were too far away from downtown. He hung up on them. One young girl was suspicious, said he sounded too young, and he hung up on her too. But for the most part it was just routine business—call, place the order, give the address and phone number, and allow free enterprise to handle the rest.

When Doreen knocked on the door twenty minutes later, he was ordering Klickman some Chinese food from Wong Boys. He quickly hung up and walked to the bunks. She took great satisfaction in removing the phone, like taking toys away from bad little boys. But she was not quick enough. Detective Klickman had ordered about forty deep dish supreme deluxe large pizzas and a dozen Chinese lunches, all to be delivered around noon, at a cost of somewhere in the neighborhood of five hundred dollars.

For his hangover, Gronke sipped his fourth orange juice of the morning and washed down another headache powder. He stood at the window of his hotel room, shoes off, belt unbuckled, shirt unbuttoned, and listened painfully as Jack Nance reported the disturbing news.

"Happened less than thirty minutes ago," Nance said, sitting on the dresser, staring at the wall, trying to ignore this goon standing at the window with his back to him.

"Why?" Gronke grunted.

"Has to be youth court. They took him straight to jail. I mean, hell, they can't just pick a kid, or anybody else for that matter, and take him straight to jail. They had to file something in youth court. Cal's there now, checking it out. Maybe we'll have it soon, I don't know. Youth court records are locked up, I think."

"Get the damned records, okay."

Nance seethed but bit his tongue. He hated Gronke and his little band of cutthroats, and even though he needed the hundred bucks an hour he was tired of hanging around this dirty, smoky room like a flunky waiting to be barked at. He had other clients. Cal was a nervous wreck.

"We're trying," he said.

"Try harder," Gronke said to the window. "Now I gotta call

Barry and tell him the kid's been taken away and there's no way to get to him. Got him locked up somewhere, probably with a cop sittin' outside his door." He finished the orange juice and tossed the can in the general direction of the wastebasket. It missed and rattled along the wall. He glared at Nance. "Barry'll wanna know if there's a way to get the kid. What would you suggest?"

"I suggest you leave the kid alone. This is not New Orleans, and this is not just some little punk you can rub out and make everything wonderful. This kid's got baggage, lots of it. People are watching him. If you do something stupid, you'll have a hundred Fibbies all over your ass. You won't be able to breathe, and you and Mr. Muldanno will rot in jail. Here, not New Orleans."

"Yeah, yeah." Gronke waved both hands at him in disgust and walked back to the window. "I want you boys to keep watching him. If they move him anywhere, I wanna know it immediately. If they take him to court, I wanna know it. Figure it out, Nance. This is your city. You know the streets and alleys. At least you're supposed to. You're gettin' paid good money."

"Yes sir," Nance said loudly, then left the room.

TWENTY-THREE

FOR TWO HOURS every Thursday morning, Reggie disappeared into the office of Dr. Elliot Levin, her longtime psychiatrist. Levin had been holding her hand for ten years. He was the architect who'd figured out the pieces and helped her put the puzzle back together. Their sessions were never disturbed.

Clint paced nervously in Levin's reception area. Dianne had called twice already. She had read the summons and petition to him over the phone. He had called Judge Roosevelt, and the detention center, and Levin's office, and now he waited impatiently for eleven o'clock. The receptionist tried to ignore him.

Reggie was smiling when Dr. Levin finished with her. She pecked him on the cheek, and they walked hand in hand into his plush reception area where Clint was waiting. She stopped smiling. "What's the matter?" she asked, certain something terrible had happened.

"We need to go," Clint said, taking her arm and ushering her through the door. She nodded good-bye to Levin, who was watching with interest and concern.

They were on a sidewalk next to a small parking lot. "They've picked up Mark Sway. He's in custody."

"What! Who!"

"Cops. A petition was filed this morning alleging Mark to be a delinquent, and Roosevelt issued an order to take him into custody." Clint was pointing. "Let's take your car. I'll drive."

"Who filed the petition?"

"Foltrigg. Dianne called from the hospital, that's where they got him. She had a big fight with the cops, and scared Ricky again. I've talked to her and assured her you'll go get Mark."

They opened and slammed doors to Reggie's car, and sped from the parking lot. "Roosevelt's scheduled a hearing for noon," Clint explained.

"Noon! You must be kidding. That's fifty-six minutes from now."

"It's an expedited hearing. I talked to him about an hour ago, and he wouldn't comment on the petition. Had very little to say, really. Where are we going?"

She thought about this for a second. "He's in the detention center, and I can't get him out. Let's go to Juvenile Court. I want to see the petition, and I want to see Harry Roosevelt. This is absurd, a hearing within hours of filing the petition. The law says between three and seven days, not three and seven hours."

"But isn't there a provision for expedited hearings?"

"Yeah, but only in extreme matters. They've fed Harry a bunch of crap. Delinquent! What's the kid done? This is crazy. They're trying to force him to talk, Clint, that's all."

"So you didn't expect this?"

"Of course not. Not here, not in Juvenile Court. I've thought about a grand jury summons for Mark from New Orleans, but not Juvenile Court. He's committed no delinquent act. He doesn't deserve to be taken in."

"Well, they got him."

Jason McThune zipped his pants, and hit the lever three times before the antique urinal flushed. The bowl was stained with streaks of brown and the floor was wet, and he thanked God he worked in the Federal Building where everything was polished and spiffy. He'd lay asphalt with a shovel before he'd work in Juvenile Court.

But he was here now, like it or not, wasting time on the Boyette case because K. O. Lewis wanted him here. And K.O. took orders from Mr. F. Denton Voyles, Director of the FBI for forty-two years now. And in his forty-two years, no member of Congress and certainly no U.S. Senator had been murdered. And the fact that the late Boyd Boyette had been hidden so neatly was galling. Mr.

Voyles was quite upset, not about the killing itself but about the FBI's inability to solve it completely.

McThune had a strong hunch Ms. Reggie Love would arrive shortly, since her client had been snatched away from right under her nose, and he figured she'd be fuming when he saw her. Maybe she'd understand that these legal strategies were being hatched in New Orleans, not Memphis, and certainly not in his office. Surely she would understand that he, McThune, was just a humble FBI agent taking orders from above and doing what the lawyers told him. Perhaps he could dodge her until they were all in the courtroom.

Perhaps not. As McThune opened the rest room door and stepped into the hallway, he was suddenly face to face with Reggie Love. Clint was a step behind her. She saw him immediately, and within seconds he was backed against the wall and she was in his face. She was agitated.

"Morning, Ms. Love," he said, forcing a calm smile.

"It's Reggie, McThune."

"Morning, Reggie."

"Who's here with you?" she asked, glaring.

"Beg your pardon."

"Your gang, your little band, your little group of government conspirators. Who's here?"

This was not a secret. He could discuss this with her. "George Ord, Thomas Fink from New Orleans, K. O. Lewis."

"Who's K. O. Lewis?"

"Deputy Director, FBI. From D.C."

"What's he doing here?" Her questions were clipped and rapid, and aimed like arrows at McThune's eyes. He was pinned to the wall, afraid to move, but gallantly trying to appear nonchalant. If Fink or Ord or heaven forbid K. O. Lewis happened into the hallway and saw him huddled with her like this he'd never recover.

"Well, I, uh—"

"Don't make me mention the tape, McThune," she said, mentioning the damned thing anyway. "Just tell me the truth."

Clint was standing behind her, holding her briefcase and watching the traffic. He appeared a bit surprised by this confrontation and the speed with which it was occurring. McThune shrugged as if he'd forgotten about the tape, and now that she mentioned it, what the hell. "I think Foltrigg's office called Mr. Lewis and asked him to come down. That's all."

"That's all? Did you guys have a little meeting with Judge Roosevelt this morning?"

"Yes, we did."

"Didn't bother to call me, did you?"

"Uh, the judge said he'd call you."

"I see. Are you planning to testify during this little hearing?" She took a step back when she asked this and McThune breathed easier.

"I'll testify if I'm called as a witness."

She stuck a finger in his face. The nail on the end of it was long, curved, carefully manicured, and painted red, and McThune watched it fearfully. "You stick with the facts, okay. One lie, however small, or one bit of unsolicited self-serving crap to the judge, or one cheap shot remark that hurts my client, and I'll slice your throat, McThune. You understand?"

He kept smiling, glancing up and down the hall as if she were a pal and they were just having a tiny disagreement. "I understand," he said, grinning.

Reggie turned and walked away with Clint by her side. McThune turned and darted back into the rest room, though he knew she wouldn't hesitate to follow him in if she wanted something.

"What was that all about?" Clint asked.

"Just keeping him honest." They wove through crowds of litigants—paternity defendants, delinquent fathers, kids in trouble—and their lawyers huddled in small packs along the hallway.

"What's the bit about the tape?"

"I didn't tell you about it?"

"No."

"I'll play it for you later. It's hysterical." She opened the door with JUDGE HARRY M. ROOSEVELT painted on it, and they entered a small cramped room with four desks in the center and rows of file cabinets around the walls. Reggie went straight for the first desk on the left where a pretty black girl was typing. The plate on her desk gave the name as Marcia Riggle. She stopped typing and smiled. "Hello, Reggie," she said.

"Hi, Marcia. Where's His Honor?"

On her birthdays, Marcia received flowers from the law offices of Reggie Love, and chocolates at Christmas. She was the right arm of Harry Roosevelt, a man so overworked he had no time to remember such things as speaking commitments and appointments and anniversaries. But Marcia always remembered. Reggie had handled her divorce two years ago. Momma Love had cooked lasagna for her.

"He's on the bench. Should be off in a few minutes. You're on for noon, you know."

"That's what I hear."

"He's tried to call you all morning."

"Well, he didn't find me. I'll wait in his office."

"Sure. You want a sandwich? I'm ordering lunch for him now."

"No, thanks." Reggie took her briefcase and asked Clint to wait in the hall and watch for Mark. It was twenty minutes before twelve, and he'd be arriving soon.

Marcia handed her a copy of the petition, and Reggie entered the judge's office as if it were hers. She closed the door behind her.

Harry and Irene Roosevelt had also eaten at Momma Love's table. Few, if any, lawyers in Memphis spent as much time in Juvenile Court as Reggie Love, and over the past four years their lawyer-judge relationship had developed from one of mutual respect to one of friendship. About the only asset Reggie had been awarded in the divorce from Joe Cardoni was four season tickets for Memphis State basketball. The threesome—Harry, Irene, and Reggie—had watched many games at the Pyramid, sometimes joined by Elliot Levin, or another male friend of Reggie's. The basketball was usually followed by cheesecake at Café Expresso in The Peabody, or, depending on Harry's mood, maybe a late dinner at Grisanti's in midtown. Harry was always hungry, always planning the next meal. Irene fussed at him about his weight, so he ate more. Reggie occasionally kidded him about it, and each time she mentioned pounds or calories, he immediately asked about Momma Love and her pastas and cheeses and cobblers.

Judges are human. They need friends. He could eat and socialize with Reggie Love or any other lawyer for that matter and maintain his unbiased judicial discretion.

She marveled at the organized debris of his office. The floor was an ancient, pale carpet, most of it covered with neat stacks of briefs and other legal wisdoms all somehow cropped off at the height of twelve inches. Saggy bookshelves lined two walls, but the books could not be seen for the files and more stacks of briefs and memos tucked in front of books with inches hanging perilously in mid-air. Red and manila files were crammed everywhere. Three old wooden chairs sat pitifully before the desk. One had files on it. One had files under it. One was vacant for the moment, but would doubtless be used for some type of storage by the end of the day. She sat on this one and looked at the desk.

Though it was allegedly made of wood, none was visible except for the front and side panels. The top could be leather or chrome, no one would ever know. Harry himself could not remember what the top of his desk looked like. The upper level was another of Marcia's neat rows of legal papers, cropped at eight inches. Twelve inches for the floor, eight for the desk. Underneath and next in depth was a huge daily calendar for 1986, which Harry had once used to draw and doodle while listening to lawyers bore him with their arguments. Under the calendar was no-man's-land. Even Marcia was afraid to go deeper.

She'd stuck a dozen notes on yellow Post-it pads to the back of his chair. Evidently, these were the most urgent of the morning's emergencies.

Despite the chaos of his office, Harry Roosevelt was the most organized judge Reggie had encountered in her four-year career. He was not forced to spend time studying the law because he'd written most of it. He was known for the economy of his words, so his orders and decrees tended to be lean by judicial standards. He didn't tolerate lengthy briefs written by lawyers, and he was abrupt with those who loved to hear themselves talk. He managed his time wisely, and Marcia took care of the rest. His desk and office were somewhat famous in Memphis legal circles, and Reggie suspected he enjoyed this. She admired him immensely, not just for his wisdom and integrity, but also for his dedication to this office. He could've moved up many years ago to a stuffier place on the bench with a fancy desk, and clerks and paralegals, and clean carpet, and dependable air-conditioning.

She flipped through the petition. Foltrigg and Fink were the petitioners, their signatures at the bottom. Nothing detailed, just broad, sweeping allegations about the juvenile, Mark Sway, obstructing a federal investigation by refusing to cooperate with the FBI and the U.S. Attorney's office for the Southern District of Louisiana. She despised Foltrigg every time she saw his name.

But it could be worse. Foltrigg's name could be at the bottom of a grand jury subpoena demanding the appearance of Mark Sway in New Orleans. It would be perfectly legal and proper for Foltrigg to do this, and she was a bit surprised he had chosen Memphis as his forum. New Orleans would be next if this didn't work.

The door opened, and a massive black robe lumbered in with Marcia in pursuit, holding a list and clicking off things that had to be done immediately. He listened without looking at her, unzipped the robe and threw it at a chair, the one with the files under it.

"Good morning, Reggie," he said with a smile. He patted her on the shoulder as he walked behind her. "That'll be all," he said calmly to Marcia, who closed the door and left. He picked the little yellow notes from his chair without reading them, then fell in it.

"How's Momma Love?" he asked.

"She's fine. And you?"

"Marvelous. Not surprised to see you here."

"You didn't have to sign a custody order. I would've brought him here, Harry, you know that. He fell asleep last night in the swing on Momma Love's porch. He's in good hands."

Harry smiled and rubbed his eyes. Very few lawyers called him Harry in his office. But he rather enjoyed it when it came from her. "Reggie, Reggie. You never believe your clients should be taken into custody."

"That's not true."

"You think all's well if you can just take them home and feed them."

"It helps."

"Yes, it does. But according to Mr. Ord and the FBI, little Mark Sway could be in a world of danger."

"What'd they tell you?"

"It'll come out during the hearing."

"They must've been pretty convincing, Harry. I get an hour's notice of the hearing. That has to be a record."

"I thought you'd like that. We can do it tomorrow if you'd prefer. I don't mind making Mr. Ord wait."

"Not with Mark in custody. Release him to my custody, and we'll do the hearing tomorrow. I need some time to think."

"I'm afraid to release him until I hear proof."

"Why?"

"According to the FBI, there are some very dangerous people now in the city who may want to shut him up. Do you know a Mr. Gronke, and his pals Bono and Pirini? Ever hear of these guys?"

"No."

"Neither had I, until this morning. It seems that these gentleman have arrived in our fair city from New Orleans, and that they're close associates of Mr. Barry Muldanno, or The Blade, as I believe he's known down there. Thank god organized crime never found Memphis. This scares me, Reggie, really scares me. These men do not play games."

"Scares me too."

"Has he been threatened?"

"Yes. It happened yesterday at the hospital. He told me about it, and he's been with me ever since."

"So now you're a bodyguard."

"No, I'm not. But I don't think the code gives you the authority to order custody of children who may be in danger."

"Reggie, dear, I wrote the code. I can issue a custody order for any child alleged to be delinquent."

True, he wrote the law. And the appellate courts had long since ceased second-guessing Harry Roosevelt.

"And according to Foltrigg and Fink, what are Mark's sins?"

Harry snatched two tissues from a drawer and blew his nose. He smiled at her again. "He can't keep quiet, Reggie. If he knows something, he must tell them. You know that."

"You're assuming he knows something."

"I'm not assuming anything. The petition makes certain allegations, and these allegations are based partly on fact and partly on assumption. Same as all petitions, I guess. Wouldn't you say? We never know the truth until we have the hearing."

"How much of Slick Moeller's crap do you believe?"

"I believe nothing, Reggie, until it is told to me, under oath, in my courtroom, and then I believe about ten percent of it."

There was a long pause as the judge debated whether to ask the question. "So, Reggie, what does the kid know?"

"You know it's privileged, Harry."

He smiled. "So, he knows more than he should."

"You could say that."

"If it's crucial to the investigation, Reggie, then he must tell."

"What if he refuses?"

"I don't know. We'll deal with that when it happens. How smart is this kid?"

"Very. Broken home, no father, working mother, grew up on the streets. The usual. I talked to his fifth-grade teacher yesterday, and he makes all A's except for math. He's very bright, besides being street smart."

"No prior trouble."

"None. He's a great kid, Harry. Remarkable, really."

"Most of your clients are remarkable, Reggie."

"This one is special. He's here through no fault of his own."

"I hope he'll be fully advised by his lawyer. The hearing could get rough."

"Most of my clients are fully advised."

"They certainly are."

There was a brief knock at the door and Marcia appeared. "Your client is here, Reggie. Witness Room C."

"Thanks." She stood and walked to the door. "I'll see you in a few minutes, Harry."

"Yes. Listen to me. I'm tough on kids who don't obey me."

"I know."

He sat in a chair leaning against the wall, with his arms folded across his chest and a frustrated look on his face. He'd been treated like a convict for three hours now, and he was getting used to it. He felt safe. He hadn't been beaten by the cops or by his fellow inmates.

The room was tiny with no windows and bad lighting. Reggie entered and moved a folding chair near him. She'd been in this room under these circumstances many times. He smiled at her, obviously relieved.

"So how's jail?" she asked.

"They haven't fed me yet. Can we sue them?"

"Maybe. How's Doreen, the lady with the keys?"

"A real snot. How do you know her?"

"I've been there many times, Mark. It's my job. Her husband is serving thirty years in prison for bank robbery."

"Good. I'll ask her about him if I see her again. Am I going back there, Reggie? I'd like to know what's going on, you know."

"Well, it's very simple. We'll have a hearing before Judge Harry Roosevelt in a few moments, in his courtroom, that may last a couple of hours. The U.S. Attorney and the FBI are claiming you possess important information, and I think we can expect them to ask the judge to make you talk."

"Can the judge make me talk?"

Reggie was speaking very slowly and carefully. He was an eleven-year-old child, a smart one with plenty of street sense, but she'd seen many like him and knew that, at this moment, he was nothing but a scared little boy. He might hear her words, and he might not. Or, he might hear what he wanted to hear, so she had to be careful.

"No one can make you talk."

"Good."

"But the judge can put you back in the same little room if you don't talk."

"Back in jail!"

"That's right."

"I don't understand. I haven't done a damned thing wrong, and I'm in jail. I just don't understand this."

"It's very simple. If, and I emphasize the word *if,* Judge Roosevelt instructs you to answer certain questions, and *if* you refuse, then he can hold you in contempt of court for not answering, for disobeying him. Now, I've never known an eleven-year-old kid to be held in contempt, but if you were an adult and you refused to answer the judge's questions, then you'd go to jail for contempt."

"But I'm a kid."

"Yes, but I don't think he'll allow you to go free if you refuse to answer the questions. You see, Mark, the law is very clear in this area. A person who has knowledge of information crucial to a criminal investigation cannot withhold this information because he feels threatened. In other words, you can't keep quiet because you're afraid of what might happen to you or your family."

"That's a stupid law."

"I don't really agree with it either, but that's not important. It is the law, and there are no exceptions, not even for kids."

"So I get thrown in jail for contempt?"

"It's very possible."

"Can we sue the judge, or do something else to get me out?"

"No. You can't sue the judge. And Judge Roosevelt is a very good and fair man."

"I can't wait to meet him."

"It won't be long now."

Mark thought about all this. His chair rocked methodically against the wall. "How long would I be in jail?"

"Assuming, of course, you're sent there, probably until you decide to comply with the judge's orders. Until you talk."

"Okay. What if I decide not to talk. How long will I stay in jail? A month? A year? Ten years?"

"I can't answer that, Mark. No one knows."

"The judge doesn't know?"

"No. If he sends you to jail for contempt, I doubt if he has any idea how long he'll make you stay."

Another long pause. He'd spent three hours in Doreen's little room, and it wasn't such a bad place. He'd seen movies about prison in which gangs fought and rampaged and homemade weapons were used to kill snitches. Guards tortured inmates. Inmates attacked each other. Hollywood at its finest. But this place wasn't so bad.

And look at the alternative. With no place to call home, the Sway family now lived in Room 943 of St. Peter's Charity Hospital. But the thought of Ricky and his mother all alone and struggling without him was unbearable. "Have you talked to my mother?" he asked.

"No, not yet. I will after the hearing."

"I'm worried about Ricky."

"Do you want your mother present in the courtroom when we have this hearing? She needs to be here."

"No. She's got enough stuff on her mind. You and I can handle this mess."

She touched his knee, and wanted to cry. Someone knocked on the door, and she said loudly, "Just a minute."

"The judge is ready," came the reply.

Mark breathed deeply and stared at her hand on his knee. "Can I just take the Fifth Amendment?"

"No. It won't work, Mark. I've already thought about it. The questions will not be asked to incriminate you. They will be asked for the purpose of gathering information you may have."

"I don't understand."

"I don't blame you. Listen to me carefully, Mark. I'll try to explain it. They want to know what Jerome Clifford told you before he died. They will ask you some very specific questions about the events immediately before the suicide. They will ask you what, if anything, Clifford told you about Senator Boyette. Nothing you tell them with your answers will in any way incriminate you in the murder of Senator Boyette. Understand? You had nothing to do with it. And, you had nothing to do with the suicide of Jerome Clifford. You broke no laws, okay? You're not a suspect in any crime or wrongdoing. Your answers cannot incriminate you. So, you cannot hide under the protection of the Fifth Amendment." She paused and watched him closely. "Understand?"

"No. If I didn't do anything wrong, why was I picked up by the cops and taken to jail? Why am I sitting here waiting for a hearing?"

"You're here because they think you know something valuable, and because, as I stated, every person has a duty to assist law enforcement officials in the course of their investigation."

"I still say it's a stupid law."

"Maybe so. But we can't change it today."

He rocked forward and sat the chair on all fours. "I need to know something, Reggie. Why can't I just tell them I know nothing? Why can't I say that me and old Romey talked about suicide and going to heaven and hell, you know, stuff like that."

"Tell lies?"

"Yeah. It'll work, you know. Nobody knows the truth but Romey, me, and you. Right? And Romey, bless his heart, ain't talking."

"You can't lie in court, Mark." She said this with all the sincerity she could muster. Hours of sleep had been lost trying to formulate the answer to this inevitable question. She wanted so badly to say "Yes! That's it! Lie, Mark, lie!"

Her stomach ached and her hands almost shook, but she held firm. "I cannot allow you to lie to the court. You'll be under oath, so you must tell the truth."

"Then it was a mistake to hire you, wasn't it?"

"I don't think so."

"Sure it was. You're making me tell the truth, and in this case the truth might get me killed. If you weren't around, I'd march in there and lie my little butt off and me and Mom and Ricky would all be safe."

"You can fire me if you like. The court will appoint another lawyer."

He stood and walked to the darkest corner of the room, and began crying. She watched his head sink and his shoulders sag. He covered his eyes with the back of his right hand, and sobbed loudly.

Though she'd seen it many times, the sight of a child scared and suffering was unbearable. She couldn't keep from crying too.

TWENTY-FOUR

TWO DEPUTIES escorted him into the courtroom from a side door, away from the main hallway where the curious were known to lurk, but Slick Moeller anticipated this little maneuver and watched it all from behind a newspaper just a few feet away.

Reggie followed her client and the deputies. Clint waited outside. It was almost a quarter after noon, and the jungle of Juvenile Court had quieted a bit for lunch.

The courtroom was of a shape and design Mark had never seen on television. It was so small! And empty. There were no benches or seats for spectators. The judge sat behind an elevated structure between two flags with the wall just behind him. Two tables were in the center of the room, facing the judge, and one was already occupied with men in dark suits. To the judge's right was a tiny table where an older woman was flipping through a stack of papers, very bored with it all, it seemed, until he entered the room. A gorgeous young lady sat ready with a stenographic machine directly in front of the judge's bench. She wore a short skirt and her legs were attracting a lot of attention. She couldn't be older than sixteen, he thought as he followed Reggie to their table. A bailiff with a gun on his hip was the final actor in the play.

Mark took his seat, very much aware that everyone was staring at him. His two deputies left the room, and when the door closed behind them the judge picked up the file again and flipped through it. They had been waiting on the juvenile and his lawyer, and now it was time for everyone to wait for the judge again. Rules of courtroom etiquette must be followed.

Reggie pulled a single legal pad from her briefcase and began writing notes. She held a tissue in one hand, and dabbed her eyes with it. Mark stared at the table, eyes still wet but determined to suck it up and be tough through this ordeal. People were watching.

Fink and Ord stared at the court reporter's legs. The skirt was halfway between knee and hip. It was tight and seemed to slide upward just a fraction of an inch every minute or so. The tripod holding her recording machine sat firmly between her knees. In the coziness of Harry's courtroom, she was fewer than ten feet away, and the last thing they needed was a distraction. But they kept staring. There! It slipped upward another quarter of an inch.

Baxter L. McLemore, a young attorney fresh from law school, sat nervously at the table with Mr. Fink and Mr. Ord. He was a lowly assistant with the county Attorney General's office, and it had fallen to his lot to prosecute on this day in Juvenile Court. This was certainly not the glamorous end of prosecution, but sitting next to George Ord was quite a thrill. He knew nothing about the Sway case, and Mr. Ord had explained in the hallway just minutes earlier that Mr. Fink would handle the hearing. With the court's permission, of course. Baxter was expected to sit there and look nice, and keep his mouth shut.

"Is the door locked?" the judge finally asked in the general direction of the bailiff.

"Yes sir."

"Very well. I have reviewed the petition, and I am ready to proceed. For the record, I note the child is present along with counsel, and that the child's mother, who is alleged to be his custodial parent, was served with a copy of the petition and a summons this morning. However, the child's mother is not present in the courtroom, and this concerns me." Harry paused for a moment and seemed to read from the file.

Fink decided this was the appropriate time to establish himself in this matter, and he stood slowly, buttoning his jacket, and addressed the court. "Your Honor, if I may, for the record, I'm Thomas Fink, Assistant U.S. Attorney for the Southern District of Louisiana."

Harry's gaze slowly left the file and settled on Fink, who was standing stiff-backed, very formal, frowning intelligently as he spoke, still fiddling with the top button of his jacket.

Fink continued. "I am one of the petitioners in this matter, and, if I may, I would like to address the issue of the presence of the child's mother." Harry said nothing, just stared as if in disbelief. Reggie couldn't help but smile. She winked at Baxter McLemore.

Harry leaned forward, and rested on his elbows as if intrigued by these great words of wisdom flowing from this gifted legal mind.

Fink had found an audience. "Your Honor, it's our position, the position of the petitioners, that this matter is of a nature so urgent that this hearing must take place immediately. The child is represented by counsel, quite competent counsel I might add, and none of the child's legal rights will be prejudiced by the absence of his mother. From what we understand, the mother's presence is required by the bedside of her youngest son, and so, well, who knows when she might be able to attend a hearing. We just think it's important, Your Honor, to proceed immediately with this hearing."

"You don't say?" Harry asked.

"Yes sir. This is our position."

"Your position, Mr. Fink," Harry said very slowly and very loudly with a pointed finger, "is in that chair right there. Please sit, and listen to me very carefully, because I will only say this once. And if I have to say it again, I will do so as they are putting the handcuffs on you and taking you away for a night in our splendid jail."

Fink fell into his chair, mouth open, gaping in disbelief.

Harry scowled over his reading glasses and looked straight down at Thomas Fink. "Listen to me, Mr. Fink. This is not some fancy courtroom in New Orleans, and I am not one of your federal judges. This is my little private courtroom, and I make the rules, Mr. Fink. Rule number one is that you speak only in my courtroom when you are first spoken to by me. Rule number two is that you do not grace His Honor with unsolicited speeches, comments, or remarks. Rule number three is that His Honor does not like to hear the voices of lawyers. His Honor has been hearing these voices for twenty years, and His Honor knows how lawyers love to hear themselves talk. Rule number four is that you do not stand in my courtroom. You sit at that table and say as little as possible. Do you understand these rules, Mr. Fink?"

Fink stared blankly at Harry and tried to nod.

Harry wasn't finished. "This is a tiny courtroom, Mr. Fink, designed by myself a long time ago for private hearings. We can all see and hear each other just fine, so just keep your mouth shut and your butt in your seat, and we'll get along fine."

Fink was still trying to nod. He gripped the arms of the chair, determined never to rise again. Behind him, McThune, the lawyer hater, barely suppressed a smile.

"Mr. McLemore, I understand Mr. Fink wants to handle this case for the prosecution. Is this agreeable?"

"Okay with me, Your Honor."

"I'll allow it. But try and keep him in his seat."

Mark was terrified. He had hoped for a kind, gentle old man with lots of love and sympathy. Not this. He glanced at Mr. Fink, whose neck was crimson and whose breathing was loud and heavy, and he almost felt sorry for him.

"Ms. Love," the judge said, suddenly very warm and compassionate, "I understand you may have an objection on behalf of the child."

"Yes, Your Honor." She leaned forward and spoke deliberately in the direction of the court reporter. "We have several objections we'd like to make at this time, and I want them in the record."

"Certainly," Harry said, as if Reggie Love could have anything she wanted. Fink sank lower and felt even dumber. So much for impressing the court with an initial burst of eloquence.

Reggie glanced at her notes. "Your Honor, I request the transcript of these proceedings be typed and prepared as soon as possible to facilitate an emergency appeal if necessary."

"So ordered."

"I object to this hearing on several grounds. First, inadequate notice has been given to the child, his mother, and to his lawyer. About three hours have passed since the petition was served upon the child's mother, and though I have represented the child for three days now, and everyone involved has known this, I was not notified of this hearing until seventy-five minutes ago. This is unfair, absurd, and an abuse of discretion by the court."

"When would you like to have the hearing, Ms. Love?" Harry asked.

"Today's Thursday," she said. "What about Tuesday or Wednesday of next week?"

"That's fine. Say Tuesday at nine." Harry looked at Fink, who still hadn't moved and was afraid to respond to this. "Of course, Ms. Love, the child will remain in custody until then."

"The child does not belong in custody, Your Honor."

"But I've signed a custody order, and I will not rescind it while we wait on a hearing. Our laws, Ms. Love, provide for the immediate taking of alleged delinquents, and your client is being treated no differently from others. Plus, there are other considerations for Mark Sway, and I'm sure these will be discussed shortly."

"Then I cannot agree on a continuance if my client will remain in custody."

"Very well," His Honor said properly. "Let the record reflect a continuance was offered by the court and declined by the child."

"And let the record also reflect the child declined a continuance because the child does not wish to remain in the Juvenile Detention Center any longer than he has to."

"So noted," Harry said with a slight grin. "Please proceed, Ms. Love."

"We also object to this hearing because the child's mother is not present. Due to extreme circumstances, her presence is not possible at this time, and keep in mind, Your Honor, the poor woman was first notified barely three hours ago. The child here is eleven years old and deserves the assistance of his mother. As you know, Your Honor, our laws strongly favor the presence of the parents in these hearings, and to proceed without Mark's mother is unfair."

"When can Ms. Sway be available?"

"No one knows, Your Honor. She is literally confined to the hospital room with her son who's suffering from post-traumatic stress. Her doctor allows her out of the room only for minutes at a time. It could be weeks before she's available."

"So you want to postpone this hearing indefinitely?"

"Yes sir."

"All right. You've got it. Of course, the child will remain in custody pending the hearing."

"The child does not belong in custody. The child will make

himself available any time the court wants. There's nothing to be gained by keeping the child locked up until a hearing."

"There are complicating factors in this case, Ms. Love, and I'm not inclined to release this child before we have this hearing and it's determined how much he knows. It's that simple. I'm afraid to release him at this time. If I did so, and if something happened to him, I'd carry the guilt to my grave. Do you understand this, Ms. Love?"

She understood, though she wouldn't admit it. "I'm afraid you're making this decision based on facts not in evidence."

"Maybe so. But I have wide discretion in these matters, and until I hear the proof I'm not inclined to release him."

"That'll look good on appeal," she snapped, and Harry didn't like it.

"Let the record reflect a continuance was offered to the child until his mother could be present, and the continuance was declined by the child."

To which Reggie quickly responded, "And also let the record reflect the child declined the continuance because the child does not wish to remain in the Juvenile Detention Center any longer than he has to."

"So noted, Ms. Love. Please continue."

"The child moves this court to dismiss the petition filed against him on the grounds that the allegations are without merit and the petition has been filed in an effort to explore things the child *might* know. The petitioners, Fink and Foltrigg, are using this hearing as a fishing expedition for their desperate criminal investigation. Their petition is a hopeless mishmash of maybes and what ifs, and filed under oath without the slightest hint of the real truth. They're desperate, Your Honor, and they're here shooting in the dark hoping they hit something. The petition should be dismissed, and we should all go home."

Harry glared down at Fink, and said, "I'm inclined to agree with her, Mr. Fink. What about it?"

Fink had settled into his chair and watched with comfort as Reggie's first two objections had been shot down by His Honor. His breathing almost returned to normal and his face had gone from crimson to pink, when suddenly the judge was agreeing with her and staring at him.

Fink bolted to the edge of his chair, almost stood but caught himself, and started stuttering. "Well, uh, Your Honor, we, uh, can prove our allegations if given the chance. We, uh, believe what we've said in the petition—"

"I certainly hope so," Harry sneered.

"Yes sir, and we know that this child is impeding an investigation. Yes sir, we are confident we can prove what we've alleged."

"And if you can't?"

"Well, I, uh, we, feel sure that—"

"You realize, Mr. Fink, that if I hear the proof in this case and find you're playing games, I can hold you in contempt. And, knowing Ms. Love the way I do, I'm sure there will be retribution from the child."

"We intend to file suit first thing in the morning, Your Honor," Reggie added helpfully. "Against both Mr. Fink and Roy Foltrigg. They're abusing this court and the juvenile laws of the state of Tennessee. My staff is working on the lawsuit right now."

Her staff was sitting outside in the hallway eating a Snickers bar and sipping a diet cola. But the threat sounded ominous in the courtroom.

Fink glanced at George Ord, his co-counsel, who was sitting next to him making a list of things to do that afternoon, and nothing on the list had anything to do with Mark Sway or Roy Foltrigg. Ord supervised twenty-eight lawyers working thousands of cases, and he just didn't care about Barry Muldanno and the body of Boyd Boyette. It wasn't in his jurisdiction. Ord was a busy man, too busy to waste valuable time playing gofer for Roy Foltrigg.

But Fink was no featherweight. He'd seen his share of nasty trials and hostile judges and skeptical juries. He was rallying quite nicely. "Your Honor, the petition is much like an indictment. Its truth cannot be ascertained without a hearing, and if we can get on with it we can prove our allegations."

Harry turned to Reggie. "I'll take this motion to dismiss under advisement, and I'll hear the petitioners' proof. If it falls short, then I'll grant the motion and we'll go from there."

Reggie shrugged as if she expected this.

"Anything else, Ms. Love?"

"Not at this time."

"Call your first witness, Mr. Fink," Harry said. "And make it brief. Get right to the point. If you waste time, I'll jump in with both feet and speed things along."

"Yes sir. Sergeant Milo Hardy of the Memphis Police is our first witness."

Mark had not moved during these preliminary skirmishes. He wasn't sure if Reggie had won them all, or lost them all, and for some reason he didn't care. There was something unfair about a system in which a little kid was brought into a courtroom and surrounded by lawyers arguing and sniping at each other under the scornful eye of a judge, the referee, and somehow in the midst of this barrage of laws and code sections and motions and legal talk the kid was supposed to know what was happening to him. It was hopelessly unfair.

And so he just sat and stared at the floor near the court reporter. His eyes were still wet and he couldn't make them stay dry.

The courtroom was silent as Sergeant Hardy was fetched. His Honor relaxed in his chair and removed his reading glasses. "I want this on the record," he said. He glared at Fink again. "This is a private and confidential matter. This hearing is closed for a reason. I defy anyone to repeat any word uttered in this room today, or to discuss any aspect of this proceeding. Now, Mr. Fink, I realize you must report to the U.S. Attorney in New Orleans, and I realize Mr. Foltrigg is a petitioner and has a right to know what happens here. And when you talk to him, please explain that I am very upset by his absence. He signed the petition, and he should be here. You may explain these proceedings to him, and only to him. No one else. And you are to tell him to keep his big mouth shut, do you understand, Mr. Fink?"

"Yes, Your Honor."

"Will you explain to Mr. Foltrigg that if I get wind of any breach in the confidentiality of these proceedings that I will issue a contempt order and attempt to have him jailed?"

"Yes, Your Honor."

He was suddenly staring at McThune and K. O. Lewis. They were seated immediately behind Fink and Ord.

"Mr. McThune and Mr. Lewis, you may now leave the courtroom," Harry said abruptly. They grabbed the armrests as their feet hit the floor. Fink turned and stared at them, then looked at the judge.

"Uh, Your Honor, would it be possible for these gentlemen to remain in the—"

"I told them to leave, Mr. Fink," Harry said loudly. "If they're gonna be witnesses, we'll call them later. If they're not witnesses, they have no business here and they can wait in the hall with the rest of the herd. Now, move along, gentlemen."

McThune was practically jogging for the door, without the slightest hint of wounded pride, but K. O. Lewis was pissed. He buttoned his jacket and stared at His Honor, but only for a second. No one had ever won a staring contest with Harry Roosevelt, and K. O. Lewis was not about to try. He strutted for the door, which was already open as McThune dashed through it.

Seconds later, Sergeant Hardy entered and sat in the witness chair. He was in full uniform. He shifted his wide ass in the padded seat, and waited. Fink was frozen, afraid to begin without being told to do so.

Judge Roosevelt rolled his chair to the end of the bench and peered down at Hardy. Something had caught his attention, and Hardy sat like a fat toad on a stool until he realized His Honor was just inches away.

"Why are you wearing the gun?" Harry asked.

Hardy looked up, startled, then jerked his head to his right hip as if the gun was a complete surprise to him also. He stared at it as if the damned thing had somehow stuck itself to his body.

"Well, I—"

"Are you on duty or off, Sergeant Hardy?"

"Well, off."

"Then why are you wearing a uniform, and why in the world are you wearing a gun in my courtroom?"

Mark smiled for the first time in hours.

The bailiff had caught on and was rapidly approaching the witness stand as Hardy jerked at his belt and removed the holster. The bailiff carried it away as if it were a murder weapon.

"Have you ever testified in court?" Harry asked.

Hardy smiled like a child and said, "Yes sir, many times."

"You have?"

"Yes sir. Many times."

"And how many times have you testified while wearing your gun?"

"Sorry, Your Honor."

Harry relaxed, looked at Fink, and waved at Hardy as if it was now permissible to get on with it. Fink had spent many hours in courtrooms during the past twenty years, and took great pride in his trial skills. His record was impressive. He was glib and smooth, quick on his feet.

But he was slow on his ass, and this sitting while interrogating a witness was such a radical way of finding truth. He almost stood again, caught himself again, and grabbed his legal pad. His frustration was apparent.

"Would you state your name for the record?" he asked in a short, rapid burst.

"Sergeant Milo Hardy, Memphis Police Department."

"And what is your address?"

Harry held up a hand to cut off Hardy. "Mr. Fink, why do you need to know where this man lives?"

Fink stared in disbelief. "I guess, Your Honor, it's just a routine question."

"Do you know how much I hate routine questions, Mr. Fink?"

"I'm beginning to understand."

"Routine questions lead us nowhere, Mr. Fink. Routine questions waste hours and hours of valuable time. I do not want to hear another routine question. Please."

"Yes, Your Honor. I'll try."

"I know it's hard."

Fink looked at Hardy and tried desperately to think of a brilliantly original question. "Last Monday, Sergeant, were you dispatched to the scene of a shooting?"

Harry held up his hand again, and Fink slumped in his seat. "Mr. Fink, I don't know how you folks do things in New Orleans, but here in Memphis we make our witnesses swear to tell the truth before they start testifying. It's called, 'Placing them under oath.' Does that sound familiar?"

Fink rubbed his temples and said, "Yes sir. Could the witness please be sworn?"

The elderly woman at the desk suddenly came to life. She sprang to her feet and yelled at Hardy, who was less than fifteen feet away. "Raise your right hand!"

Hardy did this, and was sworn to tell the truth. She returned to her seat, and to her nap.

"Now, Mr. Fink, you may proceed," Harry said with a nasty little smile, very pleased that he'd caught Fink with his pants down. He relaxed in his massive seat, and listened intently to the rapid question and answer routine that followed.

Hardy spoke in a chatty voice, eager to help, full of little details. He described the scene of the suicide, the position of the body, the condition of the car. There were photographs, if His Honor would like to see them. His Honor declined. They were completely irrelevant. Hardy produced a typed transcript of the 911 call made by Mark, and offered to play the recording if His Honor would like to hear it. No, His Honor said.

Then Hardy explained with great joy the capture of young Mark in the woods near the scene, and of their ensuing conversations in his car, at the Sway trailer, en route to the hospital, and over dinner in the cafeteria. He described his gut feelings that young Mark was not telling the complete truth. The kid's story was flimsy, and through skillful interrogation with just the right touch of subtlety, he, Hardy, was able to poke all sorts of holes in it.

The lies were pathetic. The kid said he and his brother stumbled upon the car and the dead body; that they did not hear any gunshots; that they were just a couple of kids playing in the woods, minding their own business, and somehow they found this body. Of course, none of Mark's story was true, and Hardy was quick to catch on.

With great detail, Hardy described the condition of Mark's face, the swollen eye and puffy lip, the blood around the mouth. Kid said he'd been in a fight at school. Another sad little lie.

After thirty minutes, Harry grew restless and Fink took the hint. Reggie had no cross-examination, and when Hardy stepped down and left the room there was no doubt that Mark Sway was a liar who'd tried to deceive the cops. Things would get worse.

When His Honor had asked Reggie if she had any questions for Sergeant Hardy, she simply said, "I've had no time to prepare for this witness."

McThune was called as the next witness. He gave his oath to tell the truth and sat in the witness chair. Reggie slowly reached into her briefcase and withdrew a cassette tape. She held it casually in her hand, and when McThune glanced at her she tapped it softly on her legal pad. He closed his eyes.

She carefully placed the tape on the pad, and began tracing its edges with her pen.

Fink was quick, to the point, and by now fairly adept at avoiding even vaguely routine questions. It was a new experience for him, this efficient use of words, and the more he did it the more he liked it.

McThune was as dry as cornmeal. He explained the fingerprints they found all over the car, and on the gun and the bottle, and on the rear bumper. He speculated about the kids and the garden hose, and showed Harry the Virginia Slims cigarette butts found under the tree. He also showed Harry the suicide note left behind by Clifford, and again gave his thoughts about the additional words added by a different pen. He showed Harry the Bic pen found in the car, and said there was no doubt Mr. Clifford had used this pen to scrawl these words. He talked about the speck of blood found on Clifford's hand. It wasn't Clifford's blood, but was of the same type as Mark Sway's, who just happened to have a busted lip and a couple of wounds from the affair.

"You think Mr. Clifford struck the child at some point during all this?" Harry asked.

"I think so, Your Honor."

McThune's thoughts and opinions and speculations were objectionable, but Reggie kept quiet. She'd been through many of these hearings with Harry, and she knew he would hear it all and decide what to believe. Objecting would do no good.

Harry asked how the FBI obtained a fingerprint from the child to match those found in the car. McThune took a deep breath, and told about the Sprite can at the hospital, but was quick to point out that they were not investigating the child as a suspect when this happened, just as a witness, and so therefore they felt it was okay to lift the print. Harry didn't like this at all, but said nothing. McThune emphasized that if the child had been an actual suspect, they would never have dreamed of stealing a print. Never.

"Of course you wouldn't," Harry said with enough sarcasm to make McThune blush.

Fink walked him through the events of Tuesday, the day after the suicide, when young Mark hired a lawyer. They tried desperately to talk with him, then to his lawyer, and things just deteriorated.

McThune behaved himself and stuck to the facts. He left the room in a quick dash for the door, and he left behind the undeniable fact that young Mark was quite a liar.

From time to time, Harry watched Mark during the testimony of Hardy and McThune. The kid was impassive, hard to read, preoccupied with an invisible spot somewhere on the floor. He sat low in his seat and ignored Reggie for the most part. His eyes were wet, but he was not crying. He looked tired and sad, and occasionally glanced at the witness when his lies were emphasized.

Harry had watched Reggie many times under these circumstances, and she usually sat very close to her young clients and whispered to them as the hearings progressed. She would pat them, squeeze their arms, give reassurances, lecture them if necessary. Normally, she was in constant motion, protecting her clients from the harsh reality of a legal system run by adults. But not today. She glanced at her client occasionally as if waiting for a signal, but he ignored her.

"Call your next witness," Harry said to Fink, who was resting on his elbows, trying not to stand. He looked at Ord for help, then at His Honor.

"Well, Your Honor, this may sound a bit strange, but I'd like to testify next."

Harry ripped off his reading glasses and glared at Fink. "You're confused, Mr. Fink. You're the lawyer, not a witness."

"I know that, sir, but I'm also the petitioner, and, I know this may be a bit out of order, but I think my testimony could be important."

"Thomas Fink, petitioner, lawyer, witness. You wanna play bailiff, Mr. Fink? Maybe take down a bit of stenography? Perhaps wear my robe for a while? This is not a courtroom, Mr. Fink, it's a theater. Why don't you just choose any role you like?"

Fink stared blankly at the bench without making eye contact with His Honor. "I can explain, sir," he said meekly.

"You don't have to explain, Mr. Fink. I'm not blind. You boys have rushed in here half-ass prepared. Mr. Foltrigg should be here, but he's not, and now you need him. You figured you could throw together a petition, bring in some FBI brass, hook in Mr. Ord here, and I'd be so impressed I'd just roll over and do anything you asked. Can I tell you something, Mr. Fink?"

Fink nodded.

"I'm not impressed. I've seen better work at high school mock trial competitions. Half the first-year law students at Memphis State could kick your butt, and the other half could kick Mr. Foltrigg's."

Fink was not agreeing, but he kept nodding for some reason. Ord slid his chair a few inches away from Fink's.

"What about it, Ms. Love?" Harry asked.

"Your Honor, our rules of procedure and ethics are quite clear. An attorney trying a case cannot participate in the same trial as a witness. It's simple." She sounded bored and frustrated, as if everyone should know this.

"Mr. Fink?"

Fink was regaining himself. "Your Honor, I would like to tell the court, under oath, certain facts regarding Mr. Clifford's actions prior to the suicide. I apologize for this request, but under the circumstances it cannot be helped."

There was a knock on the door, and the bailiff opened it slightly. Marcia entered carrying a plate covered with a thick roast beef sandwich and a tall plastic glass of ice tea. She sat it before His Honor, who thanked her, and she was gone.

It was almost one o'clock, and suddenly everyone was starving. The roast beef and horseradish and pickles, and the side order of onion rings, emitted an appetizing aroma that wafted around the room. All eyes were on the kaiser roll, and as Harry picked it up to take a huge bite, he saw young Mark Sway watching his every move. He stopped the sandwich in mid-air, and noticed that Fink and Ord, and Reggie, and even the bailiff were staring in helpless anticipation.

Harry placed the sandwich onto the plate, and slid it to one side. "Mr. Fink," he said, jabbing a finger in Fink's direction, "stay where you are. Do you swear to tell the truth?"

"I do."

"You'd better. You're now under oath. You have five minutes to tell me what's bugging you."

"Yes, thank you, Your Honor."

"You're so welcome."

"You see, Jerome Clifford and I were in law school together, and we knew each other for many years. We had many cases together, always on opposite sides, of course."

"Of course."

"After Barry Muldanno was indicted, the pressure began to mount and Jerome began acting strange. Looking back, I think he was slowly cracking up, but at the time I didn't think much about it. I mean, you see, Jerome was always a strange one."

"I see."

"I was working on the case every day, many hours a day, and I talked to Jerome Clifford several times a week. We had preliminary motions and such, so I saw him in court occasionally. He looked awful. He gained a lot of weight, and was drinking too much. He was always late for meetings. Rarely bathed. Often, he failed to return phone calls, which was unusual for Jerome. About a week before he died he called me at home one night, really drunk, and rambled on for almost an hour. He was crazy. Then, he called me at the office first thing the next morning and apologized. But he wouldn't get off the phone. He kept fishing around as if he was afraid he'd said too much the night before. At least twice he mentioned the Boyette body, and I became convinced Jerome knew where it was."

Fink paused to allow this to sink in, but Harry was waiting impatiently.

"Well, he called me several times after that, kept talking about the body. I led him on. I implied that he'd said too much when he was drunk. I told him that we were considering an indictment against him for obstruction of justice."

"Seems to be one of your favorites," Harry said dryly.

"Anyway, Jerome was drinking heavily and acting bizarre. I confessed to him that the FBI was trailing him around the clock, which was not altogether true, but he seemed to believe it. He grew very paranoid, and called me several times a day. He'd get drunk and call me late at night. He wanted to talk about the body, but was afraid to tell everything. During our last phone conversation, I suggested that maybe we could cut a deal. If he'd tell us where the body was, then we'd help him bail out with no record, no conviction, nothing. He was terrified of his client, and he never once denied knowing where the body was."

"Your Honor," Reggie interrupted, "this, of course, is pure hearsay and quite self-serving. There's no way to verify any of this."

"You don't believe me?" Fink snapped at her.

"No, I don't."

"I'm not sure I do either, Mr. Fink," Harry said. "Nor am I sure why any of this has any relevance to this hearing."

"My point, Your Honor, is that Jerome Clifford knew about the body and he was talking about it. Plus, he was cracking up."

"I'll say he cracked up, Mr. Fink. He put a gun in his mouth. Sounds crazy to me."

Fink sort of hung in the air with his mouth open, uncertain if he should say anything else.

"Any more witnesses, Mr. Fink?" Harry asked.

"No sir. We do, however, Your Honor, feel that, due to the unusual circumstances of this case, the child should take the stand and testify."

Harry ripped off the reading glasses again, and leaned toward Fink. If he could have reached him, he might have gone for his neck.

"You what!"

"We, uh, feel that—"

"Mr. Fink, have you studied the juvenile laws for this jurisdiction?"

"I have."

"Great. Will you please tell us, sir, under which code section the petitioner has the right to force the child to testify?"

"I was merely stating our request."

"That's great. Under which code section is the petitioner allowed to make such a request?"

Fink dropped his head a few inches and found something on his legal pad to examine.

"This is not a kangaroo court, Mr. Fink. We do not create new rules as we go. The child cannot be forced to testify, same as any other criminal or Juvenile Court proceeding. Surely you understand this."

Fink studied the legal pad with great intensity.

"Ten-minute recess!" His Honor barked. "Everyone out of the courtroom, except Ms. Love. Bailiff, take Mark to a witness room." Harry was standing as he growled these instructions.

Fink, afraid to stand but nonetheless trying, hesitated for a split second too long, and this upset the judge. "Out of here, Mr. Fink," he said rudely, pointing to the door.

Fink and Ord stumbled over each other as they clawed for the door. The court reporter and clerk followed them. The bailiff escorted Mark away, and when he closed the door Harry unzipped his robe and threw it on a table. He took his lunch and sat it on the table before Reggie.

"Shall we dine?" he said, tearing the sandwich in two and placing half of it on a napkin for her. He slid the onion rings next to her legal pad. She took one and nibbled around the edges.

"Are you going to allow the kid to testify?" he asked with a mouth full of roast beef.

"I don't know, Harry. What do you think?"

"I think Fink's a dumbass, that's what I think."

Reggie took a small bite of the sandwich and wiped her mouth.

"If you put him on," Harry said, crunching, "Fink'll ask him some very pointed questions about what happened in the car with Clifford."

"I know. That's what worries me."

"How will the kid answer the questions?"

"I honestly don't know. I've advised him fully. We've talked about it at length. And I have no idea what he'll do."

Harry took a deep breath, and realized the ice tea was still on the bench. He took two paper cups from Fink's table, and poured them full of tea.

"It's obvious, Reggie, that he knows something. Why did he tell so many lies?"

"He's a kid, Harry. He was scared to death. He heard more than he should have. He saw Clifford blow his brains out. It scared him to death. Look at his poor little brother. It was a terrible thing to witness, and I think Mark initially thought he might get in trouble. So he lied."

"I don't really blame him," Harry said, taking an onion ring. Reggie bit into a pickle.

"What are you thinking?" she asked.

He wiped his mouth, and thought about this for a long time. This child was now his, one of Harry's Kids, and each decision from now on would be based on what was best for Mark Sway.

"If I can assume the child knows something very relevant to the investigation in New Orleans, then several things might happen. First, if you put him on the stand and he gives the information Fink wants, then this matter is closed as far as my jurisdiction is concerned. The kid walks out of here, but he's in great danger. Second, if you put him on the stand, and he refuses to answer Fink's questions, then I will be forced to make him answer. If he refuses, he'll be in contempt. He cannot remain silent if he has crucial information. Either way, if this hearing is concluded here today without satisfactory answers by the child, I strongly suspect Mr. Foltrigg will move quickly. He'll get a grand jury subpoena for Mark, and away you go to New Orleans. If he refuses to talk to the grand jury, he'll certainly be held in contempt by the federal judge, and I suspect he'll be incarcerated."

Reggie nodded. She was in complete agreement. "So what do we do, Harry?"

"If the kid goes to New Orleans, I lose control of him. I'd rather keep him here. If I were you, I'd put him on the stand and advise him not to answer the crucial questions. At least not for now. He can always do it later. He can do it tomorrow, or the next day. I'd advise him to withstand the pressure from the judge, and keep his mouth shut, at least for now. He'll go back to our Juvenile Detention Center, which is probably much safer than anything in New Orleans. By doing this, you protect the child from the New Orleans thugs, who scare even me, until the Feds can arrange something better. And you buy yourself some time to see what Mr. Foltrigg will do in New Orleans."

"You think he's in great danger?"

"Yes, and even if I didn't, I wouldn't take chances. If he spills his guts now, he could get hurt. I'm not inclined to release him today, under any circumstances."

"What if Mark refuses to talk, and Foltrigg presents him with a grand jury subpoena?"

"I won't allow him to go."

Reggie's appetite was gone. She sipped her tea from the paper cup and closed her eyes. "This is so unfair to this boy, Harry. He deserves more from the system."

"I agree. I'm open to suggestions."

"What if I don't put him on the stand?"

"I'm not going to release him, Reggie. At least not today. Maybe tomorrow. Maybe the next day. This is happening awfully fast, and I suggest we take the safest route and see what happens in New Orleans."

"You didn't answer my question. What if I don't put him on the stand?"

"Well, based on the proof I've heard, I'll have no choice but to find him to be a delinquent, and I'll send him back to Doreen. Of course, I could reverse myself tomorrow. Or the next day."

"He's not a delinquent."

"Maybe not. But if he knows something, and he refuses to tell, then he's obstructing justice." There was a long pause. "How much does he know, Reggie? If you'll tell me, I'll be in a better position to help him."

"I can't tell you, Harry. It's privileged."

"Of course it is," he said with a smile. "But it's rather obvious he knows plenty."

"Yes, I guess it is."

He leaned forward, and touched her arm. "Listen to me, dear. Our little pal is in a world of trouble. So let's get him out of it. I say we take it one day at a time, keep him in a safe place where we call the shots, and in the meantime start talking to the Feds about their witness protection program. If that falls into place for the kid and his family, then he can tell these awful secrets and be protected."

"I'll talk to him."

TWENTY-FIVE

UNDER THE STERN SUPERVISION of the bailiff, a man named Grinder, they were reassembled and directed to their positions. Fink glanced about fearfully, uncertain whether to sit, stand, speak, or crawl under the table. Ord picked at the cuticle on a thumb. Baxter McLemore had moved his chair as far away from Fink as possible.

His Honor sipped the remains of the tea and waited until all was still. "On the record," he said in the general direction of the court reporter. "Ms. Love, I need to know if young Mark will testify."

She was sitting a foot behind her client, and she looked at the side of his face. His eyes were still wet.

"Under the circumstances," she said, "he doesn't have much of a choice."

"Is that a yes or a no?"

"I will allow him to testify," she said, "but I will not tolerate abusive questioning by Mr. Fink."

"Your Honor, please," Fink said.

"Quiet, Mr. Fink. Remember rule number one? Don't speak until spoken to."

Fink glared at Reggie. "A cheap shot," he snarled.

"Knock it off, Mr. Fink," Harry said. All was quiet.

His Honor was suddenly all warmth and smiles. "Mark, I want you to remain in your seat, next to your lawyer, while I ask you some questions."

Fink winked at Ord. Finally, the kid would talk. This could be the moment.

"Raise your right hand, Mark," His Honor said, and Mark slowly obeyed. The right hand, as well as the left, was trembling.

The elderly lady stood in front of Mark and properly swore him. He did not stand, but inched closer to Reggie.

"Now, Mark, I'm going to ask you some questions. If you don't understand anything I ask, please feel free to talk to your lawyer. Okay?"

"Yes sir."

"I'll try to keep the questions clear and simple. If you need a break to step outside and talk to Reggie, Ms. Love, just let me know. Okay?"

"Yes sir."

Fink turned his chair to face Mark and sat like a hungry puppy awaiting his Alpo. Ord finished his nails, and was ready with his pen and legal pad.

Harry reviewed his notes for a second, then smiled down at the witness. "Now, Mark, I want you to explain to me exactly how you and your brother discovered Mr. Clifford on Monday."

Mark gripped the arms of his chair and cleared his throat. This was not what he expected. He'd never seen a movie in which the judge asked the questions.

"We sneaked off into the woods behind the trailer park, to smoke a cigarette," he began, and slowly led to the point where Romey stuck the water hose in the tail pipe the first time and got in the car.

"What'd you do then?" His Honor asked anxiously.

"I took it out," he said, and told the story about his trips through the weeds to remove Romey's suicide device. Although he'd told this before, once or twice to his mother and Dr. Greenway, and once or twice to Reggie, it had never seemed amusing to him. But as he told it now, the judge's eyes began to sparkle and his smile widened. He chuckled softly. The bailiff thought it was funny. The court reporter, always noncommittal, was enjoying it. Even the old woman at the clerk's desk was listening with her first smile of the proceedings.

But the humor turned sour as Mr. Clifford grabbed him, slapped him around, and threw him in the car. Mark relived this with a straight face, staring at the brown pumps of the court reporter.

"So you were in the car with Mr. Clifford before he died?" His Honor asked cautiously, very serious now.

"Yes sir."

"And what did he do once he got you in the car?"

"He slapped me some more, yelled at me a few times, threatened me." And Mark told all that he remembered about the gun, the whiskey bottle, the pills.

The small courtroom was deathly still, and the smiles were long gone. Mark's words were deliberate. His eyes avoided all others. He spoke as if in a trance.

"Did he fire the gun?" Judge Roosevelt asked.

"Yes sir," he answered, and told them all about it.

When he finished this part of the story, he waited for the next question. Harry thought about it for a long minute.

"Where was Ricky?"

"Hiding in the bushes. I saw him sneak through the weeds, and I sort of figured he'd removed the water hose again. He did, I found out later. Mr. Clifford kept saying he could feel the gas, and he asked me over and over if I could feel it. I said yes, twice I think, but I knew Ricky had come through."

"And he didn't know about Ricky?" It was a throwaway question, irrelevant, but asked because Harry couldn't think of a better one at the moment.

"No sir."

Another long pause.

"So you talked with Mr. Clifford while you were in the car?"

Mark knew what was coming, as did everyone in the courtroom, so he jumped in quickly in an attempt to divert it.

"Yes sir. He was out of his mind, kept talking about floating off to see the Wizard of Oz, off to La La Land, then he would yell at me for crying, then he would apologize for hitting me."

There was a pause as Harry waited to see if he was finished. "Is that all he said?"

Mark glanced at Reggie, who was watching him carefully. Fink inched closer. The court reporter was frozen.

"What do you mean?" Mark asked, stalling.

"Did Mr. Clifford say anything else?"

Mark thought about this for a second, and decided he hated Reggie. He could simply say "No," and the ballgame was over. No sir, Mr. Clifford did not say anything else. He just rambled on like an idiot for about five minutes, then fell asleep, and I ran like hell. If he'd never met Reggie, and had not heard her lecture about being under oath and telling the truth, then he would simply say "No sir." And go home, or back to the hospital, or wherever.

Or would he? One day in the fourth grade the cops put on a show about police work, and one of them demonstrated a polygraph. He wired up Joey McDermant, the biggest liar in the class, and they watched as the needle went berserk every time Joey opened his mouth. "We catch criminals lying every time," the cop had boasted.

With cops and FBI agents swarming around him, could the polygraph be far away? He'd lied so much since Romey killed himself, and he was really tired of it.

"Mark, I asked you if Mr. Clifford said anything else."

"Like what?"

"Like, did he mention anything about Senator Boyd Boyette?"

"Who?"

Harry flashed a sweet little smile, then it was gone. "Mark, did Mr. Clifford mention anything about a case of his in New Orleans involving a Mr. Barry Muldanno or the late Senator Boyd Boyette?"

A tiny spider was crawling next to the court reporter's brown pumps, and Mark watched it until it disappeared under the tripod. He thought about that damned polygraph again. Reggie said she would fight to keep it away from him, but what if the judge ordered it?

The long pause before his response said it all. Fink's heart was laboring and his pulse had tripled. Aha! The little bastard *does* know!

"I don't think I want to answer that question," he said, staring at the floor, waiting for the spider to reappear.

Fink looked hopefully at the judge.

"Mark, look at me," Harry said like a gentle grandfather. "I want you to answer the question. Did Mr. Clifford mention Barry Muldanno or Boyd Boyette?"

"Can I take the Fifth Amendment?"

"No."

"Why not? It applies to kids, doesn't it?"

"Yes, but not in this situation. You're not implicated in the death of Senator Boyette. You're not implicated in any crime."

"Then why did you put me in jail?"

"I'm going to send you back there if you don't answer my questions."

"I take the Fifth Amendment anyway."

They were glaring at each other, witness and judge, and the witness blinked first. His eyes watered and he sniffed twice. He bit his lip, fighting hard not to cry. He clenched the armrests and squeezed until his knuckles were white. Tears dropped onto his cheeks, but he kept staring up into the dark eyes of the Honorable Harry Roosevelt.

The tears of an innocent little boy. Harry turned to his side and pulled a tissue from a drawer under the bench. His eyes were wet too.

"Would you like to talk to your attorney, in private?" he asked.

"We've already talked," he said in a fading voice. He wiped his cheeks with a sleeve.

Fink was near cardiac arrest. He had so much to say, so many questions for this brat, so many suggestions for the court on how to handle this matter. The kid knew, dammit! Let's make him talk!

"Mark, I don't like to do this, but you must answer my questions. If you refuse, then you're in contempt of court. Do you understand this?"

"Yes sir. Reggie's explained it to me."

"And did she explain that if you're in contempt, then I can send you back to the Juvenile Detention Center?"

"Yes sir. You can call it a jail if you like, it doesn't bother me."

"Thank you. Do you want to go back to jail?"

"Not really, but I have no place else to go." His voice was stronger and the tears had stopped. The thought of jail was not as frightening now that he'd seen the inside of it. He could tough it out for a few days. In fact, he figured he could take the heat longer than the judge. He was certain his name would appear in the paper again in the very near future. And the reporters would undoubtedly learn he was locked up by Harry Roosevelt for not talking. And surely the judge would catch hell for locking up a little kid who'd done nothing wrong.

Reggie'd told him he could change his mind anytime he got tired of jail.

"Did Mr. Clifford mention the name Barry Muldanno to you?"

"Take the Fifth."

"Did Mr. Clifford mention the name Boyd Boyette to you?"

"Take the Fifth."

"Did Mr. Clifford say anything about the murder of Boyd Boyette?"

"Take the Fifth."

"Did Mr. Clifford say anything about the present location of the body of Boyd Boyette?"

"Take the Fifth."

Harry removed his reading glasses for the tenth time, and rubbed his face. "You can't take the Fifth, Mark."

"I just did."

"I'm ordering you to answer these questions."

"Yes sir. I'm sorry."

Harry took a pen and began writing.

"Your Honor," Mark said. "I respect you and what you're trying to do. But I cannot answer these questions because I'm afraid of what might happen to me or my family."

"I understand, Mark, but the law does not allow private citizens to withhold information that might be crucial to a criminal investigation. I'm following the law, not picking on you. I'm holding you in contempt. I'm not angry with you, but you leave me no choice. I'm ordering you to return to the Juvenile Detention Center where you will remain as long as you're in contempt."

"How long will that be?"

"It's up to you, Mark."

"What if I decide never to answer the questions?"

"I don't know. Right now we'll take it one day at a time." Harry flipped through his calendar, found a spot, and made a note. "We'll meet again at noon tomorrow, if that's agreeable with everyone."

Fink was crushed. He stood, and was about to speak when Ord grabbed his arm and pulled him down. "Your Honor, I don't think I can be here tomorrow," he said. "As you know, my office is in New Orleans, and—"

"Oh, you'll be here tomorrow, Mr. Fink. You and Mr. Foltrigg together. You chose to file your petition here in Memphis, in my court, and now I have jurisdiction over you. As soon as you leave here, I suggest you call Mr. Foltrigg and tell him to be here at noon tomorrow. I want both petitioners, Fink and Foltrigg, right here at twelve o'clock sharp tomorrow. And if you're not here, I'll hold you in contempt, and tomorrow it'll be you and your boss being hauled off to jail."

Fink's mouth was open but nothing came out. Ord spoke for the first time. "Your Honor, I believe Mr. Foltrigg has a hearing in federal court in the morning. Mr. Muldanno has a new lawyer who's asking for a continuance, and the judge down there has set the hearing for tomorrow morning."

"Is that true, Mr. Fink?"

"Yes sir."

"Then tell Mr. Foltrigg to fax me a copy of the judge's order setting the hearing for tomorrow. I'll excuse him. But as long as Mark is in jail for contempt, I intend to bring him back here every other day to see if he wants to talk. I'll expect both petitioners to be here."

"That's quite a hardship on us, Your Honor."

"Not as hard as it's gonna be if you don't show up. You picked this forum, Mr. Fink. Now you gotta live with it."

Fink had flown to Memphis six hours earlier without a toothbrush or change of underwear. Now it appeared as though he might be forced to lease an apartment with bedrooms for himself and Foltrigg.

The bailiff had eased his way to the wall behind Reggie and Mark, and was watching His Honor and waiting for a signal.

"Mark, I'm going to excuse you now," Harry said, scribbling on a form, "and I'll see you again tomorrow. If you have any problems in the detention center, you inform me tomorrow and I'll take care of it. Okay?"

Mark nodded. Reggie squeezed his arm, and said, "I'll talk to your mother, and I'll come see you in the morning."

"Tell Mom I'm fine," he whispered in her ear. "I'll try and call her tonight." He stood and left with the bailiff.

"Send in those FBI people," Harry said to the bailiff as he was closing the door.

"Are we excused, Your Honor?" Fink asked. There was sweat on his forehead. He was anxious to leave this room and call Foltrigg with the horrible news.

"What's the hurry, Mr. Fink?"

"Uh, no hurry, Your Honor."

"Then relax. I want to talk, off the record, with you boys and the FBI people. Just take a minute." Harry excused the court reporter and the old woman. McThune and Lewis entered and took their seats behind the lawyers.

Harry unzipped his robe, but did not remove it. He wiped his face with a tissue and sipped the last of the tea. They watched and waited.

"I do not intend to keep this child in jail," he said, looking at Reggie. "Maybe for a few days, but not long. It's apparent to me that he has some critical information, and he's duty bound to divulge it."

Fink started nodding.

"He's scared, and we can all certainly understand that. Perhaps we can convince him to talk if we can guarantee his safety, and that of his mother and brother. I'd like for Mr. Lewis to help us on this. I'm open to suggestions."

K. O. Lewis was ready. "Your Honor, we have taken preliminary steps to place him in our witness protection program."

"I've heard of it, Mr. Lewis, but I'm not familiar with the details."

"It's quite simple. We move the family to another city. We provide new identities. We find a good job for the mother, and get them a nice place to live. Not a trailer or an apartment, but a house. We make sure the boys are in a good school. There's some cash up front. And we stay close by."

"Sounds tempting, Ms. Love," Harry said.

It certainly did. At the moment, the Sways had no home. Dianne worked in a sweatshop. There were no relatives in Memphis.

"They're not mobile right now," she said. "Ricky is confined to the hospital."

"We've already located a children's psychiatric hospital in Portland that can take him right away," Lewis explained. "It's a private one, not a charity outfit like St. Peter's, and it's one of the best in the country. They'll take him whenever we ask, and, of course, we'll pay for it. After he's released, we'll move the family to another city."

"How long will it take to place the entire family into the program?" Harry asked.

"Less than a week," Lewis answered. "Director Voyles has given it top priority. The paperwork takes a few days, new driver's license, Social Security numbers, birth certificates, credit cards, things like this. The family has to make the decision to do it, and the mother must tell us where she wants to go. We'll take over from there."

"What do you think, Ms. Love?" Harry asked. "Will Ms. Sway go for it?"

"I'll talk to her. She's under enormous stress right now. One kid in a coma, the other in jail, and she lost everything in the fire last night. The idea of running away in the middle of the night could be a hard sell, at least for now."

"But you'll try?"

"I'll see."

"Do you think she could be in court tomorrow? I'd like to talk to her."

"I'll ask the doctor."

"Good. This meeting is adjourned. I'll see you folks at noon tomorrow."

The bailiff handed Mark to two Memphis policemen in plain clothes, and they took him through a side door into the parking lot. When they were gone, the bailiff climbed the stairs to the second floor and darted into an empty rest room. Empty, except for Slick Moeller.

They stood before the urinals, side by side, and stared at the graffiti.

"Are we alone?" asked the bailiff.

"Yep. What happened?" Slick had unzipped his pants and had both hands on his waist. "Be quick."

"Kid wouldn't talk, so he's going back to jail. Contempt."

"What does he know?"

"I'd say he knows everything. It's rather obvious. He said he was in the car with Clifford, they talked about this and that, and when

Harry pressed him on the New Orleans stuff the kid took the Fifth Amendment. Tough little bastard."

"But he knows?"

"Oh sure. But he's not telling. Judge wants him back tomorrow at noon to see if a night in the slammer changes his mind."

Slick zipped his pants and stepped away from the urinal. He took a folded one-hundred-dollar bill from his pocket and handed it to the bailiff.

"You didn't hear it from me," the bailiff said.

"You trust me, don't you?"

"Of course." And he did. Mole Moeller never revealed a source.

Moeller had three photographers poised at various places around the Juvenile Court Building. He knew the routines better than the cops themselves, and he figured they'd use the side door near the loading dock for a quick getaway with the kid. That's exactly what they did, and they almost made it to their unmarked car before a heavy woman in fatigues jumped from a parked van and nailed them straight on with her Nikon. The cops yelled at her, and tried to hide the kid behind them, but it was too late. They rushed him to their car, and pushed him into the backseat.

Just great, thought Mark. It was not yet 2 P.M., and so far this day had brought the burning of their trailer, his arrest at the hospital, his new home at the jail, a hearing with Judge Roosevelt, and now, another damned photographer shooting at him for what would undoubtedly be another front page story.

As the car squealed tires and raced away, he sunk low in the backseat. His stomach ached, not from hunger, but from fear. He was alone again.

TWENTY-SIX

FOLTRIGG WATCHED THE TRAFFIC on Poydras Street and waited on the call from Memphis. He was tired of pacing and checking his watch. He had tried to return phone calls and dictate letters, but it was hopeless. His mind could not leave the wonderful image of Mark Sway sitting in a witness chair somewhere in Memphis telling all his splendid secrets. Two hours had passed since the hearing was scheduled to start, and surely they'd take a recess along the way so Fink could dash to a phone and call him.

Larry Trumann was on standby, waiting for the call so they could swing into action with a posse of corpse hunters. They had become quite proficient in digging for bodies during the past eight months. They just hadn't found any.

But today would be different. Roy would take the call, walk to Trumann's office, and off they'd go to find the late Boyd Boyette. Foltrigg talked to himself, not a whisper or a mumble, but a full-blown speech in which he addressed the media with the thrilling announcement that, yes, they had indeed found the Senator, and, yes, he died of six bullet wounds to the head. The gun was a .22, and the bullet fragments were definitely, without the slightest doubt, fired from the same handgun that had been so meticulously traced to the defendant, Mr. Barry Muldanno.

It would be a wonderful moment, this press conference.

Someone knocked slightly and the door opened before Roy could turn around. It was Wally Boxx, the only person allowed such casual entries.

"Heard anything?" Wally asked, walking to the window and standing next to his boss.

"No. Not a word. I wish Fink would get to a phone. He has specific orders."

They stood in silence and watched the street.

"What's the grand jury doing?" Roy asked.

"The usual. Routine indictments."

"Who's in there?"

"Hoover. He's finishing up with the drug bust in Gretna. Should be through this afternoon."

"Are they scheduled to work tomorrow?"

"No. They've had a hard week. We promised them yesterday they could take off tomorrow. What're you thinking?"

Foltrigg shifted weight slightly and scratched his chin. His eyes had a faraway look, and he watched the cars below but didn't see them. Heavy thinking was sometimes painful for him. "Think about this. If, for some reason, the kid doesn't talk, and if Fink drills a dry hole with the hearing, what do we do then? I say we go to the grand jury, get subpoenas for both the kid and his lawyer, and drag them down here. The kid's gotta be scared right now, and he's still in Memphis. He'll be terrified when he has to come here."

"Why would you subpoena his lawyer?"

"To scare her. Pure harassment. Shake 'em both up. We get the subpoenas today, keep them sealed, sit on them until late tomorrow afternoon when everything's closing for the weekend, then we serve the kid and his lawyer. The subpoenas will require their presence before our grand jury at 10 A.M. Monday morning. They won't have a chance to run to court and quash the subpoenas because it's the weekend and everything's shut down and all the judges are out of town. They'll be too scared not to show up here Monday morning, on our turf, Wally. Right down the hall here, in our building."

"What if the kid doesn't know anything?"

Roy shook his head in frustration. They'd had this conversation a dozen times in the last forty-eight hours. "I thought that was established."

"Maybe. And maybe the kid's talking right now."

"He probably is."

A secretary squeaked through on the intercom and announced

that Mr. Fink was holding on line one. Foltrigg walked to his desk and grabbed the phone. "Yes!"

"The hearing's over, Roy," Fink reported. He sounded relieved and tired.

Foltrigg hit the switch for the speakerphone, and fell into his chair. Wally perched his tiny butt on the corner of the desk. "Wally's here with me, Tom. Tell us what happened."

"Nothing much. The kid's back in jail. He wouldn't talk, so the judge found him in contempt."

"What do you mean, he wouldn't talk?"

"He wouldn't talk. The judge handled both the direct and cross-examinations, and the kid admitted being in the car and talking with Clifford. But when the judge asked questions about Boyette and Muldanno, the kid took the Fifth Amendment."

"The Fifth Amendment!"

"That's right. He wouldn't budge. Said jail wasn't so bad after all, and that he had no other place to go."

"But he knows, doesn't he, Tom? The little punk knows."

"Oh, there's no question about it. Clifford told him everything."

Foltrigg slapped his hands together. "I knew it! I knew it! I knew it! I've been telling you boys this for three days now." He jumped to his feet and squeezed his hands together. "I knew it!"

Fink continued. "The judge has scheduled another hearing for noon tomorrow. He wants the kid brought back in to see if he's changed his mind. I'm not too optimistic."

"I want you at that hearing, Tom."

"Yes, and the judge wants you too, Roy. I explained you had a hearing on the continuance motion in the morning, and he insisted that you fax him a copy of the hearing order. He said he'd excuse you under those circumstances."

"Is he some kind of nut?"

"No. He's not a nut. He said he plans to hold these little hearings quite often next week, and he expects both of us, as petitioners, to be there."

"Then he is a nut."

Wally rolled his eyes and shook his head. These local judges could be such fools.

"After the hearing, the judge talked to us about placing the kid and his family in witness protection. He thinks he can convince the kid to talk if we can guarantee his safety."

"That could take weeks."

"I think so too, but K.O. told the judge it could be done in a matter of days. Frankly, Roy, I don't think the kid will talk until we can make some guarantees. He's a tough little guy."

"What about his lawyer?"

"She played it cool, didn't say much, but she and the judge are pretty tight. I got the impression the kid's getting a lot of advice. She's no dummy."

Wally just had to say something. "Tom, it's me, Wally. What do you think will happen over the weekend?"

"Who knows? As I said, I don't think this kid'll change his mind overnight, and I don't think the judge plans to release him. The judge knows about Gronke and the Muldanno boys, and I get the impression he wants the kid locked up for his own protection. Tomorrow's Friday, so it looks like the kid will stay where he is over the weekend. And I'm sure the judge will call us back in on Monday for another chat."

"Are you coming in, Tom?" Roy asked.

"Yeah, I'll catch a flight out in a couple of hours, and fly back here in the morning." Fink's voice was now very tired.

"I'll be waiting for you here tonight, Tom. Good work."

"Yeah."

Fink faded away and Roy hit the switch.

"Get the grand jury ready," he snapped at Wally, who bounced off the desk and headed for the door. "Tell Hoover to take a break. This won't take but a minute. Get me the Mark Sway file. Inform the clerk that the subpoenas will be sealed until they are served late tomorrow."

Wally was through the door and gone. Foltrigg returned to the window, mumbling to himself, "I knew it. I just knew it."

The cop in the suit signed Doreen's clipboard, and left with his partner. "Follow me," she said to Mark as if he'd sinned again and her patience was wearing thin. He followed her, watching her wide rear end rock from side to side in a pair of tight, black polyester pants. A thick, shiny belt squeezed her narrow waist and held an assortment of key rings, two black boxes which he assumed to be pagers, and a pair of handcuffs. No gun. Her shirt was official white with markings up and down the sleeves and gold trim around the collar.

The hall was empty as she opened his door and motioned for him to return to his little room. She followed him in and eased around the walls like a dope dog sniffing at the airport. "Sort of surprised to see you back here," she said, inspecting the toilet.

He could think of nothing to say to this, and he was not in the mood for a conversation. As he watched her stoop and bend, he thought about her husband serving thirty years for bank robbery, and if she insisted on chatting he might just bring this up. That would quiet her down and send her on her way.

"Must've upset Judge Roosevelt," she said, looking through the windows.

"I guess so."

"How long are you in for?"

"He didn't say. I have to go back tomorrow."

She walked to the bunks and began patting the blanket. "I've been reading about you and your little brother. Pretty strange case. How's he doing?"

Mark stood by the door, hoping she would just go away. "He's probably gonna die," he said sadly.

"No!"

"Yeah, it's awful. He's in a coma, you know, sucking his thumb, grunting and slobbering every now and then. His eyes have rolled back into his head. Won't eat."

"I'm sorry I asked." Her heavily decorated eyes were wide open, and she had stopped touching everything.

Yeah, I'll bet you're sorry you asked, Mark thought. "I need to be there with him," Mark said. "My mom's there, but she's all stressed out. Taking a lot of pills, you know."

"I'm so sorry."

"It's awful. I've been feeling dizzy myself. Who knows, I could end up like my brother."

"Can I get you anything?"

"No. I just need to lie down." He walked to the bottom bunk and fell into it. Doreen knelt beside him, deeply troubled now.

"Anything you want, honey, you just let me know, okay?"

"Okay. Some pizza would be nice."

She stood and thought about this for a second. He closed his eyes as if in deep pain.

"I'll see what I can do."

"I haven't had lunch, you know."

"I'll be right back," she said, and she left. The door clicked loudly behind her. Mark bolted to his feet and listened to it.

TWENTY-SEVEN

THE ROOM WAS DARK as usual; the lights off, the door shut, the blinds drawn, the only illumination the moving blue shadows of the muted television high on the wall. Dianne was mentally drained and physically beat from lying in bed with Ricky for eight hours, patting and hugging and cooing and trying to be strong in this damp, dark little cell.

Reggie had stopped by two hours ago, and they'd sat on the edge of the foldaway bed and talked for thirty minutes. She explained the hearing, assured her Mark was being fed and in no physical danger, described his room at the detention center because she'd seen one before, told her he was safer there than here, and talked about Judge Roosevelt and the FBI and their witness protection program. At first, and under the circumstances, the idea was attractive—they would simply move to a new city with new names and a new job and a decent place to live. They could run from this mess and start over. They could pick a large city with big schools and the boys would get lost in the crowd. But the more she lay there curled on one side and stared above Ricky's little head at the wall, the less she liked the idea. In fact, it was a horrible idea—living on the run forever, always afraid of an unexpected knock on the door, always in a panic when one of the boys was late getting home, always lying about their past.

This little plan was forever. What if, she began asking herself, one day, say five or ten years from now, long after the trial in New Orleans, some person she's never met lets something slip and it's heard by the wrong ears, and their trails are quickly traced? And when Mark is, say, a senior in high school, somebody waits on him after a ballgame and sticks a gun to his head? His name wouldn't be Mark, but he would be dead nonetheless.

She had almost decided to veto the idea of witness protection when Mark called her from the jail. He said he'd just finished a large pizza, was feeling great, nice place and all, was enjoying it more than the hospital, food was better, and he chatted so eagerly she knew he was lying. He said he was already plotting his escape, and would soon be out. They talked about Ricky, and the trailer, and the hearing today and the hearing tomorrow. He said he was trusting Reggie's advice, and Dianne agreed this was best. He apologized for not being there to help with Ricky, and she fought tears when he tried to sound so mature. He apologized again for all this mess.

Their conversation had been brief. She found it difficult to talk to him. She had little motherly advice, and felt like a failure because her eleven-year-old son was in jail and she couldn't get him out. She couldn't go see him. She couldn't go talk to the judge. She couldn't tell him to talk or to remain quiet because she was scared too. She couldn't do a damned thing but stay here in this narrow bed and stare at the walls and pray that she would wake up and the nightmare would be over.

It was 6 P.M., time for the local news. She watched the silent face of the anchorperson and hoped it wouldn't happen. But it didn't take long. After two dead bodies were carried from a landfill, a black-and-white still photo of Mark and the cop she'd slapped this morning was suddenly on the screen. She turned up the volume.

The anchorperson gave the basics about the taking of Mark Sway, careful not to call it an arrest, then went to a reporter standing in front of the Juvenile Court Building. He rattled on a few seconds about a hearing he knew nothing about, gushed breathlessly that the child, Mark Sway, had been taken back to the Juvenile Detention Center, and that another hearing would be held tomorrow in Judge Roosevelt's courtroom. Back in the studio, the anchorperson brought 'em up to date on young Mark and the tragic suicide of Jerome Clifford. They ran a quick clip of the mourners leaving the chapel that morning in New Orleans, and had a second or two of Roy Foltrigg talking to a reporter under an umbrella. Back quickly to the anchorperson, who began quoting

Slick Moeller's stories, and the suspicion mounted. No comments from the Memphis Police, the FBI, the U.S. Attorney's office, or the Shelby County Juvenile Court. The ice got thinner as she skated into the vast, murky world of unnamed sources, all of whom were short on facts but long on speculation. When she mercifully finished and broke for a commercial, the uninformed could easily believe that young Mark Sway had shot not only Jerome Clifford but Boyd Boyette as well.

Dianne's stomach ached, and she hit the power button. The room was even darker. She had not taken a single bite of food in ten hours. Ricky twitched and grunted, and this irritated her. She eased from the bed, frustrated with him, frustrated with Greenway for the lack of progress, sick of this hospital with its dungeon-like decor and lighting, horrified at a system that allowed children to be jailed for being children, and, above all, scared of these lurking shadows who'd threatened Mark and burned the trailer and obviously were quite willing to do more. She closed the bathroom door behind her, sat on the edge of the bathtub, and smoked a Virginia Slim. Her hands trembled and her thoughts were a blur. A migraine was forming at the base of her skull, and by midnight she would be paralyzed. Maybe the pills would help.

She flushed the skinny cigarette butt, and sat on the edge of Ricky's bed. She had vowed to get through this ordeal one day at a time, but damned if the days weren't getting worse. She couldn't take much more.

Barry The Blade had picked this dumpy little bar because it was quiet, dark, and he remembered it from his teenage years as a young and aspiring hoodlum on the streets of New Orleans. It was not one he routinely frequented, but it was deep in the Quarter, which meant he could park off Canal and dart through the tourists on Bourbon and Royal, and there was no way the Feds could follow him.

He found a tiny table in the back, and sipped a vodka gimlet while waiting for Gronke.

He wanted to be in Memphis himself, but he was out on bond and his movements were restricted. Permission was required before he could leave the state, and he knew better than to ask. Communication with Gronke had been difficult. The paranoia was eating him alive. For eight months now, every curious stare was another cop watching his every move. A stranger behind him on the sidewalk was another Fibbie hiding in the darkness. His phones were tapped. His car and house were bugged. He was afraid to speak half the time because he could almost feel the sensors and hidden mikes.

He finished the gimlet and ordered another one. A double. Gronke arrived twenty minutes late, and crowded his bulky frame into a chair in the corner. The ceiling was seven feet above them.

"Nice place," Gronke said. "How you doin'?"

"Okay." Barry snapped his fingers and the waiter walked over.

"Beer. Grolsch," Gronke said.

"Did they follow you?" Barry asked.

"I don't think so. I've zigzagged through half the Quarter, you know."

"What's happening up there?"

"Memphis?"

"No. Milwaukee, you dumbass," Barry said with a smile. "What's happening with the kid?"

"He's in jail, and he ain't talkin'. They took him in this morning, had some kinda hearing at lunch before the youth court, then took him back to jail."

The bartender carried a heavy tray of dirty beer mugs through the swinging doors into the dirty, cramped kitchen, and when he cleared the doors, two FBI agents in jeans stopped him. One flashed a badge while the other took the tray.

"What the hell?" the bartender asked, backing to the wall while staring at the badge just inches from the tip of his wide nose.

"FBI. Need a favor," said Special Agent Scherff calmly, all business. The other agent pressed forward. The bartender owned two felony convictions, and had been enjoying his freedom for less than six months. He became eager.

"Sure. Anything."

"What's your name?" asked Scherff.

"Uh, Dole. Link Dole." He'd used so many names over the years it was difficult keeping them straight.

The agents inched forward even more and Link began to fear an attack. "Okay, Link. Can you help us?"

Link nodded rapidly. The cook stirred a pot of rice, with a cigarette barely hanging from his lips. He glanced their way once but had other things on his mind.

"There are two men out there having a drink in the rear corner, on the right side where the ceiling is low."

"Yeah, okay, sure. I'm not involved, am I?"

"No, Link. Just listen." Scherff pulled a matching set of salt and pepper shakers from his pocket. "Put these on a tray with a bottle of ketchup. Go to the table, just routine, you know, and switch these with the ones sitting there now. Ask these guys if they want something to eat, or another drink. You understand?"

Link was nodding but not understanding. "Uh, what's in these?"

"Salt and pepper," Scherff said. "And a little bug that allows us to hear what these guys are saying. They're criminals, okay, Link, and we have them under surveillance."

"I really don't want to get involved," Link said, knowing full well that if they threatened even slightly he'd bust his ass to get involved.

"Don't make me angry," Scherff said, waving the shakers.

"Okay, okay."

A waiter kicked open the swinging doors and shuffled behind them with stack of dirty dishes. Link took the shakers. "Don't tell anyone," he said, trembling.

"It's a deal, Link. This is our little secret. Now, is there an empty closet around here?" Scherff asked this while looking around the cramped and cluttered kitchen. The answer was obvious. There had not been an empty square foot in this dump in fifty years.

Link thought a second or two, very anxious to help his new friends. "No, but there's a little office right above the bar."

"Great, Link. Go exchange these, and we'll set up some equipment in the office." Link held them gingerly as if they might explode, and returned to the bar.

A waiter placed a heavy green bottle of Grolsch in front of Gronke and disappeared.

"The little bastard knows something, doesn't he?" The Blade said.

"Of course. Otherwise, this wouldn't be happening. Why would he get himself a lawyer? Why would he clam up like this?" Gronke drained half his Grolsch with one, thirsty gulp.

Link approached them with a tray loaded with a dozen salt and pepper shakers and bottles of ketchup and mustard. "You guys eating dinner?" he asked, all business, as he swapped the shakers and bottles on their table.

Barry waved him off. Gronke said, "No." And Link was gone. Fewer than thirty feet away, Scherff and three more agents crowded over a small desk and flipped open heavy briefcases. One of the agents grabbed earphones and stuck them to his head. He smiled.

"This kid scares me, man," Barry said. "He's told his lawyer, so that makes two more who know."

"Yeah, but he ain't talkin', Barry. Think about it. We got to him. I showed him the picture. We took care of the trailer. The kid is scared to death."

"I don't know. Is there any way to get him?"

"Not right now. I mean, hell, the cops have him. He's locked up."

"There are ways, you know. I doubt if security is tight at a jail for kids."

"Yeah, but the cops are scared too. They're all over the hospital. Got guards sittin' in the hallway. Fibbies dressed like doctors runnin' all over the place. These people are terrified of us."

"But they can make him talk. They can put him in the mouse program, throw a buncha money at his mother. Hell, buy them a fancy new house trailer, maybe a double-wide or something. I'm just nervous as hell, Paul. If this kid was clean we would've never heard about him."

"We can't hit the kid, Barry."

"Why not?"

"Because he's a kid. Because everybody's watching him right now. Because if we do, a million cops'll hound us to our graves. It won't work."

"What about his mother or his brother?"

Gronke took another shot of beer, and shook his head in frustration. He was a tough thug who could threaten with the best of them, but, unlike his friend, he was not a killer. This random search for victims scared him. He said nothing.

"What about his lawyer?" Barry asked.

"Why would you kill her?"

"Maybe I hate lawyers. Maybe it'll scare the kid so bad he'll go into a coma like his brother. I don't know."

"And maybe killing innocent people in Memphis is not such a good idea. The kid'll just get another lawyer."

"We'll kill the next one too. Think about it, Paul, this could do wonders for the legal profession," Barry said with a loud laugh. Then he leaned forward as if a terribly private thought hit him. His chin was inches from the salt shaker. "Think about it, Paul. If we knock off the kid's lawyer, then no lawyer in his right mind would represent him. Get it?"

"You're losin' it, Barry. You're crackin' up."

"Yeah, I know. But it's a great thought, ain't it? Smoke her, and the kid won't talk to his own mother. What's her name, Rollie or Ralphie?"

"Reggie. Reggie Love."

"What the hell kinda name is that for a broad?"

"Don't ask me."

Barry drained his glass and snapped again for the waiter. "What's she sayin' on the phone?" he asked, in low again, just above the shaker.

"Don't know. We couldn't go in last night."

The Blade was suddenly angry. "You what!" The wicked eyes were fierce and glowing.

"Our man is doing it tonight, if all goes well."

"What kinda place has she got?"

"Small office in a tall building downtown. It should be easy."

Scherff pressed the earphone closer to his head. Two of his pals did likewise. The only sound in the room was a slight clicking noise from the recorder.

"Are these guys any good?"

"Nance is pretty smooth and cool under pressure. His partner, Cal Sisson, is a loose cannon. Afraid of his shadow."

"I want the phones fixed tonight."

"It'll be done."

Barry lit an unfiltered Camel and blew smoke at the ceiling. "Are they protecting the lawyer?" He asked this as his eyes narrowed. Gronke looked away.

"I don't think so."

"Where does she live? What kinda place?"

"She's got a cute little apartment behind her mother's house."

"She live alone?"

"I think so."

"She'd be easy, wouldn't she? Break in, take her out, steal a few things. Just another house burglary gone sour. What do you think?"

Gronke shook his head and studied a young blonde at the bar.

"What do you think?" Barry repeated.

"Yeah, it'd be easy."

"Then let's do it. Are you listening to me, Paul?"

Paul was listening, but avoiding the evil eyes. "I'm not in the mood to kill anyone," he said, still staring at the blonde.

"That's fine. I'll get Pirini to do it."

Several years earlier, a detainee, as they're called in the Juvenile Detention Center, a twelve-year-old, died in the room next to Mark's from an epileptic seizure. A ton of bad press and a nasty lawsuit followed, and though Doreen had not been on duty when it happened, she had nonetheless been shaken by it. An investigation followed. Two people were terminated. And a new set of regulations came down.

Doreen's shift ended at five, and the last thing she did was check on Mark. She'd stopped by on the hour throughout the afternoon, and watched with growing concern as his condition worsened. He was withdrawing before her very eyes, saying less with each visit, just lying there in bed staring at the ceiling. At five, she brought a county paramedic with her. Mark was given a quick physical, and pronounced alive and well. Vital signs were strong. When she left, she rubbed his temples like a sweet little grandmother and promised to return bright and early tomorrow, Friday. And she sent more pizza.

Mark told her he thought he could make it until then. He'd try to survive the night. Evidently she left instructions, because the next floor supervisor, a short plump little woman named Telda, immediately knocked on his door and introduced herself. For the next four hours, Telda knocked repeatedly and entered the room, staring wildly at his eyes as if he were crazy and something was about to snap.

Mark watched television, no cable, until the news started at ten, then brushed his teeth and turned off the lights. The bed was quite comfortable, and he thought of his mother trying to sleep on that rickety cot the nurses had rolled into Ricky's room.

The pizza was from Domino's, not some leathery slab of cheese someone threw in a microwave, but a real pizza Doreen had probably paid for. The bed was warm, the pizza was real, and the door was locked. He felt safe, not only from the other inmates and the gangs and violence certain to be close by, but especially from the man with the switchblade who knew his name and had the picture. The man who'd burned the trailer. He'd thought about this guy every moment of every hour since he dashed from the elevator early yesterday morning. He'd thought about him on Momma Love's porch last night, and sitting in the courtroom this afternoon listening to Hardy and McThune. He'd worried about him hanging around the hospital where Dianne was unaware.

Sitting in a parked car on Third Street in downtown Memphis at midnight was not Cal Sisson's idea of safe fun, but the doors were locked and there was a gun under the seat. His felony convictions forbade him from owning or possessing a firearm, but this was Jack Nance's car. It was parked behind a delivery van near Madison, a couple blocks from the Sterick Building. There was nothing suspicious about the car. Traffic was light.

Two uniformed cops on foot strolled along the sidewalk and stopped fewer than five feet from Cal. They stared at him. He glanced in the mirror, and saw another pair. Four cops! One of them sat on the trunk, and the car shook. Had the parking meter run out on him? No, he'd paid for an hour and been here less than ten minutes. Nance said it was a thirty-minute job.

Two more cops joined the two on the sidewalk, and Cal started sweating. The gun worried him, but a good lawyer could convince his probation officer that the gun was not his. He was merely driving for Nance.

An unmarked police car parked behind him, and two cops in plain clothes joined the others. Eight cops!

One in jeans and a sweatshirt bent at the waist and stuck his badge to Cal's window. There was a radio on the seat next to his leg, and thirty seconds ago he should have punched the blue button and warned Nance. But now it was too late. The cops had materialized from nowhere.

He slowly rolled down his window. The cop leaned forward and their faces were inches apart. "Evening, Cal. I'm Lieutenant Byrd, Memphis PD."

The fact that he called him Cal made him shudder. He tried to remain calm. "What can I do for you, Officer?"

"Where's Jack?"

Cal's heart stopped and sweat popped through his skin. "Jack who?"

Jack who. Byrd glanced over his shoulder and smiled at his partner. The uniformed cops had surrounded the car. "Jack Nance. Your good friend. Where is he?"

"I haven't seen him."

"Well, what a coincidence. I haven't seen him either. At least not for the past fifteen minutes. In fact, the last time I saw Jack was at the corner of Union and Second, less than a half an hour ago, and he was getting out of this car here. And you drove away, and, surprise, here you are."

Cal was breathing, but it was difficult. "I don't know what you're talking about."

Byrd unlocked the door and opened it. "Get out, Cal," he demanded, and Cal complied. Byrd slammed the door and shoved him against it. Four of the cops surrounded him. The other three were looking in the direction of the Sterick Building. Byrd was in his face.

"Listen to me, Cal. Accomplice to breaking and entering carries seven years. You have three prior convictions, so you'll be charged as a habitual offender, and guess how much time you're looking at."

His teeth were chattering and his body was shaking. He shook his head no, as if he didn't understand and wanted Byrd to tell him.

"Thirty years, no parole."

He closed his eyes and slumped. His breathing was heavy.

"Now," Byrd continued, very cool, very cruel. "We're not worried about Jack Nance. When he finishes with Ms. Love's phones, we've got some boys waiting for him outside the building. He'll be arrested, booked, and in due course sent away. But we don't figure he'll talk much. You follow?"

Cal nodded quickly.

"But, Cal, we figure you might want to cut a deal. Help us a little, know what I mean?"

He was still nodding, only faster.

"We figure you'll tell us what we need to know, and in return, we'll let you walk."

Cal stared at him desperately. His mouth was open, his chest pounding away.

Byrd pointed to the sidewalk on the other side of Madison. "You see that sidewalk, Cal?"

Cal took a long, hopeful look at the empty sidewalk. "Yeah," he said eagerly.

"Well, it's all yours. Tell me what I want to hear, and you walk. Okay? I'm offering you thirty years of freedom, Cal. Don't be stupid."

"Okay."

"When does Gronke return from New Orleans?"

"In the morning, around ten."

"Where's he staying?"

"Holiday Inn Crowne Plaza."

"Room number?"

"It's 782."

"Where are Bono and Pirini?"

"I don't know."

"Please, Cal, we're not idiots. Where are they?"

"They're in 783 and 784."

"Who else from New Orleans is here?"

"That's it. That's all I know."

"Can we expect more people from New Orleans?"

"I swear I don't know."

"Do they have any plans to hit the boy, his family, or his lawyer?"

"It's been discussed, but no definite plans. I wouldn't be a part of it, you know."

"I know, Cal. Any plans to bug more phones?"

"No. I don't think so. Just the lawyer."

"What about the lawyer's house?"

"No, not to my knowledge."

"No other bugs or wires or phone taps?"

"Not to my knowledge."

"No plans to kill anybody?"

"No."

"If you're lying, I'll come get you, Cal, and it's thirty years."

"I swear it."

Suddenly, Byrd slapped him on left side of his face, then grabbed his collar and squeezed it together. Cal's mouth was open and his eyes showed absolute terror. "Who burned the trailer?" Byrd snarled at him as he pushed him harder against the car.

"Bono and Pirini," he said without the slightest hesitation.

"Were you in on it, Cal?"

"No. I swear."

"Any more fires planned?"

"Not to my knowledge."

"Then what the hell are they doing here, Cal?"

"They're just waiting, listening, you know, just in case they're needed for something else. Depends on what the kid does."

Byrd squeezed tighter. He showed him his teeth and twisted the collar. "One lie, Cal, and I'm all over your ass, okay?"

"I'm not lying, I swear," Cal said in a shrill voice.

Byrd turned him loose and nodded at the sidewalk. "Go, and sin no more." The wall of cops opened, and Cal walked through them and into the street. He hit the sidewalk at full stride, and was last seen jogging into the darkness.

TWENTY-EIGHT

FRIDAY MORNING. Reggie sipped strong, black coffee in the darkness of predawn, and waited for another unpredictable day as counsel for Mark Sway. It was a cool, clear morning, the first of many in September, and the first hint that the hot, sticky days of the Memphis summer were coming to an end. She sat in a wicker rocker on the small balcony stuck to the rear of her apartment, and tried to unscramble the past five hours of her life.

The cops had called her at one-thirty, said there was an emergency at her office, and asked her to come down. She'd called Clint, and together they had gone to her office where a half dozen cops were waiting. They had allowed Jack Nance to finish his dirty work and leave the building before they nailed him. They showed Reggie and Clint the three phones and the tiny transmitters glued into the receivers, and they said Nance did pretty good work.

As she watched, they carefully removed the transmitters and kept them for evidence. They explained how Nance entered, and more than once they commented on her lack of security. She said she wasn't that concerned about security. There were no real assets in the office.

She'd checked her files, and everything appeared to be in order. The Mark Sway file was in her briefcase at home, and she kept it there when she slept. Clint examined his desk and said there was a chance Nance went through his files. But Clint's desk was not well organized to begin with, so he couldn't be certain.

The police had known Nance was coming, they had explained, but they wouldn't say how they knew. He was allowed easy access into the building—unlocked doors, absent security guards, etc.—and they had a dozen men watching him. He was in custody now, and so far had said nothing. One cop had taken her aside, and in hushed confidence explained about Nance's connection to Gronke, and to Bono and Pirini. They had been unable to find the latter two; their hotel rooms had been abandoned. Gronke was in New Orleans, and they had him under surveillance.

Nance would serve a couple of years, maybe more. For an instant, she'd wanted the death penalty.

The cops had gradually left. Around three, she and Clint were left alone with the empty offices and the startling knowledge that a professional had entered and laid his traps. A man hired by killers had been there, gathering information so there could be more killings, if necessary. The place made her nervous, and she and Clint had left shortly after the cops and found a coffee shop in midtown.

And so with three hours' sleep and a nerve-racking day about to begin, she sipped her coffee and watched the eastern sky turn orange. She thought about Mark, and how he'd arrived in her office on Wednesday, barely two days ago, wet from the rain and scared to death, and told her about being threatened by a man with a switchblade. This man was big and ugly, and waved the knife and produced a photo of the Sway family. She had listened with horror as this small, shivering child described the switchblade. It was a frightening event to hear about, but it had happened to someone else. She was not directly involved. The knife was not pointed at her.

But that was Wednesday, and this was Friday, and the same bunch of thugs had now violated her, and things were a helluva lot more dangerous. Her little client was safely tucked away in a nice jail with security guards at his beck and call, and here she was sitting alone in the darkness thinking about Bono and Pirini and who knew who else might be out there.

Though it couldn't be seen from Momma Love's house, an unmarked car was parked in the street not far away. Two FBI agents were on guard, just in case. Reggie had agreed to this.

She pictured a hotel room, clouds of cigarette smoke hanging along the ceiling, empty beer bottles littering the floor, curtains drawn, and a small group of badly dressed hoodlums hovering over a small table listening to a tape recorder. She was on the tape recorder, talking to clients, to Dr. Levin, to Momma Love, just chatting away as if everything were private. The hoods were bored for the most part, but occasionally one would chuckle and grunt.

Mark didn't use her office phones, and the strategy of bugging them was ridiculous. These people obviously believed Mark knew about Boyette, and that he and his lawyer were stupid enough to discuss this knowledge over the phone.

The phone in the kitchen rang, and Reggie jumped. She checked her watch—six-twenty. It had to be more trouble because no one called at this hour. She walked inside and caught it after the fourth ring. "Hello."

It was Harry Roosevelt. "Good morning, Reggie. Sorry to wake you."

"I was awake."

"Have you seen the paper?"

She swallowed hard. "No. What is it?"

"It's a front page spread with two big pictures of Mark, one as he's leaving the hospital, under arrest as it says, and the other as he's leaving court yesterday, cops on both sides. Slick Moeller wrote it, and he knows all about the hearing. He's got his facts straight, for a change. He says Mark refused to answer my questions about his knowledge of Boyette and such, and that I found him in contempt and sent him to jail. Makes me sound like Hitler."

"But how does he know this?"

"Cites unnamed sources."

She was counting the people in the courtroom during the hearing. "Was it Fink?"

"I doubt it. Fink would have nothing to gain by leaking this, and the risks are too great. It has to be someone who's not too bright."

"That's why I said Fink."

"Good point, but I doubt it was a lawyer. I plan to issue a subpoena for Mr. Moeller to appear in my court at noon today. I'll demand he give me his source, or I'll throw him in jail for contempt."

"Wonderful idea."

"It shouldn't take long. We'll have Mark's little hearing afterward. Okay?"

"Sure, Harry. Listen, there's something you should know. It's been a long night."

"I'm listening," he said. Reggie gave him the quick version of the bugging of her office, with particular emphasis on Bono and Pirini and the fact they had not been found.

"Good Lord," he said. "These people are crazy."

"And dangerous."

"Are you scared?"

"Of course I'm scared. I've been violated, Harry, and it's frightening to know they've been watching."

There was a long pause on the other end. "Reggie, I'm not going to release Mark under any circumstances, not today anyway. Let's see what happens over the weekend. He's much safer where he is."

"I agree."

"Have you talked to his mother?"

"Yesterday. She was lukewarm on the idea of witness protection. It might take some time. Poor thing is nothing but ragged nerves."

"Work on her. Can she be present in court today? I'd like to see her."

"I'll try."

"See you at noon."

She poured another cup of coffee and returned to the balcony. Axle slept under the rocker. The first light of dawn crept through the trees. She held the warm mug with both hands and tucked her bare feet under the heavy bathrobe. She sniffed the aroma and thought about how much she despised the press. So now the world would know about the hearing. So much for confidentiality. Her little client was suddenly more vulnerable. It was obvious now, the fact that he knew something he shouldn't know. If not, why wouldn't he simply have talked when the judge instructed him to?

This game was growing more dangerous by the hour. And she, Reggie Love, Attorney and Counselor-at-Law, was supposed to have all the answers and dispense perfect advice. Mark would look at her with those scared blue eyes, and ask what to do next. How the hell was she supposed to know?

They were after her too.

□ □ □ □

Doreen woke Mark early. She'd fixed blueberry muffins for him, and she nibbled on one and watched him with great concern. Mark sat in a chair, holding a muffin but not eating it, just staring blankly at the floor. He slowly raised the muffin to his mouth, took a tiny bite, then lowered it to his lap. Doreen watched every move.

"Are you okay, sweetheart?" she asked him.

Mark nodded slowly. "Oh, I'm fine," he said in a hollow, hoarse voice.

Doreen patted his knee, then his shoulder. Her eyes were narrow and she was very troubled. "Well, I'll be around all day," she said as she stood and walked to the door. "And I'll be checking on you."

Mark ignored her, and took another small bite of his muffin. The door slammed and clicked, and suddenly he crammed the rest of it in his mouth and reached for another.

He turned on the television, but with no cable he was forced to watch Bryant Gumbel. No cartoons. No old movies. Just Willard in a hat eating corn on the cob and sweet potato sticks.

Doreen returned twenty minutes later. The keys jangled outside, the lock popped, and the door opened. "Mark, come with me," she said. "You have a visitor."

He was suddenly still again, detached, lost in another world. He moved slowly. "Who?" he said in that voice.

"Your lawyer."

He stood and followed her into the hallway. "Are you sure you're okay?" she asked, squatting in front of him. He nodded slowly, and they walked to the stairs.

Reggie was waiting in a small conference room one floor below. She and Doreen exchanged pleasantries, old acquaintances, and the door was locked. They sat on opposite sides of a small, round table.

"Are we buddies?" she asked with a smile.

"Yeah. I'm sorry about yesterday."

"You don't need to apologize, Mark. Believe me, I understand. Did you sleep well?"

"Yeah. Much better than at the hospital."

"Doreen says she's worried about you."

"I'm fine. I'm much better off than Doreen."

"Good." Reggie pulled a newspaper from her briefcase and placed the front page on the table. He read it very slowly.

"You've made the front page three days in a row," she said, trying to coax a smile.

"It's getting old. I thought the hearing was private."

"Supposed to be. Judge Roosevelt called me early this morning. He's very upset about the story. He plans to bring in the reporter and grill him about it."

"It's too late for that, Reggie. The story is right here in print. Everybody sees it. It's pretty obvious I'm the kid who knows too much."

"Right." She waited as he read it again and studied the pictures of himself.

"Have you talked to your mother?" she asked.

"Yes ma'am. Yesterday afternoon around five. She sounded tired."

"She is. I saw her before you called, and she's hanging in there. Ricky had a bad day."

"Yeah. Thanks to those stupid cops. Let's sue them."

"Maybe later. We need to talk about something. After you left the courtroom yesterday, Judge Roosevelt talked to the lawyers and the FBI. He wants you, your mother, and Ricky placed in the Federal Witness Protection Program. He thinks it's the best way to protect you, and I tend to agree."

"What is it?"

"The FBI moves you to a new location, a very secret one, far away from here, and you have new names, new schools, new everything. Your mother has a new job, one that pays a lot more than six dollars an hour. After a few years there, they might move you again, just to be safe. They'll place Ricky in a much better hospital until he's better. Government pays for everything, of course."

"Do I get a new bike?"

"Sure."

"Just kidding. I saw this once in a movie. A Mafia movie. This informant ratted on the Mafia, and the FBI helped him vanish. He had plastic surgery. They found him a new wife, you know, the works. Sent him off to Brazil or some place."

"What happened?"

"It took them about a year to find him. They killed his wife too."

"It was just a movie, Mark. You really have no choice. It's the safest thing to do."

"Of course, I have to tell them everything before they do all these wonderful things for us."

"That's part of the deal."

"The Mafia never forgets, Reggie."

"You've watched too many movies, Mark."

"Maybe so. But has the FBI ever lost a witness in this program?"

The answer was yes, but she couldn't cite a specific example. "I don't know, but we'll meet with them and you can ask all the questions you want."

"What if I don't want to meet with them? What if I want to stay in my little cell here until I'm twenty years old and Judge Roosevelt finally dies? Then can I get out?"

"Fine. What about your mother and Ricky? What happens to them when he's released from the hospital and they have no place to go?"

"They can move in with me. Doreen'll take care of us."

Damn, he was quick for an eleven-year-old. She paused for a moment and smiled at him. He glared at her.

"Listen, Mark, do you trust me?"

"Yes, Reggie. I do trust you. You're the only person in the world I trust right now. So please help me."

"There's no easy way out, okay."

"I know that."

"Your safety is my only concern. The safety of you and your family. Judge Roosevelt feels the same way. Now, it'll take a few days to work out the details of the witness program. The judge instructed the FBI yesterday to start working on it immediately, and I think it's the best thing to do."

"Did you discuss it with my mother?"

"Yes. She wants to talk about it some more. I think she liked the idea."

"But how do you know it'll work, Reggie? Is it totally safe?"

"Nothing is totally safe, Mark. There are no guarantees."

"Wonderful. Maybe they'll find us, maybe they won't. That'll make life exciting, won't it."

"Do you have a better idea?"

"Sure. It's very simple. We collect the insurance money from the trailer. We find another one, and we move into it. I keep my mouth shut and we live happily ever after. I don't really care if they ever find this body, Reggie. I just don't care."

"I'm sorry, Mark, but that can't happen."

"Why not?"

"Because you happen to be very unlucky. You have some important information, and you'll be in trouble until you give it up."

"And then I could be dead."

"I don't think so, Mark."

He crossed his arms over his chest and closed his eyes. There was a slight bruise high on his left cheek, and it was turning brown. This was Friday. He'd been slapped by Clifford on Monday, and though it seemed like weeks ago the bruise reminded her that things were happening much too fast. The poor kid still bore the wounds of the attack.

"Where would we go?" he asked softly, his eyes still closed.

"Far away. Mr. Lewis with the FBI mentioned a children's psychiatric hospital in Portland that's supposed to be one of the best. They'll place Ricky in it with the best of everything."

"Can't they follow us?"

"The FBI can handle it."

He stared at her. "Why do you suddenly trust the FBI?"

"Because there's no one else to trust."

"How long will all this take?"

"There are two problems. The first is the paperwork and details. Mr. Lewis said it could be done within a week. The second is Ricky. It might be a few days before Dr. Greenway will allow him to be moved."

"So I'm in jail for another week?"

"Looks like it. I'm sorry."

"Don't be sorry, Reggie. I can handle this place. In fact, I could stay here for a long time if they'd leave me alone."

"They're not going to leave you alone."

"I need to talk to my mother."

"She might be at the hearing today. Judge Roosevelt wants her there. I suspect he'll have a meeting, off the record, with the FBI people and discuss the witness protection program."

"If I'm gonna stay in jail, why have the hearing?"

"In contempt matters, the judge is required to bring you back into court periodically to allow you to purge yourself of contempt, in other words, to do what he wants you to do."

"The law stinks, Reggie. It's silly, isn't it?"

"Oftentimes, yes."

"I had a wild thought last night as I was trying to go to sleep. I thought—what if the body is not where Clifford said it is. What if Clifford was just crazy and talking out of his head? Have you thought about that, Reggie?"

"Yes. Many times."

"What if all this is a big joke?"

"We can't take that chance, Mark."

He rubbed his eyes and slid his chair back. He began walking around the small room, suddenly very nervous. "So we just pack up and leave our lives behind, right? That's easy for you to say, Reggie. You're not the one who'll have the nightmares. You'll go on like nothing ever happened. You and Clint. Momma Love. Nice little law office. Lots of clients. But not us. We'll live in fear for the rest of our lives."

"I don't think so."

"But you don't know, Reggie. It's easy to sit here and say everything'll be fine. Your neck's not on the line."

"You have no choice, Mark."

"Yes I do. I could lie."

It was just a motion for a continuance, normally a rather boring and routine legal skirmish, but nothing was boring when Barry The Blade Muldanno was the defendant and Willis Upchurch was the mouthpiece. Throw in the enormous ego of the Reverend Roy Foltrigg and the press manipulation skills of Wally Boxx, and this innocuous little hearing for a continuance took on the air of an execution. The courtroom of the Honorable James Lamond was crowded with the curious, the press, and a small army of jealous lawyers who had more important things to do but just happened to be in the neighborhood. They milled about and spoke in grave tones while keeping anxious eyes on the media. Cameras and reporters attract lawyers like blood attracts sharks.

Beyond the railing that separated the players from the spectators, Foltrigg stood in the center of a tight circle of his assistants and whispered, frowning as if they were planning an invasion. He was decked out in his Sunday best—dark three-piece suit, white shirt, red-and-blue silk tie, hair perfect, shoes shined to a glow. He faced the audience, but of course was much too preoccupied to notice anyone. Across the way, Muldanno sat with his back to the gaggle of onlookers and pretended to ignore everyone. He was dressed in black. The ponytail was perfect and arched down to the bottom of his collar. Willis Upchurch sat on the edge of the defense table, also facing the press while engaging himself in a highly animated conversation with a paralegal. If it was humanly possible, Upchurch loved the attention more than Foltrigg.

Muldanno did not yet know of the arrest of Jack Nance eight hours earlier in Memphis. He did not know Cal Sisson had spilled his guts. He had not heard from either Bono or Pirini, and he had sent Gronke back to Memphis this morning in complete ignorance of the night's events.

Foltrigg, on the other hand, was feeling quite smug. Based on the taped conversation gathered from the salt shaker, he would obtain on Monday indictments against Muldanno and Gronke for obstruction of justice. Convictions would be easy. He had them in the bag. He had Muldanno facing five years.

But Roy didn't have the body. And trying Barry The Blade on obstruction charges would not generate anywhere near the publicity of a nasty murder trial complete with color glossies of the decomposed corpse and pathologists' reports about bullet entries and trajectories and exits. Such a trial would last for weeks, and Roy would shine on the evening news every night. He could just see it.

He'd sent Fink back to Memphis early this morning with the grand jury subpoenas for the kid and his lawyer. That should liven things up a bit. He should have the kid talking by Monday afternoon, and maybe, with just a little luck, he'd have the remains of Boyette by Monday night. This thought had kept him at the office until three in the morning. He strutted to the clerk's desk for nothing in particular, then strutted back, glaring at Muldanno, who ignored him.

The courtroom deputy stopped in front of the bench and yelled instructions for all to sit. Court was now in session, the Honorable James Lamond presiding. Lamond appeared from a side door, and was escorted to the bench by an assistant carrying a stack of heavy files. In his early fifties, Lamond was a baby among federal judges. One of countless Reagan appointees, he was typical—all business, no smiles, cut the crap and let's get on with it. He had been the U.S. Attorney for the Southern District of Louisiana immediately prior to Roy Foltrigg, and he hated his successor as much as anyone. Six months after taking the job, Foltrigg had embarked upon a speaking tour of the district in which he presented charts and graphs to Rotarians and Civitans and declared with statistical evidence that his office was now much more efficient than it had been in prior years. Indictments were up. Dope dealers were behind bars. Public officials were running scared. Crime was in trouble, and the public's interest was now being fiercely protected because he, Roy Foltrigg, was now the chief federal prosecutor in the district.

It was a stupid thing to do because it insulted Lamond and angered the other judges. They had little use for the Reverend.

Lamond gazed at the crowded courtroom. Everyone was seated. "My goodness," he started. "I'm delighted at the interest shown here today, but honestly, it's just a hearing on a simple motion." He glared at Foltrigg, who sat in the middle of six assistants. Upchurch had a local lawyer on each side, and two paralegals sitting behind him.

"The court is ready to proceed upon the motion of the defendant, Barry Muldanno, for a continuance. The court notes that this matter is set for trial three weeks from next Monday. Mr. Upchurch, you filed the motion, so you may proceed. Please be brief."

To the surprise of everyone, Upchurch was indeed brief. He simply stated what was common knowledge about the late Jerome Clifford, and explained to the court that he had a trial in federal court in St. Louis beginning three weeks from Monday. He was glib, relaxed, and completely at home in this strange courtroom. A continuance was necessary, he explained, with remarkable efficiency, because he needed time to prepare a defense for what would undoubtedly be a long trial. He finished in ten minutes.

"How much time do you need?" Lamond asked.

"Your Honor, I have a busy trial calendar, and I'll be happy to show it to you. In all fairness, six months would be a reasonable delay."

"Thank you. Anything else?"

"No sir. Thank you, Your Honor." Upchurch took his seat as Foltrigg was leaving his and heading for the podium directly in front of the bench. He glanced at his notes and was about to speak when Lamond beat him to it.

"Mr. Foltrigg, surely you don't deny that the defense is entitled to more time, in light of the circumstances?"

"No, Your Honor, I don't deny this. But I think six months is entirely too much time."

"So how much would you suggest?"

"A month or two. You see, Your Honor, I—"

"I'm not going to sit up here and listen to a haggle over two months or six or three or four, Mr. Foltrigg. If you concede the defendant is entitled to a delay, then I'll take this matter under advisement and set this case for trial whenever my calendar will allow."

Lamond knew Foltrigg needed a delay worse than Muldanno. He just couldn't ask for it. Justice must always be on the attack. Prosecutors are incapable of asking for more time.

"Well, yes, Your Honor," Foltrigg said loudly. "But it's our position that needless delays should be avoided. This matter has dragged on long enough."

"Are you suggesting this court is dragging its feet, Mr. Foltrigg?"

"No, Your Honor, but the defendant is. He's filed every frivolous motion known to American jurisprudence to stall this prosecution. He's tried every tactic, every—"

"Mr. Foltrigg. Mr. Clifford is dead. He can't file any more motions. And now the defendant has a new lawyer, who, as I see it, has only filed one motion."

Foltrigg looked at his notes and started a slow burn. He had not expected to prevail in this little matter, but he certainly hadn't expected to get kicked in the teeth.

"Do you have anything relevant to say?" His Honor asked, as if Foltrigg had yet to say anything of substance.

He grabbed his legal pad and stormed back to his seat. A rather pitiful performance. He should've sent an underling.

"Anything else, Mr. Upchurch?" Lamond asked.

"No sir."

"Very well. Thanks to all of you for your interest in this matter. Sorry it has been so brief. Maybe we'll do more next time. An order for a new trial setting will be forthcoming."

Lamond stood just minutes after he'd sat, and was gone. The reporters filed out, and of course were followed by Foltrigg and Upchurch, who walked to opposite ends of the hallway and held impromptu press conferences.

TWENTY-NINE

THOUGH SLICK MOELLER had reported jailhouse riots, rapes, and beatings, and though he'd stood on the safe side of the doors and bars, he'd never actually, physically, been inside a jail cell. And though this thought was heavy on his mind, he kept his cool and projected the aura of the surefooted reporter and confident believer in the First Amendment. He had a lawyer on each side, high-paid studs from a hundred-man firm that had represented the *Memphis Press* for decades, and they had assured him a dozen times in the past two hours that the Constitution of the United States of America was his friend and on this day would be his shield. Slick wore jeans, a safari jacket, and hiking boots, very much the weather-beaten reporter.

Harry was not impressed with the aura being projected by this weasel. Nor was he impressed with the silk-stocking, blue-blooded Republican mouthpieces who'd never before darkened the doors to his courtroom. Harry was upset. He sat on his bench and read for the tenth time Slick's morning story. He also reviewed applicable First Amendment cases dealing with reporters and their confidential sources. And he took his time so Slick would sweat.

The doors were locked. The bailiff, Slick's friend Grinder, stood quite nervously by the bench. Following the judge's order, two uniformed deputies sat directly behind Slick and his lawyers, and seemed poised and ready for action. This bothered Slick and his lawyers, but they tried not to show it.

The same court reporter with an even shorter skirt filed her nails and waited for the words to start flowing. The same grouchy old woman sat at her table and flipped through the *National Enquirer*. They waited and waited. It was almost twelve-thirty. As usual, the docket was packed and things were behind schedule. Marcia had a club sandwich waiting for Harry between hearings. The Sway hearing was next.

He leaned forward on his elbows and glared down at Slick, who at a hundred and thirty pounds weighed probably a third of what Harry did. "On the record," he barked at the stenographer, and she started pecking away.

Cool as he was, Slick jerked with these first words and sat upright.

"Mr. Moeller, I've brought you here under summons because you've violated a section of the Tennessee Code regarding the confidentiality of my proceedings. This is a very grave matter because we're dealing with the safety and well-being of a small child. Unfortunately, the law does not provide criminal penalties, only contempt."

He removed his reading glasses and began rubbing them with a handkerchief. "Now, Mr. Moeller," he said like a frustrated grandfather, "as upset as I am with you and your story, I am much more troubled by the fact that someone leaked this information to you. Someone who was in this courtroom during the hearing yesterday. Your source troubles me greatly."

Grinder leaned against the wall and pressed his calves against it to keep his knees from shaking. He would not look at Slick. His first heart attack had been only six years ago, and if he didn't control himself this might be the big one.

"Please sit in the witness chair, Mr. Moeller," Harry instructed with a sweep of the hand. "Be my guest."

Slick was sworn by the old grouch. He placed one hiking boot on one knee, and looked at his attorneys for reassurance. They were not looking at him. Grinder studied the ceiling tiles.

"You are under oath, Mr. Moeller," Harry reminded him just seconds after he'd been sworn.

"Yes sir," he uttered and feebly attempted to smile at this huge man who was sitting high above him and peering down over the railing of the bench.

"Did you in fact write the story in today's paper with your name on it?"

"Yes sir."

"Did you write it by yourself, or did someone assist you?"

"Well, Your Honor, I wrote every word, if that's what you mean."

"That's what I mean. Now, in the fourth paragraph of this story, you write, and I quote, 'Mark Sway refused to answer questions about Barry Muldanno or Boyd Boyette.' End quote. Did you write that, Mr. Moeller?"

"Yes sir."

"And were you present during the hearing yesterday when the child testified?"

"No sir."

"Were you in this building?"

"Uh, yes sir, I was. Nothing wrong with that, is there?"

"Be quiet, Mr. Moeller. I'll ask the questions, and you answer them. Do you understand the relationship here?"

"Yes sir." Slick pleaded with his eyes to his lawyers, but both were deep into reading at this moment. He felt alone.

"So you weren't present. Now, Mr. Moeller, how did you learn that the child refused to answer my questions about Barry Muldanno or Boyd Boyette?"

"I had a source."

Grinder had never thought of himself as a source. He was just a low-paid courtroom bailiff with a uniform and a gun, and bills to pay. He was about to be sued by Sears for his wife's credit card. He wanted to wipe the sweat from his forehead but was afraid to move.

"A source," Harry repeated, mocking Slick. "Of course you had a source, Mr. Moeller. I assumed this. You weren't here. Someone told you. This means you had a source. Now, who was your source?"

The lawyer with the grayest hair quickly stood to speak. He was dressed in standard big-firm attire—charcoal suit, white button-down, red tie but with a daring yellow stripe on it, and black shoes. His name was Alliphant. He was a partner who normally avoided courtrooms. "Your Honor, if I may."

Harry grimaced, and he slowly turned from the witness. His mouth was open as if he were shocked at this daring interruption. He scowled at Alliphant, who repeated himself. "If I may, Your Honor."

Harry let him hang there for an eternity, then said, "You haven't been in my courtroom before, have you, Mr. Alliphant?"

"No sir," he answered, still standing.

"I didn't think so. Not one of your usual hangouts. How many lawyers are in your firm, Mr. Alliphant?"

"A hundred and seven, at last count."

Harry whistled and shook his head. "That's a buncha lawyers. Do any of them practice in Juvenile Court?"

"Well, I'm sure some do, Your Honor."

"Which ones?"

Alliphant stuck one hand in one pocket while running a loose finger along the edge of his legal pad. He did not belong here. His legal world was one of boardrooms and thick documents, of fat retainers and fancy lunches. He was rich because he billed three hundred dollars an hour and had thirty partners doing the same. His firm prospered because it paid seventy associates fifty thousand a year and expected them to bill five times that. He was here ostensibly because he was chief counsel for the paper, but actually because no one in the firm's litigation section could make the hearing on two hours' notice.

Harry despised him, his firm, and their ilk. He did not trust the corporate types who came down from the tall buildings to mingle with the lower class only when necessary. They were arrogant and afraid to get their hands dirty.

"Sit down, Mr. Alliphant," he said, pointing. "You do not stand in my courtroom. Sit."

Alliphant awkwardly backed into his chair.

"Now what are you trying to say, Mr. Alliphant?"

"Well, Your Honor, we object to these questions, and we object to the court's interrogation of Mr. Moeller on the grounds that his story is protected free speech under the First Amendment of the Constitution. Now—"

"Mr. Alliphant, have you read the applicable code section dealing with closed hearings in juvenile matters? Surely you have."

"Yes sir, I have. And, frankly, Your Honor, I have some real problems with this section."

"Oh you do? Go on."

"Yes sir. It's my opinion that this code section is unconstitutional, as written. I have some cases here from other—"

"Unconstitutional?" Harry asked with raised eyebrows.

"Yes sir," Alliphant answered firmly.

"Do you know who wrote the code section, Mr. Alliphant?"

Alliphant turned to his associate as if he knew everything. But he shook his head.

"I wrote it, Mr. Alliphant," Harry said loudly. "Me. *Moi.* Yours truly. And if you knew anything about juvenile law in this state, you would know that I am the expert because I wrote the law. Now, what can you say about that?"

Slick slid down in his chair. He'd covered a thousand trials. He'd seen lawyers hammered by angry judges, and he knew their clients usually suffered.

"I contend it's unconstitutional, Your Honor," Alliphant said gallantly.

"And the last thing I intend to do, Mr. Alliphant, is to get into a long, hot-air debate with you about the First Amendment. If you don't like the law, then take it up on appeal and get it changed. I honestly don't care. But right now, while I'm missing lunch, I want your client to answer the question." He turned back to Slick, who was waiting in terror. "Now, Mr. Moeller, who was your source?"

Grinder was about to vomit. He stuck his thumbs under his belt and pressed against his stomach. By reputation, Slick was a man of his word. He always protected his sources.

"I cannot reveal my source," Slick said in an effort at great drama, the martyr willing to face death. Grinder took a deep breath. Such sweet words.

Harry immediately motioned for the two deputies. "I find you in contempt, Mr. Moeller, and order you to jail." The deputies stood beside Slick, who looked around wildly for help.

"Your Honor," Alliphant said, standing without thinking. "We object to this! You cannot—"

Harry ignored Alliphant. He spoke to the deputies. "Take him to the city jail. No special treatment. No favors. I'll bring him back Monday for another try."

They yanked Slick up and handcuffed him. "Do something!" he

yelled at Alliphant, who was saying, "This is protected speech, Your Honor. You can't do this."

"I'm doing it, Mr. Alliphant," Harry yelled. "And if you don't sit down, you'll be in the same cell with your client."

Alliphant dropped into his chair.

They dragged Slick to the door, and as they opened it, Harry had one final thing to say. "Mr. Moeller, if I read one word in your paper written by you while in jail, I'll let you sit there for a month before I bring you back. You understand."

Slick couldn't speak. "We'll appeal, Slick," Alliphant promised as they shoved him through and closed the door. "We'll appeal."

Dianne Sway sat in a heavy wood chair, holding her oldest son and watching the sunlight filter through the dusty, broken blinds of Witness Room B. The tears were gone and words had failed them.

After five days and four nights of involuntary confinement in the psychiatric ward, she at first had been happy to leave it. But happiness these days came in tiny spurts, and she now longed to return to Ricky's bed. Now that she'd seen Mark, and held him and cried with him, she knew he was safe. Under the circumstances, that was all a mother could ask.

She didn't trust her instincts or judgment. Five days in a cave takes away any sense of reality. The endless series of shocks had left her drained and stunned. The drugs—pills to sleep and pills to wake up and pills to get through it—deadened the mind so that her life was a series of snapshots thrown on the table one at a time. The brain worked, but in slow motion.

"They want us to go to Portland," she said, rubbing his arm.

"Reggie talked to you about it."

"Yes, we had a long talk yesterday. There's a good place for Ricky out there, and we can start over."

"Sounds good, but it scares me."

"Scares me too, Mark. I don't want to live the next forty years looking over my shoulder. I read a story one time in some magazine about a Mafia informant who helped the FBI and they agreed to hide him. Just like they want us to do. I think it took two years before the Mafia found him and blew him up in his car."

"I think I saw the movie."

"I can't live like that, Mark."

"Can we get another trailer?"

"I think so. I talked to Mr. Tucker this morning, and he says he had the trailer covered with plenty of insurance. He said he had another one for us. And I still have my job. In fact, they delivered my paycheck to the hospital this morning."

Mark smiled at the thought of returning to the trailer park and hanging out with the kids. He even missed school.

"These people are deadly, Mark."

"I know. I've met them."

She thought for a second, then asked, "You what?"

"I guess it's something else I forgot to tell you."

"I'd like to hear it."

"It happened a couple of days ago at the hospital. I don't know which day. They're all running together." He took a deep breath. He told her about his encounter with the man and the switchblade and their family portrait. Normally, she, or any mother, would have been shocked. But for Dianne, it was just another event in this horrible week.

"Why didn't you tell me?" she asked.

"Because I didn't want to worry you."

"You know, we might not be in this trouble if you'd told me everything up front."

"Don't fuss at me, Mom. I can't take it."

She couldn't take it either, so she dropped it. Reggie knocked on the door and it opened. "We need to go," she said. "The judge is waiting."

They followed her through the hall and around a corner. Two deputies trailed behind. "Are you nervous?" Dianne whispered.

"No. It's no big deal, Mom."

Harry was munching on the sandwich and flipping through the file when they entered the courtroom. Fink, Ord, and Baxter McLemore, the Juvenile Court prosecutor-of-the-day, were all seated together at their table, all quiet and subdued, all bored and waiting for what would undoubtedly be a quick appearance by the kid. Fink and Ord were captivated by the court reporter's legs and skirt. Her figure was obscene—tiny waist, healthy breasts, slender legs. She was the only redeeming element in this rinky-dink courtroom, and Fink had to admit to himself that he'd thought about her on the flight to New Orleans yesterday. And he'd thought about her all the way back to Memphis. She was not disappointing him. The skirt was at mid-thigh and inching upward.

Harry looked at Dianne and gave his best smile. His large teeth were perfect and his eyes were warm. "Hello, Ms. Sway," he said sweetly. She nodded and tried to smile.

"It is a pleasure meeting you, and I'm sorry it has to be under these circumstances."

"Thank you, Your Honor," she said softly to the man who'd ordered her son to jail.

Harry looked at Fink with contempt. "I trust everyone has read this morning's *Memphis Press.* It has a fascinating story about our proceedings yesterday, and the man who wrote the story is now in jail. I intend to investigate this matter further, and I am confident I will find the leak."

Grinder, by the door, was suddenly ill again.

"And when I find it, I intend to fix it with a contempt order. So, ladies and gentlemen, keep your mouths shut. Not a word to anyone." He took the file. "Now, Mr. Fink, where's Mr. Foltrigg?"

Sitting firmly in place, Fink answered, "He's in New Orleans, Your Honor. I have a copy of the court order you requested."

"Fine. I'll take your word for it. Madam Clerk, swear the witness."

Madam Clerk threw her hand in the air, and barked at Mark, "Raise your right hand." Mark stood awkwardly, and was sworn.

"You can remain in your seat," Harry said. Reggie was on his right, Dianne on the left.

"Mark, I'm going to ask you some questions, okay?"

"Yes sir."

"Prior to his death, did Mr. Clifford say anything to you about a Mr. Barry Muldanno?"

"I'm not going to answer that."

"Did Mr. Clifford mention the name of Boyd Boyette?"

"I'm not going to answer that."

"Did Mr. Clifford say anything about the murder of Boyd Boyette?"

"I'm not going to answer that."

"Did Mr. Clifford say anything about the present location of the body of Boyd Boyette?"

"I'm not going to answer that."

Harry paused and looked at his notes. Dianne had stopped breathing and was staring blankly at Mark. "It's okay, Mom," he whispered to her.

"Your Honor," he said in a strong, confident voice. "I want you to understand that I'm not answering for the same reasons I gave yesterday. I'm just scared, that's all."

Harry nodded but gave no expression. He was neither angry nor pleased. "Mr. Bailiff, take Mark back to the witness room, and keep him there until we finish. He can talk to his mother before he's transported to the detention center."

Grinder's knees were putty, but he managed to lead Mark from the courtroom.

Harry unzipped his robe. "Let's go off the record. Madam Clerk, you and Ms. Gregg can go to lunch." It was not an offer, but a demand. Harry wanted fewer ears in the courtroom.

Ms. Gregg swung her legs toward Fink, and his heart stopped. He and Ord watched with their mouths open as she stood, took her purse, and pranced from the courtroom.

"Get the FBI, Mr. Fink," Harry instructed.

McThune and a weary K. O. Lewis were fetched and took seats behind Ord. Lewis was a busy man with a thousand important items stacked on his desk in Washington, and he'd asked himself a hundred times in the past twenty-four hours why he'd come to Memphis. Of course, Director Voyles wanted him here, which clarified his priorities immensely.

"Mr. Fink, you indicated before the hearing there is an urgent matter that I should know about."

"Yes sir. Mr. Lewis would like to address it."

"Mr. Lewis. Please be brief."

"Yes, Your Honor. We've had Barry Muldanno under surveillance for several months, and yesterday we obtained by electronic means a conversation between Muldanno and Paul Gronke. It took place in a bar in the French Quarter, and I think you need to hear it."

"You have the tape?"

"Yes sir."

"Then let it roll." Harry was suddenly unconcerned with time.

McThune quickly assembled a tape player and speaker on the desk in front of Fink, and Lewis inserted a micro-cassette. "The first voice you'll hear is that of Muldanno," he explained like a chemist preparing a demonstration. "Then Gronke."

The courtroom was still and quiet as the scratchy but very clear voices squawked from the speaker. The entire conversation was captured; the suggestion by Muldanno of hitting the kid, and Gronke's doubts about getting to him; the idea of hitting the kid's mother or brother, and Gronke's protests of killing innocent people; Muldanno's talk of killing his lawyer, and the laughter about it doing wonders for the legal profession; the boasting of Gronke about taking care of the trailer; and finally the plans to bug the lawyer's phones that night.

It was chilling. Fink and Ord had heard it ten times already, so they were noncommittal. Reggie closed her eyes when the taking of her life was so nonchalantly bantered about. Dianne was rigid with fear. Harry stared at the speaker as if he could see their faces, and when the tape was finished and Lewis punched the button, he simply said, "Play it again."

They listened to it the second time, and the shock began to wear off. Dianne was trembling. Reggie held her arm and tried to be brave, but the easy talk of killing the kid's lawyer made her blood run cold. Dianne's skin broke out in goose pimples, and her eyes began to water. She thought of Ricky, who at this moment was being watched by Greenway and a nurse, and prayed he was safe.

"I've heard enough," Harry said when the tape stopped. Lewis took his seat, and they waited for His Honor to give direction. He wiped his eyes with a handkerchief, then took a long drink of ice tea. He smiled at Dianne. "Now, Ms. Sway, do you understand why we've placed Mark in the detention center?"

"I think so."

"Two reasons. The first is that he refused to answer my questions, but at the moment, that's not nearly as important as the second. He's in great danger, as you've just heard. What would you like for me to do next?"

It was an unfair question posed to a scared, deeply troubled, and irrational person, and she didn't like him asking it. She just shook her head. "I don't know," she mumbled.

Harry spoke slowly, and there was no doubt he knew exactly what should be done next. "Reggie has told me that she's discussed the witness protection program with you. Tell me what you think."

Dianne raised her head and bit her lip. She thought for a few seconds and tried to focus on the tape recorder. "I do not want those people," she said deliberately, nodding at the recorder, "following me and my children for the rest of our lives. And I'm afraid that will happen if Mark gives you what you want."

"You'll have the protection of the FBI and every necessary agency of the U.S. Government."

"But no one can completely guarantee our safety. These are my children, Your Honor, and I'm a single parent. There's no one else. If I make a mistake, I could lose, well, I can't even imagine it."

"I think you'll be safe, Ms. Sway. There are thousands of government witnesses now being protected."

"But some have been found, haven't they?"

It was a quiet question that hit hard. Neither McThune nor Lewis could deny the fact that witnesses had been lost. There was a long silence.

"Well, Ms. Sway," Harry finally said with a great deal of compassion, "what's the alternative?"

"Why can't you arrest these people? Lock them up somewhere. I mean, it looks as if they're just roaming free terrorizing me and my family, and also Reggie here. What're the damned cops doing?"

"It's my understanding, Ms. Sway, that one arrest was made last night. The police here are looking for the two men who burned your trailer, two thugs from New Orleans named Bono and Pirini, but they haven't found them. Is that correct, Mr. Lewis?"

"Yes sir. We think they're still in the city. And I might add, Your Honor, that the U.S. Attorney in New Orleans intends to indict Muldanno and Gronke early next week on charges of obstruction of justice. So they'll be in custody very soon."

"But this is the Mafia, isn't it?" Dianne asked.

Every idiot who could read the newspapers knew it was the Mafia. It was a Mafia killing by a Mafia gunman whose family had been Mafia hoods in New Orleans for four decades. Her question was so simple, yet it implied the obvious: The Mafia is an invisible army with plenty of soldiers.

Lewis did not wish to answer the question, so he waited for His Honor, who likewise hoped it would simply go away. There was a long, awkward silence.

Dianne cleared her throat and spoke in a much stronger voice. "Your Honor, when you guys can show me a way to completely protect my children, then I'll help you. But not until then."

"So you want him to stay in jail," Fink blurted.

She turned and glared at Fink, less than ten feet away. "Sir, I'd rather have him in a detention center than in a grave."

Fink slumped in his chair and stared at the floor. Seconds ticked away. Harry looked at his watch, and zipped his robe. "I suggest we meet again Monday at noon. Let's take things one day at a time."

THIRTY

PAUL GRONKE finished his unexpected trip to Minneapolis as the Northwest 727 lifted off the runway and started for Atlanta. From Atlanta, he hoped to catch a direct flight to New Orleans, and once home he had no plans to leave for a long time. Maybe years. Regardless of his friendship with Muldanno, Gronke was tired of this mess. He could break a thumb or a leg when necessary, and he could huff and puff and scare almost anybody. But he did not particularly enjoy stalking little kids and waving switchblades at them. He made a nice living off his clubs and beer joints, and if The Blade needed help, he'd just have to lean on his family. Gronke was not family. He was not Mafia. And he was not going to kill anyone for Barry Muldanno.

He'd made two phone calls this morning as soon as his flight arrived at the Memphis airport. The first call spooked him because no one answered. He then dialed a backup number for a recorded message, and again there was no answer. He walked quickly to the Northwest ticket counter and paid cash for a one-way ticket to Minneapolis. Then he found the Delta counter and paid cash for a one-way ticket to Dallas-Fort Worth. Then he bought a ticket to Chicago, on United. He roamed the concourses for an hour, watching his back and seeing nothing, and at the last second hopped on Northwest.

Bono and Pirini had strict instructions. The two phone calls meant one of two things: either the cops had them, or they were forced to pull up stakes and haul ass. Neither thought was comforting.

The flight attendant brought two beers. It was a few minutes after one, too early to start drinking, but he was edgy, and what the hell. It was 5 P.M. somewhere.

Muldanno would flip out and start throwing things. He'd run to his uncle and borrow some more thugs. They'd descend upon Memphis and start hurting people. Finesse was not Barry's long suit.

Their friendship had started in high school, in the tenth grade, their last year of formal education before they dropped out and began hustling on the streets of New Orleans. Barry's route to crime was preordained by family. Gronke's was a bit more complicated. Their first venture had been a fencing operation that had been wildly successful. The profits, however, were siphoned off by Barry and sent to the family. They peddled some drugs, ran some numbers, managed a whorehouse, all cash-rich ventures. But Gronke saw little of the cash. After ten years of this lopsided partnership, he told Barry he wanted a place of his own. Barry helped him buy a topless bar, then a porno house. Gronke made money and was able to keep it. At about this point in their careers, Barry started his killing, and Gronke established more distance between them.

But they remained friends. A month or so after Boyette disappeared, the two of them spent a long weekend at Johnny Sulari's house in Acapulco with a couple of strippers. After the girls had passed out one night, they went for a long walk on the beach. Barry was drinking tequila and talking more than usual. His name had just surfaced as a suspect. He bragged to his friend about the killing.

The landfill in Lafourche Parish was worth millions to the Sulari family. Johnny's scheme was to eventually route most of the garbage from New Orleans to it. Senator Boyette had been an unexpected enemy. His antics had attracted lots of negative publicity for the dump, and the more ink Boyette received the crazier he'd become. He'd launched federal investigations. He'd called in dozens of EPA bureaucrats who'd prepared massive volumes of studies, most of which condemned the landfill. In Washington, he'd hounded the Justice Department until it initiated its own investigation into the allegations of mob involvement. Senator Boyette became the biggest obstacle to Johnny's gold mine.

The decision had been made to hit Boyette.

Sipping from a bottle of Cuervo Gold, Barry laughed about the killing. He stalked Boyette for six months, and was pleasantly surprised to learn that the Senator, who was divorced, had an affinity for young women. Cheap young women, the kind he could find in a bordello and buy for fifty bucks. His favorite place was a seedy roadhouse halfway between New Orleans and Houma, the site of the landfill. It was in oil country, and frequented by offshore roustabouts and the cute little whores they attracted. Evidently, the Senator knew the owner and had a special arrangement. He always parked behind a garbage dumpster, away from the gravel lot crowded with monster pickups and Harleys. He always used the rear entrance by the kitchen.

The Senator's trips to Houma became more frequent. He was raising hell in town meetings and holding press conferences every week. And he enjoyed the drives back to New Orleans with his little quickies at the roadhouse.

The hit was easy, Barry said as they sat on the beach with foamy saltwater rushing around them. He trailed Boyette for twenty miles after a rowdy landfill meeting in Houma, and waited patiently in the darkness behind the roadhouse. When Boyette emerged after his little liaison, he hit him in the head with a nightstick and quickly threw him in the backseat. He stopped a few miles down the road and pumped four bullets in his head. The body was wrapped in garbage bags and placed in the trunk.

Imagine that, Barry had marveled, a U.S. Senator snatched from the darkness of a run-down bordello. He'd served for twenty-one years, chaired powerful committees, eaten at the White House, trotted around the globe searching for ways to spend taxpayers' money, had eighteen assistants and gofers working for him, and, bam!, just like that, got caught with his pants down. Barry thought it was hilarious. One of his easiest jobs, he said, as if there'd been hundreds.

A state trooper had stopped Barry for speeding ten miles outside of New Orleans. Imagine that, he said, chatting with a cop with a warm body in the trunk. He talked football and avoided a ticket. But then he panicked, and decided to hide the body in a different place. Gronke was tempted to ask where, but thought better of it.

The case against him was shaky. The trooper's records placed Barry in the vicinity at the time of the disappearance. But with no body, there was no proof of the time of death. One of the prostitutes saw a man who resembled Barry in the shadows of the parking lot while the Senator was being entertained. She was now under government protection, but not expected to make a good witness. Barry's car had been cleaned and sanitized. No blood samples, no fibers or hair. The star of the government's case was a Mafia informant, a man who'd spent twenty of his forty-two years in jail, and who was not expected to live to testify. A .22 caliber Ruger had been seized from the apartment of one of Barry's girlfriends, but, again, with no corpse it was impossible to determine the cause of death. Barry's fingerprints were on the gun. It was a gift, said the girlfriend.

Juries are hesitant to convict without first knowing for certain that the victim is indeed dead. And Boyette was such an eccentric character that rumors and gossip had produced all sorts of wild speculation about his disappearance. One published report detailed his recent history of psychiatric problems, and thus had given rise to a popular theory that he'd gone nuts and run off with a teenage hooker. He had gambling debts. He drank too much. His ex-wife had sued him for fraud in the divorce. And on and on.

Boyette had plenty of reasons to disappear.

And now, an eleven-year-old kid in Memphis knew where he was buried. Gronke opened the second beer.

Doreen held Mark's arm and walked him to his room. His steps were measured and he stared at the floor in front of them as if he'd just witnessed a car bomb in a crowded marketplace.

"Are you okay, baby?" she asked, the wrinkles around her eyes bunched together with terrible concern.

He nodded and plodded along. She quickly unlocked the door, and placed him on the bottom bunk.

"Lie right here, sweetheart," she said, pulling back the covers and swinging his legs onto the bed. She knelt beside him and searched his eyes for answers. "Are you sure you're okay?"

He nodded but could say nothing.

"Do you want me to call a doctor?"

"No," he managed to say in a hollow voice. "I'm fine."

"I think I'll get a doctor," she said. He grabbed her arm and squeezed tightly.

"I just need some rest," he mumbled. "That's all."

She unlocked the door with the key and slowly eased out, her eyes never leaving Mark. When the door closed and clicked, he swung his feet to the floor.

At three Friday afternoon, Harry Roosevelt's legendary patience was gone. His weekend would be spent in the Ozarks, fishing with his two sons, and as he sat on the bench and looked at the courtroom still crowded with deadbeat dads awaiting sentencing for nonpayment, his mind kept wandering to thoughts of long sleepy mornings and cool mountain streams. At least two dozen men filled the pews of the main courtroom, and most had either current wives or current girlfriends sitting anxiously at their elbows. A few had brought their lawyers, though there was no legal relief available at this moment. All of them would soon be serving weekend sentences at the Shelby County Penal Farm for failing to pay child support.

Harry wanted to adjourn by four, but it looked doubtful. His two sons waited in the back row. Outside, the Jeep was packed, and when the gavel finally rapped for the last time, they would rush His Honor from the building and whisk him away to the Buffalo River. That was the plan anyway. They were bored, but they had been here before many times.

In spite of the chaos in the front of the courtroom—clerks hauling bundles of files in and out, lawyers whispering as they waited, deputies standing by, defendants being shuffled to the bench then out the door—Harry's assembly line moved with determined efficiency. He glared at each deadbeat, scolded a bit, sometimes a quick lecture, then he signed an order and moved on to the next one.

Reggie eased into the courtroom and made her way to the clerk seated next to the bench. They whispered for a minute with Reggie pointing to a document she'd brought with her. She laughed at something that was probably not that funny, but Harry heard her and motioned her to the bench.

"Something wrong?" he asked with his hand over the microphone.

"No. Mark's fine, I guess. I need a quick favor. It's another case."

Harry smiled and turned off the mike. Typical Reggie. Her cases were always the most important and needed immediate attention. "What is it?" he asked.

The clerk handed Harry the file while Reggie handed him an order. "It's another snatch and run by the Welfare Department," she said in a low voice. No one was listening. No one cared.

"Who's the kid?" he asked, flipping through the file.

"Ronald Allan Thomas the Third. Also known as Trip Thomas. He was taken into custody last night by Welfare and placed in a foster home. His mother hired me an hour ago."

"Says here he's been abandoned and neglected."

"Not true, Harry. It's a long story, but I assure you this kid has good parents and a clean home."

"And you want the kid released?"

"Immediately. I'll pick him up myself, and take him home to Momma Love if I have to."

"And feed him lasagna."

"Of course."

Harry scanned the order and signed his name at the bottom. "I'll have to trust you, Reggie."

"You always do. I saw Damon and Al back there. They look rather bored."

Harry handed the order to the clerk who stamped it. "So am I. When I get this riffraff cleared from my courtroom, we're going fishing."

"Good luck. I'll see you Monday."

"Have a nice weekend, Reggie. You'll check on Mark, won't you?"

"Of course."

"Try and talk some sense into his mother. The more I think about it, the more I'm convinced these people must cooperate with the Feds and enter the witness program. Hell, they have nothing to lose by starting over. Convince her they'll be protected."

"I'll try. I'll spend some time with her this weekend. Maybe we can wrap it up Monday."

"I'll see you then."

Reggie winked at him, and backed away from the bench. The clerk handed her a copy of the order, and she left the courtroom.

THIRTY-ONE

THOMAS FINK, fresh from another exciting flight from Memphis, entered Foltrigg's office at four-thirty Friday afternoon. Wally Boxx sat like a faithful lapdog on the sofa, writing what Fink presumed to be another speech for their boss, or perhaps a press release for upcoming indictments. Roy's shoeless feet were on his desk and the phone was cradled on his shoulder. He was listening with his eyes closed. The day had been a disaster. Lamond had embarrassed him in a crowded courtroom. Roosevelt had failed to make the kid talk. He'd had it with judges.

Fink removed his jacket and sat down. Foltrigg ended his phone chat and hung up. "Where are the grand jury subpoenas?" he asked.

"I hand-delivered them to the U.S. marshal in Memphis, and gave him strict instructions not to serve them until he heard from you."

Boxx left the sofa and sat next to Fink. It would be a shame if he were excluded from a conversation.

Roy rubbed his eyes and ran his fingers through his hair. Frustrating, very frustrating. "So what's the kid gonna do, Thomas? You were there. You saw the kid's mother. You heard her voice. What's gonna happen?"

"I don't know. It's obvious the kid has no plans to talk anytime soon. He and his mother are terrified. They've watched too much television, seen too many Mafia informants blown to bits. She's convinced they won't be safe in witness protection. She's really scared. The woman's been through hell this week."

"That's real touching," Boxx mumbled.

"I have no choice but to use the subpoenas," Foltrigg said

gravely, pretending to be troubled by this thought. "They leave me no choice. We were fair and reasonable. We asked the youth court in Memphis to help us with the kid, and it simply has not worked. It's time we got these people down here, on our turf, in our courtroom, in front of our people, and made them talk. Don't you agree, Thomas?"

Fink was not in full agreement. "Jurisdiction worries me. The kid is under the jurisdiction of the Juvenile Court up there, and I'm not sure what'll happen when he gets the subpoena."

Roy was smiling. "That's right, but the court is closed for the weekend. We've done some research, and I think federal law supersedes state law on this one, don't you, Wally?"

"I think so. Yes," said Wally.

"And I've talked to the marshal's office here. I've told them I want the boys in Memphis to pick the kid up tomorrow and bring him here so he can face the grand jury Monday. I don't think the locals in Memphis will interfere with the U.S. marshal's office. We've made arrangements to house him here in the Juvenile Wing at city jail. Should be a piece of cake."

"What about the lawyer?" asked Fink. "You can't make her testify. If she knows anything, she learned it in the course of her representation of the kid. It's privileged."

"Pure harassment," Foltrigg admitted with a smile. "She and the kid will be scared to death on Monday. We'll be calling the shots, Thomas."

"Speaking of Monday. Judge Roosevelt wants us in his courtroom at noon."

Roy and Wally had a good laugh at this. "He'll be a lonely judge, won't he," Foltrigg said with a chuckle. "You, me, the kid, and the kid's lawyer will all be down here. What a fool."

Fink did not join their laughter.

At five, Doreen knocked on the door, and rattled keys until it opened. Mark was on the floor playing checkers against himself, and immediately became a zombie. He sat on his feet, and stared at the checkerboard as if in a trance.

"Are you okay, Mark?"

Mark didn't answer.

"Mark, honey, I'm really worried about you. I think I'll call the doctor. You might be going into shock, just like your little brother."

He shook his head slowly, and looked at her with mournful eyes. "No, I'm okay. I just need some rest."

"Could you eat something?"

"Maybe some pizza."

"Sure, baby. I'll get one ordered. Look, honey, I get off duty in five minutes, but I'll tell Telda to watch you real close, okay. Will you be all right till I get back in the morning?"

"Maybe," he moaned.

"Poor child. You got no business in here."

"I'll make it."

Telda was much less concerned than Doreen. She checked on Mark twice. On her third visit to his room, around eight o'clock, she brought visitors. She knocked and opened the door slowly, and Mark was about to do his trance routine when he saw the two large men in suits.

"Mark, these men are U.S. marshals," Telda said nervously. Mark stood near the toilet. The room was suddenly tiny.

"Hi, Mark," said the first one. "I'm Vern Duboski, deputy U.S. marshal." His words were crisp and precise. A Yankee. But that was all Mark noticed. He was holding some papers.

"You are Mark Sway?"

He nodded, unable to speak.

"Don't be afraid, Mark. We just have to give you these papers."

He looked at Telda for help, but she was clueless. "What are they?" he asked nervously.

"It's a grand jury subpoena, and it means that you have to appear before a federal grand jury on Monday in New Orleans. Now, don't worry, we're gonna come get you tomorrow afternoon and drive you down."

A nervous pain shot through his stomach and he was weak. His mouth was dry. "Why?" he asked.

"We can't answer that, Mark. It's none of our business, really. We're just following orders."

Mark stared at the papers Vern was waving. New Orleans! "Have you told my mother?"

"Well, you see, Mark, we're required to give her a copy of these same papers. We'll explain everything to her, and we'll tell her you'll be fine. In fact, she can go with you if she wants."

"She can't go with me. She can't leave Ricky."

The marshals looked at each other. "Well, anyway, we'll explain everything to her."

"I have a lawyer, you know. Have you told her?"

"No. We're not required to notify the attorneys, but you're welcome to call her if you like."

"Does he have access to a telephone?" the second one asked Telda.

"Only if I bring him one," she said.

"You can wait thirty minutes, can't you?"

"If you say so," Telda said.

"So, Mark, in about thirty minutes you can call your lawyer." Duboski paused and looked at his sidekick. "Well, good luck to you, Mark. Sorry if we scared you."

They left him standing near the toilet, leaning on the wall for support, more confused than ever, scared to death. And angry. The system was rotten. He was sick of laws and lawyers and courts, of cops and agents and marshals, of reporters and judges and jailers. Dammit!

He yanked a paper towel from the wall and wiped his eyes, then sat on the toilet.

He swore to the walls that he would not go to New Orleans.

Two other deputy marshals would serve Dianne, and two more would serve Ms. Reggie Love at home, and all this serving of subpoenas was carefully coordinated to happen at roughly the same time. In reality, one deputy marshal, or one unemployed concrete worker for that matter, could have served all three subpoenas at a leisurely pace and completed the job in an hour. But it was more fun to use six men in three cars with radios and telephones and guns, and to strike quickly under cover of darkness like a Special Forces assault unit.

They knocked on Momma Love's kitchen door, and waited until

the porch light came on and she appeared behind the screen. She instantly knew they were trouble. During the nightmare of Reggie's divorce and commitments and legal warfare with Joe Cardoni, there had been several deputies and men in dark suits standing at her doorway at odd hours. These guys always brought trouble.

"Can I help you?" she asked with a forced smile.

"Yes ma'am. We're looking for one Reggie Love."

They even talked like cops. "And who are you?" she asked.

"I'm Mike Hedley, and this is Terry Flagg. We're U.S. marshals."

"U.S. marshals, or deputy U.S. marshals? Let me see some ID."

This shocked them, and in perfect synchronization they reached into their pockets for their badges. "We're deputy U.S. marshals, ma'am."

"That's not what you said," she said, examining the badges held up to the screen door.

Reggie was sipping coffee on the tiny balcony of her apartment when she heard the car doors slam. She was now peeking around the corner and looking down at the two men standing under the light. She could hear the voices, but could not understand what they were saying.

"Sorry, ma'am," Hedley said.

"Why do you want one Reggie Love?" Momma Love asked with a suspicious frown.

"Does she live here?"

"Maybe, maybe not. What do you want?"

Hedley and Flagg looked at each other. "We're supposed to serve her with a subpoena."

"A subpoena for what?"

"May I ask who you are?" Flagg said.

"I'm her mother. Now what's the subpoena for?"

"It's a grand jury subpoena. She's supposed to appear before a grand jury in New Orleans on Monday. We can just leave it with you, if you like."

"I'm not accepting service of it," she said, as if she fought with process servers every week. "You have to actually serve her, if I'm not mistaken."

"Where is she?"

"She doesn't live here."

This irritated them. "That's her car," Hedley said, nodding at Reggie's Mazda.

"She doesn't live here," Momma Love repeated.

"Okay, but is she here now?"

"No."

"Do you know where she is?"

"Have you tried her office? She works all the time."

"But why is her car here?"

"Sometimes she rides with Clint, her secretary. They may be having dinner, or something."

They gave each other frustrated stares. "I think she's here," Hedley said, suddenly aggressive.

"You're not paid to think, son. You're paid to serve those damned papers, and I'm telling you she's not here." Momma Love raised her voice when she said this, and Reggie heard it.

"Can we search the house?" Flagg asked.

"If you have a warrant, you can search the house. If you don't have a warrant, it's time to get off my property."

They both took a step back, and stopped. "I hope you're not obstructing the service of a federal subpoena," Hedley said gravely. It was supposed to have an ominous, dire ring to it, but Hedley failed miserably.

"And I hope you're not trying to threaten an old woman." Her hands were on her hips and she was ready for combat.

They surrendered and backed away. "We'll be back," Hedley promised as he opened his car door.

"I'll be here," she shouted angrily, opening the front door. She stood on the small porch and watched as they backed into the street. She waited for five minutes, and when she was certain they were gone, she went to Reggie's apartment over the garage.

Dianne took the subpoena from the polite and apologetic gentleman without comment. She read it by the light of the dim lamp next to Ricky's bed. It contained no instructions, just a command for Mark to appear before the grand jury at 10 A.M. at the address below. There was no hint of how he was to get there; no clue as to when he might return; no warning of what could happen if he failed to comply or failed to talk.

She called Reggie, but there was no answer.

Though Clint's apartment was only fifteen minutes away, the drive took almost an hour. She zigzagged through midtown, then raced around the interstate going nowhere in particular, and when she was certain she was not being followed, she parked on a street crowded with empty cars. She walked four blocks to his apartment.

His nine o'clock date had been abruptly canceled, and it was a date with a lot of promise. "I'm sorry," Reggie said as he opened the door and she eased through it.

"That's okay. Are you all right?" He took her bag and waved at the sofa. "Sit down."

Reggie was no stranger to the apartment. She found a diet Coke in the refrigerator and sat on a bar stool. "It was the U.S. marshal's office with a grand jury subpoena. Ten o'clock Monday morning in New Orleans."

"But they didn't serve you?"

"No. Momma Love ran them off."

"Then you're off the hook."

"Yeah, unless they find me. There's no law against dodging subpoenas. I need to call Dianne."

Clint handed her a phone, and she punched the numbers from memory. "Relax, Reggie," he said, and kissed her gently on the cheek. He picked up stray magazines and turned on the stereo. Dianne was on the phone, and Reggie managed three words before she was forced to listen. Subpoenas were everywhere. One for Reggie, one for Dianne, and one for Mark. Reggie tried to calm her. Dianne had called the detention center, but couldn't get through to Mark. Phones were unavailable at this hour, she'd been told. They talked for five minutes. Reggie, badly shaken herself, tried to convince Dianne everything was fine. She, Reggie, was in control. She promised to call her in the morning, then hung up.

"They can't take Mark," Clint said. "He's under the jurisdiction of our Juvenile Court."

"I need to talk to Harry. But he's out of town."

"Where is he?"

"Fishing somewhere with his sons."

"This is more important than fishing, Reggie. Let's find him. He can stop it, can't he?"

She was thinking of a hundred things at once. "This is pretty slick, Clint. Think about it. Foltrigg waits until late Friday to serve subpoenas for Monday morning."

"How can he do this?"

"It's easy. He just did it. In a criminal case like this, a federal grand jury can subpoena any witness from anywhere, regardless of time and distance. And the witness must appear unless he or she can first quash the subpoena."

"How do you quash one?"

"You file a motion in federal court to void the subpoena."

"Lemme guess, federal court in New Orleans?"

"That's right. We're forced to find the trial judge early Monday morning in New Orleans and beg him to allow an emergency hearing to quash the subpoena."

"It won't work, Reggie."

"Of course it won't work. That's the way Foltrigg planned it." She gulped the diet Coke. "Do you have any coffee?"

"Sure." He began opening drawers.

Reggie was thinking out loud. "If I can dodge the subpoena until Monday, Foltrigg will be forced to issue another one. Then maybe I'll have time to quash. The problem is Mark. They're not after me, because they know they can't force me to talk."

"Do you know where the damned body is, Reggie?"

"No."

"Does Mark?"

"Yes."

He froze for a moment, then ran water in the pot.

"We have to figure out a way to keep Mark here, Clint. We can't allow him to go to New Orleans."

"Call Harry."

"Harry's fishing in the mountains."

"Then call Harry's wife. Find out where he's fishing in the mountains. I'll go get him if necessary."

"You're right." She grabbed the phone and started calling.

THIRTY-TWO

FINAL ROOM CHECK at the Juvenile Detention Center was 10 P.M., when they made sure all lights and televisions were off. Mark heard Telda rattling keys and giving commands across the hall. His shirt was soaked, unbuttoned, and sweat ran to his navel and puddled around the zipper of his jeans. The television was off. His breathing was heavy. His thick hair was watery and rows of sweat ran to his eyebrows and dripped from the tip of his nose. She was next door. His face was crimson and hot.

Telda knocked, then unlocked Mark's door. The light was on and this immediately irritated her. She took a step inside, glanced at the bunks, but he wasn't there.

Then she saw his feet beside the toilet. He was curled tightly with his knees on his chest, motionless except for rapid, heavy breathing.

His eyes were closed and his left thumb was in his mouth.

"Mark!" she shouted, suddenly terrified. "Mark! Oh my god!" She ran from the room to get help, and was back within seconds with Denny, her partner, who took a quick look.

"Doreen was worried about this," Denny said, touching the sweat on Mark's stomach. "Damn, he's soaking wet."

Telda was pinching his wrist. "His pulse is crazy. Look at him breathe. Call an ambulance!"

"The poor kid's in shock, isn't he?"

"Go call an ambulance!"

Denny lumbered from the room and the floor shook. Telda picked Mark up and carefully placed him on the bottom bunk, where he curled again and brought his knees to his chest. The thumb never left his mouth. Denny was back with a clipboard. "This must be Doreen's handwriting. Says here to check on him every half hour, and if there's any doubt, to rush him to St. Peter's and call Dr. Greenway."

"This is all my fault," Telda said. "I shouldn't have allowed those damned marshals in here. Scared the poor boy to death."

Denny knelt beside her, and with a thick thumb peeled back the right eyelid. "Damn! His eyes have rolled back. This kid's in trouble," he said with all the gravity of a brain surgeon.

"Get a washcloth over here," Telda said, and Denny did as told. "Doreen was telling me this is what happened to his little brother. They saw that shooting on Monday, both of them, and the little one's been in shock ever since." Denny handed her the cloth and she wiped Mark's forehead.

"Damn, his heart's gonna explode," Denny said, on his knees again next to Telda. "He's breathing like crazy."

"Poor kid. I should've run those marshals off," Telda said.

"I would have. They got no right coming on this floor." He jabbed another thumb into the left eye, and Mark groaned and twitched. Then he started the moaning, just like Ricky, and this scared them even more. A low, dull, pitchless sound from deep in the throat. He sucked hard on the thumb.

A paramedic from the main jail three floors down ran into the room, followed by another jailer. "What's up?" he asked as Telda and Denny moved.

"I think it's called traumatic shock or stress or something," Telda said. "He's been acting strange all day, then about an hour ago two U.S. marshals were here to give him a subpoena." The paramedic was not listening. He gripped a wrist and found the pulse. Telda rattled on. "They scared him to death, and I think it sent him into shock. I should've watched him after that, but I got busy."

"I would've run those damned marshals off," Denny said. They stood side by side behind the paramedic.

"This is what happened to his little brother, you know, the one who's been in the newspaper all week. The shooting and all."

"He's gotta go," the paramedic said, standing, frowning, and talking into his radio. "Hurry up with the stretcher to the fourth floor," he barked into it. "Got a kid in bad shape."

Denny stuck the clipboard in front of the paramedic. "Says here to take him to St. Peter's. Dr. Greenway."

"That's where his brother is," Telda added. "Doreen told me all about it. She was worried this might happen. Said she almost sent for an ambulance this afternoon. Said he's been slipping away all day. I should've been more careful."

The stretcher arrived with two more paramedics. Mark was quickly laid on it and covered with a blanket. A strap was placed across his thighs and another on his chest. His eyes never opened, but he managed to keep the thumb in his mouth.

And he managed to emit the painful, monotonous groan that frightened the paramedics and sped the stretcher along. It rolled quickly past the front station, and into an elevator.

"You ever seen this before?" one paramedic mumbled under his breath to the other.

"Not that I recall."

"He's burning up."

"The skin is normally cool and clammy with shock. I've never seen this."

"Yeah. Maybe traumatic shock is different. Check out that thumb."

"Is this the kid the mob's after?"

"Yeah. Front page today and yesterday."

"I guess he's gone over the edge."

The elevator stopped, and they pushed the stretcher hurriedly through a series of short hallways, all busy and filled with the usual Friday night madness of city jail. A set of double doors flew open, and they were at the ambulance.

The ride to St. Peter's took less than ten minutes, half as long as the wait once they arrived. Three other ambulances were in the process of depositing their occupants. St. Peter's received the vast majority of Memphis knife wounds, gunshot victims, beaten wives, and mangled bodies from weekend car wrecks. The pace was hectic twenty-four hours a day, but from sunset Friday until late Sunday, the place was in chaos.

They rolled him through the bay and onto the white-tiled floors where the stretcher stopped and the paramedics waited and filled out forms. A small army of nurses and doctors scrambled around a new patient and all yelled at the same time. People ran in every direction. A half dozen cops milled about. Three more stretchers were parked haphazardly in the wide hallway.

A nurse ventured by, stopped for a second, and asked the paramedics, "What is it?" One of them handed her a form.

"So he's not bleeding," she said, as if nothing mattered except flowing blood.

"No. Looks like stress or shock or something. Runs in the family."

"He can wait. Roll him to Intake. I'll be back in a minute." And she was off.

They wove the stretcher through heavy traffic, and stopped in a small room off the main hallway. The forms were presented to another nurse, who scribbled something without looking at Mark. "Where's Dr. Greenway?" she asked the paramedics.

They looked at each other, and shrugged at the nurse.

"You haven't called him?" she asked.

"Well, no."

"Well, no," she repeated to herself and rolled her eyes. What a couple of dumbasses. "Look, this is a war zone, okay. We're talking blood and guts. We've lost two people in that hallway right there in the past thirty minutes. Psychiatric emergencies do not get top priority around here."

"You want us to shoot him?" one of them said, nodding at Mark, and this really pissed her off.

"No. I want you to leave. I'll take care of him, but you guys just get the hell out of here."

"You signed the forms, lady. He's all yours." They smiled at her, and headed for the door.

"Is there a policeman with him?" she asked.

"Nope. He's just a juvenile." They were gone.

Mark managed to roll onto his left side and bring his knees to his chest. The straps were not tight. His eyes opened slightly. A black man was lying across three chairs in one corner of the room. An empty stretcher with blood on the sheets was by a green door next to a water fountain. The nurse answered the phone, said a few words, and left the room. Mark quickly unhooked the straps and jumped to the floor. There was no crime in walking around. He was a nut case now, so what if she caught him on his feet.

The forms she'd been holding were on the counter. He grabbed them, and pushed the stretcher through the green door, which led to a cramped corridor with small rooms on both sides. He abandoned the stretcher and threw the forms in a garbage can. The exit signs led to a door with a window in it. It opened into the madhouse of Admissions.

Mark smiled to himself. He'd been here before. He watched the chaos through the window and picked the spot where he and Hardy had stood after Greenway and Dianne disappeared with Ricky. He eased through the door, and casually made his way through the snarled throng of sick and wounded trying anxiously to get admitted. Running and darting might attract attention, so he played it cool. He rode his favorite escalator to the basement, and found an empty wheelchair by the stairs. It was adult-size, but he worked the wheels and rolled himself past the cafeteria to the morgue.

Clint had fallen asleep on the sofa. Letterman was almost over when the phone rang. Reggie grabbed it. "Hello."

"Hi, Reggie. It's me, Mark."

"Mark! How are you, dear?"

"Doing great, Reggie. Just wonderful."

"How'd you find me?" she asked, turning off the TV.

"I called Momma Love and woke her. She gave me this number. It's Clint's place, right?"

"Right. How'd you get to a phone? It's awful late."

"Well, I'm not in jail anymore."

She stood and walked to the snack bar. "Where are you, dear?"

"At the hospital. St. Peter's."

"I see. And how'd you get there?"

"They brought me in an ambulance."

"Are you okay?"

"Great."

"Why'd they take you in an ambulance?"

"I had an attack of post-traumatic stress syndrome, and they rushed me over."

"Should I come see you?"

"Maybe. What's this grand jury stuff?"

"Nothing but an attempt to scare you into talking."

"Well, it worked. I'm more scared than ever."

"You sound fine."

"Nervous energy, Reggie. I'm scared to death."

"I mean, you don't sound like you're in shock or anything."

"I recovered real quick. I faked them out, Reggie, okay? I jogged in my little cell for half an hour, and when they found me I was soaking wet and in bad shape, as they say."

Clint sat up on the sofa and listened intently.

"Have you seen a doctor?" she asked, frowning at Clint.

"Not exactly."

"What does that mean?"

"It means I walked out of the emergency room. It means I've escaped, Reggie. It was so easy."

"Oh my god!"

"Relax. I'm fine. I'm not going back to jail, Reggie. And I'm not going to see the grand jury in New Orleans. They'll just lock me up down there, won't they?"

"Listen, Mark, you can't do this. You can't escape. You must—"

"I've already escaped, Reggie. And you know something?"

"What?"

"I doubt if anyone knows it yet. This place is so crazy, I doubt if they've missed me yet."

"What about the cops?"

"What cops?"

"Didn't a cop go with you to the hospital?"

"No. I'm just a kid, Reggie. I had two huge paramedics, but I'm just a little kid and at the time I was in a coma, sucking my thumb, moaning and groaning, just like Ricky. You'd have been proud. It was like something out of a movie. Once I got here, they turned their backs, and just like that, I walked away."

"You can't do this, Mark."

"It's done, okay? And I'm not going back."

"What about your mother?"

"Oh, I talked to her about an hour ago, by phone of course. She freaked out, but I convinced her I was fine. She didn't like it, told me to come to Ricky's room. We had a big fight over the phone, but she settled down. I think she's on pills again."

"But you're at the hospital?"

"That's right."

"Where? In which room?"

"Are you still my lawyer?"

"Of course I'm your lawyer."

"Good. So if I tell you something, you can't repeat it, right?"

"Right."

"Are you my friend, Reggie?"

"Of course I'm your friend."

"That's good, because right now you're the only friend I have. Will you help me, Reggie? I'm really scared."

"I'll do anything, Mark. Where are you?"

"In the morgue. There's a little office in the corner, and I'm hiding under the desk. The lights are off. If I hang up real quick, you'll know somebody walked in. They've brought in two bodies while I've been here, but so far no one's come to the office."

"The morgue?"

Clint bolted to his feet and stood beside her.

"Yeah. I've been here before. I know this place pretty well, remember."

"Sure."

"Who's in the morgue?" Clint whispered. She frowned at him and shook her head.

"Mom said they have a subpoena for you too, Reggie. Is this true?"

"Yes, but they haven't served me. That's why I'm here at Clint's. If they don't hand me the subpoena, then I don't have to go."

"So you're hiding too?"

"I guess."

Suddenly his end clicked and the dial tone followed. She stared at the receiver, then quickly placed it on the phone. "He hung up," she said.

"What the hell's going on!" Clint asked.

"It's Mark. He's escaped from jail."

"He what!"

"He's hiding in the morgue at St. Peter's." She said this as if she didn't believe it. The phone rang, and she snatched it. "Hello."

"Sorry about that. The door to the morgue opened, then closed. I thought they were bringing in another body."

"Are you safe, Mark?"

"Hell no, I'm not safe. But I'm a kid, okay. And now I'm a psychiatric case. So if they catch me, I'll just go into shock again and they'll put me in a room. Then I'll figure out another way to escape, maybe."

"You can't hide forever."

"Neither can you."

She marveled once again at his quick tongue. "You're right, Mark. So what do we do?"

"I don't know. I really would like to leave Memphis. I'm sick of cops and jails."

"Where do you want to go?"

"Well, let me ask you something. If you come and get me, and we leave town together, then you could get in trouble for helping me escape. Right?"

"Yes. I'd be an accomplice."

"What would they do to you?"

"We'll worry about that later. I've done worse things."

"So you'll help me?"

"Yes, Mark. I'll help you."

"And you won't tell anybody?"

"We may need Clint."

"Okay, you can tell Clint. But nobody else, okay?"

"You have my word."

"And you won't try to talk me into going back to jail?"

"I promise."

There was a long pause. Clint was near panic.

"Okay, Reggie. You know the main parking lot, the one next to that big green building?"

"Yes."

"Drive into it, just like you're looking for a place to park. Go real slow. I'll be hiding between some cars."

"That place is dark and dangerous, Mark."

"It's Friday night, Reggie. Everything around here is dark and dangerous."

"But there's a guard in the exit booth."

"That guard sleeps half the time. It's a guard, not a cop. I know what I'm doing, okay?"

"Are you sure?"

"No. But you said you'd help me."

"I will. When should I be there?"

"As fast as you can."

"I'll be in Clint's car. It's a black Honda Accord."

"Good. Hurry."

"I'm on my way. Be careful, Mark."

"Relax, Reggie. This is just like the movies."

She hung up, and took a deep breath.

"My car?" Clint asked.

"They're looking for me too."

"You're crazy, Reggie. This is insane. You can't run away with an escaped, I don't know, whatever the hell he is. They'll arrest you for contributing. You'll be indicted. You'll lose your license."

"Where's my bag?"

"In the bedroom."

"I need your keys, and your credit cards."

"My credit cards! Look, Reggie, I love you, sweetheart, but my car and my plastic?"

"How much cash do you have?"

"Forty bucks."

"Give it here. I'll pay you back." She headed for the bedroom.

"You've lost your mind."

"I've lost it before, remember."

"Come on, Reggie."

"Get a grip, Clint. We're not blowing anything. I've got to help Mark. He's sitting in a dark office in the morgue at St. Peter's begging for help. What am I supposed to do?"

"Well, hell! I think you should attack the place with a shotgun and blow people away. Anything for Mark Sway."

She threw her toothbrush in a canvas bag. "Give me the credit cards and the cash, Clint. I'm in a hurry."

He reached in his pockets. "You're nuts. This is ridiculous."

"Stay by the phone. Do not leave this place, okay. I'll call you later." She grabbed his keys, cash, and two credit cards—Visa and Texaco.

He followed her to the door. "Take it easy with the Visa. It's almost to the limit."

"Why am I not surprised?" She kissed him on the cheek. "Thanks, Clint. Take care of Momma Love."

"Call me," he said, thoroughly defeated.

She eased through the door and disappeared in the darkness.

THIRTY-THREE

FROM THE MOMENT Mark jumped into the car and hid on the floor, Reggie became an accomplice to his escape. But, unless he murdered someone before they were caught, it was doubtful her crime would be punishable by incarceration. She was thinking more along the lines of community service, perhaps a bit of restitution, and forty years of probation. Hell, she'd give them all the probation they wanted. It would be her first offense. She, and her lawyer, could make a strong argument that the kid was being hunted by the Mafia, and he was all alone, and, well, dammit, somebody had to do something! She couldn't worry about legal niceties when her client was out there begging for help. Maybe she could pull strings and keep her license to practice.

She paid the parking guard fifty cents, and refused eye contact. She had circled through the lot one time. The guard was in another world. Mark was rolled into a tight coil somewhere in the darkness under the dashboard, and he remained there until she turned on Union and headed for the river.

"Is it safe now?" he asked nervously.

"I think so."

He sprang into the seat, and surveyed the landscape. The digital clock gave the time as twelve-fifty. The six lanes of Union Avenue were deserted. She drove three blocks, catching red lights at each one, while waiting for Mark to speak.

"So where are we going?" she finally asked.

"The Alamo."

"The Alamo?" she repeated without a trace of a smile.

He shook his head. Adults could be so dumb at times. "It's a joke, Reggie."

"Sorry."

"I take it you haven't seen *Pee-Wee's Big Adventure.*"

"Is that a movie?"

"Forget it. Just forget it." They waited for another red light.

"I like your car better," he said, rubbing his hand along the Accord's console and taking a sudden interest in the radio.

"That's good, Mark. This street is about to stop at the river, and I think we should discuss exactly where it is you want to go."

"Well, right now, I just want to leave Memphis, okay? I really don't care where we go, I just want to get out of Dodge."

"And once we leave Memphis, where might we be going? A destination would be nice."

"Let's cross the bridge by the Pyramid, okay?"

"Fair enough. You want to go to Arkansas?"

"Why not? Yeah, sure, let's go to Arkansas."

"Fair enough."

With that decision out of the way, he leaned forward and carefully inspected the radio. He pushed a button, turned a knob, and Reggie braced for a loud burst of rap or heavy metal. He made adjustments with both hands. Just a kid with a new toy. He should be home in a warm bed, and he should sleep late since it's Saturday. And fresh from bed he should watch cartoons, then, still in pajamas, play Nintendo with all its buttons and gadgets, much like he was doing right then with the radio. The Four Tops finished a song.

"You listen to oldies?" she asked, genuinely surprised.

"Sometimes. I thought you'd like it. It's almost one o'clock in the morning, not the best time for the loud stuff, you know."

"Why do you think I like oldies?"

"Well, Reggie, to be perfectly honest, I can't see you at a rap concert. And besides, the radio in your car was on this station last time I rode in it."

Union Avenue stopped at the river, and they sat at another red light. A police car stopped next to them, and the cop behind the wheel frowned at Mark.

"Don't look at him," Reggie scolded.

The light changed, and she turned right onto Riverside Drive. The cop followed. "Don't turn around," she said under her breath. "Just act normal."

"Damn, Reggie, why is he following us?"

"I have no idea. Just be cool."

"He recognized me. My face has been plastered all over the newspapers this week, and the cop recognized me. This is just great, Reggie. We make our big escape, and ten minutes later the cops nail us."

"Be quiet, Mark. I'm trying to drive and watch him at the same time."

He eased downward, sliding slowly until his butt was on the edge of the seat and his head was just above the door handle. "What's he doing?" he whispered.

Her eyes darted back and forth from the mirror to the street. "Just following. No, wait. Here he comes."

The police car eased by them, then sped away. "He's gone," she said, and Mark breathed again.

They entered I-40 at the downtown ramp, and were on the bridge over the Mississippi River. He gazed at the brightly lit Pyramid to the right, then spun around to admire the Memphis skyline fading in the distance. He stared in awe, as if he'd never seen it before. Reggie wondered if the poor child had ever left Memphis.

An Elvis song started. "You like Elvis?" he asked.

"Mark, believe it or not, when I was a teenager growing up in Memphis, a bunch of us girls would ride over to Elvis's house on Sundays and watch him play touch football. This was before he was really famous, and he still lived at home with his parents in a nice little house. He went to Humes High School, which is now Northside."

"I live in north Memphis. At least I did. I don't know where I live now."

"We'd go to his concerts, and we'd see him hanging out around town. He was just an average guy, at first, then things changed. He got so famous he couldn't live a normal life."

"Just like me, Reggie," he said with sudden smile. "Think of it. Me and Elvis. Pictures on the front page. Photographers everywhere. All sorts of people looking for us. It's tough being famous."

"Yeah, and wait till tomorrow, in the Sunday paper. I can see the headlines now, big, bold letters—SWAY ESCAPES."

"It's great! And they'll have my smiling face on the front page again with cops all around me like I'm some kind of serial killer. And those same cops will sound so stupid trying to explain how an eleven-year-old kid escaped from jail. I wonder if I'm the youngest kid to ever escape from jail."

"Probably."

"I do feel sorry for Doreen, though. Do you think she'll get in trouble?"

"Was she on duty?"

"No. It was Telda and Denny. Wouldn't bother me if they got fired."

"Doreen's probably okay. She's been there a long time."

"I faked her out, you know. I started acting like I was going into shock, just fading away to La La Land as Romey called it. Every time she checked on me, I acted weirder and weirder; quit talking to her, just stared at the ceiling and groaned. She knows all about Ricky, and she became convinced it was happening to me too. Yesterday, she brought in a medic from the jail, and he examined me. Said I was fine. But Doreen was worried. I guess I used her."

"How'd you get out?"

"Played like I was in shock, you know. I worked up a good sweat running around my little cell, then curled up in a ball and sucked my thumb. It scared them so bad, they called the ambulance. I knew if I could make it to St. Peter's, I was home free. That place is a zoo."

"And you just disappeared?"

"They had me on this stretcher, and when they turned their backs I got up and, yeah, just disappeared. Look, Reggie, there were people dying right and left, so no one was concerned with me. It was easy."

They were over the bridge and into Arkansas. The highway was flat and lined on both sides by truck stops and motels. He turned to admire the Memphis skyline once more, but it was gone.

"What are you looking for?" she asked.

"Memphis. I like to look at the tall buildings downtown. A teacher told me once that people actually live in those tall buildings. It's hard to believe."

"Why is it hard to believe?"

"I saw a movie once about this little rich kid who lived in a tall building in a city, and he roamed around the streets just having a great time. He knew the cops by their first names. He stopped taxis when he wanted to go somewhere. And at night, he'd sit on the balcony and watch the streets below. I've always thought that would be a wonderful way to live. No cheap house trailers. No trashy neighbors. No pickups parked in the street in front of your house."

"You can have it, Mark. It's yours, if you want it."

He gave her a long look. "How?"

"Right now the FBI will give you whatever you want. You can live in a tall building in a big city, or you can live in a cabin in the mountains. You pick the place."

"I've been thinking about that."

"You can live on a beach and play in the ocean, or you can live in Orlando and go to Disney World every day."

"That'd be okay for Ricky. I'm too old. I've heard the tickets are too expensive."

"You'd probably get a lifetime pass, if you asked for it. Right now, Mark, you and your mom can get anything you want."

"Yeah, but, Reggie, who wants it if you're afraid of your shadow. For three nights now, I've had nightmares about these people, Reggie. I don't want to be scared for the rest of my life. They'll get me one day, I know they will."

"So what do you do, Mark?"

"I don't know, but I've been thinking real hard about something."

"I'm listening."

"One good thing about jail is that it allows you to think a lot." He placed one foot on one knee and wrapped his fingers around it. "Think about this, Reggie. What if Romey told me a lie? He was drunk, taking pills, out of his mind. Maybe he was just talking to hear himself talk. I was there, remember. The man was crazy. Said all sorts of weird things, and at first I believed all of it. I was scared to death, and I wasn't thinking clearly. My head was hurting where he'd slapped me. But now, well, I'm not so sure. All week I've been remembering crazy stuff he said and did, and maybe I was too eager to believe everything."

She was driving exactly fifty-five miles per hour and hanging on every word. She had no idea where he was going with this, and she had no idea where the car was going either.

"But I couldn't take a chance, right? I mean, what if I'd told the cops everything and they found the body right where Romey said? Everybody's happy but the Mafia, and who knows what would happen to me. And what if I'd told the cops everything, but Romey was lying and they found no body. I'm off the hook, right, because in reality I didn't know anything at all. What a joker, that Romey. But it was too big of a risk." He paused for a half a mile. The Beach Boys sang "California Girls." "So I've had a brainstorm."

By now, she could almost feel this brainstorm. Her heart stopped and she managed to keep the wheels between the white lines of the right lane. "And what might that be?" she asked nervously.

"I think we should see if Romey was lying or not."

She cleared her dry throat. "You mean, go find the body."

"That's right."

She wanted to laugh at this innocent humor of a hyperactive mind, but at the moment she didn't have the strength. "You must be kidding."

"Well, let's talk about it. You and I are both expected to be in New Orleans Monday morning, right?"

"I guess. I haven't seen a subpoena."

"But I'm your client, and I've got a subpoena. So even if they didn't give you one, you'd still have to go with me, right?"

"That's true."

"And now we're on the run, right? Just you and me, Bonnie and Clyde, running from the cops."

"I guess you could say that."

"Where's the last place they'd look for us? Think about it, Reggie. Where's the last place in the world they'd expect us to run to?"

"New Orleans."

"Right. Now, I don't know anything about hiding out, but since you're dodging a subpoena and you're a lawyer and all, and you deal with criminals all the time, I figure you could get us to New Orleans and no one would know it. Right?"

"I suppose so." She was beginning to agree with him, and she was shocked by her own words.

"And if you can get us to New Orleans, then we'll find Romey's house."

"Why Romey's house?"

"That's where the body's supposed to be."

This was the last thing in the world she wanted to know. She slowly removed her glasses and rubbed her eyes. A slight headache was forming between her temples, and it would only get worse.

Romey's house? The home of Jerome Clifford, deceased? He had said this very slowly, and she had heard it very slowly. She glared at taillights in front of them but there was nothing but a red blur. Romey's house? The victim of the murder was buried at the home of the accused's lawyer. This was beyond bizarre. Her mind raced wildly in circles asking itself a hundred questions and answering none of them. She glanced in the mirror, and was suddenly aware that he was staring at her with a curious smile.

"Now you know, Reggie," he said.

"But how, why—"

"Don't ask because I don't know. It's crazy, isn't it? That's why I think Romey could've made it up. A crazy mind created this weird story about the body being at his house."

"So, you don't think it's really there?" she asked, seeking reassurance.

"We won't know until we look. If it's not there, I'm off the hook and life returns to normal."

"But what if it's there?"

"We'll worry about that when we find it."

"I don't like your brainstorm."

"Why not?"

"Look, Mark, son, client, friend, if you think I'm going to New Orleans to dig up a dead body, then you're crazy."

"Of course I'm crazy. Me and Ricky, just a couple of nut cases."

"I won't do it."

"Why not, Reggie?"

"It's much too dangerous, Mark. It's insane, and it could get us killed. I won't go, and I can't let you do it."

"Why is it dangerous?"

"Well, it's just dangerous. I don't know."

"Think about it, Reggie. We check on the body, okay. Then if it's not where Romey said, I'm home free. We'll tell the cops to drop everything against us, and in return I'll tell them what I know. And since I don't know where the body really is, the Mafia couldn't care less about me. We walk."

We walk. Too much television. "And if we find the body?"

"Good question. Think about this slowly, Reggie. Try and think like a kid. If we find the body, and then you call the FBI and tell them you know exactly where it is because you've seen it with your own eyes, then they'll give us anything we want."

"And what exactly do you want?"

"Probably Australia. A nice house, plenty of money for my mother. New car. Maybe some plastic surgery. I saw that once in a movie. They rearranged this guy's entire face. He was dog ugly to start with, and he snitched on some drug dealers just so he could get a new face. Looked like a movie star when it was over. About two years later, the drug dealers gave him another new face."

"You're serious?"

"About the movie?"

"No, about Australia."

"Maybe." He paused and looked out the window. "Maybe."

They listened to the radio and didn't speak for several miles. Traffic was light. Memphis was farther away.

"Let's make a deal," he said, looking out his window.

"Maybe."

"Let's go to New Orleans."

"I'm not digging for a body."

"Okay, okay. But let's go there. No one will expect us. We'll talk about the body when we get there."

"We've already talked about it."

"Just go to New Orleans, okay?"

The highway intersected another one, and they were on top of an overpass. She pointed to her right. Ten miles away, the Memphis skyline glowed and flickered under a half-moon. "Wow," he said in awe. "It's beautiful."

Neither of them could know that it would be his last look at Memphis.

□ □ □ □

They stopped in Forrest City, Arkansas, for gas and snacks. Reggie paid for cupcakes, a large coffee, and a Sprite, while Mark hid on the floor. Minutes later, they were back on the interstate headed for Little Rock.

Steam poured from the Styrofoam cup as she drove and watched him inhale four cupcakes. He ate like a kid—crumbs on his pants and in the seat, cream filling on his fingers, which he licked as if he hadn't seen food in a month. It was almost two-thirty. The road was empty except for convoys of tractor-trailer rigs. She set the cruise control on sixty-five.

"Do you think they're chasing us yet?" he asked, finishing the last cupcake and opening the Sprite. There was a certain excitement in his voice.

"I doubt it. I'm sure the police are searching the hospital, but why would they suspect we're together?"

"I'm worried about Mom. I called her, you know, before I called you. Told her about the escape, and that I was hiding in the hospital. She got real mad. But I think I convinced her I'm safe. I hope they don't give her a hard time."

"They won't. But she'll worry herself sick."

"I know. I don't mean to be cruel, but I think she can handle it. Look at what she's already been through. My mom's pretty tough."

"I'll tell Clint to call her later today."

"Are you going to tell Clint where we're going?"

"I'm not sure where we're going."

He thought about this as two trucks roared by and the Honda veered to the right.

"What would you do, Reggie?"

"For starters, I don't think I would have escaped."

"That's a lie."

"I beg your pardon."

"Sure it is. You're dodging a subpoena, aren't you? I'm doing the same thing. So what's the difference? You don't want to face the grand jury. I don't want to face the grand jury, so here we are on the run. We're in the same boat, Reggie."

"There's only one difference. You were in jail, and you escaped. That's a crime."

"I was in a jail for juveniles, and juveniles do not commit crimes. Isn't that what you told me? Juveniles are rowdy, or delinquent, or in need of supervision, but juveniles do not commit crimes. Right?"

"If you say so. But it was wrong to escape."

"It's done. I can't undo it. It's wrong for you to dodge the law too, isn't it?"

"Absolutely not. There's no crime in avoiding a subpoena. I was doing fine until I picked you up."

"Then stop the car and let me out."

"Oh sure. Please be serious, Mark."

"I am serious."

"Right. And what'll you do when you get out?"

"Oh, I don't know. I'll go as far as I can, and if I get caught then I'll just go into shock and they'll send me back to Memphis. I'll claim I was crazy, and they'll never know you were involved. Just stop anytime you feel like it, and I'll get out." He leaned forward and punched the Seek button on the radio. For five miles they listened to Conway Twitty and Tammy Wynette.

"I hate country music," she said, and he turned it off.

"Can I ask you something?" she said.

"Sure."

"Suppose we go to New Orleans and find the body. And, according to your plan, we then cut a deal with the FBI and you go into their witness protection plan. You, Dianne, and Ricky then fly off into the sunset to Australia or wherever, right?"

"I guess."

"Then, why not cut a deal and tell them now?"

"Now you're thinking, Reggie," he said, patronizingly, as if she'd finally awakened and was beginning to see the light.

"Thank you so much," she said.

"It took me a while to figure it out. The answer is easy. I don't completely trust the FBI. Do you?"

"Not completely."

"And I'm not willing to give them what they want until me, my mother, and my brother are already far away. You're a good lawyer, Reggie, and you wouldn't allow your client to take any chances, would you?"

"Go on."

"Before I tell these clowns anything, I want to make sure we are safely put away somewhere. It'll take some time to move Ricky. If I told them now, the bad guys might find out before we can disappear. It's too risky."

"But what if you told them now, and they didn't find the body? What if Clifford was, as you say, joking?"

"I would never know, would I? I'd be undercover somewhere, getting a nose job, changing my name to Tommy or something, and all of it would be for nothing. It makes more sense to know now, Reggie, if Romey told me the truth."

She shook her bewildered head. "I'm not sure I follow you."

"I'm not sure I follow me, either. But one thing is for certain: I'm not going to New Orleans with the U.S. marshals. I'm not going to face the grand jury on Monday and refuse to answer questions so they can throw my little butt in jail down there."

"Good point. So how do we spend our weekend?"

"How far is it to New Orleans?"

"Five or six hours."

"Let's go. We can always chicken out once we get there."

"How much trouble will it be to find the body?"

"Probably not much."

"Can I ask where it is at Clifford's house?"

"Well, it's not hanging in a tree or lying in the bushes. It'll take a little work."

"This is completely crazy, Mark."

"I know. It's been a bad week."

THIRTY-FOUR

SO MUCH for a quiet Saturday morning with the kids. Jason McThune studied his feet on the rug next to his bed, and tried to focus on the clock on the wall by the bathroom door. It was almost six, still dark outside, and the cobwebs from a late night bottle of wine blurred his eyes. His wife rolled over and grunted something he could not understand.

Twenty minutes later, he found her deep under the covers and kissed her good-bye. He might not be home for a week, he said, but doubted if she heard. Saturdays at work and days out of town were the norm. Nothing unusual.

But today would be unusual. He opened the door and the dog ran into the backyard. How could an eleven-year-old kid simply disappear? The Memphis Police had no idea. He just vanished, the lieutenant said.

Not surprisingly, traffic was light in the predawn hours as he headed for the Federal Building downtown. He punched numbers on his car phone. Agents Brenner, Latchee, and Durston were roused from sleep and instructed to meet him immediately. He flipped through his black book and found the Alexandria number for K. O. Lewis.

K.O. was not asleep, but neither was he in the mood to be disturbed. He was eating his oatmeal, enjoying his coffee, chatting with his wife, and just how in the hell could an eleven-year-old kid disappear while in police custody? he demanded. McThune told him what he knew, which was nothing, and asked him to be ready to come to Memphis. It could be a long weekend. K.O. said he would make a couple of calls, find the jet, and call him back at the office.

At the office McThune called Larry Trumann in New Orleans, and was delighted when Trumann answered the phone disoriented and obviously trying to sleep. This was Trumann's case, though McThune had worked on it all week. And just for fun, he called George Ord and asked him to come on down with the rest of the gang. McThune explained he was hungry, and could George please bring some Egg McMuffins.

By seven, Brenner, Latchee, and Durston were in his office gulping coffee and speculating wildly. Ord arrived next without the food, then two uniformed Memphis policemen knocked on the door to the outer office. Ray Trimble, Deputy Chief of Police and a legend in Memphis law enforcement, was with them.

They assembled in McThune's office, and Trimble, in fluent coptalk, got right to the point. "Subject was transported from the detention center by ambulance to St. Peter's around ten-thirty last night. Subject was signed in by the paramedics at St. Peter's ER, at which time the paramedics left. Subject was not accompanied by Memphis Police or jail personnel. Paramedics are certain a nurse, one Gloria Watts, female white, signed subject in, but no paperwork can be found. Ms. Watts has stated she had subject in ER Intake Room, and was called out of room for an undetermined reason. She was absent for no more than ten minutes, and upon her return, subject was gone. The paperwork was gone too, and Ms. Watts assumed subject had been taken to ER for examination and treatment." Trimble slowed a bit and cleared his throat as if this was somehow unpleasant. "At approximately five this morning, Ms. Watts was evidently preparing to leave her shift, and she checked the Intake records. She thought of the subject, and began asking questions. Subject could not be found in ER, and Admissions had no record of his arrival. Hospital Security was called, then Memphis PD. At this time, a thorough search of the hospital is under way."

"Six hours," McThune said in disbelief.

"I beg your pardon," Trimble said.

"It took six hours to realize the kid was missing."

"Yes sir, but we don't run the hospital, you see."

"Why was the kid transported to the hospital without security?"

"I can't answer that. An investigation will be undertaken. It looks like an oversight."

"Why was the kid taken to the hospital?"

Trimble took a file from a briefcase, and handed McThune a copy of Telda's report. He read it carefully. "Says he went into shock after the U.S. marshals left. What the hell were the marshals doing there?"

Trimble opened the file again, and handed McThune the subpoena. He read it carefully, then handed it to George Ord.

"Anything else, Chief?" he said to Trimble, who had never taken a seat and had never stopped pacing slightly. He was anxious to leave.

"No sir. We'll complete the search, and call you immediately if we find anything. We've got about four dozen men there right now, and we've been checking for a little over an hour."

"Have you talked to the kid's mother?"

"No sir. Not yet. She's still asleep. We're watching the room in case he tries to get to her."

"I'll talk to her first, Chief. I'll be over in about an hour. Make sure no one sees her before I do."

"No problem."

"Thank you, Chief." Trimble clicked his heels together, and for an instant looked as though he wanted to salute. He was gone, along with his officers.

McThune looked at Brenner and Latchee. "You guys call every available agent. Get them here right now. Immediately." They bolted from the room.

"What about the subpoena?" he asked Ord, who was still holding it.

"I can't believe it. Foltrigg's lost his mind."

"You knew nothing about it?"

"Of course not. This kid is under the jurisdiction of the Juvenile Court. I wouldn't think of trying to reach him. Would you want to piss off Harry Roosevelt?"

"I don't think so. We need to call him. I'll do it, and you call Reggie Love. I'd rather not talk to her."

Ord left the room to find a phone. "Call the U.S. marshal,"

McThune snapped at Durston. "Get the scoop on this subpoena. I want to know everything about it."

Durston left, and suddenly McThune was alone. He raced through a phone book until he found the Roosevelts. But there was no Harry. If he had a number, it was unlisted, and that was perfectly understandable with no less than fifty thousand single mothers trying to collect unpaid child support. McThune made three quick calls to lawyers he knew, and the third one said that Harry lived on Kensington Street. He would send an agent when he could spare one.

Ord returned shaking his head. "I talked to Reggie Love's mother, but she asked more questions than I did. I don't think she's there."

"I'll send two men as soon as possible. I guess you'd better call Foltrigg, the dumbass."

"Yeah, I guess you're right." Ord turned and left the office again.

At eight, McThune left the elevator on the ninth floor of St. Peter's with Brenner and Durston following close behind. Three more agents, decked out in a splendid variety of hospital garb, met him at the elevator and walked with him to Room 943. Three massive security guards stood near the door. McThune knocked gently, and motioned for his small squadron to back away. He didn't want to scare the poor woman.

The door opened slightly. "Yes," came a weak voice from the darkness.

"Ms. Sway, I'm Jason McThune, Special Agent, FBI. I saw you in court yesterday."

The door opened wider, and Dianne stepped into the crack. She said nothing, just waited for his next words.

"Can I talk to you in private?"

She glanced to her left—three security guards, two agents, and three men in scrubs and lab jackets. "In private?" she said.

"We can walk this way," he said, nodding toward the end of the hall.

"Is something the matter?" she asked, as if nothing else could possibly go wrong.

"Yes ma'am."

She took a deep breath, and disappeared. Seconds later, she eased through the door with her cigarettes, and closed it gently behind her. They walked slowly in the center of the empty hall.

"I don't suppose you've talked to Mark," McThune said.

"He called me yesterday afternoon from the jail," she said, sticking a cigarette between her lips. It was not a lie; Mark had indeed called her from the jail.

"Since then?"

"No," she lied. "Why?"

"He's missing."

She hesitated for a step, then continued. "What do you mean, he's missing?" She was surprisingly calm. She's probably just numb to all this, McThune thought. He gave her a quick version of Mark's disappearance. They stopped at the window and looked at downtown.

"My god, do you think the Mafia's got him?" she asked, and her eyes watered immediately. She held the cigarette with a trembling hand, unable to light it.

McThune shook his head confidently. "No. They don't even know. We're keeping a lid on it. I think he just walked away. Right here, in the hospital. We figured he might have tried to contact you."

"Have you searched this place? He knows it really well, you know."

"They've been searching for three hours, but it looks doubtful. Where would he go?"

She finally lit the cigarette and took a long drag, then exhaled a small cloud. "I have no idea."

"Well, let me ask you something. What do you know about Reggie Love? Is she in town this weekend? Was she planning a trip?"

"Why?"

"We can't find her either. She's not at home. Her mother ain't saying much. You received a subpoena last night, right?"

"That's right."

"Well, Mark got one, and they tried to serve one on Reggie

Love, but they haven't found her yet. Is it possible Mark's with her?"

I hope so, Dianne thought. She hadn't thought about this. In spite of the pills she hadn't slept fifteen minutes since he'd called. But Mark on the loose with Reggie was a new idea. A much more pleasant idea.

"I don't know. It's possible, I guess."

"Where would they be, you know, the two of them together?"

"How the hell am I supposed to know? You're the FBI. I hadn't thought about that until five seconds ago, and now you're asking me where they are. Give me a break."

McThune felt stupid. It was not a bright question, and she was not as frail as he thought.

Dianne puffed her cigarette, and watched the cars crawl along the streets below. Knowing Mark, he was probably changing diapers in the nursery or assisting with surgery in orthopedics, or maybe scrambling eggs in the kitchen. St. Peter's was the largest hospital in the state. There were thousands of people under its varied roofs. He'd roamed the halls and made dozens of friends, and it would take them days to find him. She expected him to call any minute.

"I need to get back," she said, sticking the filter in an ashtray.

"If he contacts you, I need to know it."

"Sure."

"And if you hear from Reggie Love, I'd appreciate a call. I'll leave two men here on this floor, in case you need them."

She walked away.

By eight-thirty, Foltrigg had assembled in his office the usual crew of Wally Boxx, Thomas Fink, and Larry Trumann, who arrived last with his hair still wet from a quick shower.

Foltrigg was dressed like a fraternity pledge in his pressed chinos, starched cotton button-down, and shiny loafers. Trumann wore a jogging suit. "The lawyer's missing too," he announced as he poured coffee from a thermos.

"When did you hear this?" Foltrigg asked.

"Five minutes ago, on my car phone. McThune called me. They

went to her house to serve her around eight, but couldn't find her. She's disappeared."

"What else did McThune say?"

"They're still searching the hospital. The kid spent three days there and knows it very well."

"I doubt if he's there," Foltrigg said with his customary quick command of unknown facts.

"Does McThune think the kid's with the lawyer?" Boxx asked.

"Who in hell knows? She'd be kind of stupid to help the kid escape, wouldn't she?"

"She's not that bright," Foltrigg said scornfully.

Neither are you, thought Trumann. You're the idiot who issued the subpoenas that started this latest episode. "McThune's spoken twice this morning with K. O. Lewis. He's on standby. They plan to search the hospital until noon, then give up. If the kid's not found by then, Lewis will zip to Memphis."

"You think Muldanno's involved?" Fink asked.

"I doubt it. Looks like the kid strung them along until he got to the hospital, and at that point he was on home turf. I'll bet he called the lawyer, and now they're hiding somewhere in Memphis."

"I wonder if Muldanno knows," Fink said, looking at Foltrigg.

"His people are still in Memphis," Trumann said. "Gronke's here, but we haven't seen Bono or Pirini. Hell, they might have a dozen boys up there by now."

"Has McThune called in the dogs?" Foltrigg asked.

"Yeah. He's got everyone in his office working on it. They're watching her house, her secretary's apartment, they've even sent two men to find Judge Roosevelt, who's fishing somewhere in the mountains. Memphis PD has the hospital choked off."

"What about the phones?"

"Which phones?"

"The phones in the hospital room. He's a kid, Larry, you know he'll try to call his mother."

"It takes approval from the hospital. McThune said they're working on it. But it's Saturday, and the necessary people are not in."

Foltrigg stood behind his desk, and walked to the window. "The kid had six hours before anyone realized he was missing, right?"

"That's what they said."

"Have they found the lawyer's car?"

"No. They're still looking."

"I'll bet they don't find it in Memphis. I'll bet the kid and Ms. Love are in the car."

"Oh really."

"Yeah. Haulin' ass."

"And where might they be haulin' ass to?"

"Somewhere far away."

At nine-thirty, a Memphis policeman called in the tag number of an illegally parked Mazda. It belonged to one Reggie Love. The message was quickly sent to Jason McThune at his office in the Federal Building.

Ten minutes later, two FBI agents knocked on the door to apartment Number 28 at Bellevue Gardens. They waited, and knocked again. Clint hid in the bedroom. If they kicked the door down, then he would simply be sleeping on this lovely and peaceful Saturday morning. They knocked the third time, and the phone started to ring. It startled him, and he almost lunged for it. But his answering machine was on. If the cops would come to his apartment, then they would certainly not hesitate to call. After the tone, he heard Reggie's voice. He lifted the receiver, and quickly whispered, "Reggie, call me right back." He hung up.

They knocked the fourth time, and left. The lights were off and the curtains covered every window. He stared at the phone for five minutes, and it finally rang. The answering machine gave its message, then the tone. Again, it was Reggie.

"Hello," he said quickly.

"Good morning, Clint," she said cheerfully. "How are things in Memphis?"

"Oh, the usual, you know, cops watching my apartment, banging on the door. Typical Saturday."

"Cops?"

"Yeah. For the past hour, I've been sitting in my closet watching my little television. The news is all over the place. They haven't mentioned you, yet, but Mark's on every channel. Right now, it's simply a disappearance, not an escape."

"Have you talked to Dianne?"

"I called her about an hour ago. The FBI had just told her he was missing. I explained he was with you, and this calmed her a bit. Frankly, Reggie, she's been shocked so much I don't think it registered. Where are you?"

"We've checked into a motel in Metairie."

"I'm sorry. Did you say Metairie? As in Louisiana? Right outside of New Orleans?"

"That's the place. We drove all night."

"Why the hell are you down there, Reggie? Of all the places to hide, why did you pick a suburb of New Orleans? Why not Alaska?"

"Because it's the last place we'd be expected. We're safe, Clint. I paid cash and registered under another name. We'll sleep a bit, then see the city."

"See the city? Come on, Reggie, what's going on?"

"I'll explain it later. Have you talked to Momma Love?"

"No. I'll call her right now."

"Do that. I'll call back this afternoon."

"You're crazy, Reggie. Do you know that? You've lost your mind."

"I know. But I've been crazy before. Good-bye now."

Clint placed the phone on the table, and stretched on the unmade bed. She had indeed been crazy before.

THIRTY-FIVE

BARRY THE BLADE entered the warehouse alone. Gone was the swaggering strut of the quickest gun in town. Gone was the smirking scowl of the cocky street hood. Gone were the flashy suit and Italian loafers. The earrings were in a pocket. The ponytail was tucked under his collar. He'd shaved just an hour ago.

He climbed the rusted steps to the second level, and thought about playing on these same stairs as a child. His father was alive then, and after school he'd hang around here until dark, watching containers come and go, listening to the stevedores, learning their language, smoking their cigarettes, looking at their magazines. It was a wonderful place to grow up, especially for a boy who wanted to be nothing but a gangster.

Now, the warehouse was not as busy. He walked along the runway next to the dirty, painted windows overlooking the river. His steps echoed through the vast emptiness below. A few dusty containers were scattered about, and hadn't been moved in years. His uncle's black Cadillacs were parked together near the docks. Tito, the faithful chauffeur, polished a fender. He glanced up at the sound of footsteps, and waved at Barry.

Though he was quite anxious, he walked deliberately, trying not to strut. Both hands were stuck deep in his pockets. He watched the river through the ancient windows. An imitation paddle wheeler hauled tourists downriver for a breathtaking tour of more warehouses and perhaps a barge or two. The runway stopped at a metal door. He pushed a button and looked directly into the camera above his head. A loud click, and the door opened. Mo, a former stevedore who'd given him his first beer when he was twelve, stood there, wearing a dreadful suit. Mo had at least four guns either on him or within reach. He nodded at Barry, and waved him on. Mo had been a friendly guy until he'd started wearing suits, which happened about the same time he saw *The Godfather,* and he hadn't smiled since.

Barry walked through a room with two empty desks, and knocked on a door. He took a deep breath. "Come in," a voice said gently, and he entered his uncle's office.

Johnny Sulari was aging nicely. A big man, in his seventies, he stood straight and moved quickly. His hair was brilliantly gray, and not a fraction of the hairline had receded. His forehead was small, and the hair started two inches above the eyebrows and was slicked back in shiny waves. As usual, he wore a dark suit, with the jacket hanging on a rack by the window. The tie was navy and terribly boring. The red suspenders were his trademark. He smiled at Barry and waved to a worn leather chair, the same one Barry had sat in as a child.

Johnny was a gentleman, one of the last in a declining business being quickly overrun by younger men who were greedier and nastier. Men like his nephew here.

But it was a forced smile. This was not a social call. They'd talked more in the past three days than in the past three years.

"Bad news, Barry?" Johnny asked, knowing the answer.

"You might say so. The kid's disappeared in Memphis."

Johnny stared icily at Barry, who, for one of the few times in his life, did not stare back. The eyes failed him. The lethal, legendary eyes of Barry The Blade Muldanno were blinking and watching the floor.

"How could you be so stupid?" Johnny asked calmly. "Stupid to leave the body around here. Stupid to tell your lawyer. Stupid. Stupid. Stupid."

The eyes blinked faster and he shifted his weight. He nodded in agreement, now penitent. "I need help, okay."

"Of course you need help. You've done a very stupid thing, and now you need someone to rescue you."

"It concerns all of us, I think."

Johnny's eyes flashed pure anger, but he controlled himself. He was always under control. "Oh, really. Is that a threat, Barry?

You're coming into my office to ask for help and you're threatening me? Are you planning to do some talkin'? Come on, boy. If you're convicted, you'll take it to your grave."

"That's true, but I'd rather not be convicted, you know. There's still time."

"You're a dumbass, Barry. Have I ever told you that?"

"I think so."

"You stalked the man for weeks. You caught him sneaking out of a dirty little whorehouse. All you had to do was hit him over the head, coupla bullets, clean out his pockets, leave the body for the whores to trip over, and the cops would say it's just another cheap murder. They woulda never suspected anybody. But, no, Barry, you're too dumb to keep it simple."

Barry shifted again and watched the floor.

Johnny glared at him and unwrapped a cigar. "Answer my questions slowly, okay? I don't wanna know too much, you understand?"

"Yeah."

"Is the body here in the city?"

"Yeah."

Johnny clipped the end of the cigar and licked it slowly. He shook his head in disgust. "How stupid. Is it easy to get to?"

"Yeah."

"Have the Feds been close to it?"

"I don't think so."

"Is it underground?"

"Yeah."

"How long will it take to dig it up or whatever you have to do?"

"An hour, maybe two."

"So it's not in dirt?"

"Concrete."

Johnny lit the cigar with a match, and relaxed the wrinkles above his eyes. "Concrete," he repeated. Maybe the boy wasn't quite as stupid as he thought. Forget it. He was plenty stupid. "How many men?"

"Two or three. I can't do it. They're watching every move I make. If I go near the place, I'll just lead them to it."

Plenty stupid, all right. He blew a smoke ring. "A parking lot? A sidewalk?"

"Under a garage." Barry shifted again, and kept his eyes on the floor.

Johnny blew another smoke ring. "A garage. A parking garage?"

"A garage behind a house."

He studied the thin layer of ashes at the end of the cigar, then slowly placed it between his teeth. He wasn't stupid, he was dumb. He puffed it twice. "When you say house, do you mean a house on a street with other houses near it?"

"Yeah." At the time of the burial, Boyd Boyette had been in his trunk for twenty-five hours. Options were limited. He was near panic, and was afraid to leave the city. It wasn't such a bad idea, at the time.

"And these other houses have people living in them, right? People with ears and eyes?"

"I haven't met them, you know, but I would assume so."

"Don't get cute with me."

Barry slid an inch in his chair. "Sorry," he said.

Johnny stood and walked slowly to the tinted windows directly above the river. He shook his head in disbelief, and puffed his cigar in frustration. Then he turned and walked back to his seat. He placed the cigar in the ashtray and leaned forward on his elbows. "Whose house?" he asked, stonefaced and ready to explode.

Barry swallowed hard and recrossed his legs. "Jerome Clifford's."

There was no eruption. Johnny was known to have ice water in his veins, and took great pride in staying cool. He was a rarity in this profession, but his level head had made him lots of money. And kept him alive. He placed his left hand completely over his mouth as if there was no way he could believe this. "Jerome Clifford's house," he repeated.

Barry nodded. At the time, Clifford had been skiing in Colorado, and Barry knew this because Clifford had invited him to go. He lived alone in a big house with dozens of shady trees. The garage was a separate structure sitting by itself in the backyard. It was a perfect place, he had thought, because no one would ever suspect it.

And he'd been right—it was a perfect place. The Feds hadn't been near it. It was not a mistake. He'd planned to move it later. The mistake had been to tell Clifford.

"And you want me to send in three men to dig it up, without making a sound, and dispose of it properly?"

"Yes sir. It could save my ass."

"Why do you say this?"

"Because I'm afraid this kid knows where it is, and he's disappeared. Who knows what he's doing? It's just too risky. We gotta move the body, Johnny. I'm begging you."

"I hate beggars, Barry. What if we get caught? What if a neighbor hears something and calls the cops, and they show up, just checkin' on a prowler, you know, and, son of a bitch, there's three boys diggin' up a corpse."

"They won't get caught."

"How do you know! How'd you do it? How'd you bury him in concrete without getting caught?"

"I've done it before, okay."

"I wanna know!"

Barry straightened himself a bit, and recrossed his legs. "The day after I hit him, I unloaded six bags of ready-mix at the garage. I was in a truck with bogus tags, dressed like a yard boy, you know. No one seemed to notice. The nearest house is a good thirty yards away, and there's trees everywhere. I went back at midnight in the same truck and unloaded the body in the garage. Then I left. There's a ditch behind the garage, and a park on the other side of the ditch. I just walked through the trees, climbed across the ditch, and sneaked into the garage. Took about thirty minutes to dig a shallow grave, put the body in it, and mix the concrete. The floor of the garage is gravel, white rock, you know. I went back the next night, after the stuff had dried, and covered it with the gravel. He's got this old boat, and so I rolled the boat back over it. When I left, everything was perfect. Clifford never had a clue."

"Until you told him, of course."

"Yeah, until I told him. It was a mistake, I admit."

"Sounds like a lot of hard work."

"I've done it before, okay. It's easy. I was gonna move it later, but then the Feds got involved and they've followed me for eight months."

Johnny was nervous now. He relit the cigar and returned to the window. "You know, Barry," he said, looking at the water, "you've got some talent, boy, but you're an idiot when it comes to removing the evidence. We've always used the Gulf out there. Whatever happened to barrels and chains and weights?"

"I promise it won't happen again. Just help me now, and I'll never make this mistake again."

"There won't be a next time, Barry. If you somehow survive this, I'm gonna let you drive a truck for a while, then maybe run a fence for a year or so. I don't know. Maybe you can go to Vegas and spend a little time with Rock."

Barry stared at the back of the silver head. He'd lie for the moment, but he would not drive a truck or fence or kiss Rock's ass. "Whatever you say, Johnny. Just help me."

Johnny returned to his seat behind the desk. He pinched the bridge of his nose. "I guess it's urgent."

"Tonight. This kid's on the loose. He's scared, and it's just a matter of time before he tells someone."

Johnny closed his eyes and shook his head.

Barry continued. "Give me three men. I'll tell them exactly how to do it, and I promise they won't get caught. It'll be easy."

Johnny nodded slowly, painfully. Okay. Okay. He stared at Barry. "Now get the hell outta here."

After seven hours of searching, Chief Trimble declared St. Peter's to be free of Mark Sway. He huddled in the lobby near Admissions with his officers, and pronounced the search over. They would continue to patrol the tunnels and walkways and corridors, and stand guard at the elevators and stairwells, but they were all now convinced the kid had eluded them. Trimble called McThune at his office with the news.

McThune was not surprised. He had been briefed periodically throughout the morning as the search fizzled. And there was no sign of Reggie. Momma Love had been bothered twice, and now she refused to answer the door. She'd told them to either produce a search warrant, or get the hell off her property. There was no probable cause for a search warrant, and he suspected Momma Love knew this. The hospital had consented to the wiring of the phone in Room 943. Less than thirty minutes earlier, two agents, posing as orderlies, had entered the room while Dianne was down the hall talking to the Memphis Police. Instead of inserting the device, they simply switched phones. They were in the room less than a minute. The child, they reported, was asleep and never moved. The line was direct to the outside, and tapping in through the hospital switchboard would've taken at least two hours and involved other people.

Clint had not been found, but there was no valid reason to obtain a search warrant for his apartment, so they simply watched it.

Harry Roosevelt had been located in a rented boat somewhere along the Buffalo River in Arkansas. McThune had talked to him around eleven. Harry was livid, to say the least, and was now en route back to the city.

Ord had called Foltrigg twice during the morning, but, uncharacteristically, the great man had little to say. The brilliant strategy of ambush by subpoena had blown up in his face, and he was plotting some serious damage control.

K. O. Lewis was already on board Director Voyles's jet, and two agents had been dispatched to meet him at the airport. He would arrive around two.

An All-Points-Bulletin for Mark Sway had been on the national wire since early morning. McThune was reluctant to add the name of Reggie Love to it. Though he hated lawyers, he found it difficult to believe one would actually help a child escape. But as the morning dragged on and there was no sign of her, he became convinced that their disappearances were more than coincidental. At eleven, he added her name to the APB, along with a physical description and a comment that she was probably traveling with Mark Sway. If they were in fact together, and if they had crossed a state line, the offense would be federal and he'd have the pleasure of nailing her.

There was little to do but wait. He and George Ord feasted on cold sandwiches and coffee for lunch. Another phone call, another reporter asking questions. No comment.

Another phone call, and Agent Durston walked into the office and held up three fingers. "Line three," he said. "It's Brenner at the hospital." McThune hit the button. "Yeah," he barked at the phone.

Brenner was in Room 945, next door to Ricky. He spoke in a guarded voice. "Jason, listen, we just heard a phone call from Clint Van Hooser to Dianne Sway. He told her he had just talked to Reggie, that she and Mark were in New Orleans, and everything was fine."

"New Orleans!"

"That's what he said. No indication of exactly where, just New Orleans. Dianne said almost nothing, and the entire conversation lasted under two minutes. He said he was calling from his girlfriend's apartment in East Memphis, and he promised to call back later."

"Where in East Memphis?"

"We can't determine that, and he didn't say. We'll try and trace it next time. He hung up too quick. I'll send the tape over."

"Do that." McThune punched another button, and Brenner was gone. He immediately called Larry Trumann in New Orleans.

THIRTY-SIX

THE HOUSE was in the bend of an old, shady street, and as they approached it Mark instinctively slid downward in the seat until only his eyes and the top of his head were visible in the window. He was wearing a black-and-gold Saints cap Reggie had bought him at a Wal-Mart along with a pair of jeans and two sweatshirts. A street map was folded badly and stuffed beside the hand brake.

"It's a big house," he said from under the cap as they drove through the bend without the slightest decrease in speed. Reggie saw as much as she could, but she was driving on a strange street and trying desperately not to appear suspicious. It was 3 P.M., hours before dark, and they could drive and look for the rest of the afternoon if they wished. She, too, wore a Saints cap, solid black, and it covered her short gray hair. Her eyes hid behind large sunglasses.

She held her breath as they passed the mailbox with the name Clifford on the side in small, gold, stick-on lettering. It certainly was a big house, but nothing spectacular for this neighborhood. It was of English Tudor design, with dark wood and dark brick, and ivy covering all of one side and most of the front. It was not particularly pretty, she thought as she remembered the newspaper article in which Clifford was described as a divorced father of one. It was obvious, to her at least, that the house did not have the advantage of a woman living in it. Though she could glance at it only as she made the bend and cut her eyes in all directions, looking at once for neighbors, cops, thugs, the garage, and the house, she noticed there were no flowers in the beds and the hedges needed trimming. The windows were covered with dark, drab curtains.

It was not pretty, but it was certainly peaceful. It sat in the center of a large lot with dozens of heavy oaks around it. The driveway ran along a thick hedge and disappeared somewhere around back. Though Clifford had been dead for five days, the grass was neatly trimmed. There was no clue that the house was now uninhabited. There was no hint of any suspicion. Perhaps it was the perfect place to hide a body.

"There's the garage," Mark said, peeking now. It was a separate structure, fifty or so feet from the house, obviously built much later. A small sidewalk led to the house. A red Triumph Spitfire was on blocks next to the garage.

Mark jerked and stared at the house through the rear window as they eased down the street. "What do you think, Reggie?"

"Looks awfully quiet, doesn't it?"

"Yeah."

"Is it what you expected?" she asked.

"I don't know. I watch all those cop shows, you know, and for some reason I could just see Romey's house with yellow police line tape strung all over the place."

"Why? No crime was committed there. It's just the home of a man who committed suicide. Why would the cops be interested?"

The house was out of sight, and Mark turned around and sat straight in the seat. "Do you think they've searched it?" he asked.

"Probably. I'm sure they got a search warrant for his house and office, but what could they find? He carried his little secret with him."

They stopped at an intersection, then continued their tour of the neighborhood.

"What happens to his house?" Mark asked.

"I'm sure he had a will. His heirs will get the house and his assets."

"Yeah. You know, Reggie, I guess I need a will. With everybody after me and all. What do you think?"

"What, exactly, do you own?"

"Well, now that I'm famous and all, I figure the Hollywood people will be knocking on my door. I realize we don't have a door at the present time, but something's gotta happen about that, Reggie, don't you think? I mean, we gotta have a door, of some sort?

Anyway, they'll want to do this big movie about the kid who knew too much, and, I hate to say this for obvious reasons, but if these goons put me away, then the movie will be huge and Mom and Ricky will be on easy street. Follow me?"

"I think so. You want a will so Dianne and Ricky will get the movie rights to your life story?"

"Exactly."

"You don't need one."

"Why not?"

"They'll get all your assets anyway."

"Just as well. Saves me attorney's fees."

"Could we talk about something other than wills and death?"

He shut up and watched the houses on his side of the street. He'd slept most of the night in the backseat, then napped for five hours in the motel room. She, on the other hand, had driven all night and napped less than two hours. She was tired, scared, and beginning to snap at him.

They zigzagged at a leisurely pace through the tree-lined streets. The weather was warm and clear. At every house, people were either mowing grass or pulling weeds or painting shutters. Spanish moss hung from stately oaks. It was Reggie's first tour of New Orleans, and she wished the circumstances were better.

"Are you getting tired of me, Reggie?" he asked without looking at her.

"Of course not. Are you tired of me?"

"No, Reggie. Right now, you're my only friend in the entire world. I just hope I'm not bugging you."

"I promise."

Reggie had studied the street map for two hours. She completed a wide loop, and now they were on Romey's street again. They eased by the house without slowing, both gawking at the double garage with a pitched gable above the retractable doors. It needed painting. The concrete drive stopped twenty feet from the doors and turned to the rear of the house. A ragged hedgerow over six feet high ran along one side of the garage and blocked the view of the nearest house, which was at least a hundred feet away. Behind the garage, the small rear lawn stopped at a chain-link fence, and beyond the fence was a heavily wooded area.

They said nothing during the second viewing of Romey's house. The black Accord wandered aimlessly through the neighborhood and stopped near a tennis court in an open area called West Park. Reggie unfolded the street map, and twisted and flipped it until it covered most of the front seat. Mark watched two heavy housewives engage in truly horrible tennis. But they were cute, with their pink and green socks and matching sun visors. A biker approached on a narrow asphalt trail, then disappeared deep into the woods.

Once again, Reggie attempted to fold the map. "This is the place," she said.

"Do you want to chicken out?" he asked.

"Sort of. What about you?"

"I don't know. We've come this far. Seems kinda silly to run away now. The garage looked harmless to me."

She was still folding the map. "I guess we can try, and if we get spooked, we'll just run back here."

"Where are we now?"

She opened her door. "Let's go for a walk."

The bike trail ran beside a soccer field, then cut through a dense section of woods. The branches of the trees met above it, giving a tunnel-like darkness. The bright sunlight flickered through intermittently. An occasional biker forced them from the asphalt for a few seconds.

The walk was refreshing. After three days in the hospital, two days in jail, seven hours in the car, and six hours in the motel, Mark could barely restrain himself as they rambled through the woods. He missed his bike, and he thought how nice it would be if he and Ricky were here on this trail, racing through the trees without a worry in the world. Just kids again. He missed the crowded streets of the trailer park with kids running everywhere and games of all sorts materializing without a moment's notice. He missed the private little trails of his own woods around Tucker Wheel Estates and the long, solitary walks he had enjoyed all his life. And, strange as it seemed, he missed his hiding places under his own personal trees and beside creeks that belonged to him where he could sit and think, and, yes, sneak a cigarette or two. He hadn't touched one since Monday.

"What am I doing here?" he asked, barely audible.

"It was your idea," she said, hands stuck deep in her new jeans, also from Wal-Mart.

"It's been my favorite question this week—'What am I doing here?' I've asked it everywhere, the hospital, the jail, the courtroom. Everywhere."

"You want to go home, Mark?"

"What's home?"

"Memphis. I'll take you back to your mother."

"Yeah, but I won't stay with her, will I? In fact, we probably wouldn't even make it to Ricky's room before they grabbed me, and off I'd go, back to jail, back to court, back to see Harry, who'd really be ticked, wouldn't he?"

"Yeah, but I can work on Harry."

Nobody worked on Harry, Mark had decided. He could see himself sitting in court trying to explain why he'd escaped. Harry would send him back to the detention center where his sweetheart Doreen would be a different person. No pizza. No television. They'd probably put leg chains on him and throw him in solitary.

"I can't go back, Reggie. Not now."

They had discussed their various options until both were tired of the subject. Nothing had been settled. Each new idea immediately raised a dozen problems. Each course of action ran in all directions and eventually led to disaster. They had both reached, through different routes, the unmistakable conclusion that there was no simple solution. There was no reasonable thing to do. There was no plan even remotely attractive.

But neither believed they would actually dig for the body of Boyd Boyette. Something would happen along the way to spook them, and they'd run back to Memphis. This was yet to be admitted by either.

Reggie stopped at the half-mile marker. To the left was an open, grassy area with a pavilion in the center for picnics. To the right, a small foot trail ventured deeper into the trees. "Let's try this," she said, and they left the bike route.

He followed close behind. "Do you know where you're going?"

"No. But follow me anyway."

The trail widened a bit, then suddenly gave out and disappeared. Empty beer bottles and chip bags littered the ground. They wove through trees and brush until they found a small clearing. The sun was suddenly bright. Reggie shielded her eyes with her hand and looked at a straight row of trees stretching before them.

"I think that's the creek," she said.

"What creek?"

"According to the map, Clifford's street borders West Park, and there's a little green line that appears to be a creek or bayou or something running behind his house."

"It's nothing but trees."

She shuffled sideways for a few feet, then stopped and pointed. "Look, there are roofs on the other side of those trees. I think it's Clifford's street."

Mark stood beside her and strained on tiptoes. "I see them."

"Follow me," she said, and they headed for the row of trees.

It was a beautiful day. They were out for a stroll in the park. This was public property. Nothing to be afraid of.

The creek was nothing but a dry bed of sand and litter. They picked their way down through the vines and brush, and stood where the water once ran many years before. Even the mud had dried. They climbed the opposite bank, a much steeper one but with more vines and saplings to grab on to.

Reggie was breathing hard when they stopped on the other side of the creek bed. "Are you scared?" she asked.

"No. Are you?"

"Of course, and you are too. Do you want to keep going?"

"Sure, and I'm not afraid. We're just out for a hike, that's all." He was terrified and wanted to run, but they had made it this far without incident. And there was a certain thrill in sneaking through the jungle like this. He'd done it a thousand times around the trailer park. He knew to watch for snakes and poison ivy. He'd learned how to line up three trees ahead of him to keep from getting lost. He'd played hide-and-seek in rougher terrain than this. He suddenly crouched low and darted ahead. "Follow me."

"This is not a game," she said.

"Just follow me, unless, of course, you're scared."

"I'm terrified. I'm fifty-two years old, Mark. Now slow down."

The first fence they saw was made of cedar, and they stayed in the trees and moved behind the houses. A dog barked in their general direction, but they could not be seen from the house. Then a chain-link fence, but it was not Clifford's. The woods and underbrush thickened, but from nowhere came a small trail that ran parallel to the fence row.

Then, they saw it. On the other side of a chain-link fence, the red Triumph Spitfire sat alone and abandoned next to Romey's garage. The edge of the woods stopped less than twenty feet from the fence, and between it and the rear wall of the garage a dozen or so oaks and elms with Spanish moss shaded the backyard.

Not surprisingly, Romey was a slob. He had piled boards and bricks, buckets and rakes, all sorts of debris behind the garage and out of sight of the street.

There was a small gate in the chain-link fence. The garage had a window and a door in the rear wall. Sacks of unused and ruined fertilizer were stacked against it. An old lawn mower with the handles off was parked by the door. On the whole, the yard was overgrown and had been for some time. Weeds along the fence were knee-high.

They squatted in the trees and stared at the garage. They would get no closer. The neighbor's patio and charcoal grill were a stone's throw away.

Reggie tried to catch her breath, but it was not possible. She clutched Mark's hand, and found it impossible to believe that the body of a United States Senator was buried less than a hundred feet from where she was now hiding.

"Are we gonna go in there?" Mark asked. It was almost a challenge, though she detected a trace of fear. Good, she thought, he is scared.

She caught her breath long enough to whisper. "No. We've come far enough."

He hesitated for a long time, then said, "It'll be easy."

"It's a big garage," she said.

"I know exactly where it is."

"Well, I haven't pressed you on this, but don't you think it's time to share it with me?"

"It's under the boat."

"He told you this?"

"Yes. He was very specific. It's buried under the boat."

"What if there's no boat?"

"Then we haul ass."

He was finally sweating and breathing hard. She'd seen enough. She stayed low and began backing away. "I'm leaving now," she said.

K. O. Lewis never left the plane. McThune and company were waiting when it landed, and they rushed aboard as it refueled. Thirty minutes later, they left for New Orleans where Larry Trumann now waited anxiously.

Lewis didn't like it. What the hell was he supposed to do in New Orleans? It was a big city. They had no idea what she was driving. In fact, they didn't know if Reggie and Mark had driven, flown, or taken a bus or a train. It was a tourist and convention city with thousands of hotel rooms and crowded streets. Until they made a mistake, it would be impossible to find them.

But Director Voyles wanted him on the scene, and so off he went to New Orleans. Find the kid and make him talk—those were his instructions. Promise him anything.

THIRTY-SEVEN

TWO OF THE THREE, Leo and Ionucci, were veteran leg-breakers for the Sulari family, and were actually related by blood to Barry The Blade, though they often denied it. The third, a huge kid with massive biceps, a wide neck, and thick waist, was known simply as the Bull, for obvious reasons. He'd been sent on this unusual errand to perform most of the grunt work. Barry assured them it would not be difficult. The concrete was thin. The body was small. Chip a little here, and chip a little there, and before they knew it they'd see a black garbage bag.

Barry had diagrammed the floor of the garage, and marked with exact confidence the position of the grave. He had drawn a map with a line starting at the parking lot of West Park and running between the tennis courts, across the soccer field, through a patch of trees, then across another field with a picnic pavilion, then along the bike route for a ways until a footpath led to the ditch. It would be easy, he had assured them all afternoon.

The bike trail was deserted, and with good reason. It was ten minutes after eleven, Saturday night. The air was muggy, and by the time they reached the footpath they were breathing heavily and sweating. The Bull, much younger and fitter, followed the other two and smiled to himself as they bitched quietly in the blackness about the humidity. They were in their late thirties, he guessed, chain-smokers of course, abusive drinkers, sloppy eaters. They were griping about sweating, and they hadn't walked a mile yet.

Leo was in charge of this expedition, and he carried the flashlight. They were dressed in solid black. Ionucci followed like a bloodhound with heartworms, head down, breathing hard, lethargic, mad at the world for being here. "Careful," Leo said as they eased down the ditch bank in heavy weeds. They were not exactly woodsy types. This place had been frightening enough at 6 P.M. when they first walked it off. Now it was terrifying. The Bull expected at any moment to step on a thick, squirming snake. Of course, if he was bitten, he could turn around with justification, and, he hoped, find the car. His two buddies would then be forced to go it alone. He tripped on a log, but kept his balance. He almost wished for a snake.

"Careful," Leo said for the tenth time, as if saying it made things safer. They eased along the dark and weedy creek bed for two hundred yards, then climbed the other bank. The flashlight was turned off, and they crouched low through the brush until they were behind Clifford's chain-link fence. They rested on their knees.

"This is stupid, you know," Ionucci said between loud breaths. "Since when do we dig up bodies?"

Leo was surveying the darkness of Clifford's backyard. Not a single light. They had driven by only minutes earlier, and noticed a small gas light burning in a globe near the front door, but the rear was complete darkness. "Shut up," he said without moving his head.

"Yeah, yeah," Ionucci mumbled. "It's stupid." His screaming lungs were almost audible. Sweat dripped from his chin. The Bull knelt behind them, shaking his head at their unfitness. They were used primarily as bodyguards and drivers, occupations that required little exertion. Legend held that Leo did his first killing when he was seventeen, but was forced to quit a few years later when he served time. The Bull had heard that Ionucci had been shot twice over the years, but this was unconfirmed. The people who generated these stories were not known for telling the truth.

"Let's go," Leo said like a field marshal. They scooted across the grass to the gate in Clifford's fence, then through it. They darted between the trees until they landed against the rear wall of the garage. Ionucci was in pain. He fell to all fours and heaved mightily. Leo crawled to a corner and looked for movement next door. Nothing. Nothing but the sounds of Ionucci's impending cardiac arrest. The Bull peeked around the other corner and watched the rear of Clifford's house.

The neighborhood was asleep. Even the dogs had called it a night.

Leo stood and tried to open the rear door. It was locked. "Stay here," he said, and slid low around the garage until he came to the front door. It was locked also. Back to the rear, he said, "We gotta break some glass. It's locked too."

Ionucci produced a hammer from a pouch on his waist, and Leo began tapping lightly on the dirty pane just above the doorknob. "Watch that corner," he said to the Bull, who crawled behind him and looked in the direction of the Ballantine home next door.

Leo pecked and pecked until the pane was broken. He carefully removed broken pieces and tossed them aside. When the jagged edges were clear, he slid his left arm through and unlocked the door. He turned on the flashlight, and the three eased inside.

Barry said he remembered the place being a mess, and Clifford obviously had been too busy to tidy things up before he passed on. The first thing they noticed was that the floor was gravel, not concrete. Leo kicked at the white rocks beneath his feet. If Barry had told them about the gravel flooring, he didn't remember it.

The boat was in the center of the garage. It was a sixteen-foot outboard ski rig with a heavy layer of dust over it. Three of the four trailer tires were flat. This boat had not touched water in years. Layers of junk were piled against it. Garden tools, sacks of aluminum cans, stacks of newspapers, rusted patio furniture. Romey didn't need a garbage service. Hell, he had a garage. Thick spiderwebs were strung in every corner. Unused tools hung from the walls.

Clifford, for some reason, had been a prodigious collector of wire clothes hangers. Thousands of them hung on strands of wire above the boat. Rows and rows of clothes hangers. At some point, he'd grown weary of running the wire, so he'd simply driven long nails into the wall studs and packed hundreds of hangers on them. Romey, the environmentalist, had also collected cans and plastic containers, obviously with the lofty goal of recycling. But he'd been a busy man, and so a small mountain of green garbage bags stuffed with cans and bottles filled half of the garage. He'd been such a slob, he'd even thrown some of the bags into the boat.

Leo aimed the small light at a point directly under the main beam of the trailer. He motioned for the Bull, who eased onto all fours and began brushing away the white rock gravel. From the waist pouch, Ionucci produced a small trowel. The Bull took it and scraped away more gravel. His two partners stood over his shoulders.

Two inches down, the scraping sound changed when he struck concrete. The boat was in the way. The Bull stood, slowly lifted the hitch, and with a mighty strain rolled the front of the trailer five feet to the side. The side of the trailer brushed against the mountain of aluminum cans, and there was a prolonged racket. The men froze, and listened.

"You gotta be careful." Leo whispered the obvious. "Stay here, and don't move." He left them standing in the dark beside the boat, and eased through the rear door. He stood beside a tree behind the garage and watched the Ballantine house next door. It was dark and quiet. A patio light cast a dim glow around the grill and flower beds, but nothing moved. Leo watched and waited. He doubted the neighbors could hear a jackhammer. He crept back inside the garage and aimed the flashlight at the spot of concrete under the gravel. "Let's clear it off," he said, and the Bull returned to his knees.

Barry had explained that he'd first dug a shallow grave, approximately six feet by two feet, and no more than eighteen inches deep. Then he'd stuffed the body into it. Then he'd packed the pre-mix concrete around the body, which was wrapped in black plastic garbage bags. Then he'd added water to his little recipe. He'd returned the next day to cover it all with gravel and put the boat in place.

He'd done a fine job. Given Clifford's talent for organization, it would be another five years before the boat was moved. Barry had explained that this was just a temporary grave. He'd planned to move it, but the Feds started trailing him. Leo and Ionucci had disposed of a few bodies, usually in weighted barrels over water, but they were impressed with Barry's temporary hiding place.

The Bull scraped and brushed, and soon the entire concrete surface was clear. Ionucci knelt on the other side of it, and he and the Bull began chipping away with chisels and hammers. Leo placed the flashlight on the gravel beside them, and eased again through the rear door. He crouched low and moved to the front of the garage. All was quiet. The chiseling could be heard, all right. He walked quickly to the rear of Clifford's house, maybe fifty feet away, and the sounds were barely audible. He smiled to himself. Had the Ballantines been awake, they could not have heard it.

He darted back to the garage, and sat in the darkness between a corner and the Spitfire. He could see the empty street. A small, black car eased around the bend in front of the house, and was gone. No other traffic. Through the hedge, he could see the outline of the Ballantine house. Nothing moved. The only sounds were the muffled chippings of concrete from the grave of Boyd Boyette.

Clint's Accord stopped near the tennis courts. A red Cadillac was parked near the street. Reggie turned off the lights and the engine.

They sat in silence and stared through the windshield at the dark soccer field. This is a wonderful place to get mugged, she thought to herself, but didn't mention it. There was plenty to fear without thinking of muggers.

Mark hadn't said much since dark. They had napped, together on one bed, for an hour after the pizza had been delivered to their motel room. They had watched television. He had asked her repeatedly about the time, as if he had an appointment with a firing squad. At ten, she was convinced he would chicken out. At eleven, he was pacing around the room, and going back and forth to the bathroom.

But here they were at eleven-forty, sitting in a hot car on a dark night, planning an impossible mission that neither really wanted.

"Do you think anybody knows we're here?" he asked softly.

She looked at him. His gaze was lost somewhere beyond the soccer field. "You mean, here in New Orleans?"

"Yeah. Do you think anyone knows we're in New Orleans?"

"No. I don't think so."

This seemed to satisfy him. She'd talked to Clint around seven. A Memphis TV station had reported that she was missing as well, but things appeared to be quiet. Clint hadn't left his bedroom in twelve hours, he said, so would they please hurry up and do whatever the hell they were planning. He'd called Momma Love. She was worried, but doing okay under the circumstances.

They left the car and walked along the bike trail.

"Are you sure you want to do this?" she asked, looking around nervously. The trail was pitch black, and in places only the asphalt beneath their feet kept them from wandering into the trees. They walked slowly, side by side, and held hands.

As she took one uncertain step after another, Reggie asked herself what she was doing here on this trail, in these woods of this city, at this moment, with this kid whom she loved dearly but was not willing to die for. She clutched his hand and tried to be brave. Surely, she prayed, something would happen very soon and they would dash back to the car and leave New Orleans.

"I've been thinking," Mark said.

"Why am I not surprised?"

"It might be too hard to actually find the body, you know. So, this is what I've decided. You'll stay in the trees close to the ditch, you see, and I'll sneak through the backyard and into the garage. I'll look under the boat, you know, just to make sure it's there, then we'll get out of here."

"You think you can just look under the boat and see the body?"

"Maybe I can see where it is, you know?"

She squeezed his hand tighter. "Listen to me, Mark. We're sticking together, okay. If you go to the garage, then I'm going too." Her voice was remarkably firm. Surely, they wouldn't make it to the garage.

There was a break in the trees. A light on a pole revealed the picnic pavilion to their left. The footpath started to the right. Mark pressed a switch, and the beam from a small flashlight hit the ground in front of them. "Follow me," he said. "Nobody can see us out here."

He moved deftly through the woods without a sound. Back in the motel room, he had recounted many stories of his late night walks through the woods around the trailer park, and of the games the boys played in the darkness. Jungle games, he called them. With the light in his hand, he moved faster now, brushing past limbs and dodging saplings.

"Slow down, Mark," she said more than once.

He held her hand and helped her down the ditch bank. They climbed to the other side, and crept through the woods and underbrush until they found the mysterious trail that had surprised them hours earlier. The fences started. They moved slowly, quietly, and Mark turned off the flashlight.

They were in the dense trees directly behind Clifford's house. They knelt and caught their breath. Through the brush and weeds they could see the outline of the rear of the garage.

"What if we don't see the body?" she asked. "What then?"

"We'll worry about that when it happens."

This was not the moment for another long discussion about his options. On all fours, he crawled to the edge of the thick underbrush. She followed. They stopped twenty feet from the gate in thick, wet weeds. The backyard was dark and still. Not a light or sound or movement. The entire street was sound asleep.

"Reggie, I want you to stay here. Keep your head down. I'll be back in a minute."

"No sir!" she whispered loudly. "You can't do this, Mark!"

He was already moving. This was a game to him, just another jungle game with his little buddies giving chase and shooting guns with colored water. He slid through the grass like a lizard, and opened the gate just wide enough to slide through.

Reggie followed on all fours through the weeds, then stopped. He was already out of sight. He stopped behind the first tree, and listened. He crawled to the next one, and heard something. Chink! Chink! He froze on his hands and knees. The sounds were coming from the garage. Chink! Chink! Very slowly, he peeked around the tree and stared at the rear door. Chink! Chink! He glanced back at Reggie, but the woods and underbrush were black. She was nowhere in sight. He looked at the door again. Something was different. He crawled to the next tree, ten feet closer. The sounds were louder. The door was open slightly, and a windowpane was missing.

Somebody was in there! Chink! Chink! Chink! Somebody was hiding in there with the lights off, and he was digging! Mark breathed deeply, and crawled behind a pile of debris less than ten feet from the rear door. He hadn't made a sound, and he knew it.

The grass was taller around the debris, and he crawled through it like a chameleon, very slowly. Chink! Chink!

He crouched low, and started for the rear door. The ragged end of a rotted two-by-four caught his ankle and he tripped. The pile of debris rattled and an empty paint bucket fell to the ground.

Leo bounced to his feet and darted to the rear of garage. He yanked a .38 with a silencer from his waist, and scooted in the darkness until he was at the corner where he squatted and listened. The chiseling had stopped inside. Ionucci peeked through the rear door.

Reggie heard the racket behind the garage, and fell to her stomach in the wet grass. She closed her eyes and said a prayer. What the hell was she doing here?

Leo sneaked to the pile of debris, then cut around it with the gun drawn and ready to fire. He squatted again, and patiently studied the darkness. The fence was barely visible. Nothing moved. He slid next to a tree fifteen feet behind the garage, and waited. Ionucci watched him closely. Long seconds passed without a sound. Leo stood upright and crept slowly toward the gate. A twig snapped under his foot, freezing him in place for a second.

He moved around the backyard, bolder now but with the gun still ready, and leaned against a tree, a thick oak with limbs hanging low near the Ballantine property line. In the unkempt hedgerow less than twelve feet away, Mark crouched on all fours and held his breath. He watched the dark figure move between the trees in the darkness, and he knew if he kept still he would not be found. He exhaled slowly, his eyes glued to the silhouette of the man by the tree.

"What is it?" a deep voice asked from the garage. Leo slid the gun into the waist of his pants and eased backward. Ionucci was standing outside the door. "What is it?" he repeated.

"I don't know," Leo said in a half-whisper. "Maybe just a cat or something. Get back to work."

The door closed softly, and Leo paced silently back and forth behind the garage for five minutes. Five minutes, but it seemed like an hour to Mark.

Then the dark figure eased around the corner and was gone. Mark watched every move. He slowly counted to one hundred, then crawled along the hedgerow until it stopped at the fence. He paused at the gate and counted to thirty. All was quiet except for the distant, muffled chiseling. Then he darted to the edge of the brush where Reggie was crouching in terror. She grabbed him as they ducked into the heavier undergrowth.

"They're in there!" he said, out of breath.

"Who?!"

"I don't know! They're digging up the body!"

"What happened!?"

He was breathing rapidly. His head bobbed up and down as he swallowed and tried to speak. "I tripped on something, and this one guy, I think he had a gun, almost found me. God I was scared!"

"You're still scared. And so am I! Let's get outta here!"

"Listen, Reggie. Wait a minute. Listen! Can you hear it?"

"No! Hear what?"

"That chinking noise. I can't hear it either. We're too far away."

"And I say we get farther away. Let's go."

"Just wait a minute, Reggie. Dammit!"

"They're killers, Mark. They're Mafia people. Let's get the hell out of here!"

He breathed through his teeth, and glared at her. "Settle down, Reggie. Just settle down, okay. Look, no one can see us here. You can't even see these trees from the garage. I tried, okay. Now settle down."

She fell to her knees, and they stared at the garage. He placed his finger to his lips. "We're safe here, okay," he whispered. "Listen."

They listened, but the sounds could not be heard.

"Mark, these are Muldanno's people. They know you've escaped. They're panicking. They've got guns and knives and who knows what else. Let's go. They beat us. It's all over. They win."

"We can't let them take the body, Reggie. Think about it. If they get away with it, it'll never be found."

"Good. You're off the hook, and the Mafia forgets about you. Now let's go."

"No, Reggie. We gotta do something."

"What! You want to pick a fight with Mafia thugs? Come on, Mark. This is crazy."

"Just wait a minute."

"Okay. I'll wait exactly one minute, then I'm gone."

He turned and smiled at her. "You won't leave me, Reggie. I know you better than that."

"Don't push me, Mark. Now I know how Ricky felt when you were playing around with Clifford and his little water hose."

"Just be quiet, okay. I'm thinking."

"That's what scares me."

She sat on her butt with her legs crossed in front of her. Leaves and vines rubbed her face and neck. He rocked gently on all fours like a lion ready to kill, and finally said, "I've got an idea."

"Of course you do."

"Stay here."

She suddenly grabbed the back of his neck and pulled his face to hers. "Listen, buster, this is not one of your little jungle games where you shoot rubber darts and throw dirt clods. Those are not your little buddies in there playing hide-and-seek, or GI Joe, or whatever the hell you play. This is life and death, Mark. You just made one mistake, and you got lucky. One more, and you'll be dead. Now let's get the hell outta here! Now!"

He was still for a few seconds as she scolded him, then he jerked viciously away. "Stay here, and don't move," he said with stiff jaws. He crept from the brush, through the grass to the fence.

Just inside the gate was an abandoned flower bed outlined with sunken timbers and covered with weeds. He crawled to it, and picked out three rocks with all the fussiness of a chef selecting tomatoes at the market. He watched both corners of the garage, then made a silent retreat into the darkness.

Reggie was waiting, and she had not moved a muscle. He knew she could not find her way to the car. He knew she needed him. They huddled again in the brush.

"Mark, this is insane, son," she pleaded. "Please. These people are not playing games."

"They're too busy to worry about us, okay. We're safe here, Reggie. Look, if they came tearing out of that door right now, they could never find us. We're safe here, Reggie. Trust me."

"Trust you! You'll get yourself killed."

"Stay here."

"What! Please, Mark! No more games!"

He ignored her and pointed to a spot near three trees, about thirty feet away. "I'll be right back," he said, and he disappeared.

He crawled through the brush until he was behind the Ballantine house. He could barely see the edge of Romey's garage. Reggie was lost in the dark undergrowth.

The patio was small and dimly lit. There were three white wicker chairs and a charcoal grill. A large plate-glass window overlooked it, and it was this window that attracted his attention. He stood behind a tree, and measured the distance, which he estimated to be the length of two house trailers. The rock would have to be low enough to miss the branches, yet high enough to clear a row of hedges. He took a deep breath, and threw it as hard as he could.

Leo jumped at the sound from next door. He crept in front of the garage and peeked through the hedge. The patio was quiet and still. It sounded like a rock landing on wooden decking and rattling around next to the brick. Maybe it was just a dog. He watched for a long time, and nothing happened. They were safe. Another false alarm.

Mr. Ballantine rolled over and stared at the ceiling. He was in his early sixties, and sleep had been difficult since the removal of the disc a year and a half ago. He had just dozed off, and was awakened by a sound. Or was it a sound? No place was safe in New Orleans anymore, and he'd paid two thousand dollars for an alarm system six months earlier. Crime was everywhere. They were thinking about moving.

He rolled to one side, and had just closed his eyes when the window crashed. He bolted to the door, turned on the bedroom light, and yelled, "Get up, Wanda! Get up!" Wanda was reaching for her robe, and Mr. Ballantine was grabbing the shotgun from the closet. The alarm was wailing. They raced down the hall, yelling at each other and flipping on light switches. The glass had scattered throughout the den, and Mr. Ballantine aimed the shotgun at the window as if to prevent another attack. "Call the police!" he barked at her. "911!"

"I know the number!"

"Hurry up!" He tiptoed in his house shoes around the glass,

crouching low with the gun as if a burglar had chosen to enter the house through the window. He fought his way to the kitchen where he punched numbers on a control panel, and the sirens stopped.

Leo had just resettled into his guard post next to the Spitfire when the crash shattered the stillness. He bit a hole in his tongue as he scrambled to his feet and darted once again to the hedge. A siren screamed briefly, then stopped. A man in a red nightshirt down to his knees was running onto the patio with a shotgun.

Leo crept quickly to the rear door of the garage. Ionucci and the Bull were crouched in terror beside the boat. Leo stepped on a rake, and the handle landed on a bag full of aluminum cans. The three stopped breathing. Voices could be heard next door.

"What the hell is it?" Ionucci demanded through clenched teeth. He and the Bull were shiny with sweat. Their shirts were stuck to their bodies. Their heads were soaking wet.

"I don't know," Leo bristled, spitting blood, inching toward the window facing the hedge that separated the Ballantine property. "Something went through a window, I think. I don't know. Crazy bastard's got a shotgun!"

"A what!" Ionucci almost shrieked. He and the Bull slowly raised their heads to the window and joined Leo there. The crazy man with the shotgun was stomping around his backyard, yelling at the trees.

Mr. Ballantine was sick of New Orleans and sick of drugs and sick of punks trying to rob and pillage, and he was sick of crime and living in fear like this, and he was just so damned sick of it all he raised his shotgun and fired once at the trees for good measure. That'll teach the slimy little bastards that he meant business. Come back to his house, and you'll leave in a hearse. BOOM!

Mrs. Ballantine stood in the doorway in her pink robe, and screamed when he fired and wounded the trees.

The three heads in the garage next door hit the dirt when the shooting started. "Sumbitch is crazy!" Leo screeched. Slowly, they raised their heads again in perfect unison, and at precisely that instant, the first police car pulled into the Ballantine driveway with blue and red lights flashing wildly.

Ionucci was the first one out the door, followed by the Bull, then Leo. They were in a huge hurry, but at the same time careful not to attract attention from the idiots next door. They scooted along, close to the ground, dashing from tree to tree, trying desperately to make it to the woods before there was more gunfire. The retreat was orderly.

Mark and Reggie huddled deep in the brush. "You're crazy," she kept muttering, and it was not idle talk. She honestly believed that her client was mentally unbalanced. But she hugged him anyway, and they squeezed close together. They didn't see the three silhouettes scampering along until they crossed through the fence.

"There they are," Mark whispered, pointing. Not thirty seconds earlier, he had told her to watch the gate.

"Three of them," he whispered. The three leaped into the underbrush, less than twenty feet from where they were hiding, and disappeared into the woods.

They squeezed closer together. "You're crazy," she said again.

"Maybe so. But it's working."

The shotgun blast had almost sent Reggie over the edge. She'd been trembling when they arrived here. She'd been mortified when he returned with news that someone was in the garage. She'd damned near screamed when he threw the rock through the window. But the shotgun was the final straw. Her heart was pounding and her hands were trembling.

And oddly, at this moment, she knew they couldn't run. The three grave robbers were now between them and their car. There was no escape.

The shotgun blast brought the neighborhood to life. Floodlights filled backyards as men and women in bathrobes walked onto patios and looked in the direction of the Ballantines'. Voices shouted inquiries across fences. Dogs came to life. Mark and Reggie withdrew deeper into the brush.

Mr. Ballantine and one of the cops walked along the rear fence, searching perhaps for more felonious rocks. It was hopeless. Reggie and Mark could hear voices, but they could not understand what was being said. Mr. Ballantine yelled a lot.

The cops settled him down, then helped him tape clear plastic over the window. The red and blue lights were turned off, and after twenty minutes, the cops left.

Reggie and Mark waited, trembling and holding hands. Bugs crawled over their skin. The mosquitoes were brutal. The weeds and burrs stuck to their dark sweatshirts. The lights in the Ballantine house finally went off, and they waited some more.

THIRTY-EIGHT

A FEW MINUTES AFTER ONE, the clouds broke and the half-moon lightened Romey's backyard and garage for a moment. Reggie glanced at her watch. Her legs were numb from squatting. Her back ached from sitting on her tail. Oddly, though, she had become accustomed to her little spot in the jungle, and after surviving the thugs, the cops, and the idiot with the shotgun, she was feeling remarkably safe. Her breathing and pulse were normal. She was not sweating, though her jeans and shirt were still wet from exertion and humidity. Mark swatted and slapped mosquitoes, and said little. He was eerily calm. He chewed on a weed, watched the fence row, and acted as if he and he alone knew precisely when to make the next move.

"Let's go for a little walk," he said, rising from his knees.

"Where to? The car?"

"No. Just down the trail. My leg is about to cramp."

Her right leg was numb below the knee. Her left leg was dead below the hip, and she stood with great difficulty. She followed him through the brush until they were on the small trail parallel to the creek. He moved deftly through the darkness without the benefit of the flashlight, swatting mosquitoes and stretching his legs.

They stopped deep in the woods, out of sight of the fence rows of Romey's neighbors.

"I really think we should leave now," she said, a bit louder since the houses were no longer in view. "I have this fear of snakes, you see, and I don't want to step on one."

He did not look at her, but stared in the direction of the ditch. "I don't think it's a good idea to leave now," he whispered.

She knew he had a reason for saying this. She'd not won an argument in the past six hours. "Why?"

"Because those men could still be around here. In fact, they could be close by waiting for things to settle down so they can return. If we head for the car, we might meet them."

"Mark, I can't take any more of this, okay? This may be fun and games for you, but I'm fifty-two years old and I've had it. I can't believe I'm hiding in this jungle at one o'clock in the morning."

He put his forefinger over his lips. "Shhhhhh. You're talking too loud. And this isn't a game."

"Dammit, I know it's not a game! Don't lecture me."

"Keep your cool, Reggie. We're safe now."

"Safe my ass! I won't feel safe until I lock the door at the motel."

"Then leave. Go on. Find your way back to the car, and leave."

"Sure, and let me guess. You'll stay here, right?"

The moonlight disappeared, and suddenly the woods were darker. He turned his back to her and began walking toward their hiding place. She instinctively followed him, and this irritated her because at this moment she was depending on an eleven-year-old. But she followed him anyway, along a trail invisible to her, through the dense woods to the undergrowth, to about the same point where they'd waited before. The garage was barely visible.

The blood had returned to her legs, though they were very stiff. Her lower back throbbed. She could rub her hand across her forearm and feel the bumps from the mosquito bites. There was a thin sliver of blood on the back of her left hand, probably from a sticker in the brush or perhaps a weed. If she ever made it back to Memphis, she vowed to join a health club and get in shape. Not that she planned any more ventures like this, but she was tired of aching and gasping for breath.

Mark lowered onto one knee, stuck another weed in his mouth to chew on, and watched the garage.

They waited, almost in silence, for an hour. When she'd reached the point of leaving him and running wildly through the woods, Reggie said, "Okay, Mark, I'm leaving. Do what you've got to do, because I'm leaving now." But she didn't move.

They crouched together, and he pointed at the garage as if she didn't know where it was. "I'm crawling up there, okay, with the flashlight, and I'm looking at the body, or the grave, or whatever they were digging at, okay?"

"No."

"It won't take but a second, maybe. If I'm lucky, I'll be right back."

"I'm going with you," she said.

"No. I want you to stay here. I'm worried that those guys are watching too, somewhere along the tree line. If they come after me, I want you to start yelling and run like crazy."

"No. No way, sweetheart. If you're looking at the body, then I'm looking at the body, and I'm not arguing about it. That's final."

He looked at her eyes, four or five inches away, and decided not to argue. Her head was shaking and her jaw was tight. She looked cute under the cap.

"Then follow me, Reggie. Stay low, and listen. Always listen, okay."

"All right, all right. I'm not totally helpless. In fact, I'm getting pretty good at crawling."

They attacked from the brush on all fours again, two figures sliding in the still darkness. The grass was wet and cool. The gate, still open from the hasty retreat of the grave robbers, squeaked slightly when Reggie hooked it with a foot. Mark glared at her. They stopped behind the first tree, then eased to the next. Not a sound from anywhere. It was 2 A.M., and the neighborhood was silent. Mark, however, was worried about the nut next door with the gun. He doubted the man would sleep well with a thin sheet of plastic over the window, and he could envision him sitting in the kitchen watching the patio and waiting for the snap of a twig before he began blasting away again. They stopped at the next tree, then crawled to the junk pile.

She nodded once, taking small, quick breaths. They crouched and darted to the rear door of the garage, which was slightly open. Mark stuck his head inside. He turned on the flashlight and aimed it at the floor. Reggie eased in behind him.

The odor was thick and pungent, like a dead animal rotting in the sun. Reggie instinctively covered her nose and mouth. Mark breathed deeply, then held his breath.

The only open space in the cluttered room was in the center, where the boat had been parked. They crouched over the concrete slab. "I'm getting sick," Reggie said, barely opening her mouth.

Another ten minutes, and the body would have been out. They had started in the center, somewhere around the torso, and chipped away at each side. The black garbage bags, partially decomposed by the cement, had been ripped away. A ragged little trench had been cut away toward the feet and knees.

Mark had seen enough. He picked up a chisel, one that had been left behind, and jabbed it into black plastic.

"Don't!" Reggie whispered loudly, backing away but still seeing it all.

He ripped through the garbage bag with the chisel, and followed it closely with the light. He made a slow turn, then pulled the plastic with his hand. He bolted upright in horror, then slowly placed the light squarely into the decaying face of the late Senator Boyd Boyette.

Reggie took another step backward, and fell onto a pile of bags filled with aluminum cans. The racket was deafening in the still air. She scrambled and fought to get up in the darkness, but the thrashing and kicking created more noise. Mark grabbed a hand, and pulled her toward the boat. "I'm sorry!" she whispered, standing two feet from the corpse without thinking about it.

"Shhhhh," Mark said as he stepped onto a box and peeked through the window. A light came on next door. The shotgun could not be far behind.

"Let's go," he said. "Stay low."

They eased through the rear door, and Mark closed it behind them. A door slammed at the neighbor's. He hit his hands and knees and slid around the debris pile, past the trees, and through the gate. Reggie was on his heels. They stopped crawling when they reached the brush. They crouched low and scampered like squirrels until they found the trail. Mark turned on the flashlight, and they didn't slow until they were at the creek. He ducked into some weeds, and turned off the light.

"What's the matter?" she asked, breathing hard, terrified, and damned sure not willing to pause in this getaway.

"Did you see his face?" Mark asked, in awe of what they'd just done.

"Of course I saw his face. Now let's go."

"I want to see it again."

She almost slapped him. Then she stood upright, hands on hips, and started walking toward the creek.

Mark ran beside her with the flashlight. "I was just kidding." She stopped and glared at him, then he took her hand and led her down the bank to the creek bed.

They entered the expressway by the Superdome and headed for Metairie. Traffic was light, though heavier than in most cities at two-thirty on a Sunday morning. Not a word had been spoken since they'd jumped in the car at West Park and left the area. And the silence bothered neither.

Reggie contemplated how close she'd been to death. Mafia hoods, snakes, crazy neighbors, police, guns, shock, heart attack—it would've made no difference. She was indeed fortunate to be here, racing along the expressway, soaked with perspiration, covered with insect bites, bloody from the wounds of nature, and dirty from a night in the jungle. It could've been so much worse. She'd take a hot shower at the motel, maybe sleep a little, then worry about the next move. She was exhausted from the fear and sudden shocks. She was in pain from the crawling and stooping. She was too old for this nonsense. The things lawyers do.

Mark gently scratched the bites on his left forearm, and watched the lights of New Orleans thin as they left downtown. "Did you see that brown stuff on his face?" he asked without looking at her.

Though the face was now forever seared into her memory, she could not, at the moment, recall any brown stuff on it. It was a small, shriveled, partially decayed face, and one that she wished she could forget.

"I saw only the worms," she said.

"The brown stuff was blood," he said with the authority of a medical examiner.

She did not wish to pursue this conversation. There were more important things to discuss now that the silence was broken.

"I think we need to talk about your plans, now that this little escapade is behind us," she said, glancing at him.

"We need to move fast, Reggie. Those guys will be back to get the body, don't you think?"

"Yes. For once I agree. They might be back now, for all we know."

He scratched the other forearm, and placed an ankle on a knee. "I've been thinking."

"I'm sure you have."

"There are two things I don't like about Memphis. The heat, and the flat land. There are no hills or mountains, you know what I mean? I've always thought it would be so nice to live in the mountains where the air is cool and the snow is deep in the wintertime. Wouldn't that be fun, Reggie?"

She smiled to herself and changed lanes. "Sounds wonderful. Any particular mountain?"

"Out west somewhere. I love to watch those old 'Bonanza' reruns with Hoss and Little Joe. Adam was okay, but it really ticked me off when he left. I've watched them since I was a little kid, and I've always thought it would be neat to live out there."

"What happened to the tall buildings and the crowded city?"

"That was yesterday. Today, I'm thinking about mountains."

"Is that where you want to go, Mark?"

"I think so. Can I?"

"It can be arranged. Right now, they'll agree to almost anything."

He stopped scratching and locked his fingers around his knee. His voice was tired. "I can't go back to Memphis, can I, Reggie?"

"No," she said softly.

"I didn't think so." He thought about this for a few seconds. "It's just as well, I guess. There's not much left there."

"Think of it as yet another adventure, Mark. A new home, new school, new job for your mother. You'll have a much nicer place to live, new friends, mountains all around you if that's what you want."

"Be honest with me, Reggie. Do you think they'll ever find me?"

She had to say no. At this moment, he had no choice. She would run and hide with him no more. They had to either call the FBI and strike a deal, or call the FBI and turn themselves in. This little trip was about to be over.

"No, Mark. They'll never find you. You have to trust the FBI."

"I don't trust the FBI, and you don't either."

"I don't completely distrust them. But right now, they've got the only game in town."

"And I have to play along with them?"

"Unless you have a better idea."

Mark was in the shower. Reggie dialed Clint's number, and listened as the phone rang a dozen times before he answered. It was almost 3 A.M.

"Clint, it's me."

His voice was thick and slow. "Reggie?"

"Yes, me, Reggie. Listen to me, Clint. Turn on the light, put your feet on the floor, and listen to me."

"I'm listening."

"Jason McThune's phone number is listed in the Memphis directory. I want you to call him, and tell him you need Larry Trumann's home phone number in New Orleans. Got that?"

"Why don't you look in the New Orleans phone book?"

"Don't ask questions, Clint. Just do as I say. Trumann's not listed down here."

"What's going on, Reggie?" His words were much quicker.

"I'll call you back in fifteen minutes. Make some coffee. This could be a long day." She hung up and unlaced her muddy sneakers.

Mark finished a quick shower, and ripped open a new package of underwear. He'd been embarrassed when Reggie bought them, but now it seemed so unimportant. He slipped into a new, yellow tee shirt, and pulled on his new but dirty Wal-Mart jeans. No socks. He wasn't going anywhere for a while, according to his attorney.

He left the tiny bathroom. Reggie was lying on the bed, shoes off, weeds and grass on the cuffs of her jeans. He sat on the edge of her bed, and stared at the wall.

"Feel better?" she asked.

He nodded, said nothing, then lay beside her. She pulled him close to her body, and placed an arm under his wet head. "I'm all messed up, Reggie," he said softly. "I don't know what happens next anymore."

The tough little boy who threw rocks through windows and outsmarted killers and cops and raced fearlessly through dark woods began to cry. He bit his lip and squinted his eyes, but couldn't stop the tears. She held him closer. Then he broke, finally, and sobbed loudly with no attempt to hold it back, no effort at being tough now. He cried without shame or embarrassment. His body shook and he squeezed her arm.

"It's okay, Mark," she whispered in his ear. "Everything's okay." With her free hand, she wiped tears from her cheeks, and squeezed him even closer. Now it was up to her. She had to be the lawyer again, the counselor who moved daringly and called the shots. His life was once again in her hands.

The television was on but the sound was off. Its gray and blue shadows cast a dim light over the small room with its double beds and cheap furniture.

Jo Trumann grabbed the phone and searched the darkness for the clock. Ten minutes before four. She handed it to her husband, who took it and sat in the center of the bed. "Hello," he grunted.

"Hi, Larry. It's me, Reggie Love, remember?"

"Yeah. Where are you?"

"Here in New Orleans. We need to talk, and the sooner the better."

He almost said something smart about the hour of the day, but thought better of it. It was important, or she wouldn't be calling. "Sure. What's going on, Reggie?"

"Well, we've found the body, for starters."

Trumann was suddenly on his feet and sliding into his house shoes. "I'm listening."

"I've seen the body, Larry. About two hours ago. I saw it with my own eyes. Smelled it too."

"Where are you?" Trumann pressed a button on the recorder by the phone.

"I'm at a pay phone, so no cute stuff, okay?"

"Okay."

"The people who buried the body tried to retrieve it last night, but they were unable to do so. Long story, Larry. I'll explain it later. I'm willing to bet they'll try again very soon."

"Is the kid with you?"

"Yes. He knew where it was, and we came, we saw, and we conquered. You'll have it by noon today if you do as I say."

"Anything."

"That's the spirit, Larry. The kid wants to cut a deal. So we need to talk."

"When and where?"

"Meet me in the Raintree Inn on Veterans Boulevard in Metairie. There's a grill that's open all night. How long will it take?"

"Give me forty-five minutes."

"The sooner you get here, the sooner you'll get the body."

"Can I bring someone with me?"

"Who?"

"K. O. Lewis."

"He's in town?"

"Yeah. We knew you were here, so Mr. Lewis flew in a few hours ago."

There was hesitation on her end. "How'd you know I was here?"

"We have ways."

"Who have you wired, Trumann? Talk to me. I want a straight answer." Her voice was firm, yet with a trace of panic.

"Can I explain it when we meet?" he asked, kicking himself in the ass for opening this can of worms.

"Explain it now," she commanded.

"I'll be happy to explain when—"

"Listen, asshole. I'm canceling the meeting unless you tell me right now who's been wired. Talk, Trumann."

"Okay. We bugged the kid's mother's room at the hospital. It was a mistake. I didn't do it, okay. Memphis did it."

"What'd they hear?"

"Not much. Your man Clint called yesterday afternoon and told her you guys were in New Orleans. That's all, I swear."

"Would you lie to me, Trumann?" she asked, thinking of the tape from their first encounter.

"I'm not lying, Reggie," Trumann insisted, thinking of the same damned tape.

There was a long pause in which he heard nothing but her breathing. "Just you and K. O. Lewis," she said. "No one else. If Foltrigg shows up, all deals are off."

"I swear."

She hung up. Trumann immediately called K. O. Lewis at the Hilton. Then he called McThune in Memphis.

THIRTY-NINE

EXACTLY FORTY-FIVE MINUTES LATER, Trumann and Lewis walked nervously into the near empty grill at the Raintree Inn. Reggie waited at a table in the corner, far away from anyone. Her hair was wet and she wore no makeup. A bulky tee shirt with LSU TIGERS in purple letters was tucked into a pair of faded jeans. She sipped black coffee, and neither stood nor smiled as they approached and sat opposite her.

"Good morning, Ms. Love," Lewis said in an attempt to be nice.

"It's Reggie, okay, and it's too early for pleasantries. Are we alone?"

"Of course," Lewis said. At that moment eight FBI agents were guarding the parking lot, and more were on the way.

"No bugs, wire, body mikes, salt shakers, or ketchup bottles?"

"None."

A waiter appeared, and they ordered coffee.

"Where's the kid?" Trumann asked.

"He's around. You'll see him soon enough."

"Is he safe?"

"Of course he's safe. You boys couldn't catch him if he was on the streets begging for food."

She handed Lewis a piece of paper. "These are the names of three psychiatric hospitals that specialize in children. Battenwood in Rockford, Illinois. Ridgewood in Tallahassee. And Grant's Clinic in Phoenix. Any one of the three will do."

Their eyes went slowly from her face to the list. They focused and studied it. "But we've already checked with the clinic in Portland," Lewis said, puzzled.

"I don't care where you've checked, Mr. Lewis. Take this list, and check again. I suggest you do it quickly. Call Washington, get them out of bed, and get it done."

He folded the list and placed it under his elbow. "You, uh, you say you've seen the body," he asked, trying to sound authoritative but failing miserably.

She smiled. "I have. Less than three hours ago. Muldanno's men were trying to get it, but we scared them off."

"We?"

"Mark and I."

They both studied her intently, and waited for the precious details of this wild, impossible little story. The coffee arrived, and they ignored both it and the waiter.

"We're not eating," Reggie said rudely, and the waiter left.

"Here's the deal," she said. "There are a few provisions, none of which are in the least bit negotiable. Do it my way, do it now, and you might get the body before Muldanno carries it away and drops it in the ocean. If you blow it, gentlemen, I doubt you'll ever get this close again."

They nodded furiously.

"Did you fly here on a private jet?" she asked Lewis.

"Yes. It's the Director's."

"How many does it seat?"

"Twenty or so."

"Good. Send it back to Memphis right now. I want you to pick up Dianne and Ricky Sway, along with his doctor and Clint. Fly them here immediately. McThune is welcome to come. We'll meet them at the airport, and when Mark is safely on board and the plane is gone, I'll tell you where the body is. How about it so far?"

"No problem," Lewis said. Trumann was speechless.

"The entire family enters the witness protection plan. First, they pick the hospital, and when Ricky is able to move, they'll pick the city."

"No problem."

"Complete change of identification, nice little house, the works. This woman needs to stay home and raise her kids for a while, so I'd suggest a monthly allowance in the sum of four thousand dollars, guaranteed for three years. Plus an initial cash outlay of twenty-five thousand. They lost everything in the fire, remember?"

"Of course. These things are easy." Lewis was so eager, she wished she'd asked for more.

"If, at some point, she wants to return to work, then I'd suggest a nice, cushy government job with no responsibilities, short hours, and a fat salary."

"We have plenty of those."

"Should they desire to move at any time, and to any place, they'll be allowed to do so, at your expense, of course."

"We do it all the time."

Trumann was smiling now, though he was trying not to.

"She'll need a car."

"No problem."

"Ricky may need extended treatment."

"We'll cover it."

"I want Mark examined by a psychiatrist, though I suspect he's in better shape than we are."

"Done."

"There are a couple of other minor matters, and they'll be covered in the agreement."

"What agreement?"

"The agreement I'm having typed as we speak. It'll be signed by myself, Dianne Sway, Judge Harry Roosevelt, and you, Mr. Lewis, on behalf of Director Voyles."

"What else is in the agreement?" Lewis asked.

"I want your assurance that you'll do everything in your power to compel the attendance of Roy Foltrigg before the Juvenile Court of Shelby County, Tennessee. Judge Roosevelt will want to discuss a few matters with him, and I'm sure Foltrigg will resist. If a subpoena is issued for him, I want it served by you, Mr. Trumann."

"Gladly," Trumann said with a nasty smile.

"We'll do what we can," Lewis added, a bit confused.

"Good. Go make your phone calls. Get the plane in the air. Call McThune and tell him to pick up Clint Van Hooser and take him to the hospital. Get that damned bug off her phone, because I need to talk to her."

"No problem." They jumped to their feet.

"We'll meet right here in thirty minutes."

□ □ □ □

Clint hammered away on his ancient Royal portable. His third cup of coffee shook each time he slapped the return and rattled the kitchen table. He studied his hurried chicken-scratch handwriting on the back of an *Esquire,* and tried to remember each provision as she'd spouted it over the phone. If he finished it, it would be, without a doubt, the sloppiest legal document ever prepared. He cursed and grabbed the Liquid Paper.

A knock on the door startled him. He ran his fingers through his unkempt and unwashed hair, and walked to the door. "Who is it?"

"FBI."

Not so loud, he almost said. He could hear the neighbors now, gossiping about him and his predawn arrest. Probably drugs, they would say.

He cracked the door and peeked under the safety chain. Two agents with puffy eyes stood in the darkness. "We were told to come get you," one said apologetically.

"I need some ID."

They stuck their badges near the door. "FBI," the first one said.

Clint opened the door wider, and waved them in. "I'll be a few more minutes. Have a seat."

They stood awkwardly in the center of the den as he returned to the table and the typewriter. He pecked slowly. The chicken scratch failed him, and he ad-libbed the rest. The important points were there, he hoped. She always found something to change in his typing at the office, but this would have to do. He pulled it carefully from the Royal, and placed it in a small briefcase.

"Let's go," he said.

At five-forty, Trumann returned alone to the table where Reggie waited. He brought two cellular phones. "Thought we might need these," he said.

"Where'd you get them?" Reggie asked.

"They were delivered to us here."

"By some of your men?"

"That's right."

"Just for fun, how many men do you have right now within a quarter of a mile of this place?"

"I don't know. Twelve or thirteen. It's routine, Reggie. They might be needed. We'll send a few to protect the kid, if you'll tell me where he is. I assume he's alone."

"He's alone, and he's fine. Did you talk to McThune?"

"Yes. They've already picked up Clint."

"That was fast."

"Well, to be honest, we've had men watching his apartment for twenty-four hours now. We simply woke them up, and told them to knock on his door. We found your car, Reggie, but we couldn't find Clint's."

"I'm driving it."

"That's what I figured. Pretty slick, but we would've found you within twenty-four hours."

"Don't be so cocky, Trumann. You've been looking for Boyette for eight months."

"True. How'd the kid escape?"

"It's a long story. I'll save it for later."

"You could be implicated, you know."

"Not if you guys sign our little agreement."

"We'll sign it, don't worry." One of the phones rang, and Trumann grabbed it. As he listened, K. O. Lewis hurried to the table and brought his own cellular phone. He jumped into his chair, and leaned across the table, his eyes glowing with excitement. "Talked to Washington. We're checking the hospitals right now. Everything looks fine. Director Voyles will call here in a minute. He'll probably want to talk to you."

"How about the plane?"

Lewis checked his watch. "It's leaving now, should be in Memphis by six-thirty."

Trumann placed a hand over his phone. "This is McThune. He's at the hospital waiting for Dr. Greenway and the administrator. They've made contact with Judge Roosevelt, and he's on his way down there."

"Have you de-bugged her phone?" Reggie asked.

"Yes."

"Removed the salt shakers?"

"No salt shakers. Everything's clean."

"Good. Tell him to call back in twenty minutes," she said.

Trumann mumbled into the phone and flipped a switch. Within

seconds, K.O.'s phone beeped. He stuck it to his head, and broke into a large smile. "Yes sir," he said, most respectfully. "Just a second."

He jabbed the phone at Reggie. "It's Director Voyles. He'd like to speak with you."

Reggie took it slowly, and said, "This is Reggie Love." Lewis and Trumann watched like two kids waiting for ice cream.

A deep and very clear voice came from the other end. Though Denton Voyles had never been fond of the press during his forty-two years as Director of the FBI, they occasionally captured a brief word or two. The voice was familiar. "Ms. Love, this is Denton Voyles. How are you?"

"Just fine. The name's Reggie, okay."

"Sure, Reggie. Listen, K.O. just brought me up to date, and I want to assure you the FBI will do anything you want to protect this kid and his family. K.O. has full authority to act for me. We'll also protect you if you wish."

"I'm more concerned about the child, Denton."

Trumann and Lewis glanced at each other. She had just called him Denton, a feat no one had dared to attempt before. And she was not the least disrespectful.

"If you want, you can fax me the agreement here and I'll sign it myself," he said.

"That won't be necessary, but thanks."

"And my plane is at your disposal."

"Thank you."

"And I promise that we'll see to it that Mr. Foltrigg has to face the music in Memphis. We had nothing to do with the grand jury subpoenas, you understand?"

"Yes, I know."

"Good luck to you, Reggie. You guys work out the details. Lewis can move mountains. Call me if you need me. I'll be at the office all day."

"Thank you," she said, and handed the phone back to K. O. Lewis, the mountain mover.

The assistant night manager of the grill, a young man of no more than nineteen with a peach fuzz mustache and an attitude, walked to the table. These people had been here for an hour, and from all indications they had set up camp. There were three phones in the center of the table. Some papers were lying about. The woman wore a sweatshirt and jeans. One of the men wore a cap and no socks. "Excuse me," he said curtly, "can I be of assistance?"

Trumann glanced over his shoulder, and snapped, "No."

He hesitated, and took a step closer. "I'm the assistant night manager, and I demand to know what you're doing here."

Trumann snapped his fingers loudly, and two gentlemen reading the Sunday paper at a table not far away jumped to their feet and whipped badges from their pockets. They stuck them into the face of the assistant night manager. "FBI," they said together as they each took an arm and led him away. He did not return. The grill was still deserted.

A phone rang, and Lewis took it. He listened carefully. Reggie opened the Sunday New Orleans paper. At the bottom of the front page was her face. The picture was taken from the bar registry, and it was next to Mark's fourth-grade class photo. Side by side. Escaped. Disappeared. On the run. Boyette and all that. She turned to the comics.

"That was Washington," Lewis reported as he placed the phone on the table. "The clinic in Rockford is full. They're checking on the other two."

Reggie nodded and sipped her coffee. The sun was making its first efforts of the day. Her eyes were red and her head was hurting, but the adrenaline was pumping. With a little luck, she would be home by dark.

"Look, Reggie, could you give us an idea how long it'll take to get to the body?" Trumann asked with great caution. He didn't want to press; didn't want to upset her. But he needed to start planning. "Muldanno's still out there, and if he gets it first, we're all up a creek." He paused and waited for her to say something. "It's in the city, right?"

"If you don't get lost, you should be able to find it in fifteen minutes."

"Fifteen minutes," he repeated slowly, as if this was too good to be true. Fifteen minutes.

FORTY

CLINT HADN'T SMOKED a cigarette in four years, but he found himself puffing nervously on a Virginia Slim. Dianne had one too, and they stood at the end of the hall and watched as the day broke over downtown Memphis. Greenway was in the room with Ricky. Next door, Jason McThune, the hospital administrator, and a small collection of FBI agents waited. Both Clint and Dianne had talked to Reggie in the past thirty minutes.

"The Director has given his word," Clint said, sucking hard on the narrow cigarette, trying to extract a little smoke. "There's no other choice, Dianne."

She stared through the window with one arm across her chest and the other hand holding the cigarette near her mouth. "We just leave, right? We just get on the plane and fly off into the sunset, and everybody lives happily ever after?"

"Something like that."

"What if I don't want to, Clint?"

"You can't say no."

"Why not?"

"It's very simple. Your son has made the decision to talk. He's also made the decision to enter the witness protection program, so like it or not, you have to go too. You and Ricky."

"I'd like to talk to my son."

"You can talk to him in New Orleans. If you can change his mind, then the deal's off. Reggie's not dropping the big news until you guys are on the plane and in the air."

Clint was trying to be firm, yet compassionate. She was scared, weak, and vulnerable. Her hands trembled as she placed the filter between her lips.

"Ms. Sway," a heavy voice said from behind. They turned to find the Honorable Harry M. Roosevelt standing behind them in a massive, bright blue jogging suit with Memphis State Tigers emblazoned across the front. It had to be a triple extra-large, and it stopped six inches above his ankles. A pair of ancient but seldom used running shoes covered his long feet. He was holding the two-page agreement Clint had typed.

She acknowledged his presence but said nothing.

"Hello, Your Honor," Clint said quietly.

"I just talked to Reggie," he said to Dianne. "I'd say they've had a rather eventful trip." He stepped between them and ignored Clint. "I've read this agreement, and I'm inclined to sign it. I think it's in the best interests of Mark for you to do the same."

"Is that an order?" she asked.

"No. I do not have the power to bind you to this agreement," he said, then flashed a huge, warm smile. "But, I would if I could."

She placed the cigarette in an ashtray on the windowsill, and stuck both hands deep into the pockets of her jeans. "And if I don't?"

"Then Mark will be returned here, placed back in detention, and beyond that, who knows. He will eventually be forced to talk. The situation is much more urgent now."

"Why?"

"Because we now know for a fact that Mark knows where the body is. So does Reggie. They could be in great danger. You're at the point, Ms. Sway, where you have to trust people."

"That's easy for you to say."

"Indeed it is. But if I were you, I'd sign this and get on the plane."

Dianne slowly took the agreement from His Honor. "Let's go talk to Dr. Greenway."

They followed her down the hall to the room next to Ricky's.

Twenty minutes later, the ninth floor of St. Peter's was sealed off by a dozen FBI agents. The waiting room was evacuated. The nurses were told to remain at their station. Three of the elevators were stopped on the ground floor. The other was held in place on the ninth by an agent.

The door to Room 943 opened, and little Ricky Sway, drugged and sound asleep, was wheeled into the hallway on a stretcher pushed by Jason McThune and Clint Van Hooser. On this, his sixth day of confinement, he was no better than when he first arrived. Greenway walked along one side, Dianne the other. Harry followed along for a few steps, then stopped.

The stretcher was pushed into the waiting elevator, which descended to the fourth floor, also secured by FBI agents. It was rushed a short distance to a service elevator, where Agent Durston held the door, then taken to the second floor, also secured. Ricky never moved. Dianne held his arm and jogged beside the stretcher.

They maneuvered through a series of short corridors and metal doors, and were suddenly on a flat roof. A helicopter was waiting. Ricky was loaded quickly, and Dianne, Clint, and McThune climbed aboard.

Minutes later, the helicopter landed near a hangar at Memphis International Airport. A half dozen FBI agents guarded the pad as Ricky was rolled to a nearby jet.

At ten minutes before seven, a cellular phone rang at the corner table of the Raintree Grill, and Trumann grabbed it. He listened and checked his watch. "They're in the air," he announced and set the phone down. Lewis was talking to Washington again.

Reggie breathed deeply and smiled at Trumann. "The body's in concrete. You'll need a few hammers and chisels."

Trumann choked on his orange juice. "Okay. Anything else?"

"Yeah. Place a couple of your boys near the intersection of St. Joseph and Carondelet."

"Close by?"

"Just do it, okay."

"Done. Anything else?"

"I'll be back in a minute." Reggie walked to the registration desk, and asked the clerk to check the fax machine. The clerk returned with a copy of the two-page agreement, which Reggie read closely. The typing was horrible, but the words were perfect. She returned to the table. "Let's get Mark," she said.

□ □ □ □

Mark finished brushing his teeth for the third time, and sat on the edge of the bed. His black-and-gold Saints canvas bag was packed with dirty clothes and new underwear. Cartoons were on, but he was not interested.

He heard a car door, then footsteps, then a knock. "Mark, it's me," Reggie said.

He opened the door, but she did not step inside. "Are you ready to go?"

"I guess." The sun was up and the parking lot was visible. A familiar face was behind her. It was one of the FBI agents from the first meeting at the hospital. Mark grabbed his bag, and stepped out into the parking lot. Three cars were waiting. A man opened the rear door of the middle car, and Mark and his attorney got in.

The little motorcade sped away.

"Everything's fine," Reggie said, taking his hand. The two men in the front seat stared straight ahead. "Ricky and your mother are on the plane. They'll be here in about an hour. Are you okay?"

"I guess. Have you told them?" he whispered.

"Not yet," she answered. "Not until you're on the plane and in the air."

"Are all these guys FBI agents?"

She nodded and patted his hand. He suddenly felt important, sitting in the rear of his own black car, being rushed to the airport to board a private jet, cops all around just to protect him. He crossed his legs and sat a bit straighter.

He'd never flown before.

FORTY-ONE

BARRY PACED NERVOUSLY before the tinted windows in Johnny's office, and watched the tugs and barges on the river. His nasty eyes were red, but not from booze or partying. He hadn't slept. He'd waited here at the warehouse for the body to be delivered to him, and when Leo and company arrived around one without it, he had called his uncle.

Johnny, on this fine Sunday morning, was wearing neither tie nor suspenders. He paced slowly behind his desk, puffing blue smoke from his third cigar of the day. A thick cloud hung not far above his head.

The screaming and ass chewing had ended hours ago. Barry had cursed Leo and Ionucci and the Bull, and Leo had cursed back. But with time, the panic subsided. Throughout the night, Leo had periodically driven by Clifford's house, always in a different vehicle, and seeing nothing unusual. The body was still there.

Johnny decided to wait twenty-four hours and try again. They would watch the place during the day, and attack with full force after dark. The Bull assured him he could have the body out of the concrete in ten minutes.

Just be cool, Johnny had told everyone. Just be cool.

Roy Foltrigg finished the Sunday paper on the patio of his suburban split-level, and walked barefooted across the wet grass with a cup of cold coffee. He had slept little. He had waited in the darkness on his front porch for the paper to arrive, then ran to fetch it in his pajamas and bathrobe. He had called Trumann, but, strangely, Mrs. Trumann wasn't sure where her husband had gone.

He inspected his wife's rosebushes along the back fence, and asked himself for the hundredth time where Mark Sway would run to. There was no doubt, at least in his mind, that Reggie had helped him escape. She'd obviously gone crazy again, and run off with the kid. He smiled to himself. He'd have the pleasure of busting her ass.

The hangar was a quarter of a mile from the main terminal, in a row of identical buildings all drab gray and sitting quietly together. The words Gulf Air were painted in orange letters above the tall double doors, which were opening as the three cars stopped in front of the hangar. The floor was sparkling concrete, painted green without a speck of dirt and covered with nothing but two private jets side by side in a far corner. A few lights were on, and their reflections glowed on the green floor. The building was big enough for a stock car race, Mark thought as he stretched his neck for a glimpse of the two jets.

With the doors out of the way, the entire front of the hangar was now open. Three men walked hurriedly along the back wall as if searching for something. Two more stood by one door. Outside, another half dozen moved slowly about, keeping their distance from the cars that had just parked.

"Who are these people?" Mark asked, in the general direction of the front seat.

"They're with us," Trumann said.

"They're FBI agents," Reggie clarified.

"Why so many?"

"They're just being careful," she said. "How much longer, do you think?" she asked Trumann.

He glanced at his watch. "Probably thirty minutes."

"Let's walk around," she said, opening her door. As if on cue, the other eleven doors in the little parade opened and the cars emptied. Mark looked around at the other hangars, and the terminal, and a plane landing on the runway in front of them. This had become terribly exciting. Not three weeks ago, he'd beaten the crap out of a subdivision kid at school after the kid taunted him because he'd never flown. If they could only see him now. Rushed to the airport by private car, waiting for his private jet to take him anywhere he wanted to go. No more trailers. No more fights with subdivision kids. No more notes to Mom, because now she would be at home. He'd decided, sitting alone in the motel room, that this was a wonderful idea. He'd come to New Orleans and outsmarted the Mafia in its own backyard, and he could do it again.

He caught a few stares from the agents by the door. They cut their eyes quickly at him, then looked away. Just checking him out. Maybe he'd sign some autographs later.

He followed Reggie into the vast hangar, and the two private jets caught his attention. They were like small, shiny toys sitting under the Christmas tree waiting to be played with. One was black, the other silver, and Mark stared at them.

A man in an orange shirt with Gulf Air on a patch above the pocket closed the door to a small office inside the hangar and walked in their direction. K. O. Lewis met him, and they talked quietly. The man waved at the office, and said something about coffee.

Larry Trumann knelt beside Mark, still staring at the jets. "Mark, do you remember me?" he asked with a smile.

"Yes sir. I met you at the hospital."

"That's right. My name's Larry Trumann." He offered his hand, and Mark shook it slowly. Children are not supposed to shake hands with adults. "I'm an FBI agent here in New Orleans."

Mark nodded and kept staring at the jets.

"Would you like to look at them?" Trumann asked.

"Can I?" he asked, suddenly friendly to Trumann.

"Sure." Trumann stood and placed a hand on Mark's shoulder. They walked slowly across the gleaming concrete, the sounds of Trumann's steps echoing upward. They stopped in front of the black jet. "Now this is a Lear Jet," Trumann began.

Reggie and K. O. Lewis left the small office with tall cups of steaming coffee. The agents who'd escorted them here had slipped into the shadows of the hangar. They sipped what must've been their tenth cups of this long morning, and watched as Trumann and the kid inspected the jets.

"He's a brave kid," Lewis said.

"He's remarkable," Reggie said. "At times he thinks like a terrorist, then he cries like a little child."

"He is a child."

"I know. But don't tell him. It may upset him, and, hell, who knows what he might do." She took a long sip. "Truly remarkable."

K.O. blew into his cup, then took a tiny sip. "We've pulled some strings. There's a room waiting for Ricky at Grant's Clinic in Phoenix. We need to know if that's the destination. The pilot called five minutes ago. He has to get clearance, file a flight plan, you know."

"Phoenix it is. Complete confidentiality, okay? Register the kid under another name. Same for the mother and Mark. Keep some of your boys nearby. I want you to pay for his doctor's trip out there and for a few days of work."

"No problem. The people in Phoenix have no idea what's coming. Have you guys talked about a permanent home?"

"A little, not much. Mark says he wants to live in the mountains."

"Vancouver's nice. We vacationed there last summer. Absolutely gorgeous."

"Out of the country?"

"No problem. Director Voyles said they can go anywhere. We've placed a few witnesses outside the States, and I think the Sways are perfect candidates. These people will be taken care of, Reggie. You have my word."

The man in the orange shirt joined Mark and Trumann, and was now in charge of the tour. He lowered the steps to the black Lear, and the three disappeared inside.

"I must confess," Lewis said after he swallowed another scalding dose of coffee, "I was never convinced the kid knew."

"Clifford told him everything. He knew exactly where it was."

"Did you?"

"No. Not until yesterday. When he first came to my office, he told me that he knew, but he didn't tell me where it was. Thank god for that. He kept it to himself until we were near the body yesterday afternoon."

"Why'd you come here? Seems awfully risky."

Reggie nodded at the jets. "You'll have to ask him. He insisted we find the body. If Clifford lied to him, then he figured he was off the hook."

"And so you just drove down here and looked for the body? Just like that?"

"It was a bit more involved. It's a long story, K.O., and I'll give you all the details over a long dinner."

"I can't wait."

Mark's small head was now in the cockpit, and Reggie half expected the engines to start, the plane to taxi slowly from the hangar, out onto the runway, and Mark to dazzle them with a perfect takeoff. She knew he could do it.

"Are you concerned about your own safety?" Lewis asked.

"Not really. I'm just a humble lawyer. What would they gain by coming after me?"

"Retribution. You don't understand the way they think."

"Indeed I don't."

"Director Voyles would like for us to stick close for a few months, at least until the trial is over."

"I don't care what you do, I just don't want to see anyone who's watching me, okay?"

"Fine. We have ways."

The tour moved to the second jet, a silver Citation, and for the moment Mark Sway had forgotten about dead bodies and bad guys lurking in shadows. The steps came down, and he climbed aboard with Trumann in tow.

An agent with a radio walked to Reggie and Lewis, and said, "They're on final approach." They followed him to the opening of the hangar near the cars. A minute later Mark and Trumann joined them, and as they watched the sky to the north a tiny plane appeared.

"That's them," Lewis said. Mark inched his way next to Reggie and took her hand. The plane grew larger as it approached the runway. It, too, was black, but much larger than the jets in the hangar. Agents, some in suits and some in jeans, began moving around as the plane taxied to them. It stopped a hundred feet away, and the engines died. A full minute passed before the door opened and the stairs hit the ground.

Jason McThune trotted down first, and when he stepped onto the tarmac a dozen FBI agents had the plane surrounded. Dianne and Clint were next. They joined McThune, and together the three walked briskly toward the hangar.

Mark released Reggie's hand and ran to meet his mother. Dianne grabbed and hugged him, and for an awkward second or two everyone else either watched or looked at the terminal in the distance.

They said nothing as they embraced. He squeezed her tightly around the neck, and finally said, through tears, "I'm sorry, Mom. I'm so sorry." She clutched his head and pressed it to her shoulder, and at the same time thought of strangling him and of never letting go.

Reggie led them into the small but clean office, and offered Dianne coffee. She declined. Trumann, McThune, Lewis, and the gang waited nervously outside the door. Trumann, especially, was anxious. What if they changed their minds? What if Muldanno got the body? What if? He paced and fidgeted, glanced at the locked door, asked Lewis a hundred questions. Lewis sipped coffee and tried to remain calm. It was now twenty minutes before eight. The sun was bright, the air humid.

Mark sat in his mother's lap, and Reggie, the lawyer, sat behind the desk. Clint stood by the door.

"I'm glad you came," Reggie said to Dianne.

"I didn't have much of a choice."

"You do now. You can change your mind, if you want. You can ask me anything."

"Do you realize how fast all this is happening, Reggie? Six days ago, I came home and found Ricky curled in his bed sucking his thumb. Then Mark and the cop showed up. Now I'm being asked to become someone else and run away to another world. My god."

"I understand," Reggie said. "But we can't stop things."

"Are you mad at me, Mom?" he asked.

"Yeah. No cookies for a week." She stroked his hair. There was a long pause.

"How's Ricky?" Reggie asked.

"About the same. Dr. Greenway is trying to bring him around so he can enjoy the plane ride. But they had to drug him slightly when we left the hospital."

"I'm not going back to Memphis, Mom," Mark said.

"The FBI has contacted a children's psychiatric hospital in Phoenix, and they're waiting for you now," Reggie explained. "It's a good one. Clint checked it out Friday. It's been highly recommended."

"So we're going to live in Phoenix?" Dianne asked.

"Only until Ricky is released. Then you go wherever you want. Canada. Australia. New Zealand. It's up to you. Or you can stay in Phoenix."

"Let's go to Australia, Mom. They still have real cowboys down there. Saw it in a movie once."

"No more movies for you, Mark," Dianne said, still rubbing his head. "We wouldn't be here if you hadn't watched so many movies."

"What about TV?"

"No. From now on, you'll do nothing but read books."

The office was silent for a long time. Reggie had nothing else to say. Clint was dead tired and about to fall asleep on his feet. Dianne's mind was moving clearly now, for the first time in a week. Frightened as she was, she had escaped the dungeon at St. Peter's. She had seen sunlight and smelled real air. She was holding her lost son, and the other one would improve. All these people were trying to help. The lamp factory was history. Employment was now a thing of the past. No more cheap trailers. No more worries about past due child support and unpaid bills. She could watch the boys grow up. She could join the PTA. She could buy some clothes and do her nails. Good gosh, she was only thirty years old. With a little effort and a little money, she could be attractive again. There were men out there.

As dark and treacherous as the future seemed, it could not be as horrible as the past six days. Something had to give. She was due a break. Have a little faith, baby.

"I guess we'd better get to Phoenix," she said.

Reggie grinned with relief. She pulled the agreement from a briefcase Clint brought with him. It had been signed by Harry and McThune. Reggie added her signature, and handed the pen to Dianne. Mark, now bored with hugs and tears, walked to the wall and admired a series of framed color photos of jets. "On second thought, I might be a pilot," he said to Clint.

Reggie took the agreement. "I'll be back in a minute," she said, opening the door and closing it behind her.

Trumann jumped when it opened. Hot coffee splashed from his trembling cup and burned his right hand. He cursed, and slung at the floor, then wiped it on his pants.

"Relax, Larry," Reggie said. "Everything's fine. Sign here." She stuck the agreement in his face, and Trumann scrawled his name. K.O. did the same.

"Get the plane ready," Reggie said. "They're going to Phoenix."

K.O. turned and flashed a hand signal at the agents by the hangar entry. McThune jogged toward them with more instructions. Reggie returned to the office and closed the door.

K.O. and Trumann shook hands and smiled goofily. They stared at the door to the office.

"What now?" Trumann mumbled.

"She's a lawyer," K.O. said. "Nothing's ever easy with lawyers."

McThune walked to Trumann and handed him an envelope. "It's a subpoena for the Reverend Roy Foltrigg," he said with a smile. "Judge Roosevelt issued it this morning."

"On Sunday morning?" Trumann asked, taking the envelope.

"Yeah. He called his clerk, and they met at his office. He's very excited about seeing Foltrigg back in Memphis."

The three chuckled at this. "It'll be served upon the Reverend this morning," Trumann said.

After a minute, the door opened. Clint, Dianne, Mark, then Reggie filed out and headed for the tarmac. The engines were started. Agents scurried about. Trumann and Lewis escorted them to the hangar doors, and stopped.

K.O., ever the diplomat, offered his hand to Dianne, and said, "Good luck, Ms. Sway. Jason McThune will escort you to Phoenix, and handle things once you get there. You are completely safe. And if we can do anything to help, please let us know."

Dianne gave a sweet smile and shook his hand. Mark offered his, and said, "Thanks, K.O. You've been a real pain in the ass." But he was smiling, and it struck everyone as being funny.

K.O. laughed. "Good luck to you, Mark, and I assure you, son, you've been a bigger pain."

"Yeah, I know. Sorry about all this." He shook hands with Trumann, and walked away with his mother and McThune. Reggie and Clint remained by the hangar door.

At some point, about halfway to the jet, Mark stopped. As if suddenly scared, he froze in place and watched as Dianne climbed the steps to the plane. At no time during the past twenty-four hours had it occurred to him that Reggie would be left behind. He had simply assumed, for whatever reason, that she would stay with them until this ordeal was over. She would fly off with them, and hang around the new hospital until they were safe. And as he stood there, a tiny figure on the vast tarmac, motionless and stunned, he realized she was not beside him. She was back there with Clint and the FBI.

He turned slowly, and stared at her in terror as this reality sunk in. He took two steps toward her, then stopped. Reggie left her small group and walked to him. She knelt on the tarmac, and looked into his panicked eyes.

He bit his lip. "You can't come with us, can you?" he asked slowly in a frightened voice. Though they had talked for hours, this subject was never touched.

She shook her head as her eyes watered.

He wiped his eyes with the back of his hand. The FBI agents were close by, but not watching. For once in his life, he was not ashamed to cry in public. "But I want you to go," he said.

"I can't, Mark." She leaned forward, took both of his shoulders, and hugged him gently. "I can't go."

Tears flooded his cheeks. "I'm sorry about all this. You didn't deserve it."

"But if it hadn't happened, Mark, I never would've met you." She kissed him on the cheek, and held his shoulders tight. "I love you, Mark. I'll miss you."

"I'll never see you again, will I?" His lip quivered and tears dripped off his chin. His voice was frail.

She gritted her teeth and shook her head. "No, Mark."

Reggie took a deep breath, and stood. She wanted to grab him, and take him home to Momma Love. He could have the bedroom upstairs, and all the spaghetti and ice cream he could eat.

Instead, she nodded at the plane where Dianne was standing in the door, waiting patiently. He wiped his cheeks again. "I'll never see you again," he said, almost to himself. He turned, and made a feeble attempt to straighten his shoulders, but he couldn't. He walked slowly to the steps, and glanced back for one last look.

FORTY-TWO

MINUTES LATER, as the plane taxied to the end of the runway, Clint eased to her side and took her hand. They watched silently as it took off and finally disappeared in the clouds.

She wiped tears from both cheeks. "I think I'll become a real estate lawyer," she said. "I can't take any more of this."

"He's quite a kid," Clint said.

"It hurts, Clint."

He squeezed her hand harder. "I know."

Trumann appeared quietly beside her, and the three of them looked at the sky. She noticed him, and pulled the micro-cassette tape from her pocket. "It's yours," she said. He took it.

"The body is in the garage behind Jerome Clifford's house," she said, still wiping tears, "886 East Brookline."

Trumann turned to his left and stuck a radio to his mouth. The agents bolted for their cars. Reggie and Clint did not move.

"Thanks, Reggie," Trumann said, now suddenly anxious to leave.

She nodded at the distant clouds. "Don't thank me," she said. "Thank Mark."